VOLUME VI/FALL 1986

EDITORS IN CHIEF
Jerry Pournelle   Jim Baen

SENIOR EDITOR
Elizabeth Mitchell

BAEN SCIENCE FICTION BOOKS

FAR FRONTIERS, Volume VI

This is a work of fiction. All the characters and events portrayed in this book are fictional, and any resemblance to real people or incidents is purely coincidental.

A Baen Books Original

Baen Publishing Enterprises
260 Fifth Avenue
New York, N.Y. 10001

First printing, September 1986

ISBN: 0-671-65590-6

Cover art by Pat Ortega

Printed in the United States of America

Distributed by
SIMON & SCHUSTER
TRADE PUBLISHING GROUP
1230 Avenue of the Americas
New York, N.Y. 10020

CONTENTS

Editor's introduction to:
THE TANK LORDS

David Drake's immensely popular stories of Colonel Alois Hammer and his armored Slammers are, the author claims, set firmly within the anti-war tradition—certainly his tightly focussed vignettes of military violence and its aftermath make no bones about the essential hellishness of war.

But though, as all sane people do, Drake loathes the prospect of war, he does not make the mistake so common among those who long for peace at any price: He knows full well that there are fates worse than battle, that sometimes the only acceptable way to peace is to fight like a demon.

—JPB

*Look for the Baen Books edition of the **original** HAMMERS SLAMMERS, including for the first time, THE TANK LORDS.*

THE TANK
LORDS

David Drake

They were the tank lords.

The Baron had drawn up his soldiers in the courtyard, the twenty men who were not detached to his estates on the border between the Kingdom of Ganz and the Kingdom of Marshall—keeping the uneasy truce and ready to break it if the Baron so willed.

I think the King sent mercenaries in four tanks to our palace so that the Baron's will would be what the King wished it to be . . . though of course we were told they were protection against Ganz and the mercenaries of the Lightning Division whom Ganz employed.

The tanks and the eight men in them were from Hammer's Slammers, and they were magnificent.

Lady Miriam and her entourage rushed back from the barred windows of the women's apartments on the second floor, squealing for effect. The tanks were so huge that the mirror-helmeted men watching from the turret hatches were nearly on a level with the upper story of the palace.

I jumped clear, but Lady Miriam bumped the chair I had dragged closer to stand upon and watch the arrival over the heads of the women I served.

"Leesh!" cried the Lady, false fear of the tanks replaced by real anger at me. She slapped with her fan of

2

painted ox-horn, cutting me across the knuckles because I had thrown a hand in front of my eyes.

I ducked low over the chair, wrestling it out of the way and protecting myself with its cushioned bulk. Sarah, the Chief Maid, rapped my shoulder with the silver-mounted brush she carried for last-minute touches to the Lady's hair. "A monkey would make a better page than you, Elisha," she said. "A gelded monkey."

But the blow was a light one, a reflexive copy of her mistress' act. Sarah was more interested in reclaiming her place among the others at the windows now that modesty and feminine sensibilities had been satisfied by the brief charade. I didn't dare slide the chair back to where I had first placed it; but by balancing on tip-toes on the carven arms, I could look down into the courtyard again.

The Baron's soldiers were mostly off-worlders themselves. They had boasted that they were better men than the mercenaries if it ever came down to cases. The fear that the women had mimed from behind stone walls seemed real enough now to the soldiers whose bluster and assault rifles were insignificant against the iridium titans which entered the courtyard at a slow walk, barely clearing the posts of gates which would have passed six men marching abreast.

Even at idle speed, the tanks roared as their fans maintained the cushions of air that slid them over the ground. Three of the Baron's men dodged back through the palace doorway, their curses inaudible over the intake whine of the approaching vehicles.

The Baron squared his powerful shoulders within his dress cloak of scarlet, purple, and gold. I could not see his face, but the back of his neck flushed red and his left hand tugged his drooping moustache in a gesture as meaningful as the angry curses that would have accompanied it another time.

Beside him stood Wolfitz, his Chamberlain; the tallest man in the courtyard; the oldest; and, despite the weapons the others carried, the most dangerous.

When I was first gelded and sold to the Baron as his

Lady's page, Wolfitz had helped me continue the studies I began when I was training for the Church. Out of
his kindness, I thought, or even for his amusement . . .
but the Chamberlain wanted a spy, or another spy, in
the women's apartments. Even when I was ten years
old, I knew that death lay on that path—and life itself
was all that remained to me.

I kept the secrets of all. If they thought me a fool and
beat me for amusement, then that was better than the
impalement which awaited a boy who was found med-
dling in the affairs of his betters.

The tanks sighed and lowered themselves the last
finger's breadth to the ground. The courtyard, clay and
gravel compacted over generations to the density of
stone, crunched as the plenum-chamber skirts settled
visibly into it.

The man in the turret of the nearest tank ignored the
Baron and his soldiers. Instead, the reflective faceshield
of the tanker's helmet turned and made a slow, arrogant
survey of the barred windows and the women behind
them. Maids tittered; but the Lady Miriam did not, and
when the tanker's faceshield suddenly lifted, the mercenary's eyes and broad smile were toward the Baron's
wife.

The tanks whispered and pinged as they came into
balance with the surroundings which they dominated.
Over those muted sounds, the man in the turret of the
second tank to enter the courtyard called, "Baron
Hetziman, I'm Lieutenant Kiley and this is my number
two—Sergeant Commander Grant. Our tanks have been
assigned to you as a Protective Reaction Force until the
peace treaty's signed."

"You do us honor," said the Baron curtly. "We trust
your stay with us will be pleasant as well as short. A
banquet—"

The Baron paused, and his head turned to find the
object of the other tanker's attention.

The lieutenant snapped something in a language that
was not ours, but the name 'Grant' was distinctive in
the sharp phrase.

The man in the nearest turret lifted himself out gracefully by resting his palms on the hatch coaming and swinging up his long, powerful legs without pausing for footholds until he stood atop the iridium turret. The hatch slid shut between his booted feet. His crisp moustache was sandy blond, and the eyes which he finally turned on the Baron and the formal welcoming committee were blue. "Rudy Grant at your service, Baron," he said, with even less respect in his tone than in his words.

They did not need to respect us. They were the tank lords.

"We will go down and greet our guests," said the Lady Miriam, suiting her actions to her words. Even as she turned, I was off the chair, dragging it toward the inner wall of imported polychrome plastic.

"But Lady . . . ," said Sarah nervously. She let her voice trail off, either through lack of a firm objection or unwillingness to oppose a course on which her mistress was determined.

With coos and fluttering skirts, the women swept out the door from which the usual guard had been removed for the sake of the show in the courtyard. Lady Miriam's voice carried back: "We were to meet them at the banquet tonight. We'll just do so a little earlier."

If I had followed the women, one of them would have ordered me to stay and watch the suite—though everyone, even the tenants who farmed the plots of the home estate here, was outside watching the arrival of the tanks. Instead, I waited for the sounds to die away down the stair tower—and I slipped out the window.

Because I was in a hurry, I lost one of the brass buttons from my jacket—my everyday livery of buff; I'd be wearing the black plush jacket when I waited in attendance at the banquet tonight, so the loss didn't matter. The vertical bars were set close enough to prohibit most adults, and few of the children who could slip between them would have had enough strength to then climb the bracing strut of the roof antenna, the only safe path since the base of the West Wing was a thicket of spikes and razor ribbon.

I was on the roof coping in a matter of seconds, three quick hand-over-hand surges. The women were only beginning to file out through the doorway. Lady Miriam led them, and her hauteur and lifted chin showed she would brook no interference with her plans.

Most of the tankers had, like Grant, stepped out of their hatches, but they did not wander far. Lieutenant Kiley stood on the sloping bow of his vehicle, offering a hand which the Baron angrily refused as he mounted the steps recessed into the tank's armor.

"Do you think I'm a child?" rumbled the Baron, but only his pride forced him to touch the tank when the mercenary made a hospitable offer. None of the Baron's soldiers showed signs of wanting to look into the other vehicles. Even the Chamberlain, aloof if not afraid, stood at arm's length from the huge tank which even now trembled enough to make the setting sun quiver across the iridium hull.

Because of the Chamberlain's studied unconcern about the vehicle beside him, he was the first of the welcoming party to notice Lady Miriam striding toward Grant's tank, holding her skirts clear of the ground with dainty, bejeweled hands. Wolfitz turned to the Baron, now leaning gingerly against the curve of the turret so that he could look through the hatch while the lieutenant gestured from the other side. The Chamberlain's mouth opened to speak, then closed again deliberately.

There were matters in which he too knew better than to become involved.

One of the soldiers yelped when Lady Miriam began to mount the nearer tank. She loosed her dress in order to take the hand which Grant extended to her. The Baron glanced around and snarled an inarticulate syllable. His wife gave him a look as composed as his was suffused with rage. "After all, my dear," said the Lady Miriam coolly, "our lives are in the hands of these brave men and their amazing vehicles. Of *course* I must see how they are arranged."

She was the King's third daughter, and she spoke now as if she were herself the monarch.

"That's right, milady," said Sergeant Grant. Instead of pointing through the hatch, he slid back into the interior of his vehicle with a murmur to the Lady.

She began to follow.

I think Lady Miriam and I, alone of those on the estate, were not nervous about the tanks for their size and power. I loved them as shimmering beasts, whom no one could strike in safety. The Lady's love was saved for other subjects.

"Grant, that won't be necessary," the lieutenant called sharply—but he spoke in our language, not his own, so he must have known the words would have little effect on his subordinate.

The Baron bellowed, "*Mir—*" before his voice caught. He was not an ungovernable man, only one whose usual companions were men and women who lived or died as the Baron willed. The Lady squeezed flat the flounces of her skirt and swung her legs within the hatch ring.

"Murphy," called the Baron to his chief of soldiers. "Get up there with her." The Baron roared more often than he spoke quietly. This time his voice was not loud, but he would have shot Murphy where he stood if the soldier had hesitated before clambering up the bow of the tank.

"Vision blocks in both the turret and the driver's compartment," said Lieutenant Kiley, pointing within his tank, "give a three-sixty-degree view at any wavelength you want to punch in."

Murphy, a grizzled man who had been with the Baron a dozen years, leaned against the turret and looked down into the hatch. Past him, I could see the combs and lace of Lady Miriam's elaborate coiffure. I would have given everything I owned to be there within the tank myself—and I owned nothing but my life.

The hatch slid shut. Murphy yelped and snatched his fingers clear.

Atop the second tank, the Baron froze and his flushed

cheeks turned slatey. The mercenary lieutenant touched
a switch on his helmet and spoke too softly for anything
but the integral microphone to hear the words.

The order must have been effective, because the
hatch opened as abruptly as it had closed—startling
Murphy again.

Lady Miriam rose from the turret on what must have
been a power lift. Her posture was in awkward contrast
to the smooth ascent, but her face was composed. The
tank and its apparatus were new to the Lady, but
anything that could have gone on within the shelter of
the turret was a familiar experience to her.

"We have seen enough of your equipment," said the
Baron to Lieutenant Kiley in the same controlled voice
with which he had directed Murphy. "Rooms have been
prepared for you—the guest apartments alongside mine
in the East Wing, not the barracks below. Dinner will
be announced—" he glanced at the sky. The sun was
low enough that only the height of the tank's deck
permitted the Baron to see the orb above the courtyard
wall "—in two hours. Make yourselves welcome."

Lady Miriam turned and backed her way to the ground
again. Only then did Sergeant Grant follow her out of
the turret. The two of them were as powerful as they
were arrogant—but neither a king's daughter nor a tank
lord is immortal.

"Baron Hetziman," said the mercenary lieutenant.
"Sir—" the modest honorific for the tension, for the
rage which the Baron might be unable to control even
at risk of his estates and his life. "That building, the
gatehouse, appears disused. We'll doss down there, if
you don't mind."

The Baron's face clouded, but that was his normal
reaction to disagreement. The squat tower to the left of
the gate had been used only for storage for a generation. A rusted harrow, up-ended to fit farther within
the doorway, almost blocked access now.

The Baron squinted for a moment at the structure,
craning his short neck to look past the tank from which
he had just climbed down. Then he snorted and said,

"Sleep in a hog byre if you choose, Lieutenant. It might be cleaner at that."

"I realize," explained Lieutenant Kiley as he slid to the ground instead of using the steps, "that the request sounds odd, but Colonel Hammer is concerned that commandos from Ganz or the Lightning Division might launch an attack. The gatehouse is separated from everything but the outer wall—so if we have to defend it, we can do so without endangering any of your people."

The lie was a transparent one; but the mercenaries did not have to lie at all if they wished to keep us away from their sleeping quarters. So considered, the statement was almost generous, and the Baron chose to take it that way. "Wolfitz," he said off-handedly as he stamped toward the entrance. "Organize a party of tenants—" he gestured sharply toward the pattern of drab garments and drab faces lining the walls of the courtyard "—and clear the place, will you?"

The Chamberlain nodded obsequiously, but he continued to stride along at his master's heel.

The Baron turned, paused, and snarled, "*Now*," in a voice as grim as the fist he clenched at his side.

"My Lord," said Wolfitz with a bow that danced the line between brusque and dilatory. He stepped hastily toward the soldiers who had broken their rank in lieu of orders—a few of them toward the tanks and their haughty crews but most back to the stone shelter of the palace.

"You men," the Chamberlain said, making circling motions with his hands. "Fifty of the peasants, *quickly*. Everything is to be turned out of the gatehouse, thrown beyond the wall for the time being. *Now. Move* them."

The women followed the Baron into the palace. Several of the maids glanced over their shoulders, at the tanks—at the tankers. Some of the women would have drifted closer to meet the men in khaki uniforms, but Lady Miriam strode head high and without hesitation.

She had accomplished her purposes; the purposes of her entourage could wait.

I leaned from the roof ledge for almost a minute further, staring at the vehicles which were so smooth-

skinned that I could see my amorphous reflection in the
nearest. When the sound of women's voices echoed
through the window, I squirmed back only instants
before the Lady reentered her apartment.

They would have beaten me because of my own
excitement had they not themselves been agog with the
banquet to come—and the night which would follow it.

The high-arched banquet hall was so rarely used that
it was almost as unfamiliar to the Baron and his household as it was to his guests. Strings of small lights had
been led up the cast-concrete beams, but nothing could
really illuminate the vaulting waste of groins and coffers
that formed the ceiling.

The shadows and lights trembling on flexible fasten-
ings had the look of the night sky on the edge of an
electrical storm. I gazed up at the ceiling occasionally
while I waited at the wall behind Lady Miriam. I had
no duties at the banquet—that was for house servants,
not body servants like myself—but my presence was
required for show and against the chance that the Lady
would send me off with a message.

That chance was very slight. Any messages Lady
Miriam had were for the second-ranking tank lord,
seated to her left by custom: Sergeant-Commander Grant.

Only seven of the mercenaries, were present at the
moment. I saw mostly their backs as they sat at the
high table, interspersed with the Lady's maids. Lieutenant Kiley was in animated conversation with the
Baron to his left, but I thought the officer wished
primarily to distract his host from the way Lady Miriam
flirted on the other side.

A second keg of beer—estate stock; not the stuff
brewed for export in huge vats—had been broached by
the time the beef course followed the pork. The serving
girls had been kept busy with the mugs—in large part,
the molded-glass tankards of the Baron's soldiers, glow-
ering at the lower tables, but the metal-chased crystal
of the tank lords was refilled often as well.

Two of the mercenaries—drivers, separated by the

oldest of Lady Miriam's maids—began arguing with increasing heat while a tall, black-haired server watched in amusement. I could hear the words, but the language was not ours. One of the men got up, struggling a little because the arms of his chair were too tight against those to either side. He walked toward his commander, rolling slightly.

Lieutenant Kiley, gesturing with his mug toward the roof peak, was saying to the Baron, "Has a certain splendor, you know. Proper lighting and it'd look like a cross between a prison and a barracks, but the way you've tricked it out is—"

The standing mercenary grumbled a short, forceful paragraph, a question or a demand, to the lieutenant who broke off his own sentence to listen.

"Ah, Baron," Kiley said, turning again to his host. "Question is, what, ah, sort of regulations would there be on my boys dating local women. That one there—" his tankard nodded toward the black-haired servant. The driver who had remained seated was caressing her thigh "—for instance?"

"Regulations?" responded the Baron in genuine surprise. "On *servants*? None, of course. Would you like me to assign a group of them for your use?"

The lieutenant grinned, giving an ironic tinge to the courteous shake of his head. "I don't think that'll be necessary, Baron," he said.

Kiley stood up to attract his men's attention. "Open season on the servants, boys," he said, speaking clearly and in our language, so that everyone at or near the upper table would understand him. "Make your own arrangements. Nothing rough. And no less than two men together."

He sat down again and explained what the Baron already understood: "Things can happen when a fellow wanders off alone in a strange place. He can fall and knock his head in, for instance."

The two drivers were already shuffling out of the dining hall with the black-haired servant between them. One of the men gestured toward another buxom server with a pitcher of beer. She was not particularly well-favored, as men describe such things; but she was close, and she was willing—as any of the women in the hall would have been to go with the tank lords. I wondered whether the four of them would get any farther than the corridor outside.

I could not see the eyes of the maid who watched the departure of the mercenaries who had been seated beside her.

Lady Miriam watched the drivers leave also. Then she turned back to Sergeant Grant and resumed the conversation they held in voices as quiet as honey flowing from a ruptured comb.

In the bustle and shadows of the hall, I disappeared from the notice of those around me. Small and silent, wearing my best jacket of black velvet, I could have been but another patch of darkness. The two mercenaries left the hall by a side exit. I slipped through the end door behind me, unnoticed save as a momentary obstacle to the servants bringing in compotes of fruits grown locally and imported from across the stars.

My place was not here. My place was with the tanks, now that there was no one to watch me dreaming as I caressed their iridium flanks.

The sole guard at the door to the women's apartments glowered at me, but he did not question my reason for returning to what were, after all, my living quarters. The guard at the main entrance would probably have stopped me for spite: he was on duty while others of the household feasted and drank the best-quality beer.

I did not need a door to reach the courtyard and the tanks parked there.

Unshuttering the same window I had used in the morning, I squeezed between the bars and clambered to the roof along the antenna mount. I was fairly certain that I could clear the barrier of points and edges at the base of the wall beneath the women's suite, but there was no need to take that risk.

Starlight guided me along the stone gutter, jumping the pipes feeding the cistern under the palace cellars. Buildings formed three sides of the courtyard, but the north was closed by a wall and the gatehouse. There was no spiked barrier beneath the wall, so I stepped to the battlements and jumped to the ground safely.

Then I walked to the nearest tank, silently from reverence rather than in fear of being heard by someone in the palace. I circled the huge vehicle slowly, letting the tip of my left index finger slide over the metal. The iridium skin was smooth, but there were many bumps and irregularities set into the armor: sensors, lights, and strips of close-range defense projectors to meet an enemy or his missile with a blast of pellets.

The tank was sleeping but not dead. Though I could hear no sound from it, the armor quivered with inner life like that of a great tree when the wind touches its highest branches.

I touched a recessed step. The spring-loaded fairing that should have covered it was missing, torn away or shot off—perhaps on a distant planet. I climbed the bow slope, my feet finding each higher step as if they knew the way.

It was as if I were a god.

I might have attempted no more than that, than to stand on the hull with my hand touching the stubby barrel of the main gun—raised at a 60° angle so that it did not threaten the palace. But the turret hatch was open and, half-convinced that I was living in a hope-induced dream, I lifted myself to look in.

"Freeze," said the man looking up at me past his pistol barrel. His voice was calm. "And then we'll talk about what you think you're doing here."

The interior of the tank was coated with sulphurous light. It was too dim to shine from the hatch, but it provided enough illumination for me to see the little man in the khaki coveralls of the tank lords. The bore of the powergun in his hand shrank from the devouring cavity it had first seemed. Even the 1 cm bore of reality would release enough energy to splash the brains from my skull, I knew.

"I wanted to see the tanks," I said, amazed that I was not afraid. All men die, even kings; what better time than this would there be for me? They would never let me, so I sneaked away from the banquet. I—it was worth it. Whatever happens now."

"Via," said the tank lord, lowering his pistol. "You're just a kid, ain'tcha?"

I could see my image foreshortened in the vision screen behind the mercenary, my empty hands shown in daylit vividness at an angle which meant the camera must be in another of the parked tanks.

"My Lord," I said—straightening momentarily but overriding the reflex so that I could meet the mercenary's eyes. "I am sixteen."

"Right," he said, "and I'm Colonel Hammer. Now—"

"Oh Lord!" I cried, forgetting in my joy and embarrassment that someone else might hear me. My vision blurred and I rapped my knees on the iridium as I tried to genuflect. "Oh, Lord Hammer, forgive me for disturbing you!"

"Blood and *martyrs*, boy!" snapped the tank lord. A pump whirred and the seat from which, cross-legged, he questioned me rose. "Don't be an idiot! Me name's Curran and I drive this beast, is all."

The mercenary was head and shoulders out of the hatch now, watching me with a concerned expression. I blinked and straightened. When I knelt, I had almost slipped from the tank; and in a few moments, my bruises might be more painful than my present embarrassment.

"I'm sorry, Lord Curran," I said, thankful for once that I had practice in keeping my expression calm after a beating. "I have studied, I have dreamed about your tanks ever since I was placed in my present status six years ago. When you came I—I'm afraid I lost control."

"You're a little shrimp, even alongside me, ain'tcha?" said Curran reflectively.

A burst of laughter drifted across the courtyard from a window in the corridor flanking the dining hall.

"Aw, Via," the tank lord said. "Come take a look, seein's yer here anyhow."

It was not a dream. My grip on the hatch coaming made the iridium bite my fingers as I stepped into the tank at Curran's direction; and besides, I would never have dared to dream this paradise.

The tank's fighting compartment was not meant for two, but Curran was as small as he had implied and I—I had grown very little since a surgeon had fitted me to become the page of a high-born lady. There were screens, gauges, and armored conduits across all the surfaces I could see.

"Drivers'll tell ye," said Curran, "the guy back here, he's just along for the ride 'cause the tank does it all for 'em. Been known t' say that myself, but it ain't really true. Still—"

He touched the lower left corner of a screen. It had been black. Now, it became gray unmarked save by eight short orange lines radiating from the edge of a two-centimeter circle in the middle of the screen.

"Fire control," Curran said. A hemispherical switch was set into the bulkhead beneath the screen. He touched the control with an index finger, rotating it slightly. "That what the Slammer's all about, ain't we? Firepower and movement, and the tricky part—movement—the driver handles from up front. Got it?"

"Yes, My Lord," I said, trying to absorb everything around me without taking my eyes from what Curran was doing. The West Wing of the palace, guest and baronial quarters above the ground-floor barracks, slid up the screen as brightly illuminated as if it were daylight.

"Now *don't* touch nothin'!" the tank lord said, the first time he had spoken harshly to me. "Got it?"

"Yes, My Lord."

"Right," said Curran, softly again. "Sorry, kid. Lieutenant'll have my ass if he sees me twiddlin' with the gun, and if we blow a hole in Central Prison here—"

he gestured at the screen, though I did not understand
the reference "—the Colonel'll likely shoot me hisself."

"I won't touch anything, My Lord," I reiterated.

"Yeah, well," said the mercenary. He touched a four-
position toggle switch beside the hemisphere. "We just
lowered the main gun, right? I won't spin the turret,
'cause they'd hear that likely inside. Matter of fact—"

Instead of demonstrating the toggle, Curran fingered
the sphere again. The palace dropped off the screen
and, now that I knew to expect it, I recognized the faint
whine that must have been the gun itself gimbaling
back up to a safe angle. Nothing within the fighting
compartment moved except the image on the screen.

"So," the tanker continued, flipping the toggle to one
side. An orange numeral 2 appeared in the upper left
corner of the screen. "There's a selector there too—"
he pointed to the pistol grip by my head, attached to
the power seat which had folded up as soon as it lowered me into the tank at Curran's direction.

His finger clicked the switch to the other side—1
appeared in place of 2 on the screen—and then straight
up—3. "Main gun," he said, "co-ax—that's the tribarrel
mounted just in front of the hatch. You musta seen it?"

I nodded, but my agreement was a lie. I had been
too excited and too overloaded with wonder to notice
the automatic weapon on which I might have set my
hand.

"And 3," Curran went on, nodding also, "straight
up—that's both guns together. Not so hard, was it?
You're ready to be a tank commander now—and—" he
grinned, "—with six months and a little luck, I could
teach ye t' drive the little darlin' besides."

"Oh, My Lord," I whispered, uncertain whether I
was speaking to God or to the man beside me. I spread
my feet slightly in order to keep from falling in a fit of
weakness.

"*Watch* it!" the tank lord said sharply, sliding his
booted foot to block me. More gently, he added, "Don't
be touching *nothing*, remember? That—" he pointed to
a pedal on the floor which I had not noticed "—that's

the foot trip. Touch it and we give a little fireworks demonstration that nobody's gonna be very happy about."

He snapped the toggle down to its original position; the numeral disappeared from the screen. "Shouldn't have it live nohow," he added.

"But—all this," I said, gesturing with my arm close to my chest so that I would not bump any of the close-packed apparatus. "If shooting is so easy, then why is—*everything*—here?"

Curran smiled. "Up," he said, pointing to the hatch. As I hesitated, he added, "I'll give you a leg-up, don't worry about the power lift."

Flushing, sure that I was being exiled from Paradise because I had overstepped myself—somehow—with the last question, I jumped for the hatch coaming and scrambled through with no need of the tanker's help. I supposed I was crying, but I could not tell because my eyes burned so.

"Hey, slow down, kid," called Curran as he lifted himself with great strength but less agility. "It's just Whichard's about due t' take over guard, and we don't need him t' find you inside. Right?"

"Oh," I said, hunched already on the edge of the tank's deck. I did not dare turn around for a moment. "Of course, My Lord."

"The thing about shootin'," explained the tank lord to my back, "ain't *how* so much's when and what. You got all this commo and sensors that'll handle any wavelength or take remote feeds. But *still* somebody's gotta decide which data t' call up—and decide what it means. And decide t' pop it er not—" I turned just as Curran leaned over to slap the iridium barrel of the main gun for emphasis. "Which is a mother-huge decision for whatever's down-range, ye know."

He grinned broadly. He had a short beard, rather sparse, which partly covered the pockmarks left by some childhood disease. "Maybe even puts tank commander up on a level with driver for tricky, right?"

His words opened a window in my mind, the frames branching and spreading into a spidery, infinite structure: responsibility, the choices that came with the power of a tank.

"Yes, My Lord," I whispered.

"Now, you better get back t' whatever civvies do," Curran said, a suggestion that would be snarled out as an order if I hesitated. "And *don't* be shootin' off yer mouth about t'night, right?"

"No, My Lord," I said as I jumped to the ground. Tie-beams between the wall and the masonry gatehouse would let me climb back to the path I had followed to get here.

"And thank you," I added, but varied emotions choked the words into a mumble.

I thought the women might already have returned, but I listened for a moment, clinging to the bars, and heard nothing. Even so I climbed in the end window. It was more difficult to scramble down without the aid of the antenna brace, but a free-standing wardrobe put that window in a sort of alcove.

I didn't know what would happen if the women saw me slipping in and out through the bars. There would be a beating—there was a beating whenever an occasion offered. That didn't matter, but it was possible that Lady Miriam would also have the openings cross-barred too straitly for even my slight form to pass.

I would have returned to the banquet hall, but female voices were already greeting the guard outside the door. I had only enough time to smooth the plush of my jacket with Sarah's hairbrush before they swept in, all of them together and their mistress in the lead as usual.

By standing against a color-washed wall panel, I was able to pass unnoticed for some minutes of the excited babble without being guilty of 'hiding' with the severe flogging that would surely entail. By the time Lady Miriam called, "Leesh? *Elisha!*" in a querulous voice, no one else could have sworn that I hadn't entered the apartment with the rest of the entourage.

"Yes, My Lady?" I said, stepping forward.

Several of the women were drifting off in pairs to

help one another out of their formal costumes and coiffures. There would be a banquet every night that the tank lords remained—providing occupation to fill the otherwise featureless lives of the maids and their mistress.

That was time consuming, even if they did not become more involved than public occasion required.

"Leesh," said Lady Miriam, moderating her voice unexpectedly. I was prepared for a blow, ready to accept it unflinchingly unless it were aimed at my eyes and even then to dodge as little as possible so as not to stir up a worse beating.

"Elisha," the Lady continued in a honeyed tone—then, switching back to acid sharpness and looking at her Chief Maid, she said, "Sarah, what *are* all these women doing here? Don't they have rooms of their own?"

Women who still dallied in the suite's common room—several of the lower-ranking stored their garments here in chests and clothes presses—scurried for their sleeping quarters while Sarah hectored them, arms akimbo.

"I need you to carry a message for me, Leesh," explained Lady Miriam softly. "to one of our guests. You—you do know, don't you, boy, which suite was cleared for use by our guests?"

"Yes, My Lady," I said, keeping my face blank. "The end suite of the East Wing, where the King slept last year. But I thought— "

"Don't think," said Sarah, rapping me with the brush which she carried on all but formal occasions. "And don't interrupt milady."

"Yes, My Lady," I said, bowing and rising.

"I don't want you to *go* there, boy," said the Lady with an edge of irritation. "If Sergeant Grant has any questions, I want you to point the rooms out to him—from the courtyard."

She paused and touched her full lips with her tongue while her fingers played with the fan. "Yes," she said at last, then continued, "I want you to tell Sergeant Grant oh-four hundred and to answer any questions he may have."

Lady Miriam looked up again, and though her voice remained mild, her eyes were hard as knife points. "Oh. And Leesh? This is business which the Baron does not wish to be known. Speak to Sergeant Grant in private. And never speak to anyone else about it—even to the Baron if he tries to trick you into an admission."

"Yes, My Lady," I said bowing.

I understood what the Baron would do to a page who brought him that news—and how he would send a message back to his wife, to the king's daughter whom he dared not impale in person.

Sarah's shrieked order carried me past the guard at the women's apartment, while Lady Miriam's signet was my pass into the courtyard after normal hours. The soldier there on guard was muzzy with drink. I might have been able to slip unnoticed by the hall alcove in which he sheltered.

I skipped across the gravel-in-clay surface of the courtyard, afraid to pause to touch the tanks again when I knew Lady Miriam would be peering from her window. Perhaps on the way back . . . but no, she would be as intent on hearing how the message was received as she was anxious to know that it had been delivered. I would ignore the tanks—

"*Freeze*, buddy!" snarled someone from the turret of the tank I had just run past.

I stumbled with shock and my will to obey. Catching my balance, I turned slowly—to the triple muzzles of the weapon mounted on the cupola, not a pistol as Lord Curran had pointed. The man who spoke wore a shielded helmet, but there would not have been enough light to recognize him anyway.

"Please, My Lord," I said. "I have a message for Sergeant-Commander Grant?"

"From who?" the mercenary demanded. I knew now that Lieutenant Kiley had been serious about protecting from intrusion the quarters allotted to his men.

"My Lord, I . . . " I said and found no way to proceed.

"Yeah, Via," the tank lord agreed in a relaxed tone. "None a' my affair." He touched the side of his helmet and spoke softly.

The gatehouse door opened with a spill of light and the tall, broad-shouldered silhouette of Sergeant Grant. Like the mercenary on guard in the tank, he wore a communications helmet.

Grant slipped his faceshield down, and for a moment my own exposed skin tingled—or my mind *thought* it perceived a tingle—as the tank lord's equipment scanned me.

"C'mon, then," he grunted, gesturing me toward the recessed angle of the building and the gate leaves. "We'll step around the corner and talk."

There was a trill of feminine laughter from the upper story of the gatehouse: a servant named Maria, whose hoots of joy were unmistakable. Lieutenant Kiley leaned his head and torso from the window above us and shouted to Grant, his voice and his anger recognizable even though the words themselves were not.

The sergeant paused, clenching his left fist and reaching for me with his right because I happened to be closest to him. I poised to run—survive this first, then worry about what Lady Miriam would say—but the tank lord caught himself, raised his shield, and called to his superior in a tone on the safe side of insolent, "All right, all right. I'll stay right here where Cermak can see me from the tank."

Apparently Grant had remembered Lady Miriam also, for he spoke in our language so that I—and the principal for whom I acted—would understand the situation.

Lieutenant Kiley banged his shutters closed.

Grant stared for a moment at Cermak until the guard understood and dropped back into the interior of his vehicle. We could still be observed through the marvelous vision blocks, but we had the miminal privacy needed for me to deliver my message.

"Lady Miriam," I said softly, "says oh-four hundred."

I waited for the tank lord to ask me for directions.

His breath and sweat exuded sour echoes of the strong
estate ale.

"Won't go," the tank lord replied unexpectedly. "I'll
be clear at oh-three *to* oh-four." He paused before
adding, "You tell her, kid, she better not be playin'
games. Nobody plays prick-tease with *this* boy and likes
what they get for it."

"Yes, My Lord," I said, skipping backward because I
had the feeling that this man would grab me and shake
me to emphasize his point.

I would not deliver his threat. My best small hope for
safety at the end of this affair required that Lady Miriam believe I was ignorant of what was going on, and a
small hope it was.

That *was* a slim hope anyway.

"Well, go on, then," the tank lord said.

He strode back within the gatehouse, catlike in his
grace and lethality, while I ran to tell my mistress of
the revised time.

An hour's pleasure seemed a little thing against the
risk of two lives—and my own.

My 'room' was what had been the back staircase
before it was blocked to convert the second floor of the
West Wing into the women's apartment. The dank
cylinder was furnished only with the original stone stair
treads and whatever my mistress and her maids had
chosen to store there over the years. I normally slept
on a chair in the common room, creeping back to my
designated space before dawn.

Tonight I slept *beneath* one of the large chairs in a
corner; not hidden, exactly, but not visible without a
search.

The two women were quiet enough to have slipped
past someone who was not poised to hear them as I
was, and the tiny flashlight the leader carried threw a
beam so tight that it could scarcely have helped them
see their way. But the perfume they wore—imported,
expensive, and overpowering—was more startling than
a shout.

They paused at the door. The latch rattled like a tocsin though the hinges did not squeal.

The soldier on guard, warned and perhaps awakened by the latch, stopped them before they could leave the apartment. The glowlamp in the sconce beside the door emphasized the ruddy anger on his face.

Sarah's voice, low but cutting, said, "Keep silent, my man, or it will be the worse for you." She thrust a gleam of gold toward the guard, not payment but a richly-chased signet ring, and went on, "Lady Miriam knows and approves. Keep still and you'll have no cause to regret this night. Otherwise . . ."

The guard's face was not blank, but emotions chased themselves across it too quickly for his mood to be read. Suddenly he reached out and harshly squeezed the Chief Maid's breast. Sarah gasped, and the man snarled, "What've they got that *I* don't, tell me, huh? You're *all* whores, that's all you are!"

The second woman was almost hidden from the soldier by the Chief Maid and the panel of the half-opened door. I could see a shimmer of light as her hand rose, though I could not tell whether it was a blade or a gun barrel.

The guard flung his hand down from Sarah and turned away. "Go on, then," he grumbled. "What do I care? Go *on*, sluts."

The weapon disappeared, unused and unseen, into the folds of an ample skirt, and the two women left the suite with only the whisper of felt slippers. They were heavily veiled and wore garments coarser than any I had seen on the Chief Maid before—but Lady Miriam was as recognizable in the grace of her walk as Sarah was for her voice.

The women left the door ajar to keep the latch from rattling again, and the guard did not at first pull it to. I listened for further moments against the chance that another maid would come from her room or that the Lady would rush back, driven by fear or conscience—though I hadn't seen either state control her in the past.

I was poised to squeeze between the window-bars again, barefoot for secrecy and a better grip, when I heard the hum of static as the guard switched his belt radio live. There was silence as he keyed it, then his low voice saying, "They've left, sir. They're on their way toward the banquet hall."

There was another pause and a radio voice too thin for me to hear more than the fact of it. The guard said, "Yes, Chamberlain," and clicked off the radio.

He latched the door.

I was out through the bars in one movement and well up the antenna brace before any of the maids could have entered the common room to investigate the noise.

I knew where the women were going, but not whether the Chamberlain would stop them on the way past the banquet hall or the Baron's personal suite at the head of East Wing. The fastest, safest way for me to cross the roof of the banquet hall was twenty feet up the side, where the builders' forms had left a flat, thirty-centimeter path in the otherwise sloping concrete.

Instead, I decided to pick my way along the trash-filled stone gutter just above the windows of the corridor on the courtyard side. I could say that my life—my chance of life—depended on knowing what was going on . . . and it did depend on that. But crawling through the starlit darkness, spying on my betters, was also the only way I had of asserting myself. The need to assert myself had become unexpectedly pressing since Lord Curran had showed me the tank, and since I had experienced what a man *could* be.

There was movement across the courtyard as I reached the vertical extension of the load-bearing wall that separated the West Wing from the banquet hall. I ducked beneath the stone coping, but the activity had nothing to do with me. The gatehouse door had opened and, as I peered through dark-adapted eyes, the mercenary on guard in a tank exchanged with the man who had just stepped out of the building.

The tank lords talked briefly. Then the gatehouse

door shut behind the guard who had been relieved while his replacement climbed into the turret of the vehicle parked near the West Wing—Sergeant Grant's tank. I clambered over the wall extension and stepped carefully along the gutter, regretting now that I had not worn shoes for protection. I heard nothing from the corridor below, although the casements were pivoted outward to catch any breeze that would relieve the summer stillness.

Gravel crunched in the courtyard as the tank lord on guard slid from his vehicle and began to stride toward the end of the East Wing.

He was across the courtyard from me—faceless behind the shield of his commo helmet and at best only a shadow against the stone of the wall behind him. But the man was Sergeant Grant beyond question, abandoning his post for the most personal of reasons.

I continued, reaching the East Wing as the tank lord disappeared among the stone finials of the outside staircase at the wing's far end. The guest suites had their own entrance, more formally ornamented than the doorways serving the estate's own needs. The portal was guarded only when the suites were in use—and then most often by a mixed force of the Baron's soldiers and those of the guests.

That was not a formality. The guest who would entrust his life solely to the Baron's good will was a fool.

A corridor much like that flanking the banquet hall ran along the courtyard side of the guest suites. It was closed by a cross-wall and door, separating the guests from the Baron's private apartment, but the door was locked and not guarded.

Lady Miriam kept a copy of the door's microchip key under the plush lining of her jewel box. I had found it but left it there, needless to me so long as I could slip through window grates.

The individual guest suites were locked also, but as I lowered myself from the gutter to a window ledge I heard a door snick closed. The sound was minuscule, but it had a crispness that echoed in the lightless hall.

Skirts rustled softly against the stone, and Sarah gave a gentle, troubled sigh as she settled herself to await her mistress.

I waited on the ledge, wondering if I should climb back to the roof—or even return to my own room. The Chamberlain had not blocked the assignation, and there was no sign of an alarm. The soldiers, barracked on the ground floor of this wing, would have been clearly audible had they been aroused.

Then I did hear something—or feel it. There had been motion, the ghost of motion, on the other side of the door closing the corridor. Someone had entered or left the Baron's apartment, and I had heard them through the open windows.

It could have been one of the Baron's current favorites—girls from the estate, the younger and more vulnerable, the better. They generally used the little door and staircase on the outer perimeter of the palace— where a guard *was* stationed against the possibility that an axe-wielding relative would follow the lucky child.

I lifted myself back to the roof with particular care, so that I would not disturb the Chief Maid waiting in the hallway. Then I followed the gutter back to the portion of roof over the Baron's apartments.

I knew the wait would be less than an hour, the length of Sergeant Grant's guard duty, but it did not occur to me that the interval would be as brief as it actually was. I had scarcely settled myself again to wait when I thought I heard a door unlatch in the guest suites. That could have been imagination or Sarah, deciding to wait in a room instead of the corridor; but moments later the helmeted tank lord paused on the outside staircase.

By taking the risk of leaning over the roof coping, I could see Lord Grant and a woman embracing on the landing before the big mercenary strode back across the courtyard toward the tank where he was supposed to be on guard. Desire had not waited on its accomplishment, and mutual fear had prevented the sort of dalliance after the event that the women dwelt on so lovingly in the privacy of their apartment . . . while Leesh, the Lady's page and no man, listened of necessity.

The women's slippers made no sound in the corridor, but their dresses brushed one another to the door which clicked and sighed as it let them out of the guest apartments and into the portion of the East Wing reserved to the Baron.

I expected shouts, then; screams, even gunfire as the Baron and Wolfitz confronted Lady Miriam. There was no sound except for skirts continuing to whisper their way up the hall, returning to the women's apartment. I stood up to follow, disappointed despite the fact that bloody chaos in the palace would endanger everyone—and me, the usual scapegoat for frustrations, most of all.

The Baron said in a tight voice at the window directly beneath me, "Give me the goggles, Wolfitz," and surprise almost made me fall.

The strap of a pair of night-vision goggles rustled over the Baron's grizzled head. Their frames clucked against the stone sash as my master bent forward with the unfamiliar headgear.

For a moment, I was too frightened to breathe. If he leaned out and turned his head, he would see me poised like a terrified gargoyle above him. Any move I made—even flattening myself behind the wall coping—risked a sound and disaster.

"You're right," said the Baron in a voice that would have been normal if it had any emotion behind it. There was another sound of something hard against the sash, a metallic clink this time.

"*No*, My Lord!" said the Chamberlain in a voice more forceful than I dreamed any underling would use to the Baron. Wolfitz must have been seizing the nettle firmly, certain that hesitation or uncertainty meant the end of more than his plans. "If you shoot him now, the others will blast everything around them to glowing slag."

"Wolfitz," said the Baron, breathing hard. They had been struggling. The flare-mouthed mob gun from the Baron's nightstand—scarcely a threat to Sergeant Grant across the courtyard—extended from the window opening, but the Chamberlain's bony hand was on the Baron's wrist. "If you tell me I must let those arrogant outworlders pleasure *my* wife in *my* palace, I will kill you."

He sounded like an architect discussing a possible staircase curve.

"There's a better way, My Lord," said the Chamberlain. His voice was breathy also, but I thought exertion was less to account for that than was the risk he took. "We'll be ready the next time the—outworlder gives us the opportunity. We'll take him in, in the crime; but quietly so that the others aren't aroused."

"Idiot!" snarled the Baron, himself again in all his arrogant certainty. Their hands and the gun disappeared from the window ledge. The tableau was the vestige of an event the men needed each other too much to remember. "No matter what we do with the body, the others will blame us. Blame *me*."

His voice took a dangerous coloration as he added, "Is that what you had in mind, Chamberlain?"

Wolfitz said calmly, "The remainder of the platoon here will be captured—or killed, it doesn't matter—by the mercenaries of the Lightning Division, who will also protect us from reaction by King Adrian and Colonel Hammer."

"But . . . " said the Baron, the word a placeholder for the connected thought which did not form in his mind after all.

"The King of Ganz won't hesitate an instant if you offer him your fealty," the Chamberlain continued, letting the words display their own strength instead of speaking loudly in a fashion his master might take as badgering.

The Baron still held the mob gun, and his temper was doubtful at the best of times.

"The mercenaries of the Lightning Division," continued Wolfitz with his quiet voice and persuasive ideas, "will accept any risk in order to capture four tanks undamaged. The value of that equipment is beyond any

profit the Lightning Division dreamed of earning when
they were hired by Ganz."

"But . . . " the Baron repeated in an awestruck voice.
"The truce?"

"A matter for the kings to dispute," said the Chamberlain off-handedly. "But Adrian will find little support among his remaining barons if you were forced
into your change of allegiance. When the troops he
billeted on you raped and murdered Lady Miriam, that
is."

"How quickly can you make the arrangements?" asked
the Baron. I had difficulty in following the words: not
because they were soft, but because he growled them
like a beast.

"The delay," Wolfitz replied judiciously, and I could
imagine him lacing his long fingers together and staring
at them, "will be for the next opportunity your—Lady
Miriam and her lover give us, I shouldn't imagine that
will be longer than tomorrow night."

The Baron's teeth grated like nutshells being ground
against stone.

"We'll have to use couriers, of course," Wolfitz added.
"The likelihood of the Slammers intercepting any other
form of communication is too high. . . . but all Ganz
and its mercenaries have to do is ready a force to dash
here and defend the palace before Hammer can react.
Since these tanks *are* the forward picket, and they'll be
unmanned while Sergeant Grant is—otherwise occupied—the Lightning Division will have almost an hour
before an alarm can be given. Ample time, I'm sure."

"Chamberlain," the Baron said in a voice from which
amazement had washed all the anger. "You think of
everything. See to it."

"Yes, My Lord," said Wolfitz humbly.

The tall Chamberlain *did* think of everything, or very
nearly; but he'd had much longer to plan than the
Baron thought. I wondered how long Wolfitz had waited
for an opportunity like this one; and what payment he
had arranged to receive from the King of Ganz if he
changed the Baron's allegiance?

A door slammed closed, the Baron returning to his suite and his current child-mistress. Chamberlain Wolfitz's rooms adjoined his master's, but my ears followed his footsteps to the staircase at the head of the wing.

By the time I had returned to the West Wing and was starting down the antenna brace, a pair of the Baron's soldiers had climbed into a truck and gone rattling off into the night. It was an unusual event but not especially remarkable: the road they took led off to one of the Baron's outlying estates.

But the road led to the border with Ganz, also; and I had no doubt as to where the couriers' message would be received.

The tank lords spent most of the next day busy with their vehicles. A squad of the Baron's soldiers kept at a distance the tenants and house servants who gawked while the khaki-clad tankers crawled through access plates and handed fan motors to their fellows. The bustle racks welded to the back of each turret held replacement parts as well as the crew's personal belongings.

It was hard to imagine that objects as huge and powerful as the tanks would need repair. I had to remember that they were not ingots of iridium but vastly complicated assemblages of parts—each of which could break, and eight of which were human.

I glanced occasionally at the tanks and the lordly men who ruled and serviced them. I had no excuse to take me beyond the women's apartment during daylight.

Excitement roused the women early, but there was little pretense of getting on with their lace-making. They dressed, changed, primped—argued over rights to one bit of clothing or another—and primarily, they talked.

Lady Miriam was less a part of the gossip than usual, but she was the most fastidious of all about the way she would look at the night's banquet.

The tank lords bathed at the wellhead in the courtyard like so many herdsmen. The women watched hungrily, edging forward despite the scandalized demands of one of the older maids that they at least stand back in the room where their attention would be less blatant.

Curran's muscles were knotted, his skin swarthy. Sergeant Grant could have passed for a god—or at least a man of half his real age. When he looked up at the women's apartments, he smiled.

The truck returned in late afternoon, carrying the two soldiers and a third man in civilian clothes who could have been—but was not—the manager of one of the outlying estates. The civilian was closeted with the Baron for half an hour before he climbed back into the truck. He, Wolfitz, and the Baron gripped one another's forearms in leave-taking; then the vehicle returned the way it had come.

The tank lord on guard paid less attention to the truck than he had to the column of steam-driven produce vans, chuffing toward the nearest rail terminus.

The banquet was less hectic that that of the first night, but the glitter had been replaced by a fog of hostility now that the newness had worn off. The Baron's soldiers were more openly angry that Hammer's men picked and chose—food at the high table and women in the corridor or the servants' quarters below.

The Slammers, for their part, had seen enough of the estate to be contemptuous of its isolation, of its low technology—and of the folk who lived on it. And yet—I had talked with Lord Curran and listened to the others as well. The tank lords were men like those of the barony. They had walked on far worlds and had been placed in charge of instruments as sophisticated as any in the human galaxy—but they were not sophisticated *men*, only powerful ones.

Sergeant-Commander Grant, for instance, made the child's mistake of thinking his power to destroy conferred on him a sort of personal immortality.

The Baron ate and drank in a sullen reverie, deaf to the lieutenant's attempts at conversation and as blind to Lady Miriam on his left as she was to him. The Chamberlain was seated among the soldiers because there were more guests than maids of honor. He watched the activities at the high table unobtrusively, keeping his own counsel and betraying his nervousness only by the fact that none of the food he picked at seemed to go down his throat.

I was tempted to slip out to the tanks, because Lord Curran was on duty again during the banquet. His absence must have been his own choice; a dislike for the food or the society perhaps . . . but more probably, from what I had seen in the little man when we talked, a fear of large, formal gatherings.

It would have been nice to talk to Lord Curran again, and blissful to have the controls of the huge tank again within my hands. But if I were caught then, I might not be able to slip free later in the night—and I would rather have died than missed that chance.

The Baron hunched over his ale when Lieutenant Kiley gathered his men to return to the gatehouse. They did not march well in unison, not even by comparison with the Baron's soldiers when they drilled in the courtyard.

The skills and the purpose of the tank lords lay elsewhere.

Lady Miriam rose when the tankers fell in. She swept from the banquet hall regally as befit her birth, dressed in amber silk from Terra and topazes of ancient cut from our own world. She did not look behind her to see that her maids followed and I brought up the rear . . . but she did glance aside once at the formation of tank lords.

She would be dressed no better than a servant later that night, and she wanted to be sure that Sergeant Grant had a view of her full splendor to keep in mind when next they met in darkness.

The soldier who had guarded the women's apartments the night before was on duty when the Chief Maid led her mistress out again. There was no repetition of the previous night's dangerous byplay this time.

The guard was subdued, or frightened; or, just possibly, biding his time because he was aware of what was going to come.

I followed, more familiar with my route this time and too pumped with excitement to show the greater care I knew was necessary tonight, when there would be many besides myself to watch, to listen.

But I was alone on the roof, and the others, so certain of what *they* knew and expected, paid no attention to the part of the world which lay beyond their immediate interest.

Sergeant Grant sauntered as he left the vehicle where he was supposed to stay on guard. As he neared the staircase to the guest suites, his stride lengthened and his pace picked up. There was nothing of nervousness in his manner; only the anticipation of a man focused on sex to the extinction of all other considerations.

I was afraid that Wolfitz would spring his trap before I was close enough to follow what occurred. A more reasonable fear would have been that I would stumble into the middle of the event.

Neither danger came about. I reached the gutter over the guest corridor and waited, breathing through my mouth alone so that I wouldn't make any noise. The blood that pounded through my ears deafened me for a moment, but there was nothing to fear. Voices murmured, Sarah and Sergeant Grant, and the door that had waited ajar for the tank lord clicked to shut the suite.

Four of the Baron's soldiers mounted the outside steps, as quietly as their boots permitted. There were faint sounds, clothing and one muted clink of metal, from the corridor on the Baron's side of the door.

All day I'd been telling myself that there was no safe way I could climb down and watch the events through a window. I climbed down, finding enough purchase for my fingers and toes where weathering had rounded the corners of stone blocks. Getting back to the roof would be more difficult, unless I risked gripping an out-swung casement for support.

Unless I dropped, bullet-riddled, to the ground.

I rested a toe on a window ledge and peeked around the stone toward the door of the suite the lovers had used on their first assignation. I could see nothing—

Until the corridor blazed with silent light.

Sarah's face was white, dazzling with direct reflection of the high-intensity floods at either end of the hallway. Her mouth opened and froze, a statue of a scream but without the sound that fear or self preservation choked in her throat.

Feet, softly but many of them, shuffled over the stone flags toward the Chief Maid. Her head jerked from one side to the other, but her body did not move. The illumination was pinning her to the door where she kept watch.

The lights spilled through the corridor windows, but their effect was surprisingly slight in the open air: high-lights on the parked tanks; a faint wash of outline, not color, over the stones of the wall and gatehouse; and a distorted shadowplay on the ground itself, men and weapons twisting as they advanced toward the trapped maid from both sides.

There was no sign of interest from the gatehouse. Even if the tank lords were awake to notice the lights, what happened at night in the palace was no affair of theirs.

Three of perhaps a dozen of the Baron's soldiers stepped within my angle of vision. Two carried rifles; the third was Murphy with a chip recorder, the spidery wands of its audio and video pick-ups retracted because of the press of men standing nearby.

Sarah swallowed. She closed her mouth, but her eyes stared toward the infinite distance beyond this world. The gold signet she clutched was a drop from the sun's heart in the floodlights.

The Baron stepped close to the woman. He took the ring with his left hand, looked at it, and passed it to the stooped, stone-faced figure of the Chamberlain.

"Move her out of the way," said the Baron in a husky whisper.

One of the soldiers stuck the muzzle of his assault

rifle under the chin of the Chief Maid, pointing upward. With his other hand, the man gripped Sarah's shoulder and guided her away from the door panel.

Wolfitz looked at his master, nodded, and set a magnetic key on the lock. Then he too stepped clear.

The Baron stood at the door with his back to me. He wore body armor, but he can't have thought it would protect him against the Slammer's powergun. Murphy was at the Baron's side, the recorder's central light glaring back from the door panel, and another soldier poised with his hand on the latch.

The Baron slammed the door inward with his foot. I do not think I have ever seen a man move as fast as Sergeant Grant did then.

The door opened on a servants' alcove, not the guest rooms themselves, but the furnishings there were sufficient to the lovers' need. Lady Miriam had lifted her skirts. She was standing, leaning slightly backwards, with her buttocks braced against the bedframe. She screamed, her eyes blank reflections of the sudden light.

Sergeant-Commander Grant still wore his helmet. He had slung his belt and holstered pistol over the bedpost when he unsealed the lower flap of his uniform coveralls, but he was turning with the pistol in his hand before the Baron got off the first round with his mob gun.

Aerofoils, spread from the flaring muzzle by asymmetric thrust, spattered the lovers and a two-meter circle on the wall beyond them.

The tank lord's chest was in bloody tatters and there was a brain-deep gash between his eyebrows, but his body and the powergun followed through with the motion reflex had begun.

The Baron's weapon chunked twice more. Lady Miriam flopped over the footboard and lay thrashing on the bare springs, spurting blood from narrow wounds that her clothing did not cover. Individual projectiles from the mob gun had little stopping power, but they bled out a victim's life like so many knife blades.

When the Baron shot the third time, his gun was within a meter of what had been the tank lord's face. Sergeant Grant's body staggered backward and fell, the powergun unfired but still gripped in the mercenary's right hand.

"Call the Lightning Division," said the Baron harshly as he turned. His face, except where it was freckled by fresh blood, was as pale as I had ever seen it. "It's time."

Wolfitz lifted a communicator, short range but keyed to the main transmitter, and spoke briefly. There was no need for communications security now. The man who should have intercepted and evaluated the short message was dead in a smear of his own wastes and body fluids.

The smell of the mob gun's propellant clung chokingly to the back of my throat, among the more familiar slaughterhouse odors. Lady Miriam's breath whistled, and the bedsprings squeaked beneath her uncontrolled motions.

"Shut that off," said the Baron to Murphy. The recorder's pool of light shrank into shadow within the alcove.

The Baron turned and fired once more, into the tank lord's groin.

"Make sure the others don't leave the gatehouse till Ganz's mercenaries are here to deal with them," said the Baron negligently. He looked at the gun in his hand. Strong lights turned the heat and propellant residues rising from its barrel into shadows on the wall beyond.

"Marksmen are ready, My Lord," said the Chamberlain.

The Baron skittered his mob gun down the hall. He strode toward the rooms of his own apartment.

It must have been easier to climb back to the roof than I had feared. I have no memory of it, of the stress on fingertips and toes or the pain in my muscles as they lifted the body which they had supported for what seemed (after the fact) to have been hours. Minutes only, of course; but instead of serial memory of what had happened, my brain was filled with too many frozen pictures of details for all of them to fit within the real timeframe.

The plan that I had made for this moment lay so deep that I executed it by reflex, though my brain roiled.

Executed it by instinct, perhaps; the instinct of flight, the instinct to power.

In the corridor, Wolfitz and Murphy were arguing in low voices about what should be done about the mess.

Soldiers had taken up positions in the windowed corridor flanking the banquet hall. More of the Baron's men, released from trapping Lady Miriam and her lover, were joining their fellows with words too soft for me to understand. I crossed the steeply-pitched roof on the higher catwalk, for speed and from fear that the men at the windows might hear me.

There were no soldiers on the roof itself. The wall coping might hide even a full-sized man if he lay flat, but the narrow gutter between wall and roof was an impossible position from which to shoot at targets across the courtyard.

The corridor windows on the courtyard side were not true firing slits like those of all the palace's outer walls. Nonetheless, men shooting from corners of the windows could shelter their bodies behind stone thick enough to stop bolts from the Slammers' personal weapons. The sleet of bullets from twenty assault rifles would turn anyone sprinting from the gatehouse door or the pair of second-floor windows into offal like that which had been Sergeant Grant.

The tank lords were not immortal.

There was commotion in the women's apartments when I crossed them. Momentarily a light fanned the shadow of the window bars across the courtyard and the gray curves of Sergeant Grant's tank. A male voice cursed harshly. A lamp casing crunched, and from the returned darkness came a blow and a woman's cry.

Some of the Baron's soldiers were taking positions in

the West Wing. Unless the surviving tank lords could blow a gap in the thick outer wall of the gatehouse, they had no exit until the Lightning Division arrived with enough firepower to sweep them up at will.

But I could get in, with a warning that would come in time for them to summon aid from Colonel Hammer himself. They would be in debt for my warning, owing me their lives, their tanks, and their honor.

Surely the tank lords could find a place for a servant willing to go with them anywhere?

The battlements of the wall closing the north side of the courtyard formed my pathway to the roof of the gatehouse. Grass and brush grew there in ragged clumps. Cracks between stones had trapped dust, seeds, and moisture during a generation of neglect. I crawled along, on my belly, tearing my black velvet jacket.

Eyes focused on the gatehouse door and windows were certain to wander: to the sky; to fellows slouching over their weapons; to the wall connecting the gatehouse to the West Wing. If I stayed flat, I merged with the stone . . . but shrubs could quiver in the wrong pattern, and the Baron's light-amplifying goggles might be worn by one of the watching soldiers.

It had seemed simpler when I planned it; but it was necessary in any event, even if I died in a burst of gunfire.

The roof of the gatehouse was reinforced concrete, slightly domed, and as proof against indirect fire as the stone walls were against small arms. There was no roof entrance, but there was a capped flue for the stove that had once heated the guard quarters. I'd squirmed my way through that hole once before.

Four years before.

The roof of the gatehouse was a meter higher than the wall on which I lay, an easy jump but one which put me in silhouette against the stars. I reached up, feeling along the concrete edge less for a grip than for reassurance. I was afraid to leave the wall because my body was telling itself that the stone it pressed was safety.

If the Baron's men shot me now, it would warn the tank lords in time to save them. I owed them that, for the glimpses of freedom Curran had showed me in the turret of a tank.

I vaulted onto the smooth concrete and rolled, a shadow in the night to any of the watchers who might have seen me. Once I was *on* the gatehouse, I was safe because of the flat dome that shrugged off rain and projectiles. The flue was near the north edge of the structure, hidden from the eyes and guns waiting elsewhere in the palace.

I'd grown only slightly since I was twelve and beginning to explore the palace in which I expected to die. The flue hadn't offered much margin, but my need wasn't as great then, either.

I'd never needed *anything* as much as I needed to get into the gatehouse now.

The metal smoke pipe had rusted and blown down decades before. The wooden cap, fashioned to close the hole to rain, hadn't been maintained. It crumbled in my hands when I lifted it away, soggy wood with only flecks remaining of the stucco which had been applied to seal the cap into place.

The flue was as narrow as the gap between window bars, and because it was round, I didn't have the luxury of turning sideways. So be it.

If my shoulders fit, my hips would follow. I extended my right arm and reached down through the hole as far as I could. The flue was as empty as it was dark. Flakes of rust made mouselike patterings as my touch dislodged them. The passageway curved smoothly, but it had no sharp-angled shot trap as far down as I could feel from outside.

I couldn't reach the lower opening. The roof was built thick enough to stop heavy shells. At least the slimy surface of the concrete tube would make the job easier.

I lowered my head into the flue with the pit of my extended right arm pressed as firmly as I could against the lip of the opening. The cast concrete brought an electric chill through the sweat-soaked velvet of my jerkin, reminding me—now that it was too late—that I could have stripped off the garment to gain another millimeter's tolerance.

It was too late, even though all but my head and one arm were outside. If I stopped now, I would never have the courage to go on again.

The air in the flue was dank, because even now in late Summer the concrete sweated and the cap prevented condensate from evaporating. The sound of my fear-lengthened breaths did not echo from the end of a closed tube, and not even panic could convince me that the air was stale and would suffocate me. I slid farther down; down to the *real* point of no return.

By leading with my head and one arm, I was able to tip my collar bone endwise for what would have been a relatively easy fit within the flue if my ribs and spine did not have to follow after. The concrete caught the tip of my left shoulder and the ribs beneath my right armpit—let me flex forward minutely on the play in my skin and the velvet—and held me.

I would have screamed, but the constriction of my ribs was too tight. My legs kicked in the air above the gatehouse, unable to thrust me down for lack of purchase. My right arm flopped in the tube, battering my knuckles and fingertips against unyielding concrete.

I could die here, and no one would know.

Memory of the tank and the windows of choice expanding infinitely above even Leesh, the Lady's page, flashed before me and cooled my body like rain on a stove. My muscles relaxed and I could breathe again—though carefully, and though the veins of my head were distending with blood trapped by my present posture.

Instead of flapping vainly, my right palm and elbow locked on opposite sides of the curving passage. I breathed as deeply as I could, then let it out as I kicked my legs up where gravity, at least, could help.

My right arm pulled while my left tried to clamp itself within my rib cage. Cloth tore, skin tore, and my torso slipped fully within the flue, lubricated by blood as well as condensate.

If I had been upright, I might have blacked out momentarily with the release of tension. Inverted, I could only gasp and feel my face and scalp burn with the flush that darkened them. The length of a hand farther and my pelvis scraped. My fingers had a grip on the lower edge of the flue, and I pulled like a cork extracting itself from a wine bottle. My being, body and mind, was so focused on its task that I was equally unmoved by losing my trousers—dragged off on the lip of the flue—and the fact that my hand was free.

The concrete burned my left ear when my right arm thrust my torso down with real handhold for the first time. My shoulders slid free and the rest of my body tumbled out of the tube which had seemed to grip it tightly until that instant.

The light that blazed in my face was meant to blind me, but I was already stunned—more by the effort than the floor which I'd hit an instant before. Someone laid the muzzle of a powergun against my left ear. The dense iridium felt cool and good on my damaged skin.

"Where's Sergeant Grant?" said Lieutenant Kiley, a meter to the side of the light source.

I squinted away from the beam. There was an open bedroll beneath me, but I think I was too limp when I dropped from the flue to be injured by bare stone. Three of the tank lords were in the room with me. The bulbous commo helmets they wore explained how the lieutenant already knew something had happened to the guard. The others would be on the ground floor, poised.

The guns pointed at me were no surprise.

"He slipped into the palace to see Lady Miriam," I said, amazed that my voice did not break in a throat so dry. "The Baron killed them, both, and he's summoned the Lightning Division to capture you and your tanks. You have to call for help at once or they'll be here."

"Blood and martyrs," said the man with the gun at my ear, Lord Curran, and he stepped between me and the dazzling light. "Douse that, Sparky. The kid's all right."

The tank lord with the light dimmed it to a glow and said, "Which *we* bloody well ain't."

Lietenant Kiley moved to a window and peeked through a crack in the shutter, down into the courtyard.

"But . . ." I said. I would have gotten up but Curran's hand kept me below the possible line of fire. I'd tripped the mercenaries' alarms during my approach, awakened them—enough to save them, surely. "You have your helmets?" I went on. "You can call your Colonel?"

"That bastard Grant," the lieutenant said in the same emotionless, diamond-hard voice he had used in questioning me. "He slaved all the vehicle transceivers to his own helmet so Command Central wouldn't wake *me* if they called while he was—out fucking around."

"Via," said Lord Curran, holstering his pistol and grimacing at his hands as he flexed them together. "I'll go. Get a couple more guns up these windows—" he gestured with jerks of his forehead "—for cover."

"It's my platoon," Kiley said, stepping away from the window but keeping his back to the others of us in the room. "Via, *Via!*"

"Look, sir," Curran insisted with his voice rising and wobbling like that of a dog fighting a choke collar. "I was his bloody driver, I'll—"

"*You* weren't the fuck-up!" Lieutenant Kiley snarled as he turned. "This one comes with the rank, trooper, so shut your—"

"I'll go, My Lords," I said, the squeal of my voice lifting it through the hoarse anger of grown men arguing over a chance to die.

They paused and the third lord, Sparky, thumbed the light up and back by reflex. I pointed to the flue. "That way. But you'll have to tell me what to do then."

Lord Curran handed me a disk the size of a thumbnail. He must have taken it from his pocket when he planned to sprint for the tanks himself. "Lay it on the hatch—anywhere on the metal. Inside, t' the right a' the main screen—"

"Curran, *knot* it will you?" the lieutenant demanded in peevish amazement. "We can't—"

"*I* don't want my ass blown away, Lieutenant," said the trooper with the light—which pointed toward the officer suddenly, though the pistol in Sparky's other hand was lifted idly toward the ceiling. "Anyhow, kid's got a better chance'n you do. Or me."

Lieutenant Kiley looked from one of his men to the other, then stared at men with eyes that could have melted rock. "The main screen is on the forward wall of the fighting compartment," he said flatly. "That is—"

"He's used it, lieutenant," said Lord Curran. "He knows where it is." The little mercenary had drawn his pistol again and was checking the loads for the second time since I fell into the midst of these angry, nervous men.

Kiley looked at his subordinate, then continued to me, "The commo screen is the small one to the immediate right of the main screen, and it has an alphanumeric keypad beneath it. The screen will have a numeral two or a numeral three on it when you enter, depending whether it's set to feed another tank or to Grant's helmet."

He paused, wet his lips. His voice was bare of affect, but in his fear he was unable to sort out the minimum data that my task required. The mercenary officer realized that he was wandering, but that only added to the pressure which already ground him from all sides.

"Push numeral one on the keypad," Lieutenant Kiley went on, articulating very carefully. "The numeral on the visor should change to one. That's all you need to do—the transceiver will be cleared for normal operation, and we'll do the rest from here." He touched his helmet with the barrel of his powergun, a gesture so controlled that the iridium did not clink on the thermoplastic.

"I'll need," I said, looking up at the flue, "A platform—tables or boxes."

"We'll lift you," said Lieutenant Kiley, "and we'll cover you as best we can. Better take that shirt off now and make the squeeze easier."

"No, My Lord," I said, rising against the back wall—out of sight, though within a possible line of fire. I stretched my muscles, wincing as tags of skin broke loose from the fabric to which blood had glued them. "It's dark-colored, so I'll need it to get to the tank. I, I'll use—"

I shuddered and almost fell; as I spoke, I visualized what I had just offered to do—and it terrified me.

"Kid—" said Lord Curran, catching me; though I was all right again, just a brief fit.

"I'll use my trousers also," I said. "They're at the other—"

"Via!" snapped Lord Sparky, pointing with the light which he had dimmed to a yellow glow that was scarcely a beam. "What *happened* t' you?"

"I was a servant in the women's apartments," I said. "I'll go now, if you'll help me. I must hurry."

Lord Curran and Lieutenant Kiley lifted me. Their hands were moist by contrast with the pebbled finish of their helmets, brushing my bare thighs. I could think only of how my nakedness had just humiliated me before the tank lords.

It was good to think of that, because my body eased itself into the flue without conscious direction and my mind was too full of old anger to freeze me with coming fears.

Going up was initially simpler than worming my way down the tube had been. With the firm fulcrum of Lieutenant Kiley's shoulders beneath me, my legs levered my ribs and shoulder past the point at which they caught on the concrete.

Someone started to shove me farther with his hands.

"No!" I shouted, the distorted echo unintelligible even to me and barely heard in the room below. Someone understood, though, and the hands locked instead into a platform against which my feet could push in the cautious increments which the narrow passage required.

Sliding up the tube, the concrete hurt everywhere it rubbed me. The rush of blood to my head must have dulled the pain when I crawled downward. My right arm now had no strength and my legs, as the knees cramped themselves within the flue, could no longer thrust with any strength.

For a moment, the touch of the tank lord's lifted hands left my soles. I was wedged too tightly to slip back, but I could no more have climbed higher in the flue than I could have shattered the concrete that trapped me. Above, partly blocked by my loosely-waving arm, was a dim circle of the sky.

Hands gripped my feet and shoved upward with a firm, inexorable pressure that was now my only chance of success. Lord Curran, standing on his leader's shoulders, lifted me until my hand reached the outer lip. With a burst of hysterical strength, I dragged the rest of my body free.

It took me almost a minute to put my trousers on. The time was not wasted. If I had tried to jump down to the wall without resting, my muscles would have let me tumble all the way into the courtyard—probably with enough noise to bring an immediate storm of gunfire from the Baron's soldiers.

The light within the gatehouse must have been visible as glimmers through the same cracks in the shutters which the tank lords used to desperately survey their position. That meant the Baron's men would be even more alert . . . but also, that their attention would be focused even more firmly on the second-floor windows— rather than on the wall adjacent to the gatehouse.

No one shot at me as I crawled backwards from the roof, pressing myself against the concrete and then stone hard enough to scrape skin that had not been touched by the flue.

The key to the tank hatches was in my mouth, the only place from which I could not lose it—while I lived.

My knees and elbows were bloody from the flue already, but the open sky was a relief as I wormed my way across the top of the wall. The moments I had been stuck in a concrete tube more strait than a coffin convinced me that there were worse deaths than a bullet.

Or even than by torture, unless the Baron decided to bury me alive.

I paused on my belly where the wall mated with the corner of the West Wing. I knew there were gunmen waiting at the windows a few meters away. They could not see me, but they might well hear the thump of my feet on the courtyard's compacted surface.

There was no better place to descend. Climbing up to the roofs of the palace would only delay my danger, while the greater danger rushed forward on the air cushion vehicles of the Lightning Division.

Taking a deep breath, I rolled over the rim of the wall. I dangled a moment before my strained arms let me fall the remaining two meters earlier than I had intended to. The sound my feet, then fingertips, made on the ground was not loud even to my fearful senses. There was no response from the windows above me— and no shots from the East Wing or the banquet hall, from which I was an easy target for any soldier who chanced to stare at the shadowed corner in which I poised.

I was six meters from the nearest tank—Lord Curran's tank, the tank from which Sergeant Grant had surveyed the women's apartments. Crawling was pointless—the gunmen were above me. I considered sprinting, but the sudden movement would have tripped the peripheral vision of eyes turned toward the gatehouse.

I strolled out of the corner, so frightened that I could not be sure my joints would not spill me to the ground because they had become rubbery.

One step, two steps, three steps, four—

"Hey!" someone shouted behind me, and seven powerguns raked the women's apartments with cyan lightning.

Because I was now so close to the tank, only soldiers in the West Wing could see me. The covering fire sent them ducking while glass shattered, fabrics burned, and flakes spalled away from the face of the stone itself. I heard screams from within, and not all of the throats were female.

A dozen or more automatic rifles—the soldiers elsewhere in the palace—opened fire on the gatehouse with a sound like wasps in a steel drum. I jumped to the bow slope of the tank, trusting my bare feet to grip the metal without delay for the steps set into the iridium.

A bolt from a powergun struck the turret a centimeter from where my hand slapped it. I screamed with dazzled surprise at the glowing dimple in the metal and the droplets that spattered my bare skin.

Only the tank lords' first volley had been aimed. When they ducked away from the inevitable return fire, they continued to shoot with only their gun muzzles lifted above the protecting stone. The bolts which scattered across the courtyard at random did a good job of frightening the Baron's men away from accurate shooting, but that randomness had almost killed me.

As it was, the shock of being fired at by a friend made me drop the hatch key. The circular field-induction chip clicked twice on its way to disappear in the dark courtyard.

The hatch opened. The key had bounced the first time on the cover.

I went through the opening head first, too frightened by the shots to swing my feet over the coaming in normal fashion. At least one soldier saw what was happening, because his bullets raked the air around my legs for the moment they waved. His tracers were green sparks; and when I fell safely within, more bullets disintegrated against the dense armor about me.

The seat, though folded, gashed my forehead with a corner and came near enough to stunning me with pain that I screamed in panic when I saw there was no commo screen where the lieutenant had said it would be. The saffron glow of instruments was cold mockery.

I spun. The main screen was behind me, just where it should have been, and the small common screen—reading 3—was beside it. I had turned around when I tumbled through the hatch.

My finger stabbed at the keypad, hit **1** and **2** together. A slash replaced the **3**—and then **1**, as I got control of my hand again and touched the correct key. Electronics whirred softly in the belly of the great tank.

The West Wing slid up the main screen as I palmed the control. There was a **1** in the corner of the main screen also.

My world was the whole universe in the hush of my mind. I pressed the firing pedal as my hand rotated the turret counterclockwise.

The tribarrel's mechanism whined as it cycled and the bolts thumped, expanding the air on their way to their target; but when the blue-green flickers of released energy struck stone, the night and the facade of the women's apartments shattered. Stones the size of a man's head were blasted from the wall, striking my tank and the other palace buildings with the violence of the impacts.

My tank.

I touched the selector toggle. The numeral **2** shone orange in the upper corner of the screen which the lofty mass of the banquet hall slid to fill.

"Kid!" shouted speakers somewhere in the tank with me. "*Kid!*"

My bare toes rocked the firing pedal forward and the world burst away from the axis of the main gun.

The turret hatch was open because I didn't know how to close it. The tribarrel whipped the air of the courtyard, spinning hot vortices smoky from fires the guns had set and poisoned by ozone and gases from the cartridge matrices.

The 20 cm main gun sucked all the lesser whorls along the path of its bolt, then exploded them in a cataclysm that lifted the end of the banquet hall ten meters before dropping it back as rubble.

My screen blacked out the discharge, but even the multiple reflections that flashed through the turret hatch were blinding. There was a gout of burning stone. Torque had shattered the arched concrete roof when it lifted, but many of the reinforcing rods still held so that slabs danced together as they tumbled inward.

Riflemen had continued to fire while the tribarrel raked toward them. The 20 cm bolt silenced everything but its own echoes. Servants would have broken down the outside doors minutes before. The surviving soldiers followed them now, throwing away weapons unless they forgot them in their hands.

The screen to my left was a panorama through the vision blocks while the orange pips on the main screen provided the targeting array. Men, tank lords in khaki, jumped aboard the other tanks. Two of them ran toward me in the vehicle farthest from the gatehouse.

Only the west gable of the banquet hall had collapsed. The powergun had no penetration, so the roof panel on the palace's outer side had been damaged only by stresses transmitted by the panel that took the bolt. Even on the courtyard side, the reinforced concrete still held its shape five meters from where the bolt struck, though fractured and askew.

The tiny figure of the Baron was running toward me from the entrance.

I couldn't see him on the main screen because it was centered on the guns' point of impact. I shouted in surprise, frightened back into slavery by that man even when shrunken to a doll in a panorama.

My left hand dialed the main screen down and across, so that the center of the Baron's broad chest was ringed with sighting pips. He raised his mob gun as he ran, and his mouth bellowed a curse or a challenge.

The Baron was not afraid of me or of anything else. But he had been *born* to the options that power gives.

My foot stroked the firing pedal.

One of the mercenaries who had just leaped to the tank's back deck gave a shout as the world became ozone and a cyan flash. Part of the servants' quarters beneath the banquet hall caught fire around the three-meter cavity blasted by the gun.

The Baron's disembodied right leg thrashed once on the ground. Other than that, he had vanished from the vision blocks.

Lieutenant Kiley came through the hatch, feet first but otherwise with as little ceremony as I had shown. He shoved me hard against the turret wall while he rocked the gun switch down to safe. The orange numeral blanked from the screen.

"In the *Lord's* name, kid!" the big officer demanded while his left hand still pressed me back. "Who told you to do *that*?"

"Lieutenant," said Lord Curran, leaning over the hatch opening but continuing to scan the courtyard. His pistol was in his hand, muzzle lifted, while air trembled away from the hot metal. "We'd best get a move on unless you figure t' fight a reinforced battalion alone till the supports get here."

"Well, get in and *drive*, curse you!" the lieutenant shouted. The words relaxed his body and he released me. "*No*, I don't want to wait around here alone for the Lightning Division!"

"Lieutenant," said the driver, unaffected by his superior's anger, "we're down a man. You ride your blower. Kid'll be all right alone with me till we join up with the Colonel and come back t' kick ass."

Lieutenant Kiley's face became very still. "Yeah, get in and drive," he said mildly, gripping the hatch coaming to lift himself out without bothering to use the power seat.

The driver vanished but his boots scuffed on the armor as he scurried for his own hatch. "Gimme your bloody key," he shouted back.

Instead of replying at once, the lieutenant looked down at me. "Sorry I got a little shook, kid," he said. "You did pretty good for a new recruit." Then he muscled himself up and out into the night.

The drive fans of other tanks were already roaring when ours began to whine up to speed. The great vehicle shifted greasily around me, then began to turn slowly on its axis. Fourth in line, we maneuvered through the courtyard gate while the draft from our fans lifted flames out of the palace windows.

We are the tank lords.

Editor's introduction to:
THE NAKED CHIMP

Heretofore arguments on the subject of human racial origins have been full of sound and fury and little serious study; like its fellow tinderbox topic, psycho-sexual dimorphism, the subject of racial origins has lain nearly fallow for fear of Concerned Fascists on both ends of the political spectrum.

All that is changed now.

—JPB

THE NAKED CHIMP:

MOLECULES AND THE PROOF OF HUMAN ORIGINS

John Gribbin

Human beings share almost 99 percent of their genetic material—their DNA—with the African apes, and have followed a separate evolutionary path from the chimpanzees for only four or five million years. The evidence for this new insight into our background began to emerge almost twenty years ago. But it is only in the 1980s that the full picture has emerged of how closely Darwin's ideas are vindicated by the evidence of our own DNA.

When Charles Darwin published *On the Origin of Species* in 1859, he knew of the impact his ideas were likely to have in a society still dominated, to a large extent, by the more reactionary kind of Church teaching. Even in 1859 he tried to steer around the worst of the likely storm of controversy by keeping humankind out of the story. All he said about our own evolution, almost at the end of his great work, was, "In the distant future I see open fields for far more important researches . . . light will be thrown on the origin of man and his history." But the "distant future" closed in on Darwin almost at once, with most of the furor about the *Origin* being directly concerned with the place of human beings on the evolutionary stage. In the 1860s, Thomas Henry Huxley published an essay titled "Evidence as to Man's Place in Nature," and in 1871 Darwin himself, the ground by now prepared, published *The Descent of Man*, in which he applied his theory of evolution by natural selection of the human species.

In the *Descent* Darwin sketched out the principles of natural selection and pointed out the similarity of the human species to the living species of African apes—the gorillas and chimpanzees. He said, "We are naturally led to enquire, where was the birthplace of man?" And, pointing out that in all regions of the world today the living mammals are closely related to the extinct species of the same region, he concluded "it is therefore probable that Africa was formerly inhabited by extinct apes closely allied to the gorilla and chimpanzee; and as these two species are now man's nearest allies, it is somewhat more probable that our early progenitors lived on the African continent than elsewhere."

It would be difficult to provide a more succinct statement of modern opinion on human origins, except for changing "somewhat more probable" to read "virtually certain." During the twentieth century, our understanding of human origins has been built up almost entirely through the study of those fossil ancestors to which Darwin alluded, and fossils clearly on the human lineage have been found in Africa and received wide publicity. In recent decades, the work of the Leakey family and the publicity given to Don Johanson's famous fossil "Lucy" can have left few people—except those who, for whatever reasons, dismiss the idea of human evolution entirely—in any doubt that our ancestors evolved in Africa, and that we share a common lineage with the gorilla and chimpanzee. But there is another side to this story: an attack on the puzzle of human origins which depends on the interpretation not of fragments of fossil bone but of the molecules in the blood and tissue of living species. This part of the tale is more recent (although it has respectable scientific predecessors going back almost to Darwin's time), and has received both less public attention and less than its due share of recognition from the fossil hunters themselves, until very recently. But it provides not only direct evidence of human evolution at work but also an accurate date for the evolutionary split when the human line began to diverge from those of the other African apes. The split can be dated and calibrated from comparisons of the DNA molecules in the cells of living people, living gorillas and living chimpanzees; and the molecular clock tells us that our common ancestor lived in Africa just five million years ago.

Blood brothers

George Nuttall was born in San Francisco in 1862— right at the time, had he but known it, of the great debate about evolution stirred by the *Origin*. He grew up to do research in Germany and become Professor of Biology at the University of Cambridge. In the early 1900s he provided the first direct evidence of the blood relationships between different species.

Nuttall used the then-new discovery of the ability of the body to manufacture antibodies which protect it from attack by invaders. The first attack of a mild disease, such as chicken pox, makes the patient quite ill, but the body learns to identify the invaders that cause chicken pox and to manufacture specific antibodies to destroy them. The next time the same invaders try to attack, the appropriate antibodies are produced immediately, and the illness never becomes noticeable. The body has become immune to chicken pox. But the antibodies that protect you against chicken pox are no protection against, say, influenza—indeed, the antibodies that protect you from one kind of 'flu virus may be little use against a different 'flu virus. Nuttall used this fact to measure the relatedness of different species.

He injected laboratory animals (the ones he used were rabbits) with samples of blood protein from a different species. The animal "invaded" by the foreign material learned to manufacture antibodies against this specific invader, and the blood of the invaded animal provided a serum which reacted specifically with the blood proteins of the chosen invader. Although Nuttall knew nothing of the importance of DNA to evolution, and indeed little of antibodies themselves, he knew that this serum would react with other samples of the same blood to produce a dense precipitate in his test tubes. But the precipitation reaction was far less strong when the blood of a different species of animal was treated with the specific serum. A serum prepared from rabbits "invaded" with blood from a horse, say, reacted strongly with horse blood, but scarcely at all with cat blood. The strength of the reaction exactly followed the closeness of the similarity between different species, the Nuttall was quick to include human blood—his own—in the tests. After 16,000 tests involving species as diverse as fish and man, Nuttall reported to the London School of Tropical Medicine in 1901 that "if we accept the degree of blood reaction as an index of blood relationship within the Anthropoidea, then we find that the Old Word apes are more closely allied to man . . . exactly in accordance with the opinions expressed by Darwin." (G. F. H. Nuttall, "The new biological test for blood," *Journal of Tropical Medicine*, volume 4, page 405, 1901.)

I am not sure whether it is more surprising that this work was being carried out scarcely forty years after the publication of the *Origin* and only thirty years after the publication of the *Descent*, or that it should then have lain dormant, with its potential failing to be exploited by evolutionary biologists, for more than half a century. The fact is, however, that the technique was not taken up until the late 1950s, when Morris Goodman, at Wayne State University in Detroit, applied the much more precise techniques of modern immunology to what were essentially the same experiments that Nuttall had pioneered. Goodman was able to measure the degree of blood relationships much more accurately than Nuttall, and he had the benefit of fifty years of paleontology to draw on when comparing his measurements with the expected family tree. He found no surprises concerning the order in which different species had split off from the branch of evolution of which we are a part; the blood tests showed man and chimp to be very close relations, the gibbon to be a more distant cousin, the Old World monkeys to form a still more remote branch of the family, and the New World monkeys to be more distantly related yet. All this was very much what studies of the morphology of the living species suggested, and the fossils confirmed. The surprise came in a 1962 paper from Goodman, in which he tackled the problem of trying to sort out whether the chimp or the gorilla was more closely related to man. The short answer is that, from a variety of immunological tests, he found the three to be equally closely related. (M. Goodman, "Serological analysis of the systematics of recent hominoids," *Human Biology*, volume 35 page 377.)

This came as a bombshell to biologists. Everyone accepted at the time—and a surprising number of biologists, let alone other people, still think to this day—that although the chimp and gorilla may be our nearest relations, "obviously" they are much more closely related to each other than they are to us. That is what Goodman expected to find. But the molecules refused to conform to the expected view. They showed, and continue to show, that human, chimp, and gorilla are mutually closely related, each one being equally close to the other two. You and I are as closely related to a chimpanzee as a gorilla is related to the chimpanzee. Even though the chimp and gorilla are hairy, inarticulate creatures that wear no clothes and live in the wilds of Africa (or in our zoos), while we are sophisticated, intelligent city dwellers who watch TV and eat frozen pizza (and capture chimps and gorillas for our amusement), the evolutionary difference between me and a gorilla is no more, and no less, than the evolutionary difference between a chimpanzee and that gorilla. The big question left unanswered by this immunological work was just when the ancestral lineage (represented in part, perhaps, by those fossils being avidly dug up at the time by the Leakeys and others) had diverged, in a three-way split, to produce the three lines that led to

the three African apes, ourselves and our two hairy
sibling species. The answer wasn't long coming, although it took a long time to get the paleontologists to
begin to accept it.

Molecular evolution

In 1959 Emile Zuckerkandl (a native of Vienna who
became a French citizen in 1938 and now works in
France) came to CalTech, where he worked with the
pioneering biochemist Linus Pauling. Pauling was interested, for biochemical reasons, in the structure of
hemoglobin, the molecule that carries oxygen around in
the blood; and he enlisted Zuckerkandl's aid in a study
of this molecule.

Zuckerkandl and Pauling examined hemoglobins from
several different species, identifying exactly how they
differed from one another. Hemoglobin, like most of
the molecules in the body, is a member of the protein
family, and is made up of chains of smaller molecular
units, called amino acids, joined together. The CalTech
researchers found that the difference between human
hemoglobin and gorilla hemoglobin consists of a single
substitution in one of the protein chains—an amino acid
called aspartine in the gorilla hemoglobin where there
is one called glutamine in human hemoglobin. This is,
literally, the smallest possible difference—so small
that it is virtually certain that somewhere on Earth
there are human beings whose blood carries a mutated
form of hemoglobin identical to normal gorilla hemoglobin. At this level, the differences between man and the
other African apes appear to be no more significant than
the variations among individual members of the human
population.

But hemoglobin isn't the only molecule that can be
studied in this way. Other proteins still provide a wealth
of information about evolution at the molecular level.
From the mid-1960s onward, Walter Fitch and Eman-
uel Margoliash, of Northwestern University, near Chicago, have carried out detailed studies of the amino
acid sequences of the protein cytochrome c in many

species. Cytochromes are enzymes that are involved in the transport of energy-rich molecules around an organism, and like hemoglobin they exist in slightly different forms, doing more or less the same job, in a wide variety of species. Dog cytochrome c and horse cytochrome c, for example, differ by just ten amino acids in a chain 104 amino acids long. It is an interesting, and unresolved, question whether all of these changes are an evolutionary response to the different lifestyles of the two animals, or whether they are inconsequential mutations that have just happened by chance, so that a dog could get along just as well with horse cytochrome c as with its own.

But either way, these differences provide a measure of the differences between the two species, an indication of how far they have gone down separate evolutionary paths since they split off from some common ancestral stock.* Horse and dog are clearly less closely related than species that differ in their cytochrome c by four or five amino acids. The cytochrome c family tree now provides an indication of the evolutionary relationships between chicken and penguin, tuna fish and moth, screwfly and turtle—and, of course, between human and ape. Always, the story is the same. Changes have occurred at random, accumulating as time goes by. And human, chimpanzee, and gorilla are practically identical, as closely related as it is possible for three species to be and to remain separate species.

The molecular clock

In 1964 Vincent Sarich was a research student working in the Anthropology Department at the University of

---

*And, as Thomas Jukes pointed out in 1966 in his excellent (though now slightly out of date) book *Molecules and Evolution* (Columbia University Press, page 192), reporting Margoliash's conclusions, the overall pattern of cytochrome c similarities and variations on the same basic theme provides "striking evidence for the evolution of all the living species [so far studied] from a common ancestor."

California, Berkeley. He participated in a series of seminars conducted by the professor of physical anthropology, Sherwood Washburn. Washburn wondered whether Goodman's technique of measuring the differences—or similarities—of blood proteins in the different species might not be used to provide some indication of how long ago, or how recently, the split between man and the African apes occurred. And Sarich volunteered to read all the available scientific papers on the subject (not that many in 1964) and report on them to the seminar group.

Sarich realized that if the mutations which had led to the differences in proteins in the blood and tissues of different species today had accumulated at a steady rate during evolutionary history, then measurements of these differences could be used to indicate not only the evolutionary "distance" between two species, but the time that had elapsed since they split from a common ancestor. The molecules could be used as a clock, with the accumulating mutations ticking away the millennia. The possibilities intrigued Allan Wilson, another member of the seminar group, who was just setting up a biochemical research team at Berkeley; Washburn suggested that Sarich take up the theme for his PhD topic, and Sarich duly joined Wilson's small group, beginning a collaboration that was to rewrite our understanding of the origins of humankind.*

The first key papers were published in 1967. Using biochemical techniques far more subtle even than those used by Goodman, let alone by Nuttall, Sarich compared blood proteins from many different species, focussing particularly on the primates, our nearest relatives. He found that the difference between a human being and an ape or a chimpanzee, in terms of the number of

---

*The full story of how that collaboration developed, and what it led to, can be found in the contributions from Sarich and from J. E. Cronin, who joined the group later, in the volume *New Interpretations of Ape and Human Ancestry*, edited by Russel Ciochon and Robert Corruccini (Plenum, 1983).

amino acid substitutions in the protein chains in their blood, is just one-sixth of the difference between a human being and an Old World monkey. Now, the date of the split between Old World monkeys and apes is one of the most reliable fossil dates, well determined at around 30 million years ago. If the mutations had indeed been building up at random and at a steady rate in the lineages studied over that time, there could be only one conclusion. The split between human and chimp (and gorilla) occurred only one-sixth as far back in the past as the split between all of the apes and the monkeys—that is, just five million years ago.

The very important requirement before this interpretation could be accepted was that the mutations which produced the changes in the amino acid sequences of the proteins must be occurring at a steady rate. Suppose, for example, that the three-way split that produced human, gorilla, and chimpanzee really had happened 15 million years ago, as the paleontologists would have accepted in 1967, but that since then evolution has, in a sense, proceeded only one third as fast among the African apes as in closely related species such as the Asian apes. Such a slowing down in the rate of evolution could produce the same apparent effect as a more recent split and a continuation of evolutionary change at the old rate.

This is a crucial point, because both in 1967 and in the years since many paleontologists have failed to understand that Sarich and Wilson did not *assume* that the rate at which mutations accumulate—the rate of evolution— has stayed constant in the families of molecules they studied. They actually carried out experiments to *test* whether this was the case, and those experiments proved that the rate of mutation has stayed constant and that, therefore, these molecules can be used as a clock, reliably ticking off the timescale of human evolution.

The technique used is simple to understand, although it involves a great deal of painstaking work to carry through. Basically, it involves taking a well-established evolutionary date, such as the split between the apes and the Old World monkeys, and looking at the changes that have accumulated in a chosen protein (the first one Sarich and Wilson worked with was albumin) in living representatives of as many species as possible that are descended from the line which split at this well-known time. In this particular case, the number of differences that have accumulated in the albumins of all living apes, compared with Old World monkeys, is the same. The evolutionary distance from monkey to gibbon (which lives in Asia) is the same as from monkey to chimpanzee (which lives in Africa) or from monkey to man.

Obviously, the mutations are different in different species—the particular amino acids that have mutated in the albumin of the orangutan, for example, are different from the ones that have changed in the chimpanzee. But in all cases, including the chimp and the orang, the *number* of mutations since the split from the monkey line has been the same. The same result is found when the comparison is made with New World monkeys, or with carnivores, or with any species yet tested. The rate at which mutations accumulate in mammal albumin depends only on the time that has elapsed, regardless of any other factor. And the same is true for all the other molecules studied in this way.

Molecular anthropology, as it is now called, provides the best indication available of the date when our line first diverged from the lines leading to the gorilla and chimpanzee. That date is just five million years ago. The icing on the cake of the new interpretation of human ancestry came when it proved possible to measure the differences not only in the protein coded for by DNA, but between the DNA molecules of different species themselves. And the DNA clock came up with exactly the same timescale for human evolutions as all the other molecular clocks.

DNA itself

The technique goes back to 1960, when it was reported that DNA strands that had been broken apart by gentle heating would pair up again into double strands when allowed to cool. This, like the regularity of the molecular clock, may come as something of a surprise. The two strands in a double helix of DNA are held together only by weak hydrogen bonds, so it is no surprise that they can be parted by gentle heat. However gentle the heat, it is inevitable that the separate strands will get broken here and there in the process, and then the separate fragments of "melted" DNA are free to coil up upon themselves as they wish. Making sense out of the resulting mess might seem a hopeless task. But when the brew is allowed to cool slowly again, the affinity between complementary strands of double helix is so pronounced that the separated fragments of DNA line up with their partners once again, and re-forge the hydrogen bonds between each other. Two strands from a particular double helix are highly unlikely to find each other again, but if each one finds an exact replica of its former partner in the brew, the effect is just as if the original helix has been renewed. The process by which the DNA fragments join up again is called annealing, and it is so effective that, if handled gently, the resulting DNA has much of its biological activity restored.

Exactly complementary strands of DNA, the two halves of a whole double helix, clearly have a great affinity for each other because every molecular group (called a base) on one strand is matched by its preferred counterpart on the other. The atoms seek to form the arrangement which results in the lowest possible energy state, and in so doing they form links which are called hydrogen bonds.

What would happen if the two strands of DNA trying to anneal were not perfectly matched? Obviously, some hydrogen bonds would still form where the strands did pair up, but elsewhere the annealing would be less effective, so that the double-stranded molecules produced would not be held together so strongly. And that would mean that if they were heated again they would break apart more easily—they would melt at a lower temperature. This is the key to the use of DNA as the ultimate molecular clock.

Two researchers who use the technique today are Jon Ahlquist and Charles Sibley, of Yale University. What they do is take samples of DNA from each of two separate species—they might be man and chimp—and heat them to separate the DNA strands. The two sets of molten DNA are then mixed, and allowed to cool. As the brew cools, the single strands of DNA try to pair up. Some will find their proper partners and form tightly annealed helices; but in other cases a strand from one species will pair with a strand from the other species, forming a more loosely bound helix. When the solidified DNA is heated once again, these imperfectly combined strands will separate first, melting at a lower temperature than the rest. It is no mean feat to make the appropriate measurements and to identify just which DNA helices are melting when. But, glossing over the experimental details, two things are clear.

The first is that ordinary DNA melts at a temperature of about 85° C. The second is that hybrid DNA formed by pairing one strand from one species with one strand from another melts at a lower temperature, and that each degree lower corresponds to one percent difference along the DNA molecules. Two species that share 99 percent of their DNA form hybrid DNA which melts at about 84° C; two species that have 98 percent of their DNA bases in common (the same bases *in the same order* along the DNA) form hybrid DNA that melts at about 83° C. This test shows that human, chimpanzee, and gorilla DNA are identical along at least 98 percent of their length. The "unique" features of humanity are contained in less than 2 percent of our DNA.

The 2 percent differences between human DNA and the DNA of either chimp or gorilla indicates a splitting time a little over four million years ago. Every test tells the same story. DNA changes do accumulate at a steady rate. The first measurements of this kind, applied to human, chimp, and gorilla, indicated just the same three-way split, roughly five million years ago, that the protein clocks indicate. By now, the technique has been refined to the point where it is even more accurate for this particular task than the protein clocks. Ahlquist and Sibley carried out a study in the early 1980s which, they say, shows that the gorilla line split off first, about six million years ago, and that the split between human and chimpanzee lines occurred on the other branch of the family tree, four and a half million years ago. These figures are still entirely consistent with the protein clocks, but they shed just a little new light on human origins, and indicate, perhaps, just what the immediate ancestors of the human line looked like.

Darwin vindicated

The molecular vindication of Darwin is twofold. First, Darwin's suggestion that the human line had its origins in Africa, and that the African apes are our closest living relations, has proved more accurate than even he can have guessed. The accumulating molecular data allow for no other conclusion than that the ancestor of our own line was also the ancestor of chimpanzee and gorilla, and there is a hint—as yet, no more than a hint— that chimp and human shared a common lineage for a brief time after the gorilla line split off.

So what did the first proto-human—the first hominid— look like? The best evidence is that the chimpanzee is our closest relation, and that we both evolved from a common ancestor that was around 4½ million years ago. The oldest uniquely human ancestors were around in East Africa between 3 and 4 million years ago, and must have been rather like the oldest uniquely chimpanzee ancestors with which they shared the region. There are two species of chimpanzee alive today, *Pan troglodytes* and *Pan paniscus*, which diverged from a common line, the molecules tell us, between two and three million years ago. (*Pan paniscus*, also known as the "pygmy" chimp, has a smaller head than *Pan troglodytes*, hence its common name, but in terms of its limbs it is not as small as the image the name conjures up.) The oldest fossil hominids so far identified are the remains of species labelled *Australopithecus afarensis* and *Australopithecus africanus*, and they were around in East Africa about 3½ million years ago. Paleontologists and anthropologists are still arguing about the exact significance of these fossil finds, and whether or not either *Australopithecus* was indeed a direct ancestor of ours. But, taking these as the best examples of our likely ancestors that we have, it is possible to get a rough idea of what a typical *Australopithecus* looked like, combining features from both varieties of *Australopithecus* on the basis of the available fossil evidence. Adrienne Zihlman, of the University of California, Santa Cruz, has done just that, working with several colleagues including Sarich and Wilson, and come up with a creature very much like the modern pygmy chimp. "The earliest known hominids at 3.5 million years," she concludes, "may have been only one step away from a small ape like the living *Pan paniscus*."* And really, if we weren't prejudiced into putting man, *Homo*, into a separate category on his own evolutionary branch, it would make a lot more sense to label our own species *Pan sapiens*.

Our real origins, of course, lie back in the more distant past, along with the origins of all other forms of life on Earth. Life has been on Earth for three and a half thousand million years, but human life, as a distinct line, has been around for just five million years. Only for one seven-hundredth of our history have people walked alone. The final vindication of Darwin's theory of evolution by natural selection, the theory that explains how the present variety of life on Earth has been produced by descent from those original living cells, comes from the new understanding of molecular evolution. But the most exciting of all these developments comes from "fine tuning" the new technique to tell us

---

*A. L. Zihlman and J. M. Lowenstein, *New Interpretations*, page 691. This article, which begins on page 677, summarizes the evidence for a chimp-like first hominid and gives the references to the original research papers.

about the *immediate* ancestry of the human race, on a timescale of thousands of years rather than millions of years.

More than one flesh?

If the molecules can tell us when the human family split off from the chimpanzee line of evolution, then with just a little more skill the technique ought to be able to tell us when the different branches of the *human* family tree split off from each other. So it does—but the results make such uncomfortable reading that they have not yet been accepted in the anthropological trade.

This fine-tuning of the DNA clock depends largely on studies of DNA from semi-independent components of the human cell. Most of the human DNA, the stuff that codes for the construction and care of a human body, sits in the nucleus at the heart of the cell. But little sausage-shaped bodies called mitochondria, that are responsible for energy production in the cell, have their own DNA. Interestingly, mitochondria are inherited only from one's mother; the sperm that fertilizes the egg to make a new human being carries none of them with it. Far more important to my present tale, however, the mitochondrial DNA clock seems to tick far more rapidly than the clock of nuclear DNA, so similar studies to the ones I have just described can be used with mitochondrial DNA to measure changes over tens of thousands and hundreds of thousands of years, instead of over millions and tens of millions of years. What this clock reveals is very odd.

According to studies by Becky Cann and colleagues in Berkeley, the mitochondrial DNA from members of different varieties of human being differ in a way that corresponds to a splitting off that sets Australian aborigines and Orientals apart from the rest of humankind. The Australians split off about 400,000 years ago and the Orientals some 100,000 years ago, while the split into the other main groupings, notably the ancestors of modern blacks and whites, occurred only about 40,000 years ago.

Nobody is quite sure how best to interpret this evidence, but rather than the aboriginal population being merely yet another "living fossil" it is at least possible that the first *Homo sapiens* evolved in Australia, cut off from the rest of the world, then spread outwards, changing as he went, through the Orient and into Africa before moving on, in different varieties, to the rest of the world. This would still fit in very neatly with the fossil evidence that truly modern man, *Homo sapiens sapiens*, left Africa only about 40,000 years ago, moving up into Europe and displacing our immediate predecessor, *Homo sapiens neandertalis*, not in bloody conflict but simply by being smarter and better able to adapt to changing environmental conditions at the end of the Ice Age. On that picture, the same evolutionary step occurred at about the same time in other parts of the world, as Cro Magnon man emerged in response to the same evolutionary pressures acting on earlier varieties of man. It also fits in with another very surprising recent discovery.

At the level of DNA, not only are people much more closely related to chimps than was previously suspected, we are all much more closely related to each other than we "ought" to be. In any population, of course, there is some variation about mean values of characteristics like height or skin color. But the average stretches of DNA from members of different human populations—for example, black Africans and white Europeans—are more similar to each other than the extent of the variation *within* each population. In other words, there is no statistical significance in the differences between blacks and whites at all—the extreme possibilities of variation within, say, the white European population cover a range bigger than the difference between a typical black and a typical white! Becky Cann has suggested that this lack of variability among people might be explained if we are all descended from one woman, an "Eve" who lived in Africa about 300,000 years ago (which would be just after early man arrived there from Australia, if the story outlined above is correct). Perhaps some environmental disaster wiped out all the proto-humans except one tribe, with a matriarch; perhaps that tribe thrived because it invented some great new cultural advantage and wiped out its rivals. Such events were possible, then, because the entire "human" race probably consisted of a few thousand individuals, at most. Either way, we really could all be descended from one woman. It has to be one *woman*, because the evidence comes from the mitochondrial DNA, which isn't passed on through the male line.

This idea is so new that the details haven't yet been worked out, and the story I've told here will surely be amended over the next few years. For example, it would seem that you need more than one wave of expansion out of Africa, with Cro Magnon simply being the last. But these details are, in principle, susceptible to the modern tests.

The molecular experts are very wary of being drawn into areas of debate where their scientific findings might be misused by racial groups seeking "proof" that one kind of human being is superior to another. But serious students of human origins are eager to take up the new tool, and it might even be possible, with care, to use it to find out (for example) where the American "Indians" came from, and when. Meanwhile, we can at least say with some confidence that the last common ancestor of the Esquimaux and the Kalahari Bushmen walked the Earth just about 100,000 years ago. And we can also say, more confidently than ever before, that features such as skin color are totally insignificant and we are all literally brothers, and sisters, under the skin.

Dr. John Gribbin is the author of In Search of the Double Helix: Quantum physics and life, *published recently by Corgi, London, and McGraw-Hill, New York.*

Editor's introduction to:
TOURNAMENT

How will the descendants of those who migrate to the High Frontier differ in body and mind from their earthbound cousins? No fear of heights but stark terror at the sound of hissing air? Lacking more pedestrian function, will human feet re-learn the art of grasping? Perhaps 40,000 years from now some scientist using the techniques Dr. Gribbin describes will point to a chart and say *here* is where Solar and Terrestrial Man diverged . . .

—JPB

TOURNAMENT

Dave Smeds

He is tall and lanky, with arms like an ape, an ideal body for null-gravity karate. As soon as we hear the command to start, he launches from his side of the sphere. I see his fist heading for my face.

He is squinting, body tense, gathering all his energy into the movement. I exhale sharply, the action moving my head backward. I don't block as much as push, one hand diverting his strike, the other pressing his shoulder. The technique sends him gliding back across the combat area, and presses me more firmly against the plexiglas under my feet. I sink into a squat and leapfrog toward him.

We meet at the center. His arms are everywhere. In seconds we are in a hopeless tangle. I place one good strike to the ribs, but the judges miss it. Without fully intending it, we push away from each other once again. I get two hands on the velcro and stop my motion.

He is about one hundred twenty degrees to my left, with both feet on the velcro, ready to leap again. I see a gleam of triumph in his eyes as he realizes I will have to flip over in order to get my feet "underneath" me. He takes off.

I push off with my hands and cock my leg. The ball of my foot catches him perfectly in the midsection. He grunts in surprise. At least three of the judges give me the whistle and flag.

We settle back to our starting places and face each other.

"*Yoko geri, chu dan*," the referee announces over the p.a. system. "One half-point, red." I am the red contestant.

I have the scope of my opponent's technique now. It was a mistake to let him make the first move. As the next round begins, I plunge straight in before he can get started. A simple reverse punch gives me the score.

"*Seiken zuki, jo dan*. Two half-points, red. Winner."

We bow to each other and I, following tournament courtesy, let him open the hatch and exit the sphere first. I pause in the opening and let the referee remove the red ribbon from my belt, while I strip the velcro bands off my hands and feet. The next two contestants are sailing over from the staging area.

"Nice work, champ," says one of the statisticians as I land at the edge of the part of the bleachers reserved for contestants. I thank him, grab a squeeze bottle of Gatorade from a vendor, and float up into the seats, where some of my students have collected.

"Way to go, Aaron," one of them says; I'm not sure just who. I strap down, feeling the sweat bead and evaporate on my skin. I wait for it to trickle down the sides of my face and torso, but it never does.

No, I think. It was *not* nice work.

I smell the familiar odor of perspiring bodies and the laundry scent of freshly washed karate gis. The speakers boom with a mixture of English and Japanese, overlapping the beehive hum of the spectators' voices. My heartbeat is fast with adrenaline rush, pulling me into a hypnotic state where time seems distorted and it is almost impossible to carry on a normal conversation. I cling to the feelings. This is no different from any other tournament, I tell myself. I always start slow; I always rally in time.

The air, it strikes me, is too filtered. They forgot the dirt. They have deliberately added the essence of grass, trees, and animals to the ventilation systems, but they've left out the pollution. I practice controlled breathing, and settle in to watch the matches.

My vantage point isn't one of the best; those have been reserved for the "corner" judges, the referee, and the cameras. The folks back Earthside are getting a better view. It doesn't matter. There will be plenty of time to play it back in weeks to come, and analyze what should or shouldn't have happened. What matters now is an all too elusive state of mind.

I suppose it was inevitable that karate would move into high orbit. In many ways, it is a natural null sport. Once the dancers and racquetball players pioneered the concept, martial arts couldn't be far behind. It is one of those athletic activities that can take advantage of the ability to move in three dimensions, and it doesn't require the huge venues necessary for traditional spectator sports like baseball and football, games which will have to wait until orbital stations can afford to devote a large cubic area to such pastimes.

The spheres in which the *kumite* matches are being performed are eighteen feet in diameter, transparent, and banded along the equator and two meridians by twelve-inch-wide strips of clear velcro. The strips divide the sphere into eight equal sections. Only the contestants themselves remain within the shell; the judging personnel are positioned immediately outside, one judge over each half hemisphere. The referee, as on planetside, is able to move as he sees fit in order to best watch the action.

The current referee, a thin, effeminate Japanese, isn't moving much at all. He has that pallid shade in his complexion I've come to associate with space adaptation syndrome. Like many of the officials, he's spent less time training in zero gravity than have we contestants.

The p.a. system crackles, announcing the match and its participants. One is Joe Alexander, a Shotokan stylist, a heavyweight with a United States national championship to his credit. He faces a tall, thin Swedish player, a weight combination that wouldn't occur on Earth. Here the criterion is height.

Joe is designated as the white player. The Swede is red. *"Hajime!"* the referee shouts, and the match begins.

Joe thrusts off, a mountain of mass hurtling toward his opponent. The Swede wisely springs sideways, aiming a blade-of-foot kick at Joe's side, but failing to land it. They both miss the velcro and bounce off the sphere again, colliding in a techniqueless jumble that makes me wince. They shouldn't try to thrust; they should use snapping moves. Joe's foot automatically reaches beneath him, trying to find the ground, to gain the connection that will allow him to use his size effectively. But the collision has stolen both players' momentum, leaving them stranded at the center of the combat area, where Joe's size only means that much more target area for the Swede to take advantage of. Which he does.

"Seiken zuki, chu dan," the referee announces. "Half-point, red."

Joe opens the second engagement with a pile driver kick to the stomach. The Swede flies across the sphere, bouncing three times before he finds the velcro. The referee's whistle blares.

"Excessive contact. One warning, white," the referee calls, as the Swede struggles to catch his breath.

That is the thing about null-gravity matches; it is easy to tell when the impact has been too hard. We are using a modified version of World Union of Karate Organizations rules. This is supposed to be refined. No gloves, no full contact, no blood. Joe comes from a different tradition.

"It's the Hulk," says Mikey, my highest-ranked black belt student. The others laugh.

I almost ask them to knock it off, but they stop after the first comment. Joe doesn't deserve the mockery. He is a good, ethical player. I suspect he is as dissatisfied with his performance as was the referee.

In fact, his thunder seems to be completely stolen. He loses the second half-point in less than ten seconds.

"He looks like a whale," Mikey comments, as Joe

sails toward the viewing area. I watch him climb into a seat and strap in, stone-faced. This is only the first round. Joe can still place in the consolation matches. He will face at least one more opponent. But he will lose that match, too, as long as he remains in his present mood.

I notice the hair on my chest is sticking straight out between the lapels of my gi, and I brush it flat. I have long since given up on the hair on my scalp, adopting the crew cut so common here at the space station, even among the women.

Not a whale, I reflect. A dinosaur. Joe is from an age when power could win you matches. Any master, myself included, emphasizes the importance of speed, co-ordination, flexibility, and quick thinking, but until the arrival of the null-gravity event, simple strength and size had won many karate tournaments. Joe is a fine player, but he has never had to vary his repertoire. He is adapted to a different environment.

We all are, I tell myself, vaguely paying attention to the continuing matches. We are like rock musicians suddenly called upon to prepare a classical symphony; some may have the talent to excel at both the old art and the new, others may not. In my mind is the acrid smell of vomit, the dizziness, the frustrating urge to figure out which way is *down*: memories of my first week here. Some of the group brought up from Earth for the competition hadn't made it through those first few days; I had lost my best pupil. Some, of course, had never made it up the gravity well in the first place: bad blood pressure, lack of financial sponsor, inability to devote three months of one's life to a single sports event. Over the last few weeks, I have seen lips pursed in determination, individuals stretching their practice sessions in zero gravity right up to the eight hours permitted per day, and here and there, wild elation at a freedom impossible to the planetbound. We are part of a great experiment. Those who succeed will be the new breed of karateka; the others will be fossils. In many ways it might have been kinder for Joe to have been one of the ones eliminated early.

"Huh?" I ask, abruptly aware that someone is tapping me on the shoulder.

"Sally's coming up for her *kata*," Mikey says. "Want to watch?"

"Of course," I answer. I unbuckle and accompany the majority of my students to the other side of the arena.

Unlike sparring, forms are performed inside cubes, a design which complements their symmetrical nature. The only velcro is a small square on the "bottom" side, from which the player begins, and hopefully, finishes each kata. As I strap into a seat, a Shorin-ryu stylist dances carefully from one wall to another, executing a block and strike combination to different directions, a lower *kata*, unsophisticated if not for the unique venue. Unlike some, it closely resembles the earthbound variation.

He starts well. He stays oriented, keeps control over his momentum. It is his karate technique that suffers. His entire body lands in the right place, but his blocks are incomplete and his strikes slow. He misses the velcro at the finale.

"Three point five," the head judge announces. Average for his level.

I spot Sally at the staging area, and kick over to her. Her glance reminds me a little of a deer as it stares into oncoming headlights.

"Don't worry," I say. "Just do it the way you've done it all week."

She tugs her belt, tightening the knot. Weightlessness perversely unties everyone's belt several times a day, unless they're as old and frayed as mine. The committee has already voted to replace them with velcro-secured ones. "Yes, *sensei*."

"What's this 'sensei' shit?"

"Yes, Aaron."

"Kick ass, girl. Show them what a Goju player can do." The sentence is hardly out of my mouth when her name is announced over the loudspeaker.

She crosses her fingers once, gives me her pert, nineteen-year-old smile once again, and launches toward the cube.

I observe her gracefully sliding through the trap door to take her place on the velcro patch, and feel like a father with only one child left at home. Sally is the single one of my students who has survived the morning's qualification rounds. I'm a bit startled by the feeling. Ordinarily, watching that body of hers move brings on much more corrupt emotions. Must be getting old, I muse. Pushing the big three-five. My own instructor retired from tournament play at twenty-five.

She places the soles of her feet on the velcro and stands straight, hands at sides, gi precisely arranged, hair tied back in a neat bun. The commander announces kata *seinchin*, and gives her the cue to start.

Gradually she unfolds into the first posture of the kata, and proceeds with the opening set of slow, isotonic movements. She must try to maintain her position just above the floor. If she floats too high, she'll be unable to kick off in order to begin the fast sections of the form. I picture all too well the times during training when even I ended up rotating helplessly in the middle of the enclosure.

She hovers perfectly. I watch her hands: clenching for the double downward block, opening for the upward block, tensing for the finger strike. The hardest part is breath control. If she exhales or inhales too profoundly, it will send her traveling in directions she's not supposed to go.

Then she kicks, zooming straight "up," then back down to land on the velcro so smoothly that it holds her once more. She rotates slightly, blocking with tension, then pushes off toward a corner, performing a lower block in midair, and bouncing back to the opposite corner, blocking again. She catches herself against the sides of the cube, canceling her momentum. She stays there, executing another slow block, then kicks off to perform the same set of movements to another two corners.

She's good. She's on a streak. Furthermore, *seinchin* is the most spectacular null-gravity kata, if done with the precision that she is exhibiting. I feel a smile creeping across my lips. The judges' gazes are rapt.

She lands in cat stance dead center on the velcro, and finishes the last block in an almost leisurely fashion. She knows how well she's done.

"Hot damn," Mikey says. We wait. I wipe the slickness off my palms.

"Five point zero," we hear come out of the speakers. It's the highest score so far in Sally's class.

She shoots through the trap door like an acrobat, pivoting on one finger, and glides across the gap to the bleachers, a great big grin on her face. Then she has her arms around me, pinning me to my seat.

"Congratulations," I say.

"Oh, I'm so glad you talked me into coming here." Sally gave up a semester of college to make the trip. She waves her arms in a little dance, forgetting where she is, and I have to catch her toes and reel her back in.

"Hold on. The competition isn't over yet."

"I don't care. I *never* thought I'd get a five today."

Some time later, I leave her in the company of the others and wander back to the kumite area. I have a bye for the second round, so I have some time.

Sally is the new breed, I tell myself. She's learned the music. Whenever the next karate tournament in high orbit is held, she'll be one of the veterans there. I allow myself a spoonful of pride.

I check the scoreboard. Some of the second round has been completed, and I see that my next opponent will be another Goju player named Eunice Hershey. She is the first woman I have faced during the tournament; there aren't many in my height class. That there are any at all is a bit unusual. I can still see old Master Kawamoto's face turning purple at the thought of combining males and females in kumite matches.

Joe is off sitting by himself. He has, I note, lost the first round of the consolation series, and is now out of the tournament altogether.

I pass part of the time practicing small null-gravity maneuvers in the bleachers. I hook a finger around the grip at the top of a seat, letting my body float. I spin counterclockwise, then clockwise, flip forward, then backward. I fix my eyes on my fingers as they twist and grip at the plastic. That's the secret of keeping one's orientation, not to mention keeping one's dinner down: find a stable point and focus on it.

Later, I bounce from seat to seat, pushing off with feet, toes, elbows, knees, fingers, hands. Never has Newton's Third Law seemed more real. Even breathing, I remind myself for the thousandth time, can be a source of propulsion.

Just remember the rules, I say silently. The karate technique will take care of itself.

It seems like only a few moments later that I am hearing my students offer words of encouragement. My name has been called. I push off for the sphere. Eunice Hershey is arriving from another direction. Once more, the referee ties the red ribbon to my belt. We are inside the sphere, waiting for the command.

I glance into her eyes. She is intimidated. I haven't failed to make the quarter-finals in ten years, back on Earth. Somewhere in the distance the referee shouts.

She takes the offensive. I stay at my side of the sphere. She is leaving me an opening to the ribs just beneath her elbow. My foot takes advantage of it.

Time is moving very strangely. It seems like an hour before the whistles blow, the flags wave, the referee calls the score.

"*Yoko geri, chu dan*. One half-point, red."

More intimidation. I begin to smile. The old feeling is back. I have the mind set that has carried me through so many matches. Eunice sees it.

She tries a less direct approach this time. Off to my left, then across in front of me. Her foot licks out as she passes. Not close enough for a point; I don't block. She continues past. I launch off. We cross twice at the center of the sphere, engaging tentatively. I land again, this time on the velcro. I stop, and turn. I know she will be off to my right.

She is not.

I feel a wind brush my temple. My block is almost in time.

The whistles blow.

I tread the velcro back to my starting position, listening to it go scritch, scritch, scritch, feeling it tug at my feet.

"*Ura uchi, jo dan,*" the referee announces. "One half-point, white. One half-point, red. Continue."

Eunice seems surprised, as if uncertain she had really made the score. She shouldn't be; it was a clean technique.

She takes to the air again. I decide to move the slow way, walking the velcro. I must wait for the right opening, the one sure to be worth the point. There are no second chances at this stage. There. She is open to her face. I strike.

And miss. Not by much, but wide enough not to tempt the judges. I continue to the other side of the sphere. She is charging me again. I block her with my left leg, shoving her back across the sphere. When she returns, I am ready.

No. Her knee is in the way. I halt my technique.

I misjudge how limber she is. Her leg twists impossibly far, bringing her body with it. She makes contact with my side.

The maneuver has left a broad opening, which I take, but the whistles are already echoing.

The referee must be announcing the score, but I don't hear it. I offer Eunice my congratulations, and precede her out of the sphere. The red ribbon is removed, and I am soon in the midst of my strangely quiet group of students.

"Your strike was *much* better than her kick," Sally blurts.

"But it was *after* her kick," I reply calmly.

They offer more condolences, which I barely hear, and some part of me shuttles words back in their direction. Presently Sally is due to perform another kata, and I insist that they go on without me.

What the hell. I have enough trophies already. I spot Joe, still in his perch, and float over his way.

"Close match," he says. I decide he means mine, not the one going on in the sphere right now. We watch that one, and the next, which features a woman player. She loses.

"What do you say we get a beer?" I ask. The only alcohol available is outside the stadium, in the space station proper, where there's gravity, and an old man can tell up from down.

"Sounds good to me."

We unstrap and head for the exits, gliding like a pair of pterodactyls.

Editor's introduction to:
NEW WORLDS FOR OLD

Launch a probe, lose a planet; that's science for you. It seems like every time we learn something new about the Solar System it becomes a colder, less inviting place. Happily, our technology is surging forward at such a pace that *no* terrain remains conceptually daunting for long.

Heck, the only difference between a Luna-sized methane slushball and our heart's desire is a little solar power—even Venus, the Solar System's autoclave, is beginning to look possible. (The asteroids of course are duck soup, even with current technology.) And yet—and yet—Barsoom was such a lovely place . . .

—JPB

NEW WORLDS FOR OLD:

THE CHANGING FACE OF THE SOLAR SYSTEM

Charles Sheffield

Introduction. In the Ancient World, the Heavens were the abode of the Gods. As such, they were supposed to be perfect. And since change and decay are not perfect, the Heavens were assumed to be fixed and permanent.

The "fixed stars" seemed to fit that requirement very well. They went around the Earth every day, moving in their crystal spheres, and their relative positions never varied. You could look at the constellations any time, from any place, and they didn't change their appearance. There was just a handful of exceptions, very bright stars that kept moving around. These were named "planets," which is just the Greek word for "wanderers," and they were associated with special deities.

Little by little, humans gained more knowledge. We learned that the Earth rotated on its axis; that our planet was in an orbit around the Sun; that the other planets were whole worlds, much like the Earth; and that the fixed stars were spheres of hot gas, much like the Sun. Along the way we learned that the stars are not fixed in position any more than the planets are fixed—they are just much farther away. In one way, though, both stars and planets *were* "fixed": over long periods of time they were fixed in composition and properties, changing not at all since humans first appeared on Earth. There were the few rare exceptions, such as novas and supernovas, but most stars and planets looked just as they had always looked. A planet would have appeared the same to Alexander the Great or to Moses as it does to us. The solar system and the stars are *stable,* over vast periods of time.

This is the current view; but in one curious way, there is still rapid change. There have been enormous and fundamental changes in the solar system, not just over the past few thousand years, but in the past few *tens* of years. That change has been in our state of knowledge, and our ideas as to what the solar system is like. Not a single planet looks the same to us now as it did at the end of the Second World War, forty years ago; and the changes are not minor—they are profound.

I will discuss changes in our knowledge and perception of planets, moons, and other bodies that are gravitationally bound to our Sun. I will begin at the center (which since the time of Copernicus means, in most people's view, the region closest to the Sun) and work outwards.

Mercury. The planet closest to the Sun is Mercury. That was the view two hundred years ago, and it was the view in 1945. But *one* hundred years ago many people would have disputed it. They would have pressed the claim for *Vulcan,* a planet that was supposed to move closer to the Sun than the orbit of Mercury. One presumed effect of Vulcan was that it perturbed Mercury, which therefore didn't move quite the way it should. The ellipse that Mercury was travelling in was itself rotating, a little bit faster than predicted by computations based on Newtonian gravitational theory. Ever since 1846, scientists have been very aware of the fact that undiscovered planets could make a known planet appear in a position a little bit different from where it was calculated to be—this was the way that Adams and Leverrier were able to predict the existence and position of Neptune. So a good case could be made for Vulcan. It would be difficult to observe, argued its proponents, because it would be so close to the Sun; but some observers even thought that they had already seen it, moving rapidly across the Sun's bright face.

Einstein disposed of Vulcan in 1915. He showed that the general theory of relativity required just the necessary added precession rate for Mercury's orbit. Vulcan was not needed, and since then no one has said they saw it. (As Eddington remarked, the Universe we observe is the Universe of our theories.)

Let us look at Mercury, then, as astronomers saw it around 1950. The planet has been known since ancient times, and was already mentioned in a report in Nineveh made to Assurbanipal, King of Assyria. The Greeks called it "the sparkling one," a bright white planet visible only in the early morning or late evening. It is never seen more than 30 degrees away from the Sun's position, which makes for awkward viewing since we are looking at it through a lot of the Earth's atmosphere. Thirty-five or forty years ago Mercury was considered to be a hot, airless ball, moving around the Sun in a rather elongated ellipse every 88 days. It was thought to present the same face to the Sun all the time, so that one side would be fiercely hot and the other chillingly cold. Astronomers knew that Mercury had little or no atmosphere. One advantage of a planet being closer to the Sun than Earth is that when it is passing between us and the Sun, sunlight would be refracted by any substantial atmosphere. There was no sign of that, so the surface of Mercury must be close to a perfect vacuum.

Until the early 1970s, that simple picture of Mercury prevailed: hard to observe, small, hot, and with no atmosphere.

The big difference to our state of knowledge came with the Mariner 10 spacecraft, which in 1974-75 performed a series of Mercury fly-bys. It sent back pictures from three close encounters—and produced the first big surprise: the surface of Mercury looked at first sight exactly like the Moon's. It was cratered, barren, and airless. The spacecraft also discovered a magnetic field, about 1% of Earth's. This, together with the planet's high density, suggests a substantial iron core for Mercury, probably 1,500 kilometers in diameter (the whole planet is only 4,500 km. in diameter). At least part of that core should be fluid, allowing the existence of a permanent dynamo that generates the external magnetic field.

Mercury's rotation period was another surprise. The assumption that tidal forces would lock it to present the same face to the Sun all the time was wrong. If that were the case, the rotation period of Mercury would be the same as its year: 87.969 days. Mercury actually goes through one complete revolution on its axis in 58.646 Earth-days. Notice that 58.646 is just two-thirds of 87.969. This is not a coincidence. There is a dynamical effect known as a "resonance lock" that keeps those two periods in that exact ratio. As one odd result, a *day* on Mercury lasts just two of its *years* (because the planet turns *one and a half times* on its axis in the time it takes to make one full circuit around the Sun). Since the planet does not present the same face to the Sun all the time, it is fiercely hot; but hot all over, not just on one side as was previously thought.

Mercury has probably changed little in appearance in the past three billion years. However, it has one interesting difference from the Moon; it is more *wrinkled* in its surface, probably as a result of more cooling and contraction than the Moon has ever experienced. On the other hand, anything three billion years old has a right to be wrinkled.

Venus. If Mercury was for a long time something of a mystery to astronomers, Venus was a positive embarrassment. Galileo, back in 1610, took a look at the Planet of Love with his homemade telescope and noted that the surface seemed completely featureless. And that, improvements in telescopes and observing techniques notwithstanding, was the way that Venus obstinately remained for the next three and a half centuries. Venus was known to be about the same size as the Earth—a "sister planet," as people were fond of saying, coming closer to Earth than any other, and only a few hundred kilometers smaller in radius (6,050 km. to Earth's 6,378 km.). But if she were our sister, we knew remarkably little about her. Venus' year was known, but not its day; and the surface was a complete and total mystery because of the all-pervading and eternal cloud layer.

Naturally, that absence of facts did not stop people from speculating. A general rule applies to everything from science to religion to movie stars: the fewer the known facts, the wilder can be your speculation. In the case of Venus, until twenty years ago the theories were wild indeed. For a while the popular notion was that Venus was a younger and more primitive form of Earth. Probably hotter, and perhaps entirely covered with oceans (the logic was simple: hotter, because nearer the Sun; and clouds meant water, so more clouds than Earth meant more water than Earth). Science fiction stories were common in which Venus was a steamy, swampy planet, where it rained and rained and rained.

There were competing theories. Fred Hoyle, Britain's leading astrophysicist in the two decades after the Second World War, speculated that Venus indeed had oceans. But according to the theory he proposed for solar system formation, they would be oceans of hydrocarbons (the ultimate answer to OPEC . . .).

Hoyle's ideas may sound wild, but they were based on an extrapolation of known physical laws. Whereas, in the 1950s, there was Velikovsky, with the wildest, least scientific—and most popular—theory of all. Venus, he said, was once part of *Jupiter*. By some unspecified event it was somehow ripped out of the Jovian system and proceeded inwards. There, after a complicated game of celestial billiards with Mars and the Earth, it settled down to become Venus in its present orbit. And all this took place not at the dawn of creation of the solar system, but *recently*, only 3,500 years ago. Among other things, the multiple passages of Venus past the Earth stopped this planet in its rotation, caused a universal deluge (The Flood), parted the Red Sea, and caused numerous other annoyances.

There are so many things wrong with Velikovsky's ideas that it is tempting to trash them at length. Perhaps we should settle for just one problem with his theory, the violation of the law of conservation of angular momentum, and leave it at that. You can say one thing for Velikovsky; when he was wrong, he was wrong *big*.

The more conventional view of Venus, thirty or forty years ago, can be summarized easily: probably a hot, cloudy, perhaps water-covered planet; nature of surface, unknown; temperature, unknown; composition of atmosphere, unknown; period of revolution, unknown; internal composition, unknown; magnetic field, unknown.

In the past fifteen years space probes, largely from the Soviet Union, have changed our knowledge and understanding dramatically. The present description runs as follows:

• The period to make one complete revolution about its axis is 243 Earth-days. This is *longer* than Venus' year (225 Earth-days). Also, since the planet rotates in the opposite sense from its direction around the Sun, its *day*—the time from noon to noon for a point on the planet—is 117 Earth-days.

It is often difficult to visualize the relation between the time a planet takes to rotate on its axis (known as the *sidereal period*), the length of its day, and the length of its year. Fortunately there is a simple formula that relates the three quantities. If R is the time in Earth-days for the planet to rotate on its axis, D is the length of its day, and Y the length of its year, then $1/D = 1/R \pm 1/Y$, where the plus sign is used when the planet rotates on its axis in the opposite sense from its travel around the Sun. For Venus, Y = 225 Earth-days, R = 243 Earth-days, so D = $1/(\frac{1}{225} + \frac{1}{243})$ = 117.

• The cloud cover is real enough, but the pale yellow clouds are not water vapor. They are sulfuric acid, the result of combining sulfur dioxide and water. These sulfuric acid clouds stop about 45 kilometers above the surface, and below that everything is very clear, with almost no dust. The whole atmosphere is about 95% carbon dioxide. The lighting level at the surface is about like that of a cloudy day on Earth, though there are frequent storms in the clouds, and lots of lightning.

• The pressure down on the surface is somewhere about 90 Earth atmospheres. (This huge pressure may seem to offer impossible problems for the existence of life, but that's not the case. A sperm whale, diving in Earth's oceans to deeper than a kilometer, comfortably endures a pressure of more than a hundred atmospheres, and returns to the surface unharmed a few minutes later.)

• Venus is hot. In this way the modern picture of Venus is like the old one. It is probably hotter than anyone (with the possible exception of Velikovsky) expected. The surface temperature is somewhere between 460 and 480 degrees Celsius, and highly uniform over the whole surface. There is no relief to be had by going to the poles, or to the night side. Since the axial tilt of Venus is only about 6 degrees, there are also no seasons to speak of.

Venus is hot for the same reason that a greenhouse is hot. Solar radiation gets into the atmosphere easily enough, but the longer wavelength (heat) radiation from the surface is then trapped by that thick carbon dioxide atmosphere, and cannot escape above the clouds.

• The surface of Venus is a barren, rocky place of uplifts and shallow, melted-down craters. It is nothing like the old stories; no swamps, no intelligent amphibious life forms, no artifacts but a few burned-out spacecraft from the Soviet Union and the United States. But there are mountain ranges, well-mapped by orbiting imaging radar, and a great rift valley, bigger than any other known in the solar system.

There is an interesting difference between the general surface structure of Earth and Venus. If we plot the average altitude of surfaces on Earth (including the sea-bed) we find that there are two big peaks in the distribution: they represent the ocean floor and the continental platforms, separated by about five kilometers. This two-story world is a consequence of plate tectonics, where moving plates lift the land surfaces. When we make the same plot for Venus, a different picture emerges. We have a single peak, at the most common average elevation. There are uplands, a vast rift valley, and shallow basins, but they all cluster well around this one average value.

Why are plate tectonics not a major force on Venus? Here we are on speculative ground. Theorists argue that the high surface temperature gives rise to a thick, light crust, which is too buoyant to be subducted (forced under) even if plates collide. Others argue that Venus is like a very young Earth, where we have yet to see the effects of plate tectonics. In perhaps a billion years Venus will see the rise of continents, and conditions may perhaps change to ones more congenial to life.

• Venus possesses no appreciable magnetic field. This is strange, since the planet is so like Earth in size and composition. However, the lack of field may be related to the planet's slow rotation, which would greatly reduce the dynamo effects of a liquid iron core.

• There remains one general question: why is our sister planet so different from Earth in so many ways? It is difficult to offer an answer, but a comment is appropriate. The Earth has a large moon; Venus has none. More and more, the presence of the Moon seems important.

The Earth. I will say little about this planet. Not because we know it so well, but because the study of Earth *as a planet* is in its early days.

Consider just a couple of examples of changing perceptions. The theory of plate tectonics, already referred to, was geological heresy forty years ago. Wegener proposed the theory over half a century ago, but he was laughed away. Only when the evidence of sea-floor spreading became undeniable did geologists begin to

accept the ideas of plate tectonics—which today under-
pin almost all serious geomorphological work.

The second example is the Gaia theory proposed by
Lovelock and extended by Margulies. According to that
theory, Earth is the way that it is *because of the existence of life upon it*. It is life that regulates the temperature, decides the composition of the atmosphere, and
controls the rate of erosion and land formation. Life is
usually a strong stabilizing influence against rapid or
disastrous change (although it was the agent that trans-
formed the planet from one with a hydrogen-rich reduc-
ing atmosphere to one with an oxygen-rich atmosphere).
If the Gaia theory proves to be true, the role of life in
the Universe becomes much more important.

We know remarkably little about our own Earth—
and what we "know" seems to change with every
generation.

The Moon. This surely ought to be the most familiar
and best-known planet (or satellite) in the solar system.
Humans have been looking up at it and studying it for
all of history. Its influence on Earth, and on each of us
individually, is profound. There are lunar tides running
within our bodies, just as they ebb and flow in the seas
of Earth. Ask any policeman—the rate of occurrence of
violent crimes peaks at the full moon, and the admission to mental institutions is maximum. We are very
familiar with our own 24-hour circadian rhythms, and
how we feel at different times of day. But we are also
affected by the more subtle lunar rhythm, imposing its
cycles on our bodies in ways we have still to understand.

A generation ago, our ignorance of the Moon was
quite striking. For example, the Moon always presents
approximately the same hemisphere to Earth (small
oscillations, known as librations, allow us to see a little
more than half the Moon's surface). Thirty years ago we
had no information to tell us what lay on the far side of
the Moon. Again, this permitted wild speculation. It
was even possible to imagine a deep depression on the

back of the Moon, where there could be atmosphere and perhaps even life.

That idea went away in 1959, when a Russian spacecraft took and transmitted to Earth pictures of the far side of the Moon. It looked, disappointingly, rather like the side that we already knew.

However, there were still plenty of things to speculate about. For example, the craters: were they caused by volcanoes, or were they meteor impacts? Thirty years ago no one had any proof one way or the other. The flat, dark "seas" on the Moon: they were certainly not water, but might they be deep dust pools, ready to swallow up any spacecraft unwise enough to attempt to land on one of them?

Today we have at least some of the answers. First, we know that the surface of the Moon is *old*. The measured ages of lunar rock samples brought back in the Apollo program are in the billions of years—half of them are older than any rocks ever found on Earth. Even the "new" craters, like Tycho, measure their ages in hundreds of millions of years. The dust pools are gone. Astronauts who landed on the Moon reported a layer of dust, but no sign of the deep, dangerous seas of an earlier generation's speculations.

The Moon is of great interest to scientists; but it seems fair to say that to most other people it is a dull place. There are no interesting known deposits of minerals, no air, no water. Human colonies on the Moon seem likely within a generation, but they may exist mainly to send materials out into space. The biggest advantage of the Moon may turn out to be its low escape velocity (only 2.4 kms/sec.), allowing cheap shipment of materials from the Moon to Earth orbit.

I do not think that a lunar base will satisfy our urge to develop the planets. The Moon is too much an offshore island of Earth. We have already paddled our dugout canoes there a few times, and we will be going back. But it is not our new continent, our "new-found-land."

* * *

Mars. That new-found-land is Mars.

The Red Planet has had some bad publicity over the years. There were the *canals* of Mars, that Percival Lowell could see very well and believed were of artificial origin, but which many people had trouble seeing at all. The original observer of linear features on the Martian surface had never *said* "canals"; what Schiaparelli, who reported them back in 1877, had actually said was "canali," which is Italian for *channels*. But most people didn't care for such a fine distinction. Canals were more interesting.

And of course there were the Martians, given very poor press by H.G. Wells in *The War of the Worlds*. They were sitting up there on Mars, with their "vast, cool, and unsympathetic" minds set on taking over Earth.

Regardless of whether the Martians were good guys or bad guys, at the turn of the century almost everyone agreed that there was life on Mars. Although Venus is Earth's sister planet, from many points of view Mars is a more convincing Earth look-alike. It has a day just a few minutes longer than Earth's (24 hrs. 37 mins.). It has an axial tilt almost the same as Earth's, so the cycle of the seasons should be similar. And it has an observable atmosphere, although one that a generation ago was of unknown composition and density. There are also noticeable seasonal changes in both the planet's color and the size of its polar caps.

And as recently as 1945, Mars still had canals. A scientific text written at that time could confidently make the assertion that the color changes on the Mars surface were "presumably due to vegetation, since they change to russet brown with the approach of autumn on the planet." The same book adds that "The climate would appear to be very mild"; and "The reason for the prodigious enterprise of this complicated canal system is found in the fact that as there are no mountains and clouds on Mars, there can be no rain, and consequently no rivers. In view of the permanent water famine, water must be brought from the melting polar caps to irrigate the Martian desert with the semi-annual un-locking of the polar snows."

Intelligence, maybe; life, a sure thing. That seemed to be the common attitude towards Mars forty years ago.

And the modern Mars? No canals, but a cratered sand-worn surface that looks more like the Moon than Earth. Months-long sand storms. No surface water, but lots of mysterious signs of ancient water run-off. Stupendous mountains, twice as high as any on Earth; a vast canyon (the Vallis Marineris) that would easily swallow the Grand Canyon whole; and plenty of jagged surface rocks. That was the report that came back from the Mariner, Mars (Soviet) and Viking spacecraft, and from the Viking Lander. In 1976 the Lander also looked for life with its on-board experiment package. The first results were outstandingly positive, too good to be true—there seemed to be chemical indicators of life everywhere. Then the investigators decided, yes, those results are too good to be true—and they're *not* true. There are still optimists to be found, but today the most widely held view is that Mars probably lacks life completely.

The Mars atmosphere was also a bit of a disappointment. The pressure at the surface is only one percent of an Earth atmosphere, and it is made up of mostly carbon dioxide and nitrogen. Surface temperatures range from a little above the freezing point of water, at high noon, to maybe −100 degrees C. That is not most people's idea of a "very mild" climate. On the other hand, there are terrestrial organisms that could stand those temperatures, and even thrive, if they have access to water. And there is water on Mars, mostly locked up in the polar caps. Those caps are thought to be water ice and "dry ice" (solid carbon dioxide).

In spite of everything, humans could live on Mars. One day they almost certainly will. The available land area is roughly equal to the land area of Earth. The atmosphere is dense enough to be useful for aerobraking spacecraft or flying an aircraft. The low gravity, only ⅖ of Earth gravity, helps a lot. If there are no Martians now, some day there will be.

The moons of Mars: Phobos and Deimos. Mars has its own moons, two of them. However, if attention to objects in the solar system were to be given in proportion to their size, Phobos and Deimos would deserve to be totally ignored. They are tiny objects, each only tens of kilometers across.

In one of the oddities of literature, Jonathan Swift "predicted" the existence and major characteristics of these moons long before there was any chance of discovering them. Writing in *Gulliver's Travels* of the Voyage to Laputa, Swift in 1726 remarked that the astronomers of the flying island of Laputa, with their superior telescopes, had "discovered two lesser stars, or 'satellites,' which revolve around about Mars, whereof the innermost is distant from the center of the primary planet exactly three of its diameters, and the outermost, five; the former revolves in the space of ten hours and the latter in twenty-one and a half."

The little moons themselves would not be discovered for another century and a half. They were finally seen by Asaph Hall, in 1877. Later observations, between 1877 and 1882, gave estimates of their distances from Mars and their orbital periods. The modern values of these are 1.35 Mars-diameters and 7 hrs. 39 mins. for Phobos, and 3.5 diameters and 30 hrs. 18 mins. for Deimos. Swift had missed by a little bit—but it was an uncanny piece of fortuitous prediction.

Until thirty years ago, distances from Mars and orbital periods were all that anyone knew of Phobos and Deimos. In 1956, Gerald Kuiper estimated their diameters, giving figures of 12 km for Phobos and 6 km for Deimos. But the real quantum leap in our knowledge had to wait until 1977, one hundred years exactly after Asaph Hall's discovery. In that year, the Viking 2 spacecraft took a close-up look at both moons.

Neither Phobos nor Deimos looks anything like a sphere. They are triaxial ellipsoids of similar shape—

Phobos has principal diameters of 27, 21, and 19 kilometers, and Deimos 15, 12, and 11 km. They are both tidally locked to Mars, so that they always have their longest axes pointed towards the planet. They have battered, cratered surfaces, and Phobos has one huge crater, Stickney (named after Asaph Hall's wife, Angelina Stickney, who encouraged him to keep looking when he was about ready to give up). Stickney is about ten kilometers across—nearly half the size of the moonlet. Both moons have a regolith, a dusty surface layer of fine-grained material, and both are thought to be captured asteroids. There is some suggestion that Phobos may have water locked within it, because some of its surface features suggest steam has escaped there after past meteor impacts.

Phobos looks more and more like a tempting target for anyone interested in conducting a manned Mars expedition. There is serious suggestion that the Soviet Union has set just such an objective for the 1990s.

The Asteroids. Like the moons of Mars, the asteroids are another piece of "modern" astronomy, unknown to the ancient world prior to the discovery of Ceres, on January 1, 1801. And yet a good case can be made for the idea that people *expected* at least one of the asteroids long before that.

In 1766, a German named Johann Titius noticed and announced a curious numerical relationship. In 1772 the idea was picked up and promoted by another German, Johann Bode, and the result became known as *Bode's Law*. It looks at first sight like no more than an odd piece of numerology, and *Bode's Rule* would be a better name for it. Here it is:

Write down the numbers 0, 3, 6, 12, 24, 48, 96, 192 . . . , doubling each time after the first. Now add 4 to each of them, to get 4, 7, 10, 16, 28, 52, 100, 196 . . . Now divide by 10, to get 0.4, 0.7, 1.0, 1.6, 2.8, 5.2, 10.0, 19.6 . . . Now interpret these numbers as *distances* of planets from the Sun. Thus the Earth, third planet out, has a distance of 1.0. (It is often very convenient to use a standard value of the Earth's average distance from the Sun as a yardstick of measurement. It is done so often that this unit is called an *astronomical unit*, abbreviated to a.u., and equal to about 150 million kilometers.) After the above manipulations, the Titius-Bode Law then gives a good fit to the distances of all the planets known to Titius and Bode. Here's how the table looks:

Planet	Bode's Number	Predicted distance using Bode's Law	Actual mean distance (millions of km.)
Mercury	0.4	60	58
Venus	0.7	105	108
Earth	1.0	150	150
Mars	1.6	239	228
? ? ?	2.8	419	? ?
Jupiter	5.2	778	778
Saturn	10.0	1,500	1,427
? ? ?	19.6	2,900	? ?

No one seemed to worry that Bode's Law suggested a possible planet out beyond Saturn. It was the *gap* that seemed significant. And there was no reason offered as to why there should be a planet in that missing fifth spot, except that a couple of hundred years ago numerology was perhaps even more popular than it is now. But then Uranus was discovered, in 1781, at an observed distance from the Sun of 2.817 billion kilometers—just as Bode's Law predicted. The search for the "missing fifth planet" began in earnest.

When that planet was finally discovered, it was perhaps a bit of a disappointment. The astronomers had been fishing for a shark and caught only a herring. Ceres was a little tiddler of a world, only 750 km. in diameter. It is today labelled a "planetoid," rather than a planet, to show our disdain. On the other hand,

Bode's Law had done its job. It predicted a distance of 419 million kilometers, and Ceres had come in on the nose at 414.

Any disappointment felt at the small size of Ceres must have diminished when the rest of the asteroids began to roll in: Pallas (480 km. diameter), Juno (206 km.), Vesta (390). . . . After 1830, the list of new discoveries just went on and on. It continues today, with several thousand known asteroids. If you are willing to contribute enough money, you can even have one named after you. For it turns out that Ceres was not only the first, it was also the biggest; and apart from the first few and biggest of them, there seems to be a good rule of thumb to describe asteroid size: no matter how many there are of a particular diameter, there will be ten times as many with one-third that diameter.

What do we know about the asteroids now that we didn't know thirty or forty years ago? For one thing, we know the shapes, rotation periods, and light-reflectance curves of several hundred of them. Most of them are not spherical. They are oddly shaped, and a few may even have moons of their own. We also know that many of them have left the main belt, between Mars and Jupiter, and swing in on orbits much closer to the Sun. This class of so-called *Earth-crossing asteroids* includes its own subgroups: the *Apollo* asteroids have orbits crossing Earth's orbit; the *Aten* asteroids are on average closer to the Sun than is the Earth (their semi-major axis is less than Earth's); and the *Amor* asteroids cross the orbits of both Earth and Mars. There are approaching a hundred known asteroids of these three types. Finding such asteroids is today an active business, because these bodies are more accessible from Earth than most of the solar system. It takes less fuel to match velocities with them. And we think they may contain very valuable materials; for we now have a much better idea of asteroid composition than we did a generation ago.

The asteroids are classified today by their light-reflectance characteristics for both visible and reflective infra-red radiation. There are four basic categories, which we may term carbon-rich, silicon-rich, metal-rich, and mixed. It would be nice to mine a metal-rich asteroid. A small one, maybe a mile across, should contain as much nickel as all Earth's known commercial deposits, in quite a pure form.

People have also proposed other uses for Earth-crossing asteroids apart from mining them. Moved to Earth orbit (feasible if the necessary volatile material for fuel can be found on the asteroid itself), such bodies could be used to protect other satellites and installations, or as a threat to ground-based facilities. A dangerous threat to both parties, given the destructive power of even a small asteroid collision with Earth.

There is an old controversy surrounding the asteroids: are they fragments of matter that never got together to form a planet, or were they once a planet that for some reason catastrophically disintegrated? Forty years ago, no one could offer firm evidence one way or the other. Today, most astronomers would argue strongly that the planet never formed. Jupiter's powerful gravitational field prevented the separate bodies from ever coalescing.

However, there have been recent other opinions. In 1972, the Canadian astronomer Ovenden examined the rate of change of planetary orbits, and concluded that they are changing too rapidly for a solar system that has supposedly been fixed in major components for hundreds of millions of years. Ovenden looked at the changes, and found they were consistent with the disappearance from the system of an object of planetary dimensions in the fairly recent past. He concluded that a body of about 90 Earth masses (the size of Saturn) had vanished from the solar system about sixteen million years ago. Three years later, Van Flandern at the U.S. Naval Observatory analyzed the orbits of long-period comets. He found many with periods of about sixteen million years, and also found that they seemed to have left the solar system from a particular region between the orbits of Mars and Jupiter.

Where do I stand on this question? Reluctantly (for I like the idea of the exploding planet, and even named it *Loge* in my first novel, *Sight of Proteus*) I have concluded that the asteroids were never a single body. They date back to the origin of the solar system, and have lived their lives in the present form ever since that time.

Jupiter. The difference between what we know today about Jupiter and its moons and what we knew as recently as twenty years ago is so great that it is hard to know where to begin. We will start by summarizing our knowledge of Jupiter as it existed about 1960.

Jupiter was already well known as the biggest planet, the bully of the solar system, whose gravitational field affected every other body orbiting the Sun. With a diameter eleven times that of Earth and a mass 320 times as big, Jupiter contains more material than all the rest of the planets put together. Its density was estimated more than a century ago, at 1.3 gms/cc. This is a low value compared to Earth, so astronomers knew that Jupiter ought to contain a large fraction of the lighter elements, such as hydrogen and helium.

Jupiter was known to be in rapid rotation, spinning on its axis once every ten hours. This, together with its great size, means that it bulges noticeably at the equator, and the equatorial radius is about 6% bigger than the polar radius.

The Great Red Spot on Jupiter was already observed in the seventeenth century (it was first noted by Robert Hooke, in 1664). The feature has dimmed and brightened over the years, but is known to have been there continuously since at least 1831. And it has been observed regularly since 1878. The size varies quite a bit. At the beginning of this century it was about 45,000 km. by 25,000 km.—twice today's size. But even in its present shrunken state, the Great Red Spot could easily swallow up Earth.

Thirty years ago the nature of the Great Red Spot was quite unknown. One theory, still acceptable in the

1940s, held that the spot was a new satellite of Jupiter in the process of formation, ready to split away from its parent planet (shades of Velikovsky!). Other ideas from the 1960s include a floating island of a particular form of water-ice (Ice VII), or an atmospheric cloud cap over a deeper floating island. The spot moves around on the surface of Jupiter, so it certainly had to be a floating *something*.

The other long-observed features of Jupiter were the striped bands that circle the planet parallel to the lines of latitude. Their appearance naturally also suggested clouds. Given Jupiter's known low density, those clouds were assumed to be very deep, but their composition was largely a matter of guesswork. Speculation based on the known composition of the Sun suggested that Jupiter ought to be mainly hydrogen and helium, but the direct observations of the 1960s showed only methane and ammonia.

It had also been known since the 1950s that Jupiter is an intense emitter of radio noise, but the mechanism for its production was vague, though it was known that somehow it seemed to correlate with the position of Io.

As for satellites, in 1960 a round dozen of them were known. These included the four major ones discovered by Galileo in that marvelous year of 1610, when he first applied his telescope to astronomy. Now termed the Galileian satellites, they are, in increasing distance from the planet, Io, Europa, Ganymede, and Callisto. In 1892 a fifth satellite was found, inside the orbit of Io. It was named by its discoverer, E. E. Barnard, simply "V", the Roman numeral for five. Later it became known as Amalthea. The other satellites, all more distant than Callisto, were simply numbered in the order of their discovery. Other than size estimates and orbit parameters, not much was known about any of the moons of Jupiter in 1960. The larger ones showed a few light and dark spots, and none seemed to have an atmosphere. The four outermost moons are much farther from Jupiter. They are in retrograde orbits, moving around Jupiter in the opposite direction from the planet's spin, and were generally thought to be captured asteroids.

The four Galileian satellites are all pretty substantial bodies. A generation ago, their radii were estimated as followed: Io, 1,600 km.; Europa, 1,450 km.; Ganymede, 2,500 km.; and Callisto, 2,250 km. In 1960, it was thought that Jupiter's biggest satellites, Ganymede and Callisto, were both rather smaller than Saturn's big moon, Titan.

Today's picture of the Jovian system is vastly different from that of just twenty years ago. What then were mere points of light are now well-mapped worlds, each with its own unique features and composition. The atmosphere of Jupiter has been looked at in great detail, and is now known as complex churning cloud patterns, with infinitely detailed vortices. The Great Red Spot has given up its secrets: it is a vast semi-permanent storm system—a hurricane, fueled by Jupiter's rapid rotation and lasting for hundreds of years.

We still know less than we would like about Jupiter's interior. That will remain true for a long time, despite the Galileo mission probe planned for later this decade. The escape velocity from Jupiter is about 60 km./sec., versus 11 km./sec for Earth. Once you go to Jupiter, it is hard to get away. The present picture of the planet's interior is of a deep, slushy ocean of metallic hydrogen under fabulous pressure, with perhaps a small Earth-like core of rock and iron at the very center. However, we now have confirmation that Jupiter is composed largely of hydrogen and helium, with an observed 19% percent helium in the upper atmosphere. And we have confirmation that Jupiter gives off more energy than it receives, a result that was still tentative ten years ago. Since the planet is a net emitter of energy, that energy must be produced somewhere in the deep interior. And there must be adequate convection mechanisms to bring the heat to the outer layers. In fact, Jupiter is almost a star—a bit bigger, and it could support its own fusion reactions. (Jupiter is about

$\frac{1}{1,000}$ the mass of the Sun; fusion reactions are thought to operate at $\frac{1}{100}$ solar mass and larger.)

Jupiter has electric and magnetic fields quite in keeping with its size. The powerful magnetic field captures and accelerates the "solar wind," the stream of energetic charged particles emitted by the Sun. As the nearest big moon, Io, moves through that swarm of particles, it generates and sustains a "flux tube"—a tube of current, five million amperes strong, that connects Io and the atmosphere of Jupiter. This in turn stimulates intense electrical activity in the Jovian cloud systems. The cloud tops seethe with super-bolts of lightning, and they generate powerful radio emissions from the planet. The night side shimmers with aurorae, also observed by the electronic eyes of the Voyager spacecraft in their 1979 inspection of the planet.

The two Voyager spacecraft also sent back quite extraordinary images of the major moons of Jupiter. Amalthea, the smallest and nearest-in of the previously known Jupiter satellites, proved to be a lumpy, irregular ellipsoid, about $265 \times 170 \times 155$ km. The longest axis always points towards Jupiter. Amalthea is tidally locked to face the parent planet.

Io, the next one out, is tidally locked also. Io is a spectacular sight. It looks like a smoking hot pizza, all oranges and reds and yellows. As it sweeps its way through that high-energy particle field surrounding Jupiter, tidal forces from the parent planet and its companion satellites generate powerful seismic forces within it. Io is a moon of volcanoes. Seven active ones were observed by Voyager, spewing out sulfur from the deep interior.

Europa is my own favorite of the Galileian satellites. It is the smallest of the four, with a mass about $\frac{2}{3}$ of our own Moon's. And it seems to be an ice world. There is a smooth, flat surface of water-ice, fractured by long linear cracks, ridges, and fissures. Underneath those there is probably liquid water, kept from freezing by the tidal heating forces from Jupiter and the other Galileian satellites. Europa has an estimated radius of

1,565 km., and an estimated density of 3 gm./cc. It is believed to possess a rocky silicon core, with an outer ice/water layer maybe 100 kilometers thick. There has been speculation that the ice-locked waters of Europa could support anaerobic life-forms which would derive their energy from ocean-floor vents, much like similar life-forms in Earth's deep oceans.

Ganymede is now known to be the biggest moon in the solar system, with an estimated radius of 2,650 km. It has a low density, about 1.9 gm./cc, and is thought to be about 50% water. The high reflectivity of Ganymede in fact suggests that its surface may be largely water-ice. The surface generally is a mixture of plains, craters, and mountains, not unlike the Moon.

Callisto, the outermost of the Galileian satellites, is all craters—the most heavily cratered body in the Jovian system. It has a radius of about 2,200 km., which makes it slightly smaller than Saturn's moon, Titan. It has the lowest density of any of Jupiter's moons, again suggesting that we will find lots of water and ice there. The surface of Callisto seems to be very stable. It has probably not changed much in four billion years—in contrast to Io's fuming surface, which changes daily.

As for the other satellites of Jupiter, we still know next to nothing about them. However, the Voyager mission did add one to their number—a small one, less than 40 km. across. That moonlet orbits at the outer edge of Jupiter's ring system.

All this, and rings too? Yes. Ten years ago, Saturn was thought to be the only ringed planet. Now we know that Jupiter has one as well. A thin ring, well inside the orbit of Amalthea, was seen by the Voyager spacecraft. It has a sharply defined outer edge, and it sits about 120,000 km. out from the center of Jupiter.

Saturn. This planet is about twice as far away from us as Jupiter; it is a little smaller (58,000 km. radius, to Jupiter's 70,000); and it is twice as far from the Sun and hence less strongly illuminated. For all these reasons, Saturn is more difficult to observe from ground-based telescopes, and our knowledge of a generation ago reflects that fact. Again, we will first summarize the state of knowledge around 1960.

The first thing that most people think of when Saturn is mentioned is the ring system. Those rings were first observed, like so much else in the solar system, by Galileo in 1610, but he was baffled by them and had no idea what they might be. Huygens, working 45 years later with a much better telescope, was the first person to deduce the nature of the rings. And nearly two hundred years after that, in 1857, Maxwell showed that the rings could not be solid. They have to be a swarm of particles. However, the size and composition of those particles was unknown even as recently as ten years ago, though already the popular theory was of small chunks of ice. The rings of Saturn were thought to be made of snowballs.

It was also known that there was not one ring, but several. In 1675 Cassini observed that there were at least two rings, separated by what we now call the Cassini division. A third ring, the Crape ring, was observed in 1838 and again in 1850.

As for the planet itself, Saturn looked to be a smaller, lighter version of Jupiter. Its radius was close to Jupiter's, but its density was only 0.7 gm./cc, and it was therefore only 95 Earth masses, versus 320 for Jupiter. The surface showed the same banding as Jupiter's, but with less detail visible. The equatorial bulge was even more pronounced, with a polar radius of 54,000 km. and an equatorial radius of 60,000 km. The planet's volume was known to be about 750 times that of Earth, and the rotation period was estimated at 10 hours and 15 minutes (although that period was not the same at all latitudes—Saturn was seen to rotate faster at the equator than near the poles). Based on the same general argument as was used for Jupiter, Saturn was expected to be composed largely of hydrogen and helium. Saturn's axis is inclined at 26.75 degrees to its orbit, so that unlike Jupiter it has substantial "seasons."

By 1960, nine satellites of Saturn had been discov-

ered. In order, moving outward from the planet, these
were named Mimas, Enceladus, Tethys, Dione, Rhea,
Titan, Hyperion, Iapetus, and Phoebe (Percival Lowell
thought he saw a tenth one in 1905, and he named it
Themis; but no one else has ever seen it). The sizes of
these moons were poorly known, if at all; but Titan,
with an estimated radius of 2,900 km., was thought to be
the largest satellite in the solar system. However, by
1944 Titan was also known to have an atmosphere. And
since a planet's size is measured from its solid or liquid
surface, Titan's true radius was still in doubt.

Methane and ammonia were both observed in Titan's
atmosphere, but their amounts, and the other components of that atmosphere, were unknown. The temperature within the atmosphere had not been measured.
And the pressure estimates for Titan's surface varied
over a wide range, from 0.02 to 2 Earth atmospheres.

We had little information, one generation ago, on
Saturn's other moons, though Hyperion was known to
be very small; Iapetus was seen to be much brighter on
one side than on the other; and Phoebe was tiny, very
distant from Saturn, and in a retrograde orbit highly
inclined to the parent planet's equator.

Today, we know that the atmosphere of Saturn is
mostly hydrogen, with rather less helium than Jupiter
(11% above the clouds, versus 19% for the larger planet).
Methane, ammonia, ethane, and acetylene have also
been observed in the atmosphere; and like Jupiter,
Saturn gives off more energy than it receives from the
Sun, so there must be internal sources of heat. The
clouds of Saturn show a number of long-lived features,
including atmospheric cyclonic patterns like the Great
Red Spot on Jupiter. Saturn has nothing of that size,
though it does have one red spot about 6,000 km. long in
its southern hemisphere.

The rings of Saturn are known to be infinitely more
complex than anyone dreamed ten years ago. There are
not two or three rings, but thousands of them, each one
very narrow. And they are not just simple rings. Sometimes there are radial gaps in them, "spokes" that come

and go within a period of a few hours. Some of the rings are interwoven, plaited together in ways that seem to defy the laws of classical celestial mechanics. Others are "herded" along in their orbits by small satellites that serve to control the location of ring boundaries. The composition of the rings has been confirmed. They are indeed mostly water-ice—bands of snowballs, hundreds of thousands of kilometers across.

The count of satellites for Saturn, not including the rings, has gone up substantially. It is now thought to be at least 18, including one that actually seems to share the same orbit as Mimas. Not surprisingly, the new satellites tend to be on the small side, though one of them, circling Saturn at about 150,000 km., is comparable in size with little Phoebe.

We have size and density estimates now for all the major satellites of Saturn (see the Table), and the surface radius of Titan, now given as 2,575 km., makes it a little bit smaller than Ganymede, though still bigger than Callisto or anything else in the solar system. Good quality images of the nine major moons have been obtained.

The Moons of Saturn

Satellite	Radius (km.)	Mean distance from center of Saturn	Density (gm/cc)
Mimas	196	185,540	1.44
Enceladus	250	238,040	1.16
Tethys	530	294,670	1.21
Dione	560	377,420	1.43
Rhea	765	527,100	1.33
Titan	2,575	1,221,860	1.88
Hyperion	205	1,481,000	?
Iapetus	730	3,560,800	1.16
Phoebe	220	12,954,000	?

Naturally, of these moons Titan has received much the most attention. We now know that it has a substantial atmosphere, with a surface pressure of 1.6 Earth atmospheres. It is composed mainly of nitrogen with a good fraction of methane (as much as 10% down at the surface, less higher up). The dark-red color of Titan is known to be due to a photochemical smog of organic (i.e. carbon-containing) compounds, and ethane, acetylene, hydrogen cyanide, and ethylene have all been detected there. The surface temperature has been measured as about –180 degrees Celsius. One plausible current conjecture is that Titan has an ocean—but an ocean of ethane and methane, rather like liquefied natural gas. All water on Titan will be well-frozen, but water-ice may lie below that frigid sea. Just as the canals of Mars have shown up as linear features on Europa, the petroleum oceans of Venus are here, on Titan.

The rest of the satellites are all much smaller, devoid of all signs of atmosphere, and have low densities to suggest that they contain a good deal of water-ice. All the known moons are cratered, and Mimas has one gigantic crater on it, nearly 130 km. across. Iapetus shows dark-red material on its leading face, suggesting that water-ice may have been eroded from that hemisphere by meteor impact as the moon moves in its orbit around Saturn. Alternatively, another argument is that water-ice has been preferentially deposited on the trailing hemisphere.

Uranus.
(Note: Most of this article was written before Voyager-2's encounter with the Uranus system. I decided in the case of this planet that I should say what we knew or suspected about Uranus in late 1985, before Voyager-2's arrival, and then report what we learned in the encounter of January 1986. Remember, everything from here *until the section "Voyager-2 and the Uranus Encounter" is suspect—the encounter modified our ideas about Uranus in a number of fundamental ways.)*

*   *   *

Before 1781 the solar system ended at Saturn. William Herschel's discovery of Uranus changed that forever, and now no one is sure where the "edge" of the solar system should be placed.

Once the planet had been sighted and recognized, the search for moons began. The first and second to be found, Titania and Oberon, were discovered by Herschel himself in 1787. And in 1851–52 William Lassell found two more, Ariel and Umbriel. No one else could see those two for over twenty years, and many wondered if they existed; but Lassell was at last proved right. The fifth and final moon, Miranda, was discovered by Gerald Kuiper in 1948. It is the closest of the five to Uranus. Their distances, periods, and estimated sizes are as follows:

Satellite	Distance from center of Uranus (km.)	Period (days)	Size (radius) in km.)
Miranda	124,000	1.4	250
Ariel	191,000	2.52	665
Umbriel	267,000	4.14	555
Titania	439,000	8.71	800
Oberon	587,000	13.46	815

The "day" on Uranus is somewhere between 10.5 and 18 hours. The large uncertainty in this figure shows the difficulty of making observations of Uranus from the surface of the Earth. We cannot see *any* features on the planet's surface; the estimate of rotation period has to be based on some indirect means. There are three methods available:

1. We can measure the difference between the planet's radius at the pole and at the equator. This equatorial bulge, plus a model of the planet's composition, allows a rotation rate to be computed.

2. We can measure the rate of precession of the orbits of the moons of Uranus. This precession is caused by the equatorial bulge of the planet, and allows a second estimate of rotation rate.

3. We can measure the "Doppler broadening" of spectral measurements of Uranus. The broadening reflects the fact that in a rotating object, one edge will have an extra velocity towards us, the other edge an extra velocity away from us. These two Doppler shifts cannot be separately measured, but an otherwise sharp line in the spectrum appears broader than it would for a non-rotating object, and the broadening can be measured.

Each of these methods calls for a very difficult observation, with lots of uncertainty. And unfortunately, each gives a different answer.

The rotation axis of Uranus is highly tilted relative to the orbital plane, so the planet progresses around the Sun "on its side," rolling along like a ball. The planet is a greenish color, with an atmosphere that is mainly hydrogen and helium, plus some methane and ammonia. It is much smaller than its two giant neighbors to sunward, with a radius of about 25,000 km. Like Saturn and Jupiter, it is thought to have a small, dense core, maybe the size of Earth, under extensive slushy oceans of water, methane, ammonia, and nitrogen. But unlike Saturn and Jupiter, Uranus seems to have no source of internal heating. It radiates away only as much energy as it receives from the Sun.

Most of the above information, with the exception of the final point of the last paragraph, was available a generation ago. The area where our knowledge has increased considerably is not on Uranus itself. It is on the bodies that gravitate around it.

The most interesting new information is perhaps the Uranus rings. These were found in 1977, before we knew that Jupiter also had a ring, and they provided the first evidence that ringed planets might be much more common than we thought. There seem to be nine rings, all circling the planet well inside the orbit of Miranda. They are narrow, and extremely dark in color, so they cannot be water-ice like Saturn's rings. In addition, six of the rings are elliptical, which was unexpected and suggests that they may have been created recently (i.e. no more than a few million years ago).

Information on the moons of Uranus also came only in the past few years. A generation ago their sizes were completely unknown. Now we have estimates for radii, together with temperature measurements and some information on their composition. They all seem to have a surface temperature of about −190 degrees Celsius, and we believe that their surfaces are largely covered with water-ice, perhaps coated with dark organic polymers formed from photo-dissociated methane. Oberon and Titania have guess-timated densities of 2.6 gm./cc, and Ariel and Umbriel about 1.3 gm./cc. Oberon and Titania probably have rocky material mixed in with the ice in their interiors. The density of Miranda is anyone's guess—no figures are available.

There is some recent evidence that Uranus may have a magnetic field. The Ultraviolet Explorer Satellite observed what might be aurorae, presumably caused by charged particles spiralling into the planet's atmosphere along magnetic field lines.

Voyager-2 and the Uranus Encounter.

Voyager-2 was launched late in 1977. It took more than eight years to reach Uranus, enjoying productive fly-bys with Jupiter and Saturn along the way. Data about Uranus began to arrive from Voyager-2 at the beginning of the "Observatory" phase of its encounter, dating from 4 November 1985. The "Near Encounter" lasted from January 22–26, 1986, including the moment of closest approach to the planet on January 24 (about 80,000 km. from the surface—which may not sound very close, until you realize that to see as much detail from the Earth you would need a diffraction-limited telescope with a 10-km. diameter mirror).

The Near Encounter phase ended just a couple of

days ago. New results and refinements of old results are still coming in, and will be for months. But already there's enough to tell us we have a planetary system with unique properties and some new unique mysteries.

First, the moons. Prior to Voyager, five moons were known. Now we are up to 15, with the new ones in the 25- to 75-km. radius range. Voyager-2 obtained good resolution images of the "big five": Miranda, Ariel, Umbriel, Titania, and Oberon. We can update the earlier estimates of their sizes, as follows:

Moon	Old	New
Miranda	250	245
Ariel	665	595
Umbriel	555	595
Titania	800	800
Oberon	815	775

(radii, in kilometers)

Most of the moons show far more evidence of internal activity than anyone expected, though at −210 C they are even colder than the previous estimate of −190 C. They show what look like old impact craters, fault structures, and newer extruded material in crater floors. The exception is Umbriel, which presented a bland, dark, featureless disk to Voyager's sensors. The estimates of satellite densities are quite a bit different from earlier numbers. With the exception of Miranda, for which a density figure is not yet available, data for the moons suggest densities for each of about 1.6 gm./cc.

The images of Miranda are strikingly good—maybe the best images ever taken by the Voyager spacecraft. The estimated best resolution of the Miranda images is about 300 meters per line pair, which means that the picture element size is about 150 meters. They show Miranda to be an amazing object, with unexpectedly complex and quite inexplicable surface geology. Voyager came within 29,000 km. of Miranda's surface, the space-craft's closest approach to anything in the Uranus system.

Another ring was discovered, bringing the total to ten. The pattern of light-scattering from the rings suggests that there is very little fine dust in them, which makes them quite unlike the rings of Saturn. The estimates of particle distribution size in the rings are not yet available.

The images of the planet itself have been visually disappointing. Uranus continues to look like a hazy billiard ball, with high-lying hazy clouds (probably of methane). The rotation of those clouds, plus the direct measurement of the time-varying magnetic field—a source of observations previously quite unavailable—implies a planetary day of about 15.6 hours. Beneath the haze there ought to be atmospheric zonal bands, as there are on Jupiter and Saturn; but we have not yet seen anything of them. Observations at other wavelengths might show a lot more, but they are not yet available.

The first figures on atmospheric composition *are* available, in particular the helium/hydrogen ratio. There had been conjectures that the atmosphere of Uranus might be as much as 40% helium. The observations don't support that. The figure looks to be in the 10–15% range, which is much the same as is estimated for Jupiter. The atmosphere is pretty cold—about 63 degrees K, or –210 C.

Although there has been little sign of surface detail, other exciting things were found down on Uranus itself. There is a phenomenon for which the term "electroglow" has been coined. It was seen also on Jupiter and Saturn, and it is thought to be the effect of electrons hitting neutral hydrogen atoms in the atmosphere of the planet. In the case of Uranus, however, the electroglow is much stronger than it ought to be if it is a direct consequence of the solar wind.

The explanation of that fact may lie in what is to me the most fascinating result of all the observations made so far in the Uranian system. One conjecture that we hoped the encounter would answer concerned the existence of a magnetic field. Now we know there is definitely a magnetic field, and it is a big one—the value at the planet's surface is estimated as 0.25 gauss, compared with the value of 0.31 gauss at the surface of the Earth. The oddest thing about this magnetic field is its orientation. The magnetic axis does not line up close to the axis of planetary rotation, as it does for Earth, Jupiter, and Saturn. Instead it is inclined at 55 degrees to it. Thus Uranus in its rotation creates a substantial time-varying magnetic field in space, with a period of about 16 hours. It is a "planetary pulsar," unique in the Solar System. The size and geometry of the magnetic field will have profound effects on the possible size and composition of any dense core of Uranus, but so far no one at JPL has been willing to comment publicly on the implications.

Let's for the fun of it speculate on some possible effects of the strong, highly inclined magnetic field. The rotating field will induce diurnal inductive heating in all the moons of Uranus. The size of that heating will depend on the material composition of the moons, and could be enough to account for the unusually active nature of their surfaces. Is the heating enough to provide the nearer moons with liquid interiors? I don't know. It seems unlikely, because the surfaces are so cold. But it might provide the energy for tectonic activity in the solid satellite interiors.

The rotating magnetic field may also be the explanation of the absence of fine dust in the rings. If the rings are dark because they are coated with dark organic polymers formed from, say, photo-dissociated methane, very small particles with a high charge-to-mass ratio will be cleared out of the rings by the diurnal magnetic field variation. Only the big stuff will be left, and the light-scattering profiles will change accordingly.

Before the encounter I made a personal list of questions that I hoped might be answered while I was at JPL for the encounter. They were:

1. Why does Uranus move around the Sun with its polar axis practically in the plane of its orbit? None of

the other planets do that. 2. Why has it, alone of all the gas giants, no apparent internal sources of heat? 3. Why are its rings so dark—just about the least reflective materials in the solar system? 4. What is the atmospheric composition, particularly the hydrogen/helium ratio? 5. Does Uranus possess a dense Earth-like core and a magnetic field? 6. Does it have other satellites, beyond the five previously known?

As you see, Voyager has already provided answers to half these questions. Information on the axial tilt and the composition of the rings may be forthcoming from the data, but they will take more analysis.

The most interesting thing of all about the Uranus encounter may be the Voyager-2 spacecraft itself. Begun as a project in 1971, launched in 1977, it is now a venerable antique—think of the progress in computers alone in that time frame. But the old machine seems to do better at each encounter, improving with time like a fine wine. In the encounter with the Uranian system, it appeared to behave absolutely flawlessly.

Neptune. Any difficulties in observing Uranus are even greater for Neptune. It is about the same size, but half as far again away.

Yes, Bode's Law predicts that Neptune should be almost exactly *twice* as far away as Uranus—but in this case, Bode's Law doesn't work. That didn't stop it being used—successfully!—by Adams and Leverrier, in their independent calculations of Neptune's position, based on its perturbations of the orbit of Uranus. They both assumed that Neptune would be out nearly six billion kilometers from the Sun; it is actually more like 4.5 billion. Fortunately, that assumption was not a critical one, and the planet was discovered in 1846, just where they had predicted it to be.

There are two known satellites of Neptune: Triton and Nereid. Triton was found in 1846 by William Lassell, who also found Ariel and Umbriel (he found Triton only ten days after the planet Neptune had been discovered!). Nereid was first seen by Gerald Kuiper, in 1948.

Triton is a substantial satellite, and its radius of about
1,750 km. makes it the size of our Moon. It travels in
an almost circular retrograde orbit, with period 5.9
days. Nereid is in a very elliptical orbit, far out from
the planet, and is probably only about 150 km. in
radius.

Recent information on Neptune and its moons has
come in three areas. First, we believe that like Saturn
and Jupiter, and unlike Uranus, Neptune gives off more
energy than it receives. It is a couple of degrees warmer
than it should be, given the sunlight that falls onto it.
There must be internal sources of heat, and some way of
transporting it out to the surface.

Second, there is evidence for frozen methane on
Triton, so that unlike most of the other major satellites of
the solar system, water-ice may not be a dominant
substance. At least part of its surface may be an ocean
of liquid nitrogen, which means that the temperature
must be −196 degrees Celsius, or less. Triton also seems
to have an atmosphere, of nitrogen and methane. The
pressure at the surface is perhaps one-tenth to one-
third of an Earth atmosphere, but it should be emphasized that these numbers are very imprecise, and even
the existence of nitrogen there is not certain. Since
Triton is also reddish in color, there is also a chance of a
photochemical smog there, like that on Titan.

Third, there is a possible ring around Neptune—or
maybe a *piece* of a ring. One good way of finding rings
(it worked for Uranus) is to look for evidence of a star
dimming and then brightening again, just before it is
occulted by the body of a planet. And of course, if there
is a ring, the same thing should happen again when the
star reappears from behind the planet.

Trying this technique for Neptune gave distinctly
odd results. There was a dimming of the star for a
couple of seconds, and then a brightening before it
vanished from sight behind the planet. But there was
no dimming when it reappeared! It looks as though there
is not a ring around Neptune, but the *arc* of a ring.
That would be a phenomenon never before encoun-

tered in the solar system, and a very strange one that would call for new theories. Arcs of rings should be very unstable, too unstable to exist unless something else is going on that we don't know about.

Voyager 2 gets to Neptune in 1989. Until then we'll probably just have to wait for an answer.

Pluto. This planet, usually described as "the most distant planet from the Sun," is today actually closer to the Sun than Neptune, and will be until 1999. Pluto has a very eccentric orbit, so for a good part of each 248-year period it lies within the orbit of Neptune.

The existence of Pluto was predicted to explain discrepancies between the computed and observed positions of Neptune. Like Uranus in the previous century, Neptune was a few seconds of arc away from its calculated position. Pluto's final discovery, by Clyde Tombaugh in 1930, seemed at first to resolve the discrepancy; but it soon was clear that Pluto could do no such thing. It is simply too small to manage much disturbing of any planet. When it was first found it was thought to be maybe the size of Earth, but that estimate was gradually whittled down to something only about 2,000 km. in radius.

Pluto is so small and far away that observation of it is always difficult, and unfortunately this planet is not on Voyager 2's itinerary. However, there is some evidence that the surface of Pluto is at least partly covered with methane ice, and it is conjectured that, like Triton which it resembles in size and distance from the Sun, Pluto might have a nitrogen sea.

Little Pluto, itself smaller than some satellites of the giant planets, surprisingly has a moon of its own. It was discovered in 1978 by J.W. Christy of the U.S. Naval Observatory, who named it Charon. The moon, maybe 425 km. in radius, is only 19,000 km. from the surface of Pluto, and orbits it in 6.39 days. Charon must be a substantial fraction of the mass of Pluto, because tidal forces seem to have changed the rotation of both bodies so that they permanently present the same face to each other. It has perhaps a third to a fifth of Pluto's mass.

The discovery of Charon also allowed us to put an upper limit on the mass of Pluto. That mass turns out to be small indeed—no more than 1/400 of Earth's mass. Pluto now seems to be only about 1,350 km. in radius. Some other planet, still undiscovered, is needed to explain the discrepancies in Neptune's orbit.

Beyond Pluto. Should we now look for a "tenth planet", out beyond Pluto—maybe at 12 billion kilometers, which is where Bode's Law would tell us to expect it? That search is being seriously discussed. However, even without that new planet we are not at the current limit of the solar system.

Forty years ago Pluto was thought to define that outer limit, which took us to about 40 a.u. from the Sun (a.u. = astronomical unit—see the section on the asteroids). In 1950, the Dutch astronomer Jan Oort enormously increased the size of that proposed outer boundary. He suggested a new source for the comets that from time to time sweep in close to the Sun and then vanish again into space. Oort proposed that there must be a "cometary reservoir," a huge cloud of comets that lives out from 30,000 to 100,000 a.u. distant from the Sun. (This idea had actually been proposed back in 1932 by Ernst Opik, and unfortunately totally ignored.)

To give an idea of the distances we are talking about, 100,000 astronomical units is one and a half lightyears, more than a third of the way to the nearest star. The Voyager 2 spacecraft will be on its way to the Oort Cloud after its encounter with Neptune. But it will not reach the Oort Cloud for tens of thousands of years.

The roughly spherical Oort Cloud of comets drifts slowly around the Sun, weakly bound by the solar gravitational attraction. Sometimes a comet will be perturbed by the gravitational field of another star, or perhaps by a close encounter with another Cloud member. Then its orbit will change, and it may fall inwards towards the Sun, to become an object visible to us.

Clearly, if bright comets are to be fairly common occurrences, there must be a lot of them in the cloud—
because the chance of a particular one being disturbed
as we have described is very small. There *are* lots of
them. Estimates put the number of comets in the Oort
Cloud as somewhere between a hundred billion and a
trillion.

Each comet is thought to be a loose aggregate of
water, gravel, and other volatile substances such as
ammonia and hydrocarbons. This "dirty snowball" theory of a comet's composition was introduced by Fred
Whipple in 1950, the same year that Jan Oort wrote
about the cometary cloud. If it is correct, then the
Cloud represents a very distant and very abundant
source of materials—perhaps our "New-found-land" a
thousand years from now.

Are we finally at the edge of the solar system? Well,
there is still Nemesis—a star-like object that is suggested
to be a dark companion to the Sun, and one that comes
back every 28 million years to disturb the system and
shower us with species-extinguishing meteorites. Is Nemesis real?

I think not, but who knows? A better question is,
how can we look at such things, to know how real they
might be?

Probes like the Voyager spacecraft will not do. They
are fine for objects out as far as Neptune and Pluto,
but beyond that they are too slow and take far too
long.

We will have to use other methods. We are already
using new instruments and getting results that an earlier generation would have sworn to be impossible:
interferometers, that allow us to measure stellar diameters directly; image intensifiers, that can examine the
disk of a star like Betelgeuse and see sunspots on its
face at a distance of 520 lightyears; bolometers, that let
us estimate the size of satellites from the tiny amounts
of heat that they radiate; and all the tools that orbiting
labs, beginning with the Hubble Telescope in 1988,

will bring us—measurements in the ultra-violet, in the far infra-red, in microwave regions, and in X-ray regions.

With any luck, our view of the solar system will change as much in the next twenty-five years as it has since 1960.

Editor's introduction to:
A FIELD TO PLAY ON

It has been said many times that the universe is not only stranger than we imagine, it's stranger than we *can* imagine. If it's stranger than the reality hinted at in this story then it is strange indeed . . . or could it be that this story has less to do with imagination than with perception?

—JPB

If you find the notion underpinning this story intriguing we also recommend Dalmas's The Reality Matrix *(August 1986, Baen Books) and* The Playmasters, *Dalmas and Martin (Spring 1987, Baen Books).*

A FIELD TO PLAY ON

John Dalmas

1

With the tailwind, the airspeed indicator read 150 mph; the plane dated from before the Pentagon take-over and the switch to metric. The cliffs and breaks of the Mogollon Rim passed beneath me, and I was over the high plateau.

There was still snow in the woods below me. In Phoenix the April wind had been dry and warm; at Showlow it would feel like winter. I knew Arizona: As a kid I'd lived in Gila Bend and Flagstaff and the reformatory at Fort Grant, and I still got back to the state now and then.

Up here in the Sitgreaves country there were two kinds of towns. One was full of hicks with nothing but a pickup truck and a chainsaw. The other was Senile City. The only reason a guy like Sanberg would come up here was to hide.

From the air, Showlow looked bigger than I remembered—maybe five or six thousand people. The airport was away from the timber, in juniper scrub northeast of town. The snow was melted there, but the wind was raw, like I knew it would be. The kid who came out to service the plane was a skinny punk with an IQ about half his weight. I put a look on him, shoved him ten, and walked toward the little office and shop. A car parked in front of it had WHITE MTN CAB stenciled on the door; they'd made my call for me, too. If you tell people right, you get things done.

The cabby would have been more at home in a logging truck; the recession must have hit the lumber mills along with everything else. When I told him to take me to the Rocking-R Ranch, I half expected him to say "where the hell is that?", but he just put the hack in gear and wheeled her onto the road.

I paid enough attention to find the place myself if I ever wanted to, which seemed doubtful. The assignment never had felt real to me. But Don Bruno Randazzo was a smart—*really smart*—operator. "Why not?" he'd said. "They fly around in space, eh? Three guys on their way to Mars? Why not travel in time, too? Maybe it's a false lead, maybe not." He'd shrugged. "Use your imagination, Stevie. If it's real, it's worth plenty, and if it ain't, what the hell. Eh? I leave it to you to find out."

He'd reached up and mussed my hair, laughing. "That's what we pay you a retainer for—to be our own little Polack gumshoe when we want one."

So here I was.

Manny Gold, one of old Bruno's idea boys with degrees in about three different fields, had read where the inventor and electronics manufacturer, Robert Sanberg, had dropped out of sight. They'd let out that Sanberg had a serious illness, and he was supposed to be on an around-the-world recovery cruise on his yacht. But the yacht got in trouble near Australia and it turned out he wasn't on it; just his sister and her husband. And then Manny remembered reading a thing by Sanberg a few years earlier about a theory of space-time structure, and that it might be possible to build a time machine someday.

So Manny put two and two together and got twenty-

seven. Manny was only bright, not smart. But he didn't
have to be smart; he was just an idea man.

And one thing about it—Sanberg had gone to a lot of
trouble to hide *something*. I'd run through quite a few
thousand dollars of Syndicate money unraveling his cover.

We turned off the blacktop onto a dirt road marked
private. There were too many holes and bumps to be
accidental; they wanted to discourage people from driv-
ing it. After about four slow bouncing miles that had
the driver swearing, we came out of the junipers and
down a slope to a gate in a chain link fence. The guard
who came out of the gatehouse wore Levis and a cowboy
hat, but he looked like some of the muscle that old
Bruno had hanging around. Interesting.

I rolled down the window as he walked over. He
stopped five or six feet away.

"Stan Nevens," I said. "Mr. Sanberg is expecting
me."

He nodded and opened the gate. The house was in a
sort of basin about a mile farther on, and I looked it
over as we drove down. It sprawled big and low inside
a partial wall of bare cottonwoods. There was a wind-
mill behind it, and a big metal water tank on a platform. The walls were adobe, stuccoed over and probably
a foot or so thick. I'd known old ranch houses like it
when I was a kid. The big wing in back had the same
paint job and general appearance as the rest of the
place, but it looked like poured concrete.

A short guy was waiting by the porch steps and
walked over as I got out. "I'm John Haslett," he said,
"Dr. Sanberg's secretary. Dr. Sanberg will see you
inside." He said it like I was a kid and Sanberg was the
principal. Then he turned to the cabby. "Don't wait,"
he told him. "We'll take Mr. Nevens back when he's
done here."

I paid the fare, then followed Haslett inside as the
cab left. *A hard case at the gate and the twerp sends
the cab away; interesting,* I thought. But it probably
didn't mean anything. Stan Nevens was the number-
one news snoop for Joseph P. Krause, the syndicated

columnist, and nobody wanted to get Krause down on them.

Still, the flat 6 mm under my left arm was reassuring.

Sanberg's front room had a big fireplace with a wood fire in it, genuine rough-squared roof beams, and the world's biggest Navajo rug. Haslett, in his four-button suit, looked as out of place as a fairy in the Raiders' dressing room.

"Dr. Sanberg will see you in a few minutes," he said, then sat down behind his desk while I found a big stuffed chair. Prissy bastard. I'd listened to enough of that "doctor" bullshit in college.

"You must expect him to be a little, ah, cool toward you," Haslett added. "He has always been jealous of his privacy, and he especially dislikes threatening innuendoes. He prefers directness."

"What do you prefer?" I asked him.

"That is beside the point."

"The hell it is. It was you who played games on the phone, not Sanberg, and I don't like being grilled by some goddamn flunky. When I talk to Sanberg I'll be direct enough."

Haslett couldn't hold my eyes. He just thinned his lips and shuffled papers. I could read him like a book. Small, IQ around one-fifty, and making maybe thirty thou a year—a lot of corn since the reconstruction. Number-one flunkies are *worth* a lot. But beneath that four-button front he hated it. He figured with his brains, he ought to be top dog somewhere. What he didn't understand is, it takes more than brains. It takes what Sanberg and old Bruno had, whatever that is.

I don't have it either, Haslett, I thought, but it doesn't eat on me.

Three or four minutes later Sanberg came in. He was my age—forty-two—and fatter than the pictures I'd seen. Holed up out here, he probably ate and drank too much. I stood up.

"Dr. Sanberg, I'm . . . Stan Nevens."

For one bad moment I'd almost blown it, almost said my real name, Steve Synko. Not that the name would have meant anything to him, but it would have blown my cover. He shook my hand automatically, without seeming to notice.

"I'm glad you agreed to talk to me," I said.

He nodded. "Come back to my office. I'm sure John has useful things to do." He said it snottily, and led me down a hall toward the new concrete wing. Before we got that far, though, we turned into what had probably been a big bedroom. Now it was an office, with a large computer, bookcases, cabinets, and a desk.

"All right, Mr. Nevens, I'm a busy man. Suppose we get right down to business."

"Fine. I want to know all about your time machine."

I felt foolish saying it. His answer surprised me.

"How did you find out about it?"

"A friend of mine told me about your paper in *Science*—'Vectors of Space-Time.' Said it was one of the most interesting things he'd ever read. It sounded like science fiction to me, and I forgot about it—until I read about your yacht and started wondering what you were hiding. So I started snooping around." I sat back. "And one thing led to another."

"Mr. Krause must be proud of you," Sanberg said drily.

"Mr. Krause appreciates me. Not many investigators make the corn I do. And he's very interested in what I learn here."

In case you've been in Timbuktu the last few years, Joseph P. Krause is *big*—both on TV and in the papers. He gets something on someone who isn't in with the Pentagon and it comes out in a few hundred newspapers and on network TV. That's why I was using the name of his number-one boy: Sanberg would think he had to talk to me.

Just now, though, Sanberg looked as cool as old Bruno.

"All right, Mr. Nevens, what do you want to know about it?"

"Everything."

"Hah!" It was sort of a bark. Then he frowned, concentrating. "Put simply, some research on flunctuations of stellar emissions could be interpreted, with a little creative imagination, as meaning that time is a spiral, rather like a compressed coil spring, and that while almost everything moves through time by traveling around the coils, some particles short-cut through them, from a point on one coil to the contact point on the next. I got the basic inspiration from a science fiction story I'd read as a child—'The Coils of Time,' or something like that. It was consistent with the data."

He paused, and I nodded to keep him going.

"Actually, I didn't take the idea too seriously, myself, but it was interesting, and I enjoy shaking up the scientific establishment. But once I'd written it, I kept having ideas relating to it, and testing them. Finally, I'd had enough positive results that it started to seem real, and I began working on it in earnest. When it began to look as if I might end up with an operational time machine, I started to think what such a thing might mean in a world like this one."

He paused, pursing his lips.

"So you moved out here to work on it secretly," I said.

He nodded. "And wasted a year and a couple of million dollars."

"What do you mean?"

He shrugged. "Basically, it's not possible to receive coherent images from the past. As a matter of fact, we're about done dismantling the equipment."

Our eyes met for just a second before his slid away. "Sanberg," I told him, "as a liar you're plausible, but not convincing. You lack that certain something. Joe Krause is going to rape you anyway; you might as well relax and enjoy it. How about demonstrating it for me?"

I expected him to stall or get mad. What he did was nod and stand up. "I was afraid you'd say that," he said, and went over to a door. Not the hall door. I was wary now; something wasn't right about his reaction.

He led me through into the new wing—a single big room. Inside was a lot of complicated-looking apparatus, with things like stretched-out ceramic concertinas that suggested high voltages. In the middle was a rectangular thing like a shiny tubular door frame with no door, and he gestured at it.

"That's it," he said, and pulled a switch on an instrument panel. Then he stepped into the frame and disappeared. I stared for ten or fifteen seconds, getting edgier with each of them.

When he reappeared, he looked upset. "I thought you wanted a demonstration," he said. "Why didn't you follow me?"

"That was demonstration enough. Where the hell were you?"

The question settled him down. "In one of the only two times it can take me. Remember, it puts you in the adjacent point on an adjacent coil. The only choice is forward or backward. I've got it on forward."

"How far forward?"

"I don't know."

"What's it like there? What'd you find?"

"People. It's not what you see, though. It's what it means. I really absolutely do intend to take it apart and trash everything to do with it. Honest to god!"

And he meant it. He really meant it. I could see why, too, or thought I could. We could screw up the future bad enough from right there in present time. Anyway, his answer introverted me enough that I didn't see his moment of decision, or see him pull the gun from inside his sweater.

"Who are you really?" he said, pointing it at me.

"What the hell's wrong with you, Sanberg?" I countered. "You know who I am." I might be able to handle Sanberg, but if something had gone wrong with my cover, and they'd been laying for me, then some muscle might easily be standing ready in the hall or the next room with another gun.

Sanberg shook his head. "You should watch the news, Mr. whoever you are. Yesterday morning Stanley Nevens was shot to death by one of his and Mr. Krause's victims."

All that saved me was his grimace as he started to pull the trigger. I dropped for the floor a split second before the blast, clawing for my gun, and Sanberg stepped back into the time door and disappeared. For a moment I lay there, 6 mm in hand. He'd missed at point-blank range. Then I heard the door to the hall and saw a shotgun barrel pushing it open. I scrambled to my feet and through the time door after Sanberg, and as I went through, I stumbled and fell. At the same time, I'd heard a loud bang behind me that could have been a door effect or someone shooting after me.

I got up and looked around. I was alone in a small bare room, and it felt real as hell, as real as any place or time I'd ever been. But there was no Sanberg, no time machine, no nothing. Not even a chair. Just concrete walls, floor, and ceiling, and a window and a closed wooden door. I opened the door and looked down an empty hall. Sanberg must have hit running, I decided. My ears were still ringing as I closed the door again.

I wasn't sure what to do next, but I couldn't stay there. I'd have to go back through and hit the dirt ready to shoot. I sized up the approximate place I'd come out and couldn't see a thing. What would happen if I half missed it? Cut me in two maybe? But Sanberg hadn't seemed worried. If there'd been any danger he'd have marked the floor as a guide. Wouldn't he? My mouth was like cotton as, gun ready, I stepped crouching into the place I thought it ought to be.

Nothing happened.

I started stepping around then, less and less careful, and ended up crisscrossing all through the damn room, until I realized I wasn't going to get back that way.

Suddenly I felt like a man made out of glass, afraid to breathe, as if I might break into a thousand pieces. I don't know how long I stood there with my gun in my hand. They wouldn't have turned the door off and stranded Sanberg; there was something I didn't know about how to get back. The only way I was going to get back was with Sanberg.

Something felt wrong, wronger than hell, but I couldn't get a look at what it was.

Gradually, my mind started to work again. If Sanberg wanted to get back home, he'd have to come here. This was where the time door was. I walked to the single window and looked out. It was cloudy. Ten feet below was an alley paved with brick. Hell! This was supposed to be the future. Brick pavements had already disappeared anyplace I knew about, replaced by concrete or blacktop. And the hall door had a heavy, old-fashioned slide bolt. Why, the sonofabitch had aimed his machine backward, and it came out in old San Francisco or Chicago or someplace! Hell yes!

I began to feel a little better. The past I knew something about.

I sized the room up again. About fifteen by fifteen feet, gray unpainted concrete, and absolutely bare except for a grill by one wall. Not even a wall socket.

I sat down next to the door, where it would bump me if anyone opened it more than a foot or so, and lit a cigarette. Then I put it out because Sanberg might smell it under the door when he came back. I dozed off sitting there, then sort of half woke up—enough to realize it was getting dark—and lay down on the floor.

2

It was dark when I woke up again. My watch said 1600 hours, which had to be "other side" time—Arizona time. I was hungry and thirsty, and most of all I had to take a leak. I opened the window and looked out. It was dead quiet—no traffic noise, no distant siren.

Well hell, I thought, life goes on. I can't just sit and wait. Sanberg might have contacts here and not come back for two or three days. I walked around in the room again, and when nothing happened, bolted the door. Slow him down if he came back while I was out. Then I climbed out the window, held myself up on one forearm for a moment while I lowered the sash, and dropped into the alley. After taking a leak, I paced off the distance to the alley's end so I could find the right door if I needed to, then went back and counted windows as insurance, figuring one window per room.

I couldn't see a light in the whole building.

The alley opened onto an unlighted side street. There was no traffic, and I couldn't see any cars. I wondered if they were invented yet. There was what looked like candle light in windows along the street. About two and a half blocks to my right, the street intersected one with electric lights, and I started toward it. A little way down I passed people sitting and standing around some entryway steps, talking quietly. They stopped as I approached, and I felt their eyes on me as I passed.

It felt bad. It wasn't as if they were thinking about jumping me; it just felt bad.

The lighted street had some life, but not much. Again there weren't any cars, nor was there anything else on wheels. It was a low-class business district. The signs weren't lit up, they were just lettered boards over the entrances. And not in any alphabet I recognized. The letters weren't flowing like Arabic or some East Asian characters, and not complicated like Russian or Armenian, but most of the letters weren't quite familiar.

So I was in trouble; the people here wouldn't speak English. And while I do a half-assed job of speaking Polish, and talk enough Mexican to get by in the barrios, that wasn't going to help.

Maybe, I thought, this *was* the future, way ahead, and things had come to this. I shivered. If so, no wonder Sanberg wanted to trash his machine.

In a neighborhood like that I'd expect to see teenage punks hanging around the street lamps, but all I saw were adults. Ordinary-looking whites with hangdog looks, their clothes enough alike to be uniforms—solid gray, loose-fitting trousers and shirts, mostly with the tails out. And no one even looked at me, in spite of my umber and orange threads that stood out around there even at night.

The whole damn thing seemed unreal, yet nothing

like a dream. The air was mild and damp, the sidewalk was hard beneath my feet, and my right knee hurt where I'd fallen on it coming through the door.

Most of the businesses were closed. I turned into one that was open, a bar, small and half lit. There wasn't any music or TV, the booths were made of unstained plywood, and the people weren't talking much louder than outside; damnedest bar I'd ever seen.

But the language they were talking was English! It didn't strike me for a couple of seconds, it seemed so natural, but they were talking American English, hardly any different from at home. Apparently they just wrote it differently. I looked around for a booth with only one person in it, someone I could pump for information, and found one. She was youngish, overweight, and dull looking, and she didn't brighten up much when I moved in across from her.

"Okay if I sit here?" I asked her.

She shrugged. "I don't care, but my husband might not like it."

A husband sounded interesting. I needed something to make me feel better, like punching somebody around. "Where's he at? The men's room?"

"Where else?" She looked me over. "What're you doing in a gray bar?"

"I'm new around here, seeing the town. Any reason I shouldn't be in here?"

Her eyes left me, and I followed them back over my left shoulder where the bartender was standing looking down at me. He was big and placid looking, with relaxed but very large hands. In his black pants and black-and-white-striped shirt, he looked like an overweight hockey referee. They were pretty gaudy threads among all these sparrows.

"What're you looking for?" he asked me. The way he said it wasn't threatening; he just wanted to know what I was looking for.

"A drink," I answered, "but I don't know if my money is any good in your country."

"Money? We get gray scrip in here." He put out a thick palm. "Let's see it."

I pulled a one out of my wallet and handed it to him. He squinted at it, frowned, and took it behind the bar where the light was better. After a few seconds he brought it back and gave it to me.

Another guy came up beside him and stared at me. The husband, I thought, although he didn't look mad or anything, just worried.

"Your being a foreigner," the bartender said, "I can make allowances, but you still ought to know better." He stood waiting for me to do or say something, but I didn't know what, so I said, "Yeah?"

He scowled, still more puzzled than irritated, then went for the direct solution. "Out," he said calmly, and thumbed toward the door.

On second thought, one thing I couldn't afford was to get in trouble; I had enough of that already. So I nodded, slid out of the booth and left, trying not to look like I was being kicked out.

The air outside was close to a mist now. I had no idea what to do next. It didn't make sense to go back to the time-door room as thirsty and hungry as I'd left it. While I stood there, a guy came up to me. He looked more like a canary than a sparrow, and there was something about him that told me what he was before he opened his mouth.

"Waiting for someone?" he asked softly.

"Looking for help," I said.

"Maybe I can help you."

"I wouldn't be surprised. The first thing I need is a meal."

He just looked at me.

"I'm a stranger here," I went on. "I need information and advice. And a friend."

He was still looking me over. Maybe he thought I was with the morals squad, like in the days before fag lib. "I know a place," he said at last.

He strode out like a heel-and-toe racer then, so we didn't do any talking while we walked. After four blocks the neighborhood changed abruptly. It didn't exactly turn into Vegas, but it wasn't downbeat anymore, just quiet, with small, low-key neon or electric-lit signs, and no one wore gray. We went into a small restaurant, to a corner booth, and sat down. I reached across the table.

"I'm Steve Synko," I said.

He held my hand longer than he needed to. "I'm Jared Dunne. I'm happy to know you, Steven."

The waitress was already headed for us, and handed us menus. She looked good enough, but under the circumstances I didn't make a pass. And a glance told me the menu wasn't going to do me any good.

Dunne looked his over for a minute or so. "What are you going to have?" he asked.

I lowered my eyes and let my voice drop to a monotone. "I don't know. I can't read it."

He stared, not saying anything.

"Something happened to me," I went on. "I don't know what. But except for my name—I think it's mine anyway, it feels like it—I can't remember anything, including where I'm at. Or how to read. Nothing." I glanced up at him; he was looking at me uncertainly, and I dropped my eyes again. "I swear it," I said. "I'm probably lucky I remember how to talk."

He bought it. One of the mentally disabled, with a compulsion to feel sorry for people and a setup for a story like that. I was lucky to run into him.

"Haven't you been to the authorities?" he asked.

"I'm afraid to. I don't know how I got this way or who I am. Not even who I am, for god's sake!" I looked up at him and shivered. "Only my name. God, man!"

I'm a fair actor—good enough to play the con game a time or two. "I'm scared," I added. "What if God's punishing me for something?"

"You're in Deevers," he said softly.

"Deevers?" I let it hang for a few seconds. "Is that a city or a country?"

He really stared then, and for a minute I thought I'd laid it on too thick. But the fact was, of course, that I didn't know, and he bought that, too. Over the next forty minutes I learned a lot. Deevers, with a population of 300,000, was a seaport and the capital of Wesland. Wesland, he told me, was five hundred miles from north to south and three hundred east to west. A mile was about ten city blocks, about like a mile in my own time.

And there were no civilian cars! In towns there were streetcars, and between towns there were trains, but only the government—the police, the military, and so forth—had cars. People with enough money, and farmers, had horses. Other people rode public transportation or walked. He didn't mention bicycles.

I couldn't figure how there could be cars around without everybody insisting on having one.

He frowned. "Why should anyone—why should I, for example—want an automobile? Outside the Gray Quarter, buses go anywhere in the city you want to go."

"But suppose you want to go some place in the mountains?"

"Trains go to the mountains."

"Say you want to go somewhere a train doesn't go."

"Why should I want to go somewhere a train doesn't go?"

I nodded as if that made sense; I didn't want to bug him. "You said the Gray Quarter. Is that where we ran into each other? Where everyone wore gray?"

"That's right. The Gray Quarter is where people live who opt the gray game. They live at public expense."

"And they have to live in a certain part of town?"

He nodded.

It sounded interesting. People like that are generally not too fond of the law. "Quite a bit of crime there?" I asked, keeping it casual.

He looked at me quizzically. "There isn't much crime anywhere in Wesland," he said, "with the guillotine or Stone's Island waiting."

The guillotine? Heavy duty! "But in a place like the Gray Quarter—don't the people there stick together? How would the police ever get anything on a criminal in a place like that?"

He frowned. "You really have forgotten! There are snoops and sweeps and . . . You don't know what I'm talking about, do you? Snoops are police telepaths. Scene sweepers are clairvoyants who can go to the scene of a crime and see exactly what happened, as if they'd been there at the time. And spotters—spotters can often tell when a crime is going to take place, and where.

"There used to be a lot more crime a few generations ago, but it's pretty rare now."

I decided I'd better change the subject. I didn't want him wondering. "What's it like, I wonder, living in the Gray Quarter? As far as I know, I don't have a job. Maybe I'll end up there."

"You won't, and you wouldn't like it. Not a big vital man like you. They live in bare little rooms and use public restrooms. They eat wretched food in big mess halls. Adequate, I suppose, but wretched. They get two dollars a week for spending, in gray scrip, and almost no medical care. Their children are taken from them and . . ."

"Jesus!" I said. I was shocked. I'd never heard of anything so bad, not even from behind the Iron Curtain.

"It's not as if they can't leave, though," he added. "They can get out anytime by accepting a job, and the government makes sure there are always *some* kinds of jobs just about everywhere. A person *chooses* to wear gray; it's for people who can't cope with much of anything, actually, and it's certainly no place for children to grow up."

He shuddered. "The worst things would be the total lack of privacy and beauty. I could never be gray."

"Does every town have a Gray Quarter?"

"No, just the capital. If you choose gray, they move you here."

"Hm-m. All the people I saw there were whites. Where are the blacks?"

He looked puzzled.

"You know, negroes." He didn't know. "People with black skin and kinky hair."

Now he looked worried. "Black skin? There are no people with black skin, Steven."

"Dark brown?"

He shook his head. He was starting to get nervous; I was getting too weird for him. So I asked him about himself. It turned out he was a haberdasher who liked to read his own poetry to a poetry group—a genuine stereotype.

"What were you doing in the Gray Quarter?" I asked.

It was his turn to lower his eyes. "I get—lonely sometimes. There aren't many—people like me. People in gray sometimes get lonely, too, and they're always susceptible to gifts."

"Are they allowed to go outside the Quarter?"

"If they're accompanied. It's frowned on, though, to be seen with one except in an official capacity."

"Where do you go with them?"

"I live only a block from the Quarter," he said in a small voice. "After dark . . . we go down the alley and take the freight elevator to my floor."

Well, it was his choice if he wanted to live that way. In my case I had no goddamn choice, only necessity. I wasn't lonely, not for any puking faggot. What I needed was a place to stay and a supply of the local pesos. And me he wouldn't have to smuggle up the freight elevator.

But I hoped Don Bruno never found out. Not likely. Time was I'd have beat up this Jared Dunne and cleaned out his wallet, or run him off, depending on whether he could go to the local fuzz or not. But I didn't know what I could get away with here, and he was my only contact for help and information.

For the first time I looked squarely at the possibility that I might be cut off and never get home. It made my guts shrink. I *had* to get back, that's all there was to it. This was a bad place, with its snoops and sweeps and— what? Spotters. God! That goddamn Sanberg! When I got back I'd kill the sonofabitch.

3

I don't usually dream but I had some bastards that night. Sanberg was in them, and Dunne. I can't recall any details, only that they were bad. Really bad. I'd never in my life drank in the morning—that's a loser's game—but the first thing I did was find Dunne's whiskey and down a stiff slug.

Even a shower didn't help much. Things kept running through my head—all the things wrong with this place. Like, what happened to the blacks? Not that I'd miss them. But if they'd gotten blended into the population through interbreeding so long ago that they'd been forgotten, then most people should show strong signs of it, and from what I'd seen, they didn't. And we were on the west coast, but the mountains lay two hundred miles east. Where in hell *was* this place?

And police telepaths and all that crap! After I'd toweled off, I went in and had another shot.

Dunne had wakened me when he left for work and kissed me on the mouth. It hadn't even made me feel mad, just dirty, which shows how bad off I was.

From the few guys I'd seen outside the Gray Quarter, the style of my clothes would be conspicuous here, so I tried on some of Dunne's: a pair of light blue knit flairs, snug in the thighs and about the right size, and a shirt that was more like an embroidered gold blouse. Being cut loose, it didn't fit too bad, and the shoulder holster fitted under my left arm without a sign.

I looked in the mirror and my morale moved up a notch: Not half bad. Then I looked at the clock and came back down again: The damn thing only had ten hours on it, for chrissake! I didn't even know whether it went around twice a day, like a twelve-hour clock, or once, like the new twenty-four-hour jobs.

And that brought up a whole bunch of other crap that had been sitting there waiting to be looked at. Like the language thing. How come they spoke what amounted to American English when enough time had passed for even the geography to be different? Especially the goddamn geography! And they'd dropped the metric system to go back to feet and miles but had a ten-hour clock! And the people—the people didn't want cars! Something was awfully damn wrong with this place!

I fought down the temptation to finish off Dunne's whiskey. Getting drunk wasn't what I needed; getting home was.

I looked more closely at the clock. There were ten small marks between the hours; one hundred minutes per hour then, and one hundred seconds per minute. It had a second hand that moved in jerky ticks—it wasn't electric—and a second was a little quicker than on my watch. There'd be something under 10,000 of our seconds in one of their hours, instead of 3,600; ten hours would still give them a longer day than back home.

I poked around in the cupboard and refrigerator. The stuff in the box looked and tasted like cornflakes, and milk came in the kind of bottle it had when my folks were young. When I'd eaten, I left, backtracking my route of the night before.

There was no law against my being in the Gray Quarter, but I was conspicuous there. And Dunne had told me that everyone was required to carry ID here. If a cop were to ask me for mine, my California driver's license would never pass. And if they took me in for some mind reader to examine, I'd probably get locked up in the nuthouse.

In the daytime there were quite a few people walking the streets in the Gray Quarter, and it was surprising how little attention they paid to me, or to anything else, as far as I could see. A truck with a chain drive rolled down the street, like something out of a World War One movie, carrying a work crew in back. They wore coveralls, blue or tan or striped . . . anything but gray.

It was plain what the time-door room had to be—an empty room in a gray dormitory. It had felt like a whole empty building. How come the time-door came out there? Why not in an occupied room? Or fifty feet above the ground? Or underground? It almost looked as if Sanberg had been able to move it around at this end, to aim it.

The thought gave me a lump in my chest. If he got back to it before I got to him, and moved the door, I'd really be screwed. But hell, he'd said he was going to trash it anyway. And if he did, no way would I ever get home.

It was hard not to break into a run.

When I got there, the building was abandoned all right, and unlocked, too. Pacing the distance down the hall and counting doors, I came to what seemed like the right one. It was bolted, and the doors to either side weren't, so it had to be the one, and Sanberg hadn't come back.

So now what? I wanted to stay there and wait, as long as it took, but I'd need food and water, because if he had a contact here, it could be days before he came back. I'd need to get some rations and a water jug. But I didn't want to be seen carrying stuff like that here, so it would have to wait till night.

Meanwhile, I sat down in the room next to it, with the door ajar so I could hear if anyone came. After an hour by my watch I was bored as hell, after two hours I was thirsty, after five I was dozing, and after six I left.

I noticed the sign in front of the beer joint I'd been in the night before. The word on it had three letters. I slowed, looking at them carefully, drawing them in my mind, and guessed that the first letter probably stood for the sound of *b*, and the last for *r*. The middle could stand for an *ah* sound or for the sound of double *e*. I went in. Not that I was looking for a drink there. Dunne had told me that all they served in gray bars was weak beer that supposedly bloated you before you got half a buzz on. The rumor was, it had a tranquilizer in it. Like the food in the Quarter was supposed to have a birth control drug in it: It figured.

What I was interested in was information, not bad beer.

The barkeep wasn't the same one I'd talked to the

night before; this one looked surly. As I stepped to the bar he raised an eyebrow.

"You lost?" he asked.

"My ID card's what's lost."

"Well, I ain't found it."

I kept my temper. "You know where I can get another one?"

He looked even more irritated. "Registry. You ought to know that."

"Suppose I don't want something official. Suppose I'd rather get something, ah, made to order. Who around here can fix me up?"

He looked like I'd thrown beer in his face. "You goddamn Red! Get out of here before I call the police!" He was talking loud now, and people were turning to watch. He also looked scared—his face had gone pale— and there was a night stick in his hand. "You got your own place!" His voice was hoarse. "We don't want your kind in decent society, and the grays don't want you, either! I'm going to report you; now beat it!"

I beat it. Back home I'd have watched for him, followed him when he left, and tromped the seeds out of him in some nice alley. Here I couldn't afford to. All I could do was make tracks, feeling shaky, putting the first corner between me and the bar, and walk as fast as I dared to get outside the Quarter.

I didn't like this time.

And he'd called me a Red! I wouldn't have thought Communism would still be around after all this time.

When I got out of the Quarter I still felt shaky, so I walked around Dunne's neighborhood for a while to get over it. It looked respectably middle-class, well-kept, but the buildings were old. I came to a place with a *bar* sign, and the language thing hit me again. Why *bar?* Why not *cantina*, or *gospoda*, or even *saloon?*

It was nearly empty, and I took a stool as far from anyone as possible. Above the back bar was what looked like a bar list. One of the items was another three-letter word that began and ended with my new friends, the letters *b* and *r*. The middle was different though. *Beer*, I thought.

The bartender looked a lot more polite than the last one. "Beer," I said. He nodded, drew me a mug, and I gave him one of the bills Dunne had given me. Dunne had called it a "one," but I didn't know what "one" was worth. The guy handed me change; I looked around while I put it in my pocket.

"Thanks," I said.

"You're welcome, friend. You new around here? I don't think I've seen you before."

"Yeah, I'm new." I lowered my voice. "Do me a favor, will you?"

He lowered his voice to match mine. "Sure, if I can."

"Where can I get a forgery done? A counterfeit ID. A friend of mine blew his cork over a girl, and I'm not sure what he told her, but he's got himself in a situation where he needs false ID. You got any suggestions?"

He looked uncomfortable. "I'd be awfully careful, talking about something like that, friend. If he has to have one, he'd better try the Red Quarter. And good luck."

The way he said "good luck," he thought I'd need it. Then he went back to polishing glasses at the far end of the bar.

The Red Quarter. That was something Dunne hadn't told me about. Maybe *Red* didn't mean what it used to. I went to Dunne's place, ate, and looked around for something I could carry water in when I went back to the time-door room.

Dunne came in then, cheery as a goddamn bird, maybe because he had someone there waiting for him. Fixing supper, he hummed and sang around the kitchen like a goddamn bride, except he was a baritone.

I looked through a pile of magazines I found on a shelf. With the help of pictures and something I remembered out of Sherlock Holmes about *e* being the most common letter and *t* next, I started out to learn the alphabet. I was beginning to have my doubts about *e* and *t* here, but with *b*, *a*, *r*, and the *ee* letter to start with, I made progress. Not for long, though; I had too many things on my mind.

"What's the Red Quarter, Jared?" I asked.

He turned from the kitchen counter and looked at me. "Where did you learn about the Red Quarter?" His voice was guarded.

"I went for a walk and stopped in a bar. The bartender mentioned it."

He bit at his lip. "Do you think it's a good idea to be wandering around? With your memory the way it is . . . If you had a relapse, you might not be able to find your way back."

I was doing a good job of controlling my temper, even around a faggot. "I felt like I had to get out," I told him. "I thought maybe if I moved around some, things might start coming back to me. What's the Red Quarter?"

"It's . . . where the Reds live." He looked thoughtful, as if he was thinking about how to start, so I waited. "The Reds are—different from the rest of us, and a lot different from the Grays. They're people who can't— who can't behave themselves like other people. They have something inside them that makes them cheat or rob or trick or beat up people, or even kill them, and they can't help themselves."

Yeah, I thought, they're like faggots that way—can't help themselves.

"And because they're so incompatible with other people," he went on, "they have their own quarter in the northwest part of town. If anyone in Wesland is like that, they have to register and go there to live, or else be subject to the common law. In the Red Quarter they don't have many laws to worry about, and other people don't have to worry about them."

"You mean they've got all the hoods in one part of town?"

"Hoods?"

"Criminals. I thought you said they hanged all the criminals or put them on an island somewhere."

"Oh, criminals are people who break the law outside

the Red Quarter. So the Reds aren't criminals. Most of them had misdemeanors or disturbance charges as juveniles, before they turned Red, but they're not criminals as long as they stay in their own quarters, because hardly any laws apply there. Inside the Red Quarter they can do pretty much as they please, as long as they don't cause any trouble outside the Red Quarter. Of course, if anyone *does* . . ." He made a chopping motion with his hand. "That's the end of him.

"They do have laws of a sort in the Red Quarter—mostly rules they make themselves. But the laws there are a lot different from ours. Beatings, killings—all sorts of things go on legally there all the time."

He looked psyched out thinking about it. It didn't sound like anyplace I'd want to be either.

"How come they're called Reds?"

"Because they wear red. Bright red. It's something they do, like a badge. Of course, that still leaves various shades of red, and different cuts; there are lots of possibilities for dress."

Possibilities for dress! You silly fag bastard! I thought. But what I said was, "Where do they get their income? You can't have a place like the Red Quarter without input from the outside."

"They have businesses," he answered. "Small factories and warehouses. A few of them, the big bosses, have gotten quite rich. But lots of them are just men who like to fight or do other vicious things, and they do the work.

"You or I can go to any of their outlets at the wall markets and buy things. There are some really nice things, and some real bargains, but you'd better know who you're dealing with or else know merchandise, because you buy strictly at your own risk. Unless you get it through an outside retailer, of course."

The wall. I'll *bet* there's a wall, I thought. "What's to keep them from ganging up and coming out to raise hell?" I asked him. "Raiding through the streets, or coming out at night in twos and threes and mugging people?"

"Oh, that happened once about seventy years ago when the Quarter was new. A huge gang of about two hundred came out and began doing all kinds of horrible things, beating people and raping women and starting fires. Then, when the police and the Army came, most of the Reds ran back inside the Quarter and locked the gates. So the Army just surrounded the place and started firing mortar shells over the wall. Not heavily, but methodically.

"After a few hours, naked bodies started being thrown over the wall. Not killed by shells; their throats had been cut and their—parts cut off. They were *supposed* to be the ones who had made the trouble, but no one believed that. For one thing, the Army kept shelling anyway until about four hundred had been thrown out. Then the government had a conference with the rulers of the Quarter, and after a few days they signed an agreement and the Army went home."

He paused long enough to pour us both tea. "And that took care of it?" I asked.

Dunne sat down across the table from me. "There've been a few cases since then when two or three came out and did things to people, but they've always either been caught outside and beheaded"—Dunne shuddered again—"or turned over alive from inside, castrated. You see, whenever it happens, their trade gets shut down for some period or other.

"And the snoops know if the right ones get turned over.

"Of course, the spotters—the clairvoyants who can spot crimes ahead of time—pay a lot of attention to the Red Quarter, even if nothing is done about most of the things they spot. Spotters can't help themselves; that's the sort of thing they tend to pick up."

It occurred to me that if Sanberg had a contact here, in a country with snoops and spotters, it almost had to be in the Red Quarter.

"Twice in my lifetime," Dunne went on, "an Army commando unit has raided the Red Quarter. The details are never released to the papers, of course, but there was a lot of automatic weapons fire from inside, and sounds like grenades, and that has to be the commandos. One of the strictest prohibitions on the Reds is against automatic weapons, rifles, or actually any propulsion weapons except pistols and shotguns."

He served supper then and we talked about other things, and afterward he taught me to read. It was easy, mainly just learning the sounds of their letters. When it got dark we went up on the roof garden. The cloud cover was breaking up and you could see patches of starry sky. Before long we went to bed.

After Dunne went to sleep, I lay there thinking for a while. He wasn't a bad guy, except for being a faggot, I told myself. I was going to have to split before I started liking him.

Then the thought hit me, right in the gut! *Christ! I should have been in the time-door room right then! How in hell could I have forgotten that?* It shook hell out of me! Tomorrow morning for sure, broad daylight or not, as soon as Dunne went to work, I'd load up a sack with food and take a flat bottle I'd found for water. I could probably refill the bottle somewhere in the gray building.

Just before I drifted off, something Dunne had said came into my mind: "forensic psionics." They used telepaths in court here. What bothered me about it just then was the language thing again. *Forensic* and *psionics* were twentieth century words. Well, maybe forensic was older. But this was—what? The fortieth century? The thousandth? The English language started out as Old Saxon, a dialect of ancient German. It picked up a little bit of Celtic and Roman from the old Britons, some Latin from the church, and later some Old Norse from the Vikings. Later on it added a bunch of French from the Normans and from the French themselves, and after that some Old Danish. And it kept changing right along after that, from century to century.

So how in hell had it stopped?

I should never have taken college English, I told

myself, and shivered. I'd have given anything to be back in L.A.

4

I woke up gasping. Whatever the dream had been, it was gone, but my heart was still thudding. I sat up slowly and put my feet on the floor.

It wasn't as dark as it had been; there was moonlight out. I needed a cigarette, and to get out of the room, so I pulled on slacks, a shirt, and my shoes, and started for the roof garden, feeling brittle and shaky.

On the roof I leaned against a parapet, feeling the night air and smelling the flowers. There were still scattered clouds catching the moonlight, and I turned to look up. I felt the skin draw tight on my face, and my scalp crawled. My mouth began to open, squared off, and stretched. I listened for the scream but nothing came out. I started to shake, shook so hard I sank to my knees, and still couldn't pull my eyes away. There were two of them, two moons about fifteen degrees apart in the sky, one looking about half as big as the real moon and the other maybe a third. The real moon, Earth's moon with its familiar face, wasn't there at all.

Not time; space-time! Now I knew, right out front; Sanberg hadn't just sent me into the past or future. He'd sent me someplace else, someplace bad, where the people spoke English and had feet and miles and. . . . The last thing I heard was my own stretched-thin voice going a-a-a-a-a-a-a in a long nasal moan.

I woke up on the floor of Dunne's apartment with a cover thrown over me and a savage pain in my head. I couldn't remember anything after passing out on the roof, but obviously I'd made my way down again, and I'd found a bottle of Dunne's booze. Maybe more than one.

I started to sit up and my head split. Very carefully I rolled over onto my knees and very, very carefully got up. Abruptly I lurched not carefully at all into the bathroom. It felt like guts, throat, eyeballs, and all came out, and it kept on. When it stopped it was as if all the blood in my body was in my face, swelling it like a painful balloon. My head was pounding, and I was too weak for a while to get off my knees.

Finally I got myself together, rinsed my mouth, and walked gently into the kitchen, feeling grateful to Jared for having pulled my shoes off. It must have been him; obviously I'd been in no condition to do it for myself.

I turned the burner on under the coffee pot. *Coffee!* Jesus, God, and Mary! They even had coffee in this place! I strained to see the clock but my eyes didn't want to focus. The clock blurred, partially sharpened, then blurred again, but I got enough of a look between blurs to tell it was after six o'clock—midafternoon, the way they figured things.

Then I did a quick shuffle back to the bathroom.

Even warmed over, the coffee seemed weak, but I made up for that with quantity. Then I pawed through the refrigerator and found some tomato juice. Oh God, I thought, tomato juice, too! I wanted to cry. How could they have tomato juice?

But it put out the fire the way coffee couldn't.

Then, because I didn't want to leave Jared too disgusted, I went into the bathroom and cleaned up what I had missed, and that started it all over again, mostly green. After that I looked for a bottle, but either I'd finished it all, which seemed likely, or Jared had hidden it. So I showered, and when I was done I got down on my knees and prayed. Those were my first *Hail Marys* since I was nine years old, and my first ever with feeling.

Finally I got dressed. I was weak as a cat, but there was something I had to do. I had to get back to the— God, what could I call it now? To the time door!

No way could I eat, but I put bread and cheese in a bag, along with a bottle of tap water. Two moons! I wanted to leave a note for Jared, thanking him, but it was too much to do. I just left. Because I was afraid of what the elevator would do to my stomach, I took the stairs, each step like being stabbed in the forehead. On the sidewalk the glare of sunlight half blinded me, and I stood with my eyes squinted until they adjusted. I'd never known before what a really bad hangover was, and the world's safest bet was that once would be enough.

But right then I needed something to ease it, so I went to the nearest bar and ordered a double. After downing it I felt a lot more human, and I could see better. The bartender saw my empty glass and came back with the bottle and a questioning look. I could see the label; it said BRBN! Named after a county in Kentucky! I wanted to cry. I still didn't dare shake my head, so I put my hand over my glass and he turned away. Carefully I got off the stool and walked out.

My pace was a compromise between my headache and the need to hurry. If the room was still locked, I'd get in through the window and unlock the door. The room next to it was too risky; I could fall asleep in there and miss my chance.

By the time I'd walked the mile and a half or whatever, I felt a lot better. The door was still bolted, so I wasn't too late. Leaving my sack in the next room where I could pick it up later, I went back out. The alley was barer than any alley I'd ever seen; people who don't have anything at all don't have anything to throw away. There wasn't even a trash can to stand on, so I went back to the sidewalk and waited till five or six people had shuffled past. The last was big and chunky.

"Excuse me, friend," I said.

He stopped and stared warily. "You talking to me?"

"How'd you like to make a dollar?"

His eyes turned suspicious. "How?"

"In the alley here." I gestured. "I need someone to boost me up to a window."

"That building's empty," he said. "Ain't nothing in there. And anyway the doors is all open; you can just walk in."

"The room I want is locked. Come on."

He shrugged and we walked down the alley, me counting windows. "Here," I said. "Hunker down and I'll stand on your shoulders."

"Gimme my money first."

I dug out my wallet and handed him a one.

"I want two," he said. I grabbed him by the shirt and jammed him hard against the concrete wall. "I'll give you this," I snarled, and held my fist in front of his face. It worked like a charm.

He turned out to be less strong than he looked, and had trouble standing up with me, but he made it. I got the window open enough to get my head and shoulders in, then pulled the rest of me through. He stood watching for a few seconds, then started to turn away. I didn't want him to leave pissed off though; he might go straight to the fuzz.

"Ps-s-st," I hissed after him.

He looked back at me.

"Here, pal, and thanks. Maybe again sometime." I tossed another bill to him. He picked it up and, without another look, shuffled away.

With the sunshine outside, the room was brighter than it had been before. First I tried walking around in the middle of it, just in case, but nothing happened. Then something caught my eye. Staring, I felt like I'd known all along it was there. A vacuum filled my gut, and kneeling, I picked it up. After that there was nothing left to do but unbolt the door and leave.

I walked slowly now, dazed, hollow, like a thin shell that would cave in any minute. I didn't follow any route, just walked in the right general direction. When I got outside the Quarter, I went to the first bar I came to.

The bartender was a blur. "You okay, friend?" he asked.

"How do I get to the Red Quarter?"

He didn't say anything for a minute. "You sure you're all right?" he asked. When I didn't answer, he shrugged. "Okay. Go to Belder and . . ."

"I don't know the streets around here."

"Right. Okay, go out, turn left, walk two blocks, and you'll see a streetcar platform. Take the Tanner Park car; that's the Tanner Park car. The motorman will tell you where to get off."

I nodded and left.

I not only didn't know what I was doing, I didn't even wonder. I just let something inside push me along. I don't know how long I waited for the streetcar. I stood there looking at the little brass cylinder in my hand— the empty .32 caliber cartridge case I'd picked up off the floor. A streetcar pulled up and I got on without even checking to see if it was the right one. I just told the motorman what I wanted and he asked me which gate. I said whichever came first. Then I sat down.

Tears were running down my cheeks, but it didn't matter. I was dead; I couldn't look away from it anymore. Sanberg had gone through the door ahead of me and *stepped behind it*. I'd come through then and he'd shot at me again from behind as I appeared in front of him. That was the explosion I'd heard; that was the ejected cartridge case I'd found. When I stumbled and fell, he thought he'd hit me, and stepped back through into his lab and shut the power off.

But the door had been between us when he'd fired, and instead of the bullet hitting me, it had gone through the door into his lab. It probably hit the concrete wall there and he never knew the difference.

And it didn't *make* any difference. I was stuck here forever, whatever forever meant. For me, not long.

People were looking at me. The goddamn tears were dripping off my face, and I looked down at the wet spots on my shirt and pants. To hell with them. I was going to the Red Quarter. Nobody ever gave a shit about me but my grandmother, and I hadn't seen her since we left Chicago when I was ten. She was dead now, and pretty soon I'd be dead too, because I was going into the Red Quarter.

5

And I'd thought the hangover was bad. This time I
felt like I'd been in a plane wreck. My head roared and
throbbed, my body didn't want to move at all, and my
mouth. . . . I could only open one eye, just enough to
squint through. A broad was on her knees beside me,
making little mewling noises: "Oh God, blessed God,
the poor, poor thing!"

That's what I was: a poor, poor thing. I moaned
again. My mouth would hardly open at all, it was so
swollen. Inside it felt ragged, like I'd been chewing
razor blades. The broad made a sound that was half sob
and half whimper. "Here. Can you get up? Oh God,
you poor, poor thing. Let me help you."

Somehow I managed to get on my hands and knees.
With my face turned down, it felt as if my poor damn
mouth was hanging to the pavement. I was on the
sidewalk next to a fifteen-foot stone wall, although I
didn't know it at the time; I'd probably been thrown off
it. She tried to help me up, grunting with the effort and
still crying. "There," she said. "Oh God, oh God, you're
hurt so bad!"

Among God knows where else, I'd been kicked in the
worst possible place and couldn't straighten very much.
She was trying to help me walk. She seemed to know
where we were going and was willing to go half a step
at a time to get me there. Gradually I became aware
that birds were singing, real birds in the trees, telling
me it was just daybreak.

They hadn't liked me in Lumpy's Bar. They didn't
like guys that didn't belong there—that weren't wearing red.

It was a good thing her apartment was less than a
block away; at that it took us fifteen minutes. I needed
another four or five minutes, hanging on the railing, to
make it up the open back stairs to the service landing
and into her kitchen. She wasn't so unwound that she'd
take me up the front way; I'd have left drops of blood
all over the hall carpet.

And besides, I was naked except for my shoes. No clothes, no billfold, no gun, nothing.

She got me into her living room, threw back the spread, and helped me down on her bed. I closed my eye again and lay there while she drew a pan of warm water and dabbed my face. It hurt like hell, but I lay as still as I could, wincing and groaning. She was crying again. After a bit she finished or gave up, and I could hear her rattling things in the kitchen.

Suddenly I could feel it coming up, all the blood I'd swallowed, and rolled over to try missing the bed. I passed out.

The next time I woke up, I had a wet rag over my left eye, with ice wrapped in it. My shoes were off. I groaned, and right away she was there. I could sense her hovering, and opened my slit to look at her. After about half a minute she said, "My name is Ruth."

Ruth. Like in the Bible. Ruth. Her eyes welled with sympathy and her hand reached out to almost touch me. "Oh gentle God," she whispered, "how could anyone do such a thing?"

With an ax, I thought. With a hammer. "Help up," I mumbled. I hoped she could understand me. "Got to go can."

"You can't." She wrung her hands. "You're hurt too bad. I'll get something. You don't realize how bad you're hurt."

She disappeared back into the kitchen.

I realized all right. Jesus, I thought, why'd they have to bust me up like this and leave me alive? Why couldn't they just kill me? She brought a bucket, but there was no way that was going to work so she helped me into the bathroom after all. I had trouble there, too; it hurt really bad, and when it finally started flowing I passed blood. My balls were all swollen and black. The thought came to me that I'd never be all right again.

When I was finally done, after several little installments that nearly made me pass out, I leaned on the washbowl and peered into the mirror with my one eye.

It was even worse than I'd thought. My lips were like
overripe plums—swollen and purple-black and split. I
couldn't part them enough to see inside. My nose was
swollen all over my face, and my forehead looked like
someone had used a wood rasp on it. My left eye was so
swollen it hung down. The right was the one I could
see through; the brow above it was laid wide open. My
right ear looked like a big mushroom.

Looking back, I'd have to say that the guys who did it
were real craftsmen. You don't get a job like that done
on you in a brawl; it's an art form. But looking at it
then, I didn't think. I just felt despair.

"Please," she was saying, "please come in and lie
down. If you pass out, you may hit your face on the
washbowl or something. Please!" She took my arm, and
my head started swimming; I braced myself against the
doorway until the dizziness passed. Then I let her help
me to bed again.

She checked my covers before she left. I didn't
sleep—I just lay there and hurt. When she came back
she had some paper bags. She ground up a pill in a cup,
mixed it with water, and helped me sit up. Then she
gave me the water through a straw. After that I *did*
sleep.

Most of the next four days she kept me pretty well
doped up, but not so doped I didn't learn a few things.
I spent the daytime hours on her bed, but at night I
slept on a quilt-padded folding cot in the little kitchen,
which was the only other room she had.

It wasn't that she was a prude; it was economics. She
made her living on that bed in the evenings. A couple
of times I'd had to move off it during the day, too.
Mostly when a guy would come to the door in the
daytime, she'd tell him "no," but a couple of them
offered double the going rate and she couldn't turn it
down.

She always apologized to me afterward—not that she
needed to—and took care of me better than any professional nurse would have.

On the fourth day I could open my mouth enough to look inside it. I just stared, fascinated and sick: All my front teeth were broken or gone. My tongue had told me it was bad, but to see them like that. . . . A couple had broken stubs showing above the gums. My teeth that had always been so healthy, so white and pretty; the tears started to flow, even from the closed eye. Jesus, Jesus, I thought, sweet gentle Jesus!

But it was Ruth who answered, not Jesus. She came in and walked me back to bed, and gave me another pill, and fed me broth through a straw.

Ruth was like a chicken; she always woke up when it started to get light in the morning. And if the weather was nice, like it almost always was in summer, she'd take a walk before breakfast. That's how she'd found me. You'd think that, less than a block from the Red Quarter, it would be dangerous to go walking like that, but it wasn't.

On the morning of the fifth day I got up to go to the can—my kidneys didn't work right anymore and I went in little squirts—and she was in there brushing her hair. So when she went out for her walk, I went with her.

Although I was still sore and couldn't walk very well, it felt good to get out and hobble around. But Ruth seemed depressed.

"What's the matter?" I asked.

She shook her head and I knew it was about me. There was a little park on the corner, about the size of a small building lot, with trees and benches and flower-beds, and we sat down there. "Please," I said. "Can't you tell me?"

She looked at me and then at the ground. "I'm going to have to take you to a dentist," she answered, "and he's going to hurt you terribly bad. And I can't bear to think of you having to suffer any more than you have."

"Aw no." It still hurt to talk, so it took a while to mumble it all. "That'll cost you too much. I'll be okay Ruth, honest to God. I still got my back teeth."

She shook her head. "No," she said, "you won't be all right without help. Those broken ones—if something isn't done their roots will rot." She thought for a moment. "I'll go to the dentist today and make an appointment. After that we'll just have to see how you get along—see what else needs doing."

I had to wait twelve days before I could see the dentist, but only six before I went to bed with Ruth. I honest to God hadn't been thinking about it, but this scrawny little dude came knocking at the door at noon and when she told him "no" he offered her double. He was pretty agitated. So I ducked into the kitchen and she let him in. There was a hole in the kitchen door where a lock had been, and the next thing I knew I was watching. It really turned me on; I could hardly wait until he left.

I was a lot more presentable by the time I went to the dentist. The swelling was gone from my eyes and nose, as well as my mouth, and the cuts were healed. My right ear had gone down about as far as it was going to, and the cauliflowering wasn't really so noticeable unless you were looking for it. My face still had a greenish-yellow tinge from bruises, but as long as I kept my mouth shut I didn't look too bad.

I wasn't feeling so good, though. I still couldn't pee right, my back hurt, and eczema had broken out on my hands that itched pretty badly sometimes. My head buzzed all the time, and I got earaches.

And my nerves were shot. When the jaw butcher had finished getting the broken teeth out, I was pretty rocky again. Ruth made another appointment to get me fitted for bridges and we left.

She did a lot of reading, but her books weren't my cup of tea so I napped a lot. Even after the painkiller was gone, I could still sleep a lot more than I ever had before. In the evenings I'd stroll around the neighborhood to keep out of her way, and I started spending time in the neighborhood library, reading fiction until closing time.

Not long afterward, Ruth rented a two-room apartment in the same building. She was making better money now than she had before—doing more different stuff, charging more, and getting more business. She laughed and cried when she told me we were moving—that we could have a room to ourselves.

I started feeling blue then because I wasn't bringing in any money. In this country you needed ID to get a job. If you lost your ID, you went to a local registry and gave your name and number. Then they'd take your prints and check the register, and if everything checked out, they gave you a new ID. All very simple, except that I wasn't on the register.

She thought I wasn't and I knew I wasn't. She'd seemed to buy the amnesia story, but I got the idea that she thought I was really a Red, and that if I went to the registry they'd find out and send me back. That didn't make sense, because a guy could always stop being a Red just by asking to be reclassified. But I suspect that's what she thought; Ruth wasn't all that bright.

And anyway, what kind of job could I do, all stove up and with my nerves shot.

So I started feeling blue about being a deadbeat, but she hugged me and kissed me and smiled and told me it was all right, that she'd take care of me and things would be better after we moved the next day. Then she dialed the doorplate to "not at home," and got out a bottle of wine, and we had a little party, just the two of us.

Some things were better after we moved, but not my health. My kidneys stayed about the same, and while the earaches weren't any worse, the buzzing in my head bothered me even more, and the eczema spread. Ruth took care of me though, and when I'd get feeling especially low, she was always there with sympathy and "poor dear." I'd graduated up from "poor thing."

Meanwhile, I learned how to drink like a real pro: Watered wine, so I wouldn't get drunk, or even tight, just rummy enough to keep things off me. I felt the lowest when I'd start thinking about how there was no way I could ever get back home, and I couldn't tell Ruth about that, so I'd drink. And she never complained about keeping me supplied, not even once.

Since I'd got beaten up, I'd hardly even looked in the mirror to shave. Those couple of looks the first week had been enough. But when I finally got my partial plates I went in the bathroom and gave myself a good look. That's when I realized how old I'd gotten. A few weeks earlier I'd been forty-two and looked thirty-five. Now I looked fifty-five.

It wasn't the plates; actually, they looked okay. But my skin had gotten loose and old-looking, my hair was showing more gray, and I'd *shrunk*. I flexed my muscles and what I saw left me numb: I was getting to be an old wreck.

When I went back out, Ruth asked me what was wrong, and at first I couldn't tell her. When I did, she cried. Then she took me to bed and I couldn't make it. We wanted to, but for the first time in my life I couldn't get it up. She told me it was all right, not to worry about it, that she'd love me and care for me regardless of anything.

That evening I did get kind of drunk.

Over the next few weeks I still couldn't, and it broke my heart. Ruth had been a talented but fairly ordinary-looking broad to start with, but lately she'd looked prettier and more alive. I overheard other guys, regular customers, tell her that, too.

Now that I couldn't, I hated to hear the sounds from the next room, so I started wearing earplugs when anyone was in there with her while I was home. Funny how sounds would go right through the buzzing in my head. Now and then the buzzing got almost like a dull roar, although it never stayed that bad for long. And the eczema spread up over my elbows onto my upper arms. Ruth bought me some salve, and that kept it softer so it didn't crack and scale so bad.

I was afraid she'd get fed up and throw me out, now that we weren't lovers anymore and I was going downhill so bad, but she was sweeter and more sympathetic than ever.

Then, thank God, it finally happened. I'd been at the library, and when it closed I walked around a while and sat in the park a little bit, but pretty soon I had to go to the can. I went up the outside stairs and slipped quietly into the kitchen, where I could hear Ruth in the front room talking with some guy. I used the can without flushing, to not make any noise, then went out on the service landing with my wine bottle and sat on the top step for a while. When I went back in, I could still hear them, so I put my earplugs in and went to bed.

Her moving around next morning woke me up. I pulled my pants on and went in the kitchen.

"Hi," she said. "Want some coffee?"

"Yeah. It doesn't do my kidneys any good, but yeah, I want some." I sat at the table watching her move around, and wondering if I'd ever be able to screw again. "That guy you had when I came home was around a long time. What was he, a two-timer?"

She laughed. "No, but he'd like to be. He was a talker, and he'd been drinking." She stirred cream and sugar into my coffee and set it in front of me. "Here," she said, "let me show you what he gave me besides twenty dollars."

Twenty dollars! That was high in this world! She went into the bedroom and came out smiling, with a watch on her wrist. "Isn't it pretty?" she said. "I never saw one so tiny."

It was small, for this world.

"But the crazy thing is," she went on, "it's got *twelve hours*. Look at it." She took it off and handed it to me. I was stunned. "See?" she said. "Twelve hours. Isn't that crazy?"

I was staring, and the stun was fading out. It had

BULOVA written on the face in tiny Roman letters. *Roman letters!* That was the clincher.

"What did he look like?"

"Just some guy. I never saw him before."

I had to be careful now; I was almost shaking. "Huh! Twenty dollars and this! Did he say he was coming back?"

"No, and I don't think he will. He said he's leaving the country."

God, and I'd been within fifteen feet of the sonofabitch! "Tell me what he looked like!" I said.

"Please, Steve, let go of my arm. You're hurting me."

"Tell me what he looked like, what he talked like!"

"He was ordinary looking, smallish, maybe fifty-five. Like a lot of guys. Please, Steve."

Not Sanberg. I let go and she rubbed her arm.

"What else did he tell you? Did he say where he got it? The watch?"

She decided to act like everything was all right. Her eyes moved away as she tried to pull her thoughts together. "He said someone gave it to him, someone he sees in his government job. To give this girl he wanted to impress, but she wouldn't take it."

She looked up at me then and smiled. "It's awfully pretty. See? It's got diamonds in it. But the hours aren't even the right length. It said eleven when he gave it to me three hours ago, and now it says . . ."

I hit her. I gave her the flat of my hand and knocked her against the wall. She sat there on the floor with her hand on her cheek and her mouth a little round *O*, without a clue to what was happening. She didn't even know what she was, any more than I had till then. I grabbed her arm, hauled her to her feet, marched her into the bedroom, and took her. I didn't even take her skirt off to do it. She was crying while I finished getting dressed, but I never said a word. Then I took a twenty and some change out of the jar she kept her cash in, and left.

I knew just what I was going to do. It came to me from something Dunne had said about the police here.

Whether it would work or not—that was something else. But I was done with waiting to die. If it hadn't been for that wristwatch, she might have been able to keep me there the rest of my life, her blooming while I rotted away bit by bit. A vampire that fed on the spirit without even knowing it.

6

A guy on the street told me how to get to the Government District, so I went to a streetcar island and waited.

The traffic wasn't bad: the street was wide, there weren't any cars, and not many carriages. Traffic was mainly commercial or public: horse-drawn wagons and cabs, and now and then a truck. And lots of electric streetcars on their midstreet tracks; I only had to wait a couple of minutes.

The only other time I'd ridden a streetcar on this world, I hadn't paid much attention. They had advertising panels above the windows, like you could see in buses on Earth—familiar except for the names. Soft drinks, shoes, politicians. . . . Apparently an election was coming up, because one read, "Vote for Fred L. Mallon, Congress, Second District. Help keep your game clean!"

That was a poser: *Help keep your game clean!* Deevers was cleaner than any big American city I'd ever seen, except maybe Salt Lake.

And there were flowerbeds, red and white and yellow and violet, in front of the houses and apartment buildings. In the business blocks they had terraces and planters with flowers and flowering shrubs, and as we got close to the Government District the street became a boulevard with a broad, landscaped center strip. The architecture wasn't much—old-fashioned, with nothing really big—but everything was clean and green. It wouldn't be a half-bad place to live if a guy could come up with a decent racket.

I'd asked the motorman to let me know when we were coming to where the STB, the *Special Talents Branch*, was officed. He'd raised an eyebrow and said it ought to be in the Justice Building, so that's where I got off.

The Justice Building wasn't the kind of building you might expect—no hundred-foot-wide flight of stairs, or row of tall pillars across the front. It looked more like an old four-story office building, sand-blasted clean, with big windows.

My plan was simple. I'd get them to come to me instead of me to them. After that I'd play it by ear. Across the street from it was a little park—trees, grass, flowerbeds—that I learned later was Justice Park. It wasn't much wider than the expanded boulevard dividers. A bench faced the main entrance of the Justice Building, with a woman sitting at one end, reading in the sun; I sat down on the other end and looked across the street.

How do you shout with your mind? Try it sometime. It felt like shouting, even though I didn't make a sound, and I had the notion that if there was a telepath anywhere around, he'd hear it: *"I'm from a different world,"* I yelled, *"a different planet, and I have news for the police! I'm from a different planet and I have news for the police."*

Then there was nothing to do but wait and see if anyone showed. Maybe it would be men in white coats, bringing a little canvas jacket with sleeves that tied in back. But it seemed like I had a better chance than if I went in to some desk sergeant and said, "Hey, I'm from a different planet, where we speak the same language, and I have something important to tell your leader."

This way only a telepath could hear me, and hopefully a telepath could tell I was for real. If I was.

Nothing happened in any hurry, and I had to remind myself that anything the government does takes time, at least anything you want them to do. I tried again. *"I'm from a different planet and I have news for the*

police! My name is Steve Synko and I come from a
world with only one moon!"

What the hell; why not?

I wished I had a newspaper to kill time with. People
went in and out of the building. After a few more
minutes I tried again. I'd hardly finished when this guy
came out, and I spotted him as a cop right away. He
didn't start right down the stairs like the others had,
eyes on the steps. Instead he stopped for a few seconds
at the top, stuffing his pipe, and I knew his eyes were
making a sweep of the park. Then he came down the
stairs, slowly, lighting the curve-stemmed pipe, and
crossed the street.

Sherlock Holmes in person, I thought.

He came right up to the bench and sat down a couple
of feet from me, where he stared at the sky, drawing on
the pipe now and then to keep it lit.

"Okay," I thought to him, "you're here. Now what?"

Now nothing. I started feeling irritated. "You just
going to sit there, Fart Face?"

He didn't even slide an eye at me, and I began to
wonder if I'd been wrong and he wasn't fuzz, or not a
telepath, anyway. There was a simple test; I got up like
I was going to leave.

"Excuse me, friend," he said. "Have you seen this?"

I looked at the hand he held out; there was an open
wallet in it, with a shield. I nodded and sat back down.
"So what the hell are we waiting for?" I wondered at
him.

It didn't take much longer to find out. A light open
carriage came down the street, the horse's rubber-shod
hooves thudding softly on the concrete, and stopped
right in front of us. The horse was a big, classy-looking
animal. The carriage had a little seat out front for the
driver and two double seats behind. The wheels were
high, with thin wooden spokes and narrow rubber tires.
A woman sat in the middle seat, on the tall side, heavy,
pushing fifty. She looked like her corset was boilerplate.

"Mr. Synko," she said, and patted the seat beside
her. I got up and climbed aboard. My friend with the

pipe got in the seat behind us. "Around River Park, Weldon," she said. The driver clucked to the horse and we started off.

"My name is Regina Blake," she told me. "I'm chief of the Special Talents Branch, and the gentleman behind us is Lieutenant Glasgow." I shook the hand she reached across to me. "What planet are you from?" she asked.

All very matter of fact.

"We call it Earth," I told her, "same as you call this one. But it's different—continents are different, only one big moon . . ." I felt suddenly silly saying it, and half pissed off at feeling that way.

"Interesting. Picture your sky with a full moon for me. I'd like to see that. Then picture your planet as a classroom globe."

I closed my eyes and saw the moon again the way it looked one night from a sleeping bag nearly twelve thousand feet up on top of Baldy Mountain, back in Arizona. For a few seconds I was homesick, not for Earth, but to be fifteen years old in the Baldy wilderness, with my life ahead of me.

I opened my eyes, looking at this big telepathic broad in an old-fashioned carriage on a strange world. She nodded and I looked inside my mind again at a globe, its countries different colors—the U.S. yellow, Canada pink, Mexico orange—letting it turn slowly to show the blue seas. It was the globe in Miss Wozniak's fourth grade room, with the seam running down the Pacific about on the International Date Line. Little snot-nosed punk, I'd been in love with Miss Wozniak.

Then I gave the big broad a look at Earth the way the astronauts had photographed it from lunar orbit, partway full above the horizon of the moon. "That last was Earth," I said, "my Earth, the way it looks from the moon. It's a famous photograph taken by one of our spacemen."

"Spacemen," she said thoughtfully, and looked me over. "How did you get here?"

"You believe all this?"

"In the light of recent events, yes. Tentatively. Any experienced telepath can tell when someone's putting out a deliberate lie. You could be telling untruths that you believe, of course, but your mental imagery is exceptionally vivid and real. Now back to my question: How did you get here?"

Back home you wouldn't get that much answer out of a cop in a week. But then, she didn't seem like a cop.

"If I told you how I got here, you wouldn't . . . Hell, you would though, wouldn't you. Okay, I came here through what was supposed to be a time machine. I know that sounds crazy, and maybe it is. Or I am. Anyway, I didn't even know this was a different planet until I saw two moons in the sky. Until then I thought it was just a different time."

"When was that?"

"A couple of months ago, or a little more."

"What date?" she pushed. "What hour?"

I gave her the date in terms of their calendar, and a rough guess at the hour. She nodded as if it meant something to her. "What have you been doing since then?"

"Not much, believe me."

"Run through it for me—the time you've spent here. Don't think about it; simply be the projectionist. Go back to your arrival and let the subsequent interval rerun to the present."

I stared at her.

"You said you had information for us," she said. "Let's have it, beginning with your arrival."

Now she was sounding like a cop. I started with Sanberg's lab, actually, and ended with the park bench, doing it like she'd said, speeding through without really looking at much of it myself, slowing for the highlights. It took ten minutes at most. When I was done she spoke to her driver.

"Government Hospital, Weldon, and move it!" The hooves clopped faster, and so did my heart. I felt a hand on my shoulder from behind.

"Relax," Glasgow said, "we're not putting you away. We want you to identify someone for us."

The big broad's eyes were on me. "I gather that police telepaths aren't used on your world. Why not?"

"Because we don't have telepaths. Well, maybe we do at that—we've got the idea of them, anyway—but it's probably an off-and-on thing with them. If we had any do-it-on-demand telepaths with the police, I'd know it."

She sat there frowning, and I got the notion that she'd been handsome, maybe beautiful, twenty-five years and eighty pounds earlier. Regina Blake, she'd called herself. We were out of River Park now, jogging along a street past more government buildings, then turned into a drive through landscaped grounds, and parked in front of Government Hospital.

Glasgow and I waited in the lobby while Regina went into an office. A minute later she was back with a guy in white. An elevator took us up five floors, which meant all the way up, and let us out.

There were uniformed guards in the hall; one of them went with us down the corridor and another let us into a room. Regina and I went over to the bed. Even with his bandaged head and sagging cheeks, I knew him when I saw him. His eyes were closed, and I got the notion he was not just asleep.

I turned to Regina and nodded. "Sanberg," I said. Then we trooped back out.

"I'd have sworn he shot at me from behind and went back through the time door." We were back in the carriage, riding to the Justice Building. "When I found that cartridge case, it was like I *knew!*"

She nodded. "He probably did. I'm sure he went back, because he returned here eight days ago."

"Returned?"

"One of our clairvoyants had a premonition that something was going to happen at Berriton Square in the Red Quarter on a certain morning. She had no idea what it would be, which made it highly unusual, but it felt urgent to her that we have people there. And that it had something to do with . . . I'll go into that later. And she thought we'd need an ambulance."

In the Red Quarter I could believe that.

"We have authority to send officers into the Red Quarter whenever we need to," she went on, "but we have to submit a justification statement to the Clean Games Authority no later than three hours afterward, and it had better be good. The Reds have their rights, too, you know. So we very rarely do it.

"In this case, though, we decided quite promptly, and on the morning predicted we had three uniformed officers and an ambulance there, with our clairvoyant. Shortly before noon, Donna received a sudden, ah, jolt, and looked up, and your Mr. Sanberg appeared in the air. He just *appeared*, suddenly, seventy or eighty feet up, and fell onto a steep tiled roof that sent him chuting off into a fountain about twenty feet below it. The angle of the roof and the three feet of water in the fountain saved his life."

"How'd you connect him with me?"

"We could make nothing of his papers. There's no place in the world—those were Donna's precise words— no place in the world with writing like that. She used it as a figure of speech, of course. And his mode of arrival was unusual, to say the least. So when you came booming in with 'I'm from a different world,' I recalled her words and had an intuition. I'm not much of a clairvoyant—haven't much more ability in that area than the ordinary person—but I don't usually ignore an intuition."

"So," I said, "Sanberg walked through his time door in the wrong place without looking. Served the sonofabitch right!"

"It may possibly have served him right," she answered drily, "but it was no accident. He'd been drugged, and shot in the chest before he fell. Someone intended to kill him—apparently someone familiar with our world, who knows that the Red Quarter is the place to deposit a body with little likelihood of exciting official interest."

Heavy duty, I thought. "Okay. And that brings us to what brought me here. The watch."

"Exactly."

The carriage stopped in front of the Justice Building and we got out. Her office was on the second floor. Sunlight filled the room through the big, open south window. Hanging up her hat, she sat down behind the heavy desk; the way she leaned back, her feet probably gave her trouble. Glasgow took out a cigar; he wasn't a pipe purist after all. I eyed it and he fumbled in his jacket and held out another. Then he struck a big kitchen match with his thumbnail and lit it for me.

"About the watch, Steven," she said, "it's unfortunate you didn't see the man who gave it to her. We'll have to rely on her to identify him from photos if he is, in fact, a government employee. Two of our operatives have disappeared, a telepath and a clairvoyant, but neither is male. And I think I know what happened to them."

"Kidnapped?"

"Improbable. It would be difficult to kidnap a telepath."

"So what, then?"

She looked at me. "What do you think?"

It was a good cigar, mild. I'm not a real cigar man. "How about smuggling? Dope, maybe, and your two missing people could be in on it. They know the ropes at this end, and they could be working *from* the other end where they're not likely to get caught."

She examined it. "Improbable. Narcotics are legal and available in the Red Quarter, while in the Gray Quarter, where potential users are common, there's no money."

I shrugged. "I don't know the ropes here well enough. But listen, if there's any way I *can* help you, just ask. All I want out of it is a pad, meals, and to find that goddamn door and get back home. And maybe a few chips to spend while I'm here."

She spent a long half minute putting her thoughts together, or maybe making up her mind. "Mr. Synko," she said at last, "I sympathize, and I'll help you if I can.

I will also be open with you, because I sense that you may be able to help us. You are our expert from the other side, and we are concerned with more than a crime here.

"A few months ago, a strange thing happened, like nothing that ever happened before, to our knowledge. Every telepath in this organization experienced it at the same time: an abrupt psychic dis-ease, a feeling of fear, of something gone wrong, but without explicit content. It lasted for some minutes before ending, also abruptly. And each of us was aware that all of us felt it. The experience was essentially similar for clairvoyants."

"Fortunately it was not severe, because after a lapse of nine days it recurred frequently for a week. Then it became erratic. We have recorded the time and duration of each recurrence, but until today we had no idea, none at all, of what it was."

Absently she examined her nails. "Now I am quite confident that when I check, I'll find that one occurrence coincided with your arrival here."

She looked up at me. "No, Mr. Synko, I am not accusing you of anything. We know that it also happened briefly when Mr. Sanberg, ah, dropped in on us. I believe now that it is somehow caused by the operation of the machine which put you here—the, shall we say, time machine. When the machine is activated, the malaise occurs.

"One of our top operatives, a fine telepath with occasional clairvoyance, became particularly intrigued with the problem of the malaise, and disappeared not long before your own arrival two months ago. Perhaps she went through the door into your world. I have no evidence for this—it is another intuition—but I believe it is correct. Particularly since the other disappearance, of her closest female associate, occurred just six days later, on a day which, I seem to recall, there was a recurrence of the malaise."

Regina breathed deeply, her lips thinned. "I am not particularly concerned for their well-being. No one here has felt any sense of coercion or malevolence in connection with either disappearance, and neither Gloris nor Susan had many friends. They were not friendly people.

"The central consideration is the malaise. After a time, you see, we became aware that it was becoming worse with recurrence, even though you might think we'd grow inured to it with repeated exposure. And recently we've begun to notice something further: Between occurrences, the dis-ease has begun to persist at a low intensity between events. A few of our more sensitive people occasionally find themselves listening for something, something they cannot quite perceive but are afraid of."

As she'd talked, her voice had become softer, more of a monotone. Now, for a few seconds, she just sat there, saying nothing. But she wasn't done.

"And very recently we have had brought to our attention the worsened behavior of certain inmates in mental institutions—an intensification of depression, catatonia, anxiety, and violence. These coincide with occurrences of the malaise. So do recent disturbances in the Red Quarter. Fortunately, none of these has been sufficiently notable to have drawn the attention of the newspapers.

"I expect that if we had data, we'd also find evidence that the general populace is beginning to be touched by the malaise, but too lightly to realize it."

She turned in her swivel chair, her back to us, as if staring out the window. "Robert," she said, "take Mr. Synko to Personnel and get him on the pay roster. And see that he's advanced some expense money; he'll need to live. Then help him find clothes and arrange quarters for him."

"Right, chief," said Glasgow, and we left. I tried to make conversation as we walked down the hall.

"She's really uptight about the malaise, isn't she?"

Glasgow stopped, his face close to mine, his eyes sober. Maybe bleak would be a better word. His voice was low. "She's scared, Synko, she's scared. We all are."

7

It felt good to get up the next morning. The night before, getting ready for bed, I'd realized my head wasn't buzzing, and I hadn't noticed my earache since, hell, since I'd slapped the whore on the side of the head. I'd only had to get up once in the night, and the eczema was a lot better, too.

So much for sympathy and poor, poor thing.

The room they'd given me was pretty good: carpet, clean white walls, everything in good shape, and an east window that let the morning sun in when I opened the drapes.

I ran water to shave and looked in the mirror. The old viz didn't look too bad at that. The nose had been broken a couple of times before; this last time had just flattened it a little more. New scar tissue, new nose, a slightly thick ear—it might not be pretty but it had style.

And I'd rented some gym clothes and a locker the evening before at the gym on the top floor, and had a little workout. It wouldn't take long to get the old bod filled back out.

The place I was in was for government workers who wanted to live there, but it was run like an apartment hotel. Instead of a dining hall with a slop line, like a college dorm, they had a restaurant and a big cafeteria. I went down to the restaurant, where there'd be a waitress to make time with.

From force of habit I sat by a window where I could see around the room. The place felt good, and it was late enough that hardly anybody was there. The government work day started at 0325—a quarter after three, they called it—and the restaurant clock read 0332. I set my new watch by it.

I was in luck; the waitress had a good build. The face wasn't bad either, especially the smile. She came over and gave me a menu.

"You're new here," she said. "Coffee?"

"Sounds good."

"Cream?"

"I'll take anything you want to let me have."

She gave a quick little grin. "Careful there. Cream?"

"That, too." I put out my hand. "My name is Steve Synko. I'm going to be a regular around here."

She shook the hand. "Glad to meet you, Mr. Synko," she said, flashing the smile again, then left without telling me her name. I watched the bob of her tail as she walked away.

I still didn't have a good feel for time here. It was 0333, and I was supposed to be in Glasgow's office, two blocks away, at 0400. But that left me sixty-seven of their minutes, so I decided I had plenty of time for bacon and eggs.

Just then a little guy came in, about five-six, rimless glasses, half bald, and paunchy. I sized him up because when his eyes had reached me they'd stopped. He changed direction and came over.

"Mr. Synko, I'm Clemen Troyer. I'm with the STB, too. Glad to have you with us. May I sit with you?"

I already didn't like him. He came across oily. "Yeah, I mind," I said. "I want to get acquainted with the waitress."

He laughed a phony laugh and sat down anyway. "I saw you with Bob Glasgow yesterday, coming out of Regina's office. What's your special talent? You're not a telepath."

"Don't have one." I was starting to get pissed: He was going to ask questions and read my mind whether I wanted to or not.

"Ah, a special *skill* then," Troyer said. "Some psis are so centered on psi talents that they forget how important special *skills* are." He gave what he thought would pass for a smile. A fly cruised over the table; I flashed out a hand and caught it.

"That's my specialty," I told him. "Killing flies. I would have shot the sonofabitch but I didn't want to make a hole in the wall."

He didn't know how to take that so he made a production out of unfolding his napkin. The waitress came over and poured my coffee, then turned to Troyer. "Coffee, Mr. Troyer?"

"Yes please, Jackie."

"But not here, Jackie," I put in. "Troyer and I aren't good enough friends yet to drink together."

Troyer blushed and stood up. "Fine, Mr. Synko; perhaps another time then."

"Yeah," I said, and poured cream in my coffee. *You snoopy little cockroach,* I added mentally. That was one nice thing about him being a telepath. He went to the other end of the room and sat down with his back to me.

He'd done one thing for me, though; he'd told me the waitress's name. Jackie looked at me with interest now. Before I left, I learned her last name, Finch, that she lived here in Howard House, that she was on the Civil Service Register waiting for a secretarial job, and no, she didn't have a special boyfriend.

I also got the impression that Troyer had pestered her for a date. She seemed like a good chick: cheerful, bright, and self-reliant.

So it was an enjoyable breakfast, and I got to Glasgow's office with three minutes to spare. You work for Don Bruno Randazzo, you get in the habit of being on time.

For the first time in this world I was riding in a car. From outside it was a boxy black, like cars you see in movies about the bootlegging days. The upholstery was fuzzy light gray, it had window curtains, and there was a little inside lamp on each door post.

Glasgow and I and two women were going to Ruth's place to question her. I'm not sure why they had me along; maybe to give me something to do. Glasgow had a folder with photographs of smaller-than-average guys between forty-five and sixty who worked for the government—maybe fifty of them—with emphasis on bachelors and STB men.

When we got there, I told Glasgow I didn't think I ought to go in, so they let me stay in the car. They were back in maybe ten minutes, and Glasgow had a pleased look. As the car started away, he reached in his folder and showed me a picture.

"This is the man," he said. "STB; a weak telepath. His real talent, such as it is, is psychokinesis. He's not very powerful, but they're as rare as. . . . You know him!"

I was looking at a photo of Clemen Troyer.

"He came up to me in the restaurant this morning," I said. "Knew my name and wanted to get acquainted." I sat and remembered it for Glasgow. His satisfied look was gone; I'd spoiled his morning. I didn't have to be a telepath to know this worried him.

I browsed through a magazine in the chief's office. Glasgow had told me it bothered her for me to think of her as "the big broad." It's always been hard for me to call most people by their first names, and even harder to use mister or miss, so I was trying to use "chief," because I liked the big broad.

When Glasgow came in, he looked grim. "Troyer's gone," he said. "He's supposed to go on shift this afternoon at 0660, but he's not in his room, his toilet gear and some of his clothes are gone, and there's no suitcase in his closet."

"Then he's blown," the chief said.

Glasgow nodded. "Probably when the malaise hit, a little after four-twenty."

"Four-twenty-one; it lasted two-point-one minutes."

These people had manners. They could have run through all that and never said a word I could hear.

"Maybe it's psis they're smuggling," I offered. "In a world like mine, someone who can read minds or see what goes on in a closed room or move the tumblers in a safe door would be worth a hell of a lot. We've got all kinds of people there who'd dig deep to hire people like that—the Syndicate, politicians, the military—anyone who wants to get richer or more powerful. People like you could name your own price."

The chief nodded. "Introducing a totally new element into a game can provide major advantages, especially so long as the other players are unaware of it."

Now there was a way of looking at it. "So," I said, "whoever it is over there that's recruiting your people has one of everything now, right? Could be they'll quit; then your problem will be over."

She looked at me. "And where would that leave you, Mr. Synko?"

"Here. If that's how it is, that's how it is. I'm getting used to it here; it's not so bad." I'd taken myself by surprise, saying that, but it was true.

"And what do we do if they continue to use the machine?"

She was asking herself as much as Glasgow and me, laying the question out to look at. It was me who picked it up.

"It seems like they—whoever *they* are—aren't likely to use it without a reason," I said. "Chances are, it affects their psis the same way it affects you.

"I think I know who's in charge there," I added. "A guy named Haslett. He was Sanberg's chief flunky, the guy who took care of arrangements and paperwork. And I doubt to beat hell that anyone outside of Sanberg's private lab even knows about the machine. It's almost got to be Haslett.

"Now, if they're done with the machine, they're done, and your problem could be over. And if they're not, why not? Who put the finger on what's-her-name? Susan. Who picked her? It had to be her friend, Gloris, who left earlier, right? So if they're still looking for talent, who'd make the choices? And who would they pick?"

The chief and Glasgow were looking at each other as if sharing thoughts, but another idea came to me and I put it out. "This Gloris—is there some guy she likes?"

The question hung there for a minute or two, and I was getting tired of being left out. Then the big broad turned to me.

"Steven, you are most astute. Our silent discussion dealt with whether or not to confide in you. A telepath, by the nature of his talent and experience, is able to shield his mind from others. Few non-telepaths can do that. To tell you what we intend is to risk its becoming known to the wrong people, and endanger its success.

"On the other hand it was you, in fact, who provided the basic idea. And you are new and interesting; certain to attract eavesdropping. In a moment of carelessness you might easily recapitulate the data or elaborate your thoughts to yourself. Some of them would almost surely recur to you, and that alone might permit a curious telepath, knowing the personnel of this branch, to guess rather closely what we intend.

"So I will tell you. Gloris had a lover, Conard Harner—a telepath, and one of our most effective operatives. Fortunately Conard was sent on a—ah—foreign assignment shortly after Gloris disappeared. A very secret assignment. We will bring Conard back, and if the time machine is used again, we shall use him to bait a trap. Not to recapture or destroy Gloris; she is welcome to choose her own world. But to destroy the time machine."

She stopped then, and they watched me with more than their eyes.

"We cannot, however, afford the risk that someone will learn this from you—someone who might be indiscreet or self-serving."

My scalp began to crawl. I didn't even have a knife.

"Relax, Synko," Glasgow said. "We just want you to submit to hypnosis—a post-hypnotic suggestion not to recall any of what we, or you, have said or thought about this, until we tell you it's okay."

The chief nodded. "I regret the necessity. We find the use of hypnosis a distasteful interference in self-determinism. But the success of this operation is enormously important to us."

8

I'd always had the idea that a Polack was supposed to be tough and strong. My old man thought so, my uncles thought so, the kids in my old neighborhood in Chicago thought so. Then we moved to Gila Bend and I'd had to prove it quite a lot, because I was the only Polack in school. But growing up strong had been easy in Gila Bend and Flagstaff. I'd worked in the fields and played sports a lot, and in the reformatory they'd worked us in the woods, thinning trees, piling logging slash, and fighting fires. After the army, I'd worked out at gyms off and on and kept in pretty decent shape.

Here I'd blown it, but the weight work would get it back—I could already see the difference in just a few days. But it had been a mistake to go jogging with Glasgow, because he ran instead of jogging. I'd almost died, and staggered in way behind, while he barely worked up a good sweat in spite of the pipe and cigars.

Today, my third run, I was keeping up, although it wasn't easy. I was a Polack and wouldn't quit. And besides, I had a date with Jackie for Sixday evening, and if I got her in the sack, I wanted to look good to her.

It happened about two blocks from Joggers' Station, the low building that held showers, dressing rooms, and steam baths for joggers and runners in River Park. For a minute I thought Glasgow had a cramp; then he seemed to recover. But when we got back to the dressing room, he stood in front of his locker with his head down, like he was sick.

"What's the matter?" I asked him. He didn't say anything, and I realized it was the malaise.

Slick with sweat, I went in the shower room. There was a guy in there about my age, and seeing him, I felt better about myself. The meat on him was pork, except for the legs.

"Jogging is hard work," he said, smiling at me.

I didn't say anything, just turned on the water. The hot spray felt good on the tired bod.

"Haven't I met you somewhere before?" he asked.

"I doubt it."

"The hospital!" he said. "That's it! You were brought in to identify Mr. Sanberg. We didn't have a name for him then, and you provided one." He put out his hand. "I'm a healer there; Walser Bunt, C.H."

I took the hand, using enough pressure to show him I could put him down if I felt like it. "Synko. Steve Synko," I said. "How's Sanberg doing?"

"Improved. Distinctly improved. He's aware now. Moves his head, takes food, and follows people with his eyes. I wouldn't be surprised to see him talking this afternoon." Bunt's voice dropped to confidential. "His progress is quite largely because of you, you know. We were having to rely totally on physicians, because a healer requires communication. But when I could finally speak to him as *Mr. Sanberg*, I began to reach him, even though only at a subconscious level at first.

"You should visit him, Mr. Synko. I'm sure he'd know you, and it would be salubrious for him to see a personal friend."

I almost laughed. Then Glasgow came in, not looking sick any longer but still down. Gabby Bunt started right in on him. "Robert! Who are you going to vote for?"

Glasgow didn't look at him when he answered, which showed he was below par. He usually looks right at you when he talks. "Guess," he said, as if Bunt ought to know and as if he didn't want conversation. Bunt took the hint, and after a minute or so left. I stayed to enjoy the hot water until Glasgow finished, and we left together.

Ordinarily we went straight to the Justice Building after dressing, and caught a snack there. Then Glasgow would go to his office and I'd hit the library. They said if I was going to be on the payroll, I'd need training, and they'd given me a list of stuff to read so I'd be ready when the next training cycle started. But today we turned into a bar, a block from the building.

I hadn't been in the place before. The sign above the door called it "The Hideaway," and with the name and narrow front, I expected it to be small. Instead it was long, and toward the rear had a wing on each side. Halfway back we passed a baby grand with nobody playing it, and it occurred to me that I'd heard practically none of their music on this world.

Glasgow picked a good-sized booth, and the waitress got there almost as soon as we did. He ordered a beer and I asked for bourbon and water. The place seemed pretty empty, but it was hard to tell how empty, because it was dark even for a bar, and the booths were partly enclosed on the fourth side, almost like little rooms, some big enough for six or eight and others hardly big enough for two.

A good place to bring Jackie, I thought. And a good place for a telepath to eavesdrop. I wondered if Glasgow ever came in to eavesdrop. The waitress brought the drinks, and Glasgow took a deep draught. When he came up for air, I grinned at him.

"That take care of what ailed you?" I asked.

"It helped. One bad thing about the malaise is," he added, lowering his voice, "it usually happens in pairs— coming and going. We'll probably get another one before the day is over, and the second usually lasts longer than the first."

That made sense, if it was due to the time door.

"It might seem odd," he continued, "but we know very little about the malaise outside Wesland. We only assume it's felt in other countries. Governments are pretty jealous of their own telepaths and hostile toward others. They don't approve of our communicating or traveling outside our own countries. If a foreign psi was discovered here in the Government District, for example, he'd be arrested on the spot."

"What then?" I asked. "Shoot him?"

"Not quite that drastic. Not in this country. But he'd be on his way back to wherever he'd come from, and he wouldn't remember anything since he was five or ten years old. The treatment doesn't do anything for the talent, either, or for the mind in general, as far as that's concerned."

He paused and looked out of the booth as if to be sure no one was listening. "Anyway, we have an operative named Conard Harner who's on a secret foreign assignment and ought to be back day after tomorrow. And one of the debriefing questions I'll be asking is whether the malaise is as intense there."

I yawned, suddenly sleepy, and took another sip of the bourbon and water. I seldom get sleepy in the middle of the day, so I figured it must be the combination of running and drinking. Right now I really wanted to take a nap; even the floor looked inviting.

Then we started talking about training, and by the time we left, my drowsiness was gone.

9

The chief said she wanted me there when she talked to Sanberg. Which was fine with me; I was curious as hell. I told her he might not be happy to see me, but she said he'd be tranquilized.

The day was about perfect, and the hospital gardens were something to see. I could get hooked on open carriages on a day like that. We pulled up at the entrance and I got out and helped Regina down.

They were expecting us this time; Bunt and a doctor were waiting for us and we went right up. They weren't all that happy when the chief made them wait outside Sanberg's room and closed the door.

Sanberg was more important now; he had his own two plainclothes guards in the room with him. They didn't look especially alert—even had books in their laps—but either one could have had a gun in his hand in plenty of time. I could recognize telepaths now; I couldn't pin it down yet, but there was something about them.

Sanberg turned his face to us when we came in. His eyes stopped on me, and after a few seconds he knew me. For a minute there he looked surprised and worried.

"Synko!" he said weakly.

"Yeah," I said, "Steve Synko. How'd you know?"

He looked blank, as if he didn't understand what I meant.

"How'd you know my name is Synko? You knew it wasn't Nevens, but how'd you know it was Synko?"

He wasn't too tranked to look sheepish. "Gloris told me. She's a telepath. She was monitoring you from the moment you walked into my place."

I looked at the chief to see if she wanted to take over, but she shook her head.

"Where am I, Synko?" Sanberg asked. "No one around here will tell me anything."

"You're on the same world where you dumped me. The same place you picked Gloris up."

"Give me a little credit, Synko," he said. "I figured that much out for myself. But where on this planet, and how did I get here?"

He was sounding stronger now, feistier than he looked. "You're in the security section of Government Hospital," I told him. "Somebody did a job on you—probably Haslett. You were drugged, probably propped up in front of the time door, and shot. Then you fell through it about eighty feet or so. Those are the bad parts. The good parts are, you caromed off a steep roof and lit in a fountain, and a clairvoyant was there waiting for you, with the fuzz and an ambulance."

He turned a little green.

"What's Gloris doing back there?" I asked. "How'd you pick her up?"

"She had a precognition that something peculiar was going to happen at a certain time and place. So she was there, and when I stepped through the penetration vertex, she sensed at once what had happened. We went back together."

"Why? Why did you go back together?"

"Because she wanted to, I guess. That's the way she is. Then afterward I got ideas about bringing in a small cadre of psis and starting a secret project to identify, recruit, and train people with psi potential, with her as

project director. Something like that could get things
moving again back there."

"But Haslett had his own ideas, right?"

He looked at that. "I expect it was Gloris. But she
probably teamed up with him on it. I suppose she did."

Sanberg lay quiet for the better part of a minute,
then added softly: "I really did plan to dismantle the
vertex generator, you know, as soon as I'd completed
my team."

I glanced at the chief again, but she didn't give any
sign, so I kept going.

"Why'd you want to dismantle it? Seems like a useful
thing to have, for dumping bodies, if nothing else."

He wasn't looking at me now, or talking, either. He
was staring off blankly toward where the wall met the
ceiling.

"Okay then," I went on, "let me guess. You were
scared of it, because time didn't turn out like you
thought it would—the whole damn universe didn't.
And that scared you. Like, here we are on another
planet, supposed to be another time, and they talk
English here, and drink bourbon, and smoke cigars.
Shook you, didn't it?"

He started swearing at me in a dull voice, the worst
things he could think of. Maybe it was my grinning that
helped him run down. After that he lay quiet. Finally
he started talking again.

"Do you know what's happening, Synko? What happens to psis when the vertex is on?"

I nodded.

"It's getting worse. And it also affects people who
aren't psychic. They're not aware of it yet, but it does. I
tested my cook, my housekeeper, and John. Then,
without telling them what the real purpose was, I had
people test others in other places while the vertex was
on. We measured brain waves, skin resistance, and
respiration, and there's no question about it: Everyone's affected."

"So what?" I asked. "As long as a telepath like your
Gloris can stand it, what harm is it to the rest of us?"

This time he lay there for three times as long before answering me. "What do you suppose it is that affects people when the vertex is on, Synko? It's fear—an unconscious sense through all mankind of something gone wrong."

He was looking at me again, his eyes intense now in spite of the tranquilizer. "You wouldn't be acquainted with Bell's Theorem or Finkelstein's work, or Birkhoff and Von Neumann's paper," he said, "but anyway, there's one thing faster than light. In fact, fast isn't the word: instantaneous repositioning is. It's a matter of. . . . One thing is outside of time, and that one thing is *awareness*. And everyone in the universe is at least unconsciously aware of it when the vertex is turned on.

"For years I've been monitoring particle fluctuations; that's what started me on the damn project. And I still do. Or did. And each time the vertex is on, while it's on, the unexplained variance increases proportional to the length of time it's left on."

Sanberg was getting tired now. His intensity was fading.

"Time isn't rectilinear," he said. "I was right about that. It's helical. Also, it's distinct from space, and it's their interface that we think of as "reality." The universe is the interface of time and space. With a disjunction field that keeps times and places apart . . ."

He let it die again; he was starting to look bad. I felt wary now; I didn't really want to know what came next.

"Yeah?" I said. "What about it?"

"The disjunction field is weakening, Synko. To put it simply, the vertex makes the universe start unraveling."

I stared at him, then looked at the chief and Glasgow, hoping Sanberg was putting me on. He wasn't. He may have been crazy—I hoped so—but he wasn't kidding. "How about between times?" I said. "When it's not on? Does the damage heal up?"

"It may. I'm not sure. The analyses are statistical, and they weren't conclusive. But as long as the machine exists, or people know about it, there's a danger that others will find out—maybe take it over, or build another."

"Gloris knows your ideas about the danger," I pointed out, "and she's a telepath. She must be as concerned about it as you are. And Haslett is no dummy."

"Haslett," Sanberg said, "is probably crazy. After he'd worked for me a while, I learned he'd once had a severe breakdown, been institutionalized for months. But he was efficient and close-mouthed, and he seemed stable, so I let it pass. A sickness cured, I thought, no problem. Now—here I am."

"Yeah," I said, "here you are." Here we all were. I turned to the chief.

She nodded. "We should let Dr. Sanberg rest," she said. "This has been a stressful interview for him."

I nodded, stood up, and took a deep breath. "Hang loose, Sanberg," I said, looking down at his pale face. "Gloris isn't a fool, and she sounds like someone who can handle Haslett. If he starts to go haywire, she'll know, and she'll know what to do."

He nodded slightly. One of the guards held the door for us and we started to leave. I was in the doorway when Sanberg called after me.

"Synko!"

I stopped and looked back. "Yeah?"

"The rate of field deterioration—the variance increase per unit of time the vertex is on . . ."

"Yeah?"

"It isn't linear, Synko, it's exponential. It deteriorates faster each time the machine is on. The more it unravels, the faster it unravels."

Then he closed his eyes, and after staring at him for a few seconds, I went on out.

That wasn't the only big thing that happened that day. I noticed a small item on the front page of the paper I bought on my way home, although I didn't know it was important.

Justice agent charged. Informed sources report that Conard Harner of the National Security Branch has been charged with espionage under the Security Secrets Act and is being held in the Justice Ministry maximum security block.

Conard Harner; that was the guy Glasgow had mentioned at *The Hideaway*. I'd thought he was in the STB, not the NSB. I wondered if Glasgow had had a chance to question him about the malaise, or whether the local version of the FBI was holding Harner incommunicado.

It didn't seem important, though. We knew the malaise story pretty completely now, from Sanberg.

10

I woke up with a start, and sat up. A line of sunlight slanted across the foot of my bed from a gap where the drapes met. I turned to look at my clock and there she was.

"Good morning, Mr. Synko."

I knew her, even though I'd never seen her before, or even a picture. Her words were calm, but her face was like my ma's when she was getting one of her migraines.

"What do you use the goddamn thing for, Gloris," I asked, "if it hurts so much?"

"Can you suggest another way?"

"Another way to what? The way I've heard it, you've already got a full set."

She held what might have been Sanberg's .32 caliber, and she'd have the skill and willingness to use it. From her strained expression, the time door was open, probably right there in the room, but there was no way she'd let me get to it.

"Not quite a full set," she said. "It lacks one piece. When I've got it, I'll be done with the machine. I'll pull the plug."

"What does the rodent think of pulling the plug? Haslett, I mean."

"I'll take care of him when the time comes. Right now I want that one piece."

"Why don't you tell that to whoever has the piece?" I said. "Maybe you could make a deal. I can't do you any good; I don't even know who the hell you're talking about."

She didn't answer, just kept looking at me, waiting for me to think of . . . whatever. "Apparently they don't confide in you, Mr. Synko," she said at last, then paused. "Or perhaps—perhaps Regina hasn't come up with anything. That's possible; I've never seen her operate under this kind of stress. It's difficult."

Abruptly she gestured toward me with the gun, and a flash of fear hit me right in the gut. "Stress like this impairs the judgment, Mr. Synko. It inclines one alternately toward despondency and reckless action. Poor Susan. . . . Right now I'm inclined to shoot someone."

She didn't, though. She just stood there as if she couldn't make up her mind. A tic started jumping in one cheek, then her eyes drilled into my skull. "Or maybe you do know," she said. "You may have been given a memory block. And this is not the place to work through it; it would take too long, even if I could do it with the goddamn vertex on. Regina has never been creative or even. . . . *On your feet, goddamn you, Synko! I'm taking you back!*"

I got out of bed, naked as a jaybird. Facing a gun, a guy feels awfully damn vulnerable with no clothes on. And I didn't want to go back—not with her. On the other side I'd live just long enough for her to sort through my skull.

So I sat back down. Stall for time. And what good would that do, when she knew every thought that came to me? The hand holding the gun was whiter than I liked to see, and her eyes blazed.

"Don't play games with me!" she snapped. "Back on your feet!"

"How do I know you won't kill me after you're through messing with my mind?"

"You don't. Now UP!"

"Lady," I said, "you don't give a guy very damn much incentive."

Her voice softened. "Synko, I'm not giving you very damned much choice."

We looked at one another for five or six seconds. Five seconds can be a long time.

"I'll count to five," she said.

At two I got up, but on the other side of the bed. Turning my back on that twitchy broad while I swung my legs around and stood up took more guts than I'd thought I had anymore. But nothing happened; no bullets burst into me. I turned to face her.

Actually, she looked startled.

"Now what?" I asked.

The gun gestured toward the middle of the room. "Over there, and turn around."

"Look, lady, are you sure you can't do what you need to right here? I'd feel a hell of a lot safer."

"Safe? Here? Synko, you've never been in more danger in your life."

That was debatable, especially looking back to the dumb seventeen-year-old trooper in Nam. But the difference was academic. "You could have them turn off the machine and work on me right here," I told her. "The room is locked, you've got a burner, and I'd be glad as hell to let you tie me up first."

"One!" she counted. "Two!"

"Jesus Christ, Gloris! You could at least let me put on my pants!"

She surprised hell out of me then: She started to laugh. It wasn't funny, and it kind of pissed me off, but it was better than hearing her count. It was kind of a deep bubbling chuckle—her eyes were still on me and her hand was steady—but it was hysterical in the sense that she couldn't stop it, and her eyes were crazy.

She was still laughing when they slammed into the door. That's when I hit the carpet.

They use strong doors here. I heard two "blams" from her .32 as I rolled under the bed, and the "boom!" of one of the big .40 caliber automatics like Glasgow carried. In a moment I heard feet enter the room, and then I could see pants legs from where I lay.

"Synko! Goddamn it, Ted, he's gone!"

"No I'm not, Glasgow, I'm under the bed."

"Well, get out of there!" He sounded mad, probably from the malaise and getting shot at. And apparently they didn't want to lose me; maybe I *did* know something and just didn't appreciate what it was.

They waited while I showered, shaved, and dressed. About halfway through shaving, my alarm clock went off, so all I'd lost was maybe fifteen minutes' sleep. Glasgow asked me questions and didn't seem too happy about the answers. My guess was that Gloris was close to figuring out something they didn't want her to know.

Glasgow had already eaten breakfast and been at his office before any of this happened. Eight to five didn't mean a thing to him when he was into something. Then one of the spotters had gone to his office with something urgent, which was unusual, because spotter pickups wouldn't normally go to him. But the guy told Glasgow it was *for* him—that was part of the read. Something was about to happen at Howard House—the guy didn't know what or in what room—and Glasgow was supposed to take care of it.

So Glasgow had grabbed Ted, and about the time they hit the sidewalk, the malaise hit. And suddenly Glasgow *knew*. Poor Ted had to bust his ass to keep up with him then.

Glasgow and Ted had coffee while I ordered breakfast; they weren't about to let me out of their sight yet. Jackie waited on us, but Glasgow's mood and the breakfast crowd didn't allow for conversation. It was just as well. Glasgow told me later that that crazy Ted had it in mind to tell her they'd just been up in my room and chased some broad out, and I'd been naked. Now how in hell could I have explained that without telling her more than I was supposed to?

I decided I'd fix that sonofabitch Ted, when I'd figured out how to surprise a telepath. Maybe slug him on the spur of the moment sometime and explain afterward. Just a good one in the gut, to help him think twice about messing with me.

The chief was as calm about Gloris's visit as she was about everything else, but she said I'd have to have a bodyguard at all times. *That* I argued about; that night was my date with Jackie. Finally she agreed that the bodyguard didn't have to be right with me, just nearby, because he'd be a telepath anyway. I wasn't too happy about that either, but as long as Jackie didn't have to know. . . . After all, I *had* damn near gotten killed that morning.

The book I got into that day really turned me on. It was *The Games Concept of Social Organization*. These people may be backward in some ways, but in sociology and that bag they made the sociologists and pols and shrinks back home look like a bunch of witch doctors. And the thing that really got me was, it was so damn obvious, yet they'd missed it all those years.

The idea is that everything people do is some kind of game, and society provides rules. There are different kinds of games, and people choose. And there's a theoretical optimum set of rules for each game. If you have rules that don't make sense for a particular game, or too many rules, the game bogs down and people get frustrated and mad. Too few rules for their game, or too many rule changes too often, and people get worried and uptight because they don't know what to expect.

And people can do a lot better job of choosing their games if they think of them as games, and they can stay looser when they play them.

Each person is born with tendencies, the book said. Back home most shrinks would fight that idea to the death, but it felt right to me. People are born favoring certain kinds of games. Then, while they're growing up, some tendencies get strengthened or weakened, and some may get added. So suppose some guy has a tendency to fight or raise hell or con people. There ought to be a game set up for him too, right? Because he'll try to play it anyway.

Although there ought to be a better place for it than the Red Quarter. In fact, there was a movement to have a separate quarter for non-violent hoods.

Back home most people don't have much of a game, because there, everybody's game is supposed to go by the same rules, whether they fit or not. Everybody's but the Syndicate's, because the Syndicate is smart enough and strong enough to make its own. Now I could see why government and school and all that crap had always turned me off: So much of it didn't make any damn sense.

And a lot of people back home figure everybody else should play *their* game, so they go around preaching or pressuring or putting announcements on the tube: Vote Democrat, go to church, don't smoke, don't drink. Join the Army! See your shrink! Use dental floss for chrissake! If you don't play my game there's something wrong with you; you'd better wise up or you're a fool, or a dead man, or a traitor, or at least your goddamn armpits will sweat! The uptight society.

And on top of that, they try to get the rules changed to favor their game and screw up everybody else's. Pass a law! *Above all, pass a law!* No wonder I used to get mad so fucking easy! I lived in a damn madhouse!

Just the idea of games had made a lot of difference here, even before they amended their constitution to build it into the system. And when a kid grows up with it, knows what the choices are, sees reasonably clean games with reasonable rules, he's a lot looser about himself and everybody else.

Now I could see something else, too, that maybe the book would get into further on: There were little games inside the big ones, like the boss game and the help-others game and the dirty bastard game and the I'm-no-good game. But here people recognize games a lot better, so it's harder to fool them.

I felt better, reading that, than I had in my whole life before. I went down to the coffee room and actually put money in the kitty before I drew my cup. It was like being liberated.

And then the place blew up, or part of it did. There was a muffled explosion and the whole place jarred, which is pretty impressive, considering it's built out of rock. Someone screamed, and I jerked my head that way, but all she'd done was spill hot coffee on herself. For a few seconds everyone just stood there, and then people started drifting into the hall, talking low but earnest, wondering what had happened.

Me, I sat down to drink my coffee. After a couple minutes, though, I got antsy and went down to the chief's, but there were enough people in her office that I didn't stand a chance, so I went back up to the library.

In a minute or two, Lila, the librarian, came in and headed straight for me.

"Did you hear what it was, Mr. Synko? An explosion in the maximum security block! They're evacuating part of the east wing until they can determine if there was any structural damage."

She whispered it to me as if it were a secret. I got the feeling that there went the old ball game, although I couldn't have told you why. It just felt that way. I shelved the book—it gets Lila uptight when I do that because she doesn't trust anybody to put them in the right place—and went back down to the second floor. There were still a couple of people standing in front of the chief's desk, so I took a chair by the wall.

They were obviously telepaths because no one was talking. It seemed funny to see them looking at one another and not saying anything. I'd been around telepaths enough by now to know they can communicate from the next office or from down the hall with the doors closed, or from across the street if they put enough intention behind it. But I also knew they liked what they called "fronting with"—physically facing the person they were communicating with.

When they left, the chief looked at me without saying anything for a minute. I waited. I figured when she did say something, she'd start by answering the questions she knew I had.

Instead she clapped her hands—one, one-two-three, one—and that took care of most of the questions, because right then I started remembering. There'd been a plan, to bait a trap with Harner. Start a rumor that he was being brought back. Accuse him of espionage and lock him in a cell, which would be the only place Gloris could get to him. Let the word out so Gloris would learn where he was.

In the maximum security block, prisoners kept their gear in small foot lockers about fifteen by twenty-five by thirty-five inches. Harner's cellmate would be a non-psi cop, a big strong sonofabitch, and beneath his skivvies and toothbrush and towel, his foot locker would be filled with high explosive set to blow on impact. When Gloris or anyone else appeared there through the vertex, the cellmate was to throw his foot locker *through the time door into Sanberg's lab*.

The cellmate couldn't be a psi, because Harner would recognize a talent and that might queer the whole thing. It had to be a non-psi, with what they call a role implant so that Harner would accept him there, and an action implant keyed hypnotically to someone coming through the time door. If it worked, no more time machine. No more Sanberg's lab. Hopefully, no one alive on the other side that knew what was going on.

Only it looked like something had gone wrong.

"You're right, Steven," the chief said, "it does not look good. Although the vertex was open at the time, I suspect that the charge blew up in the cell. Otherwise the damage should have been minor or nonexistent on this side. We'll have the picture after they dig the debris out and a sweep can look the place over."

"Yeah."

There was something else that wanted to come out, and after a few seconds it came to me. "Regina," I said, and her eyes were even more sober than usual. She saw the thing too, the thing that was bothering me, but she waited for me to ask it. It was important to know. I had a different feeling toward these people, Regina and Glasgow, than I'd ever had for anyone before, a good feeling, and this threatened it. I had to get it out and answered.

"Regina," I repeated, "the non-psi cop you had in there with Harner—did he know what he was getting into? Was he a real volunteer who knew the score, or just a patsy you had hypnotized?"

Her eyes were calm and steady on mine, but not hard at all. "He volunteered, Steven. He knew in detail what the job entailed and he knew there was a fair chance he'd be killed. But he did not have full freedom of choice, because although he agreed with complete willingness, he was hypnotized right afterward as a security measure. At that point he lost his freedom to change his mind.

"On the other hand," she added, "we chose him for the proposal because we felt certain he'd accept it without reservation."

I let that soak in for a minute. That was another game some people want—the risk-your-life-for-others game. Regina had offered to let him play and told him the conditions. He'd gone for it, and it looked like he'd lost. Or maybe, for him, that was winning.

"Thanks, Regina," I said, and left. Right then I didn't feel like studying anymore so I started for home, but on the sidewalk I changed my mind. There wasn't anything at home I wanted to do either, so I went back to the library, and after a little while got into the book again.

11

It turned out that Jackie had to work late, so we didn't get to *The Hideaway* until after nine o'clock—mid-evening. I held the door and followed her in. The hostess led us to one of the smaller booths, and now I saw why Glasgow had picked a bigger one. It was intimate, the table maybe twenty inches across. Narrow enough that you could nuzzle and touch knees at the same time.

It was too dark to read the cocktail list, even with the large print, but there was a lamp on the wall and I turned it on. Two beams of light came out to read by. When we'd decided, I turned it off again. Jackie ordered something called Island Delight; it came in a glass like a little cut-glass bowl, and if there'd been any more citrus in it, the pulp would have plugged the straw.

I had bourbon and water. Each of us tried a sip of the other's, and each of us made a face and laughed.

The piano player was something special, and so was the guy playing something deep and mellow like a small bassoon. The chick on the flute wasn't bad, either. The music was different. Not the kind of difference you get with Chinese or Hindu music; in fact, the difference didn't hit me at first. It just seemed like cool jazz. But after a couple of minutes I started to feel smoothed out. It wasn't trying to lay anything on me, any mood or anything; it just relaxed me and let me feel like I wanted to feel. Or if it was laying anything on me, it was light and easy.

"What do you call that?" I asked, thumbing toward where the musicians were.

"That number? I don't know. Nice, isn't it?"

"Is that typical music here?"

It was a dumb question. There was no way for her to know that by "here" I meant this world; she assumed I meant the club. "Could be," she said. "I've never been in here before."

We just sat and listened for a while. But like any other music, even the best, after a few minutes I put my listener on automatic and started paying attention to what was in front of me. My knees were touching Jackie's. I grinned.

"The only way we could sit much closer would be if you sat on my lap," I said.

She smiled back. "If it's too crowded for you, we can ask for a bigger booth."

"Careful," I told her, "or I'll kick you. I wasn't complaining. I like being close—in present company."

"Why, thank you, Mr. Synko, you're most kind." She bobbed her head in what did for a curtsy. "Tell me, Steve, where are you from? There's something different about you, and about the way you talk, a little accent I can't put my finger on."

I didn't know what else to say, so I told her the truth. "It's what you get growing up in a Polack neighborhood in Chicago till age ten, with a grandma in the house who doesn't speak English, and then living in Gila Bend with mostly Chicanos."

She shook her head and laughed. "I understood about eighty percent of the words and still don't know what you said."

It seemed like a good time to change the subject. "Where are you from?" I asked.

"Hah!" Her face went merry on me. "I'm a cornfed farm girl from Apple Corners."

"Apple Corners? You're putting me on!"

"No, really. I grew up two miles from Apple Corners and went to Apple Corners school where I played middle guard on the girl's poleball team. Oh! And my bull calf won the blue ribbon in the district fair when I was thirteen."

"Neat!" I said, "I didn't know I was out with a celebrity! You don't look cornfed, though."

"Thank you again, sir. But I'm a big city girl now."

"How come? I wouldn't think the boys around Apple Corners would have let you get away."

"I just wasn't a country girl at heart. I got tired of being the secretary for the Farmers' Co-op, and of everyone knowing everybody's business. So I decided to taste the life of a Government District bachelor girl."

That was the most hopeful sign yet. We talked for quite a while—a little flirting, a little semi-serious talk. It kept me on my toes, carrying on a conversation without seeming totally ignorant or getting into dangerous ground. Mainly I asked questions and listened. Meanwhile, we got to know each other, liking what we learned, the drinks helping, of course, until we were nuzzling across the table.

Onward and upward, I thought. "How about a ride in the park?" I suggested.

"Sounds nice."

So we left. The horse cabs stayed busy in the evenings, becoming mostly recreation instead of transportation. The horses' shoes were hard rubber, and their hooves sounded soft and pleasant, like the night air. River Park had a system of curving streets shadowed by trees a lot like elms and maples, and all the muggers were in the Red Quarter. Now and then we'd pass another cab, but didn't pay any attention to them; we were occupied.

Jackie wasn't strong for the coy game; it was the horse that got skittish after a little. The driver talked to it quietly, trying to smooth him out, but it kept balking and sidling. It was distracting. I didn't want to blast anyone in front of Jackie, so I just asked the driver what was wrong.

"Don't know, sir," he said. "Never had trouble with him before. Something in the air."

I looked a question at Jackie, and she nodded; we could do without a neurotic horse. So I told the cabby to take us to Howard House. When we got there I didn't ask any questions, and Jackie didn't make any suggestions; we simply went to her room and picked up where we'd left off.

But something was wrong now; she wasn't relaxed the way she'd been, and her attention kept straying. I was starting to feel pissed off, but not for long because something *was* wrong. Pretty soon she rolled away and sat up.

"I'm sorry, Steve," she said. "I don't know what's the matter with me. I was looking forward to being with you, but something's . . . I feel weird."

"Yeah," I said, "I feel it, too." I got up. "Look, I think I know what the trouble is. I'm going to the Justice Building for a while." After I'd dressed I looked down at her. "I'll try to come back, maybe around midnight, okay? Can I have a key?"

She sat there looking smooth and curved and desirable, and I didn't see how I could walk out of there yet. But it hadn't been working. She nodded, got up and gave me a key, and I left.

By the time I got to the Justice Building, the malaise was pretty thick. The night guard looked fidgety and distracted. He didn't know me, but I showed him my pass and he let me in.

I found the chief in her office. From her expression, she was in communication with other telepaths around somewhere. The malaise was riding her hard: Her face was twisted into a sort of fixed wince. She nodded, then ignored me, and I sat down on the couch. Before long, Glasgow came in and sat down beside me, looking like an Asian flu case. After a while, Regina seemed to disconnect from whatever she'd been doing.

"Ninety-six minutes," she said. "It's never been left on that long since—probably since Gloris went over."

Her words were slightly slurred. It struck me that it wasn't just strain; she'd drugged herself to hold out against it. Probably all the psis had; they'd had to.

Ninety-six minutes; that's more than two hours in home time.

"I believe it," I said. "I'm getting it, too. Not like you, but I can feel it pretty strong."

She nodded. "Apparently non-psis in general are feeling it rather strongly."

Her phone rang and she picked it up. She did a lot of listening, asking occasional questions, while my head started to ache. Finally she started giving instructions, and all of a sudden I didn't understand her anymore. I thought she'd switched to some foreign language, maybe for security, but then she hung up and turned, and she was talking the same gibberish to me.

My hair felt like glass threads standing on end and sparking with electricity, and for some reason my eyes were drawn to the motto on her wall: KEEP OUR GAMES CLEAN. Only it didn't say that now. Not to me. I couldn't read it anymore.

She stopped, peering at me intently, and I could

hear myself saying "oh God, oh God, oh God." I didn't want to lose this world, not this one. Glasgow put his arm around my shoulders, flowing strength to me, and waveringly the motto was all right again. They didn't have to ask what had happened, of course, and started talking to each other, out loud to include me in.

"Have you tried the security conference room?" Glasgow asked. "It muffles tel waves; maybe it screens against the malaise."

"It doesn't. We tried. I don't believe malaise radiates from the penetration vertex anyway. I think it's present everywhere when the disjunction field is penetrated. That would be consistent with what Dr. Sanberg said."

"And no one has any idea why it's on," Glasgow said, as a statement, not a question.

"Not on this side. We're back into another tangle of unknowns. We don't know who's in charge of it or . . . anything. But Gloris must be dead. I don't think she could . . ." Regina shook her head as if it were getting hard to think. "*God!*" she said sharply, "I wish it would *stop!*"

Glasgow pretended she hadn't said it. "Any chance the riots might spread out of the Quarter?" he asked.

"If this keeps up, yes," she answered, back in control of herself. "Bendel's called in all uniformed off-duty shifts, and Number One is bringing in the commandos. It's a matter of . . ."

I saw it happen as quickly as I felt it, their eyes changing, their faces and bodies sagging with relief. The vertex had turned off. I hadn't realized how tight they'd been stretched until the change came. After a few seconds, Glasgow looked up at the clock. "One hour, to the minute. Now what?"

"Go home," she said. "There's nothing we can do for now except rest."

One hour exactly, I thought, ten o'clock midnight. Something was fishy about that.

They both looked at me, so I went on out loud. "If someone came through to do something and left the machine on for a set time, in case they needed to get back in a hurry, wouldn't it have been for an other-world period? One of their hours, or two or whatever? Why one of yours? And synchronized with your clock!"

They were looking at each other now.

"Maybe somebody over there was using the machine for something besides traveling," I went on. "Whatever the hell that could be."

There was a little bottle shop on the ground floor of Howard House. They didn't have closing-hour laws in Deevers, but usually it closed at midnight. Tonight it was still open, and there were a couple of customers looking over the shelves. I went in.

"Glad you stayed open," I said.

The proprietor nodded. "Bad night," he answered. "Bad feel to it. People keep coming in."

I bought a bottle of red port, then went back out on the sidewalk for a minute because I could hear sirens. It sounded like all the police cars in town were out. Then I went into the lobby and felt for Jackie's key while I waited for the elevator.

I was glad I'd found her, even if the world was ending. Especially if the world was ending.

12

Before going to the library the next morning, I stopped at Glasgow's office for an update. The rioters in the Red Quarter had kept their game at home, and people all over were starting to realize that everyone everywhere had felt what they had. In several countries, rioting had spread like a gasoline fire.

The chief had been called to give an early-morning briefing to the prime minister and his cabinet.

The book I got into, when I finally did, was *A History of Civilization*, and it was more interesting than it would have been a couple of days earlier because now I could see history as sets and sequences of games—the warrior game, victim game, churchman and martyr and poor-me games, to name a few. And each game always found people who were ready to play. Someone who wants to play martyr can always find someone to play persecuter, although he may have to badger him a little to get his head chopped off or the faggots lighted.

Reading history reminded me of how languages develop, and that reminded me of how Regina's office had turned into the tower of Babel for me the night before. With that on my mind, I had a hard time studying, so I got out and took a walk around a couple of blocks. I'd just gotten back and reopened the book when some sexy chick from the secretarial pool came over to me. "Mr. Synko," she said quietly, "Lieutenant Glasgow wants to see you in his office."

I followed her into the hall, staying a couple of paces back to admire the view. It turned out I'd missed the latest. The time door had opened again for a few seconds, right in the foyer of the Justice Building. Someone had stepped through, set a tape player on the floor, turned it on, and left. Several people had actually seen it happen: A man suddenly appearing out of thin air and then disappearing.

Glasgow, tight-lipped, told me about it. "I need you to listen to it, if you know how to make it work again. It said the same thing over and over, but maybe you'll get something out of it that we didn't. After all, it is your world."

"Glasgow," I told him, "you said that like I was to blame for the goddamn place. Lay off that crap, okay?" I examined the recorder, the kind that uses the new, long-play wire cassettes, with an automatic stop after a period of no sound. I pushed *rewind*, then *eject*, turned the cassette over, closed the lid, and pushed *play*. It was no surprise that the voice was Haslett's.

"I am addressing this to the Special Talents Chief," it said. "I have control of the penetration vertex generator. I know what its operation does to psychics; I've observed it. Recently one suicided here.

"In your world you are holding someone that I want back, Miss Gloris Shelmer. If you return Miss Shelmer to me, along with three psychics of her own choosing, I will destroy the machine. That is a promise. Until you do, however, I will turn it on each night for one hour longer than on the night before, and after three nights I will simply *leave* it on."

I looked at Glasgow; I'd never seen anyone look grimmer than he did. Meanwhile, Haslett continued:

"If you agree to my terms, have Miss Shelmer and her three psychics on the roof of the Justice Building at six o'clock your time, this afternoon. They must be alone. Miss Shelmer must be armed with a submachine gun; the others must be *unarmed and naked*. I will treat ruthlessly any attempt at trickery.

"If Miss Shelmer is not there at six o'clock today, your next chance will be at the same time tomorrow. You will have subsequent chances at six o'clock on subsequent days.

"I am not a psychic; I can wait in relative comfort. You who are psychic cannot afford to wait."

There was a five-second pause, then the same spiel began again. I pushed the *stop* key. "Well," I said, "we're up Shit Creek without a paddle. Both sides are, but Haslett either doesn't see it, doesn't give a damn, or he's bluffing."

"Bluffing?"

"Sure. Consider what happened in the Red Quarter last night, or better yet, in Sorvinia. The same kinds of things must have been happening on Haslett's side. New York, London, New Delhi—hell, most of the world must have been a bitch last night. On top of which, eight or ten countries have nukes, and probably five of them have long-range missiles to deliver them anywhere in the world."

I could see I'd lost him. "A nuke," I explained, "is a bomb that can devastate a whole small country. A few thousand can kill most of the people in the world and poison most of the planet.

"And if things get too much worse than last night, people are going to do crazy things, like push the buttons that launch the missiles that carry the bombs that wipe the place out. Maybe Haslett's bright enough and sane enough to see that.

"Of course, if Sanberg's right, the whole universe could go before that happens. That's what we've got to worry about here."

Glasgow wasn't talking, just thinking.

"If we had Gloris," I went on, "we could hand her over. But it's pretty damn plain that she ended up splattered all over Harner's cell when the footlocker blew, and somehow or other, Haslett doesn't know what happened. The blast must have popped the door shut or displaced it."

I stuck him with my eyes. "You know what I think, Glasgow?"

He shook his head.

"I think you'd better get going on a Gloris Shelmer look-alike contest."

There was no possible way they could be ready by six o'clock, so it looked like the universe would have to hold together through two hours of the penetration vertex that night—going on five hours of other-side time. The chief hoped to get around that. She planned to be alone on the roof, in her skivvies to show she was unarmed and to indicate surrender, hoping to get some one-on-one communication with Haslett and stall him.

It seemed to me it might work. Haslett was the kind of guy who might be gratified by seeing someone squirm, especially a wheel like Regina. She had a story for him, about Gloris being in surgery with multiple leg fractures from trying to escape, which she'd deliver in beaten, hangdog, suck-ass tones.

Of course, Haslett might also think it would be fun to turn the screw one last time tonight.

Although I didn't know it, the broken leg story would also tie in with a plan they had for their Gloris Shelmer look-alike and the three people who'd go with her the next day.

If there was a next day.

Meanwhile, they had something useful for me to do.

I was the only one who'd seen Gloris the day before. My job was to help a police artist draw her clothes, and help a tailor choose material. That was easy. One reason I was good in my profession was that I notice and remember things.

It jarred me to see Marna, the Gloris look-alike, because she didn't look that much like her. She was roughly the same size and build, and they could easily darken and shorten the hair, but the face wasn't right. Glasgow said the facial structure was close enough, though, and makeup would help. And the girl was a psi who'd known Gloris. She'd operate under the post-hypnotic suggestion that she looked and sounded exactly like her.

And her expression would be right: pained, because the vertex would be on.

"Besides," Glasgow said, "she only has to fool him long enough to herd the others through the vertex and go over herself." And that's all he'd say about it.

I thought of asking him why they didn't bandage part of her face, too, if they were going to put a cast on her leg, but as soon as I thought of it, I knew. Put anything on her face and Haslett would be suspicious right away, while the leg cast would actually draw attention away from her face.

At 0600—midafternoon—I was with Glasgow and the artist and tailor, and I knew the minute the vertex turned on. I saw it on Glasgow quicker than I felt it myself. *Good luck, Regina,* I thought. *I love you, you big broad.* Then I added, *And you too, Glasgow, you sober, mind-reading sonofabitch, I love you, too. But don't let it go to your head.*

A little later, Regina told us that a few seconds after it turned on, she saw something in the air about fifty or sixty feet up and maybe the same distance out from where she stood. Probably a video camera with a sound pickup. After half a minute or so, something else showed, which turned out too be a bullhorn, and a man's voice demanded to know where Gloris was. Regina identified herself as the chief and made her pitch, and Haslett never answered. When she was done, the equipment simply disappeared and the vertex turned off.

No one knew whether he'd hold off on giving us two more hours of the vertex or not. I had hopes he'd want to spare Gloris the malaise.

After they got the clothes right, or right enough, I got a ride to the hospital to see Sanberg. He was no help. He was still sure that the universe was unraveling— said that Bohr had missed the point and Einstein had been right after all. It didn't mean anything to me. Sanberg could have been right for all I knew, or his clutch might have been slipping because his invention was screwing things up so bad. But that was beside the point, the point being that none of it was any help.

I explained enough to Jackie that she knew what was going on. And she believed me; there had to be some explanation for what she'd felt the night before, and for all the stuff in the newspapers that day. And we agreed that tonight a club wasn't where we wanted to be, or in bed either if the malaise returned, especially if it was worse than before.

So we walked in the park.

The weather had changed. Summers are mostly clear, with showers now and then, but from fall through spring they get spells of gray drizzly weather that can last three or four days. We were getting the first one of the fall. So we wore raincoats, and walked around slowly through the mist without saying much. When we'd pass beneath a street lamp, I could see little individual droplets in Jackie's hair where it curled out from under her hood. It gave me the tenderest damn feeling. I'd never felt anything like that before.

But my thoughts kept returning to what nine o'clock might bring. Earlier I'd wondered whether Haslett would add the extra hour on the front, but eight o'clock had passed and nothing had happened. Maybe he'd bought the chief's stall after all; the malaise couldn't be very comfortable for him either.

By 0902 we knew for sure, but this time it was a little different. I felt it as fear—fear from outside, and my own fear. By 0905 it was already worse than the night before. We'd planned to stay out in the open and walk under the sky, but by 0925 we were going through the front entrance of Howard House. It was getting to Jackie worse than to me; she looked as strained as Regina had.

And we had 175 of their king-sized minutes to wait before it would be over. I stopped at the bottle shop.

As soon as we got to her room, I opened a bottle of wine, and we sat on the sofa holding hands. It took quite a while for 0950 to get there. By that time sirens were howling again. I went to the window but couldn't see anything. At 0970 we began to hear sporadic small-arms fire from the direction of the Red Quarter.

After that the malaise changed. Gradually, sitting there, I became aware of minds whispering to me, and as I listened, my fear turned into despair. I heard them more and more clearly, whispering and babbling, wailing and sobbing and cursing, all the minds in the world— all the minds in all the worlds.

The tearless desolation that came over me was way worse than when I'd found the empty cartridge case. I had a sense of space and time starting to dissolve. My guts shriveled into a knot, like a dried-up walnut, and my bones felt as though they'd turned to dust.

Distant machine guns, and what may have been grenades, pulled me out of it. Jackie was crying, hardly making any noise, her face twisted with grief. I was vaguely surprised; grief wasn't what I felt. For me it was like being dead to a level far below death.

But I wasn't dead. I got up and moved around the room. A Polack should never give up. When I'd ridden with Boleslav the Brave, we'd. . . . We'd what? I was drunk. Hell, I didn't even know any Boleslav. And there were two empty wine bottles. I opened another, and after a little, had to go to the bathroom. When I came out, Jackie wasn't crying anymore. Her face was white, her eyes blank. The word *catatonic* came to mind. I bent over, caught my balance, and put her wine glass in her hand, closing her fingers around it. But I didn't try to fill it. She couldn't drink it anyway. So I kissed her and refilled my own.

Then I listened for the gunfire again, and it had thinned noticeably. The voices in my mind were thinning, too. It was hard not to curl up and join them. That's what the gunmen must be doing, I thought. Catatonic.

I went to the window again, where I could see the glow of fires to the northwest making the clouds a dull pink-gray through the drizzle. It was 0990. Back at the sofa I tried to pour another drink, but my hands were clumsy and I missed the glass at first, splashing wine on the rug. But I would not simply swill from the bottle. I would toast from a glass the last night in the world, the last night *of* the world. And I did, more than once.

I heard a scream that seemed to be outside my head in the street below, more a wail than a scream, but I was confused, so I sat down on the floor and tipped up the bottle after all. The last thing I remember was how hard it was getting to see. I could just make out the clock face with the hands at 1002. Then I passed out.

But there was no escape in unconsciousness. It seemed that I got up and went down the hall, and the stairs, and out into the street. Cars were floating down out of the night sky. One was a '59 Chevy convertible with fins like eyebrows over the taillights, and some punks in it wearing duck-tail haircuts, gabbling like turkeys. Joe Montoya that I used to run with in Gila Bend was with me, and that seemed strange because I'd heard he'd been killed in Laos. He was excited, and trying to tell me something, but I couldn't understand him, so we started to run down the alley, and some guys were after us. All of a sudden there was this guy up ahead on a big horse, and we were in a spotlight, and he spurred his horse right at us. He wore armor and swung a club with spikes on it, and I was yelling at Joe that we had to get out of there, but he wouldn't move. I tried to drag him, then got down on my knees and looked closely at his feet. They were cemented to the bricks! I could feel the mortar with my finger.

Then I remembered the horse and rider, and screamed, and ran and vaulted over a fence.

And there was nothing on the other side. No ground. No bottom. Emptiness.

I was pinwheeling through space, the stars slowly revolving in my field of vision. And dimming. Then abruptly they were gone. There were no more stars; nothing to look at. Just blackness. No space. No universe. No field to play on. Nothing.

So of course I wasn't falling anymore. I was just there. No, not even there, because there wasn't any "there." I just was. A big glow filled me, and I felt like . . . there are no words for it. I was immense, but without dimension.

And after "a while" I decided I'd like something to look at, so I put a star "out there." Until that moment there had been no "out there." The star shone, a point of light in blackness. Then I put another off to one side, and there was distance between them, and between them and me, which made space while their persistence made time. To keep one there while I looked at the other, I put them both on automatic.

And stars were showing up that I hadn't made, so I knew that others like me were making stars, too. We were putting the universe back. It felt great. Gradually, over some unmeasured time that could have been minutes or eons if it had made any difference, space filled with stars again, thousands of billions of them. I swelled with watching, and with a knowledge of beauty and power. Then we put it all on automatic.

And I was walking in the street, the clouds gone, the stars glittering and laughing. There was a scattering of other people too, walking around, and we grinned and glowed at one another. It was only 1009 by the big clock on the corner, but there was no more malaise. Of course there wasn't. And there wasn't a shot to be heard, or any fire glow in the sky.

We hadn't put *everything* back.

Then I put myself back upstairs. Jackie's empty body lay on the floor, eyes closed, relaxed and peaceful. I sat down beside it to wait for her.

13

I woke up when the sun was just rising, rising on the cleanest-feeling day I'd ever known. There was no hangover, no empty bottles, no wine spills—nothing like that. I got around quietly, and when I'd showered, I kissed Jackie awake. She woke up pretty and sweet as I could have wished, and pulled me back into bed.

Afterwards we showered together, my second of the morning, and I asked her what she thought of the night before. And either I was crazy or she had a whole set of artificial memories, with no malaise included.

Even more interesting, it was all right with me either way; I'd never been so agreeable before in my life. But I was curious about which way it was.

We went downstairs to the dining room together, but Jackie had to work, so I sat down to eat alone. It was early enough that I was almost the only customer. But while I was looking at a menu, this heavyset guy came over and asked if he could join me—said he didn't feel like eating by himself. I told him sure. It turned out he was the fiscal director of the National Coal Board, a pretty damn high post, and he lived in one of the penthouse apartments.

His memory of the night before included supper out with his wife, and a concert at Symphony Hall. He was amazingly friendly for a big wheel, and pleased as could be when he found out he was eating with someone from STB. He didn't even seem disappointed that I wasn't a psi. He said he hoped we'd have breakfast together again sometime soon.

By the time I left, the dining room was filling up, and

everyone was acting friendly as hell to everyone. It was the same thing on the sidewalk as I went to the Justice Building; people were smiling and nodding to whoever they passed.

It was well before the start of the official workday when I arrived at Glasgow's office. He wasn't there, but his sweater was hanging on its hook so I figured he was around somewhere.

And next to his bookcase was the tape recorder— something they hadn't gotten around to inventing here— the same one I'd listened to the day before. I stashed it behind a file cabinet in the corner, then went to Regina's office, where I found the two of them drinking coffee.

I could hardly believe how she looked: probably sixty pounds lighter than I remembered. But her clothes fitted. If she'd changed, they must have, too. The first thing I did was ask how they'd enjoyed last evening. Regina said she'd gone to bed early to catch up on her sleep. Glasgow had gone to the same concert that my breakfast partner had.

Glasgow, allowing himself a peek into my mind, winked at me then and said that must have been some dream—that he was glad he didn't have nightmares. "Probably your guilty conscience," he'd added, chuckling.

It turned out that old "work is all" Glasgow had just come in to Regina's to check on whether it was all right to take a day's leave and go fishing.

"I didn't realize you were a fisherman," Regina said.

He chuckled again. "I haven't fished since I was a kid. But it seems like a good day to go down to one of the fishing piers and rent some tackle."

Of course she said okay, and he and I left together, he to get his sweater while I headed for the library. But as soon as I figured he was gone, I went back to his office and sat down with the recorder. I felt pretty sure now that I wasn't crazy, but I suppose that's not uncommon among the insane. While the cassette rewound, I wondered if just possibly it was an illusion and that I actually held a dictionary or briefcase in my lap. Then I pushed *play*, and there was Haslett's voice, the same voice with the same message.

I wouldn't have thought Regina could walk so quietly. But after the second repeat of Haslett's message, her voice spoke behind me.

"I'm glad I'm not the only one who remembers," she said. "I was beginning to wonder about my sanity." She gestured at the recorder. "I hadn't thought to look for that."

We put it in a little vault in her office and went out to a coffee shop, where we took a corner booth and talked. The unthinkably horrible had happened—Sanberg's time machine had unraveled the universe—and the results looked excellent. Certainly better than if the plan had worked that she told me about.

"All of us who were going through the vertex were to take a drug to kill the gagging reflex. Then we were each going to swallow a slender rubber balloon of nitroglycerin just before the pickup. Marna's cast"—she smiled in recollection—"was to be about ten pounds of the same stuff we had in Harner's cell, and she'd have a briefcase full of it, too. It's relatively stable, normally, but our explosives people assured me that our nitro blasts would detonate it. Marna was to spray us in the belly with her .40 caliber submachine gun as soon as we got on the other side. Human blasting caps!"

We sat there for a minute admiring the preposterous ingenuity of it. But that was the past. Next we looked to the future.

And the first thing that struck me was that Sanberg would remember, too. I had no objective reason to think so, but it just seemed like he would. So Regina and I took a horse cab to the hospital, where we found him shooting dice with his guards. He'd tried to get Regina at her office, to get him out of there, because, he said, he was healthy as a horse. But she'd already left.

He was feeling as bright and cheerful as everyone else I'd seen, but his watchful eyes told me he remembered, all right. And was keeping it to himself like we had.

After we got him out, we formed a secret alliance of three in this clean and happy world. Three but expandable, with room for others like us, and for Jackie and Glasgow if they're interested.

It doesn't feel like there's any present use for police, so Regina is looking at creating new games for special talents. Meanwhile, she'll use her telepathy to watch for anyone else who remembers, and Sanberg will invent whatever appeals to him, while I'll be the legman and the caretaker of the recorder, the only objective evidence we have of what happened.

And Sanberg and I are going to play with the puzzle of how we knew the language here so well that we thought it was our own. Play with it just for the hell of it. It's probably connected with the role of subjectivity in the universe.

Right now I'm about done recording my memoirs on the five-hour cassette, following Haslett's message. Meanwhile, Sanberg's going to reinvent the AC/DC converter so we can recharge the power cell.

Not that's it's important to save our ties to the past. It's not. Matter of fact, after what we did last night, the whole idea of importance has changed for anyone who remembers, and it seems like for everyone else too, even if they don't remember.

And meanwhile, who knows what Sanberg will come up with one of these days?

EN ROUTE

Where John Dalmas wrote of shifting realities with the observer providing the baseline of stability, relative newcomer Elaine Radford uses *reality* as the baseline against which she measures perception. Her assessment of "Better Living Through Chemistry" would have been grimmest heresy not so long ago . . .

EN ROUTE

Elaine Radford

Everyone agreed that the first solar exposition was going to be a colossal flop, and he knew they were right; grand-scale works flop as a matter of course—it's expected of them. Nevertheless, born sucker for fine advertising that he was—once, in a fit of enthusiasm after viewing a clip of the cratered wreck of the western United States, having listened intently to the caressable voice-over informing him that somewhere there are *still* barbarians who don't offer a certain brand of curacao after dinner, he'd vowed to restrict his drinking to that liqueur for life, an oath he'd never seen fit to forswear—as suddenly as that, he'd punched in the code for a ticket to the outer system, a tedious three-month voyage, his only salvation from the worst of the boredom the fact that money was really no object.

"I never get tired of looking at it." It was the well-endowed blonde who'd interrupted his thoughts, and he was marginally less irritated than he might have been.

"Tired of what?" he asked, then realized she must be referring to the receding Earth, the giant live video that the group was nominally watching.

She blushed horribly, as if she rather than he had adroitly slipped foot into mouth, and he wondered if she might be suffering an adverse reaction to a drug.

213

But before he could fumble out his concern, she skipped away to converse politely with another. Only then did he understand that she must be part of the crew.

"I never get tired of looking at it." Her throaty voice wafted over to him clearly, despite its sweet low cadence, and he saw that those words constituted the opening lines of a set performance.

At dinner, the nameplates segregated the passengers by class and status much to Marshall Thurston's satisfaction. An extreme example of the idle rich, dilettante heir to an organized crime fortune, he was gratified if not surprised to find himself assigned to the captain's table. His family took just pride in being among the first blacks to ascend to the stratosphere of a certain nameless network whose roots stretched back to the dim fastnesses of the nineteenth century. It was only proper that Thurston be seated on the captain's right.

What was not proper, what was disturbing even, was the fact that the captain turned out to be the very blushing blonde who'd spoken to him in the vid-screen room. Surely there must be some mistake. . . ? Shouldn't she have been operating the ship—or at least pretending to—during takeoff?

She laughed at his consternation. "Reality, Marshall. Why have computers if I've got to launch the damn thing?"

"Why have a live crew if the comps do it all?" He grumbled, not liking her easy familiarity with his personal name.

"Oh, that's right, I remember your file. You've never traveled out of the Earth-Luna sector before. You're a virgin." She shaped her pink face into the image of artificial cheer; he was reminded of plastic flowers. "We'll have to make this one special for you."

There was no reply to such an announcement that wouldn't sound irremediably adolescent, so Thurston sank back in his chair and sipped moodily at his curacao.

It could be a long three months.

*   *   *

At the after-dinner ball, he'd been kindly rejected by three of the most attractive passengers and was just beginning to see that cruise ship populations have less in common with his usual circles than he might have wished. Both were groups of wealthy people, but there the similarity ended. In Atlanta he hobnobbed with the sophisticated, the educated, the artistic. Here he found himself cast adrift among honeymooners too cuddlesome to want a third and aged crones whose libidos hadn't the grace to expire with their partners. (He unthinkingly resented the old woman; their lightly patterned faces cruelly reminded him that thus far, life extension techniques were really successful for females only. All the vid-screen propaganda in the world couldn't convince him to seek diversion in their ranks.)

Then, as he swung toward the apogee of despair, one of the crew noticed his distress and waltzed into his arms. A statuesque amazon, native African judging by the depth of her skin color, she revealed that she was the *Cuvier*'s midshipperson. When he'd rotated around the room with her long enough to digest this information, he realized he wasn't sure why the ship needed a midshipperson or even what one was, but it seemed a bit late to inquire. He felt obliged to shake her off, in hopes of turning up someone he was more comfortable talking to.

"Looking for me?" A soft sensual hiccup of a greeting. The captain.

"Perhaps."

She blushed. This time irritation choked his concern. "You should see the pusher about that."

"What?" She reddened even further, although he'd not have thought it possible. "Oh, you mean the way I—" She giggled like a honeymooner. "It isn't allowed, you know. One of the liner's big points is the all-natural human crew, untreated by mood-enhancing drugs. No robots, no chemicals, the whole organic service bit. You must know this, didn't you scan the ad? Oh dear, I'm running on again, aren't I?"

He resisted the urge to point out that "running on,"

too, is curable. Certainly, he'd been informed of the crew's unusual status; indeed, he'd been required to sign a form releasing the liner corporation from any responsibility for psych damage due to associating with non-optimized personnel . . . But of course his peers and his sense of adventure assured him that organic was the only way to go. After all, where else but in space could one enjoy the droll antics of the natural human? (One could hardly allow the untreated, no matter how amusing or well-championed by dissident elements, free run of a fragile planetary surface!) But this uncontrolled blushing, this marring of physical perfection in the name of psychological verisimilitude—he hadn't expected that.

"Surely blood rushing to your cheeks is a physical problem," he said. "I can't see why they'd object to your having that treated."

"Well, they do, it's in the contract. Actually, what it is, assertron is the cure and of course that also ups your self-esteem . . . not very interesting for the gossipy old ladies if the crew is all imperturbable, now is it?"

"I suppose not." He wondered if she classed him as a gossipy old lady. Perhaps all passengers fell into that category. "Must be kind of rough on you, though."

She shrugged. "Oh, everyone thinks so, clucking all over you like you're at *such* a disadvantage . . . but drug freedom isn't so bad. You get used to it, like anything. It's actually kind of fun after a while . . . everything's so intense, multiplied a thousandfold."

She'd probably delivered that spiel a million times. Call it permission not to feel guilty for being one of the people whose dollars required this sacrifice.

Abruptly he was seized with the need to convince her that he was different—more cultured, more sensitive than the usual run of cruise passenger. "Would you like to join me in my cabin for a drink?"

"Sure."

Later, he'd be stung to learn that she'd gone with him only because it was part of the job.

*   *   *

When he opened his eyes the next morning, Sapphire had vanished, leaving only a wrinkled spot in the center of the bed to mark the place where she had slept. Against his will, he felt a certain amount of pride; though common sense told him the captain must sleep somewhere at night, it struck him as rather a conquest that he'd managed to net her first. Perhaps, as a natural, she'd been able to easily intuit that he was more sophisticated (why be modest in the privacy of one's own thoughts?) than the average human.

But this was letting fantasy run away with him. Research denied the vulgar myth that naturals could be somehow more adept at grasping the reality of things. After all, weren't chemicals part of the reality? Meditating thus, he took out his morning bottles and swallowed a personalized assortment of tablets.

"Marshall . . ." A throaty voice from the comp console breathed his name.

He hunkered over the grid, punched an order, waited for the rest of the message. "If you're up before eleven, buzz me in my quarters, and we'll see about breakfast together."

Presumptuous. Almost, he was tempted not to call. But thoughts of the geriatric passengers moved his finger forward before he'd had a chance to strengthen his resolve, remind himself it wouldn't do to get too familiar with the help.

"Sapphire?"

A dark face bobbed up briefly on the screen and danced away. "Hold on."

He held. After a moment, the blonde captain swam into view. "Morning, Marshall," she said cheerfully.

"You left a message about breakfast?"

"Champagne and eggs benedict in my private quarters. What do you say?"

"I only drink curacao."

"Spoilsport."

"I'll be there in ten minutes."

"Great!" Her enthusiasm flamed her pale skin. He began to see the advantage of having a natural.

*   *   *

"Who was that in your room?" he asked, probing, over real hen's eggs perched on a thick grainy bun, the whole drowning in a viscous sauce.

"Mary," she said curtly.

"You could just say it's none of my business."

She walked her left hand around the tabletop to her glass of champagne. "No, I can't, no assertron." She smiled ruefully.

He couldn't help observing that the liner company might have chosen a more psychologically resilient staff, if they meant for their crews to do without medication.

"Oh, silly, no. I keep forgetting it's your first trip. Nobody really catches on till they've been out in the system a while. It's boring out there, the planets few and far between, you know? The whole point of us being natural is so the passengers can have fun diagnosing all our little hang-ups and stuff." She could hardly spear her next bite of food, so shaken was she with her ill-concealed amusement.

"That wasn't in the ad."

"It's the sort of thing that, um, goes without saying."

"Should you be telling me this?"

"Of course!" She tilted her glass at him, a tipsy salute. "Indiscretion is part of our charm."

Predictable as the question was, he had to ask how she'd gotten into this line of work.

"Oh, you know, the usual story. Too much video when I was a kid. I wanted to be an asteroid miner, but I flunked out of school. I don't have much of a head for math, so it was unskilled labor all the way for little old me . . . lucky thing, the liner needed people, and at least it involved free travel in space." She grinned, amazed but clearly not that unhappy with the way her life had turned out. "If I'd had any idea of how little excitement there is out here!"

"You'd have done something else?"

"I'd have missed a plush job." She giggled enticingly.

He wasn't taken in. Sure, a plush job. A plush job with psychological hazard pay. What did this act cost her? He spooned a large untidy glop of sauce over the last of his egg, suddenly restless. "Think I'll go see what's on the vid." He hadn't known he meant to leave until he was going.

She watched him walk away with neutral eyes. What had he expected? He was just a client, just a john.

His mood called for a trip to the pusher.

Out beyond Mars, Thurston started to hunger for stimulation. Somehow he'd expected to see asteroids and robo-ships out every vid-port, but the reality of space was considerably duller than its media counterpart. Once and once only, he thought he'd glimpsed a sizable chunk of rock in an extreme corner of the big screen, but no one else looked in time and Sapphire assured him it was probably his imagination. Finally he resigned himself to the prosaic fact that the cosmic void was merely an exotic backdrop for the unfolding of the psychological drama aboard the *Cuvier*.

Fine entertainment it was, actually. Thurston never ceased to be astonished by the intensity the crew brought to interpersonal interaction. The word love hung in the air like a stale perfume, and emotional extremes were the order of the day. Everywhere he looked he could see broken romance, unsuitable menages, desperate promiscuity, constricted sexuality. Amusing. But the most incredible thing, the thing that made the expense of the journey all worthwhile, was the remarkable professionalism with which the naturals approached their affairs.

How did they manage to maintain their furious serious air in face of the fact that they were actors in a metallic theater of the absurd, allowing themselves to be buffeted by emotional storms that could be settled in an instant by a judicious mixture of the proper chemicals? Thurston kept doubting their sincerity, kept hunting for the muffled snicker, but again and again found only the bawdy laugh pasted awkwardly across a stifled sob.

An excellent crew, overall.

Sapphire herself laughed (giggled, really) constantly, as if to conceal a secret sorrow. Although he didn't completely like her, Thurston was fascinated by the way she seemed driven to dance in and out of his sphere like an unformed thought. Her voice whispering his name was everywhere, homing in on every frequency, singing out from every speaker. Even when she'd skidded away toward another, she experienced some mad compulsion to keep in touch. Nights after she slept with someone else she became especially insistent on breakfasting with him. Touching, really.

On one such occasion, she spilled a drop of his precious curacao and smiled unexpectedly when he failed to scold her. "Reality, I do believe you're starting to care for me."

"There's a cure for that."

"If you take it." A challenge in the guise of flirtation.

"Why wouldn't I take it?"

"For the experience?"

An ersatz experience, on the level of that of vacationers who camped out in wilderness areas and played at being savages. But he couldn't tell her that, wasn't cruel enough to point out the falseness of her existence. An appropriate degree of compassion, too, could be parceled out in measured doses.

"Marshall . . . ?" Her tentative huskiness cut through the sweetness of the honey poured across his whole wheat pancakes.

"Yes, Sapphire?"

"Have you ever considered . . ."

"The drug-free life, you mean?" He laced his words with a subtle sardonicism he liked to think native to his personality.

"Well, yes."

Logic was a green pill, about the size of a child's thumbnail. "Have you ever considered restricting yourself to traveling in automobiles and airplanes?"

"Of course not, but—"

"Same principle."

She wrinkled her pink nose at him. "Just for a day or two?"

"I think not."

"What are you afraid of?" The emphasis with which she spoke stained her cheeks; the matter was important to her.

But of course he feared nothing. He sighed. "I'm not much for games," he said at length.

In free fall about Ganymede, Sapphire rolled off her skintights right out in front of everyone, grabbed Thurston by the hand, and with a strong push-away from the bulkhead, dragged him through the air to the vid-screen room.

One by one and two by two, the others drifted after them, until they comprised a naked, self-conscious party cavorting under the close-up of the Jovian satellite. Thurston felt keenly unreal, as if he were doing this only so that he could say later: at Ganymede, we held this big spontaneous orgy under the yellow moon . . . Popping a relaxant, he wondered idly how many blues the pusher would dispense that day.

"Marshall, honey, is something wrong?" Sapphire's worry poked at the edges of his quieting mind.

"No."

"I saw you take a pill—" Her voice trailed off uncertainly.

"Relax, Sapph, it's nothing, just that time of day for me."

"Oh."

They clung together to a slim brass bar while the nude ballet twirled before them. Couples flailed the air with their thrashing limbs, propelling themselves into others, colliding easily with good-natured curses.

Thurston felt no desire to join them. If he'd wanted such desire, an aphrodisiac would have been simple enough. But he didn't.

"All right, damn you, I'll try it!" he shouted, having already skipped the morning's dosage to celebrate his disappointment; the word on Ganymede was that the exposition was more of a flop than even a solar-sized event had any right to be. Faced with the prospect of a wasted trip, his expensive outer system voyage reduced to sad anecdote (we went all this way and the damn fair was shut down), he felt reckless enough to dare the unthinkable.

"Well, good . . ." She shrugged slightly, an apology for the tentative flavor of her enthusiasm.

He was deflated. "That's what you wanted, isn't it?"

"Well, yes, of course. I think it's wonderful." And she smiled broadly, a plastic curve as pink as a blood-soaked bandage. "Really, it's just what I wanted."

"There's no pleasing you naturals."

"I said, it's wonderful. Great."

As the day went on, his resolve weakened. His head ached, his vision swam, and his stomach churned, but the physical upset was merest nuisance compared to the psychological firestorm. For the first time, he allowed disagreeable sensations to fester within, untreated. It was horrible, unspeakable. And from what he understood, doubt that one was doing the right thing was far from the most unpleasant feeling the drug-free human was capable of experiencing.

Over a light supper spoiled by intestinal guerrilla warfare, Sapphire batted her eyes at some green-haired old bat seated two tables down. Thurston felt the blood pounding in his forehead as he deliberately lowered his fork to his plate with a threatening clink.

"Why are you acting like this?" he asked.

"Like what?" Her wide blue eyes shimmered with false innocence as she looked at him head-on for the first time all evening.

"I'm doing what you wanted, what more do you want?"

She exhaled sharply. "I don't want anything from you," she replied slowly, shaping the words into hard little bullets. "Nothing at all."

The heart, the blood, the thumping, the thumping, the thumping. For an instant he thought he was having some kind of attack. But of course it was only an emotion. Which? He slipped one on for size, an experiment. "Can't you see that I'm trying to show I care about you? Why else put myself through this?"

"You care for me, do you?" Contempt resonated throughout her throaty vowels.

"I—" Why play at all if afraid to gamble? "I love you."

She rose from her seat with a clumsy jerk, her cheeks aglow. "There's a pill for that," she said. "When it hurts too much, you'll take it."

And she was gone.

WELCOME TO BEAUTIFUL ARIEL, GATEWAY TO THE OUTER SYSTEM. Thanks to the generosity of the exposition backers, this most unimpressive moon of Uranus now boasted a flashing satellite sign some thirty kilometers across, quite the tackiest thing Thurston had ever seen. He smiled as he noticed a small jet flare from its side; apparently, its orbit was less than stable.

Sapphire, who'd crowded into the vid-screen room along with everyone else as they neared their destination, flushed pink to her décolletage in her excitement. "Got the sign up, anyway," she said. "Maybe it all got thrown together at the last minute."

"That's traditional, honey," one of the older women said. "Or at least it was when they were still world's fairs."

Thurston examined their little group: Sapphire, her latest old woman, the old woman's gigolo. And how long will that cozy situation last? he thought, not vindictively, his latest prescription having removed the need for anger. Still. Maybe the mix was off a bit, for his heart ached faintly, just enough to assert its existence. He'd have to see the pusher again.

"Look! Look!" the captain cried.

Everyone looked. Thurston could have laughed aloud. The theme of the exposition, "Concepts of the Future," was supposed to have been highlighted by a pocket

Dyson sphere formed around an asteroid-sized "star," really a controlled fusion furnace. But someone had run out of funding somewhere.

Instead of a great all-enclosing sphere encircling the hollowed-out planetoid, the ship was approaching a dark chunk of rock wearing a geodesic hemisphere like an overgrown umbrella. The slender struts connecting the inner surface of the incomplete sphere to the outer surface of the "star" winked plainly in the pale light of the faraway sun, emphasizing the embarrassing fact that the shell would never have remained in stable orbit about the asteroid anyway, not without human assistance.

Thurston turned away abruptly, but the afterimage of the grandiose failure stayed with him, odd emblem of undreamt-of strivings. Time for a blue.

I've come all this way for nothing, he thought mechanically. Why, I should demand a refund.

Laughter rumbled behind him. He wasn't ready to look; he'd paid handsomely to visit this stellar mistake. Still the others were laughing . . . in a moment, he'd join them.

But his hands closed convulsively, inadvertently bending the plastic capsule backwards and flipping it open, spilling minute multi-colored beads across the carpet.

Well, the pusher would be glad to sell him some more.

Behind him Sapphire was laughing, her deep voice an earthquake rumble. He paused.

He would salvage something from this expedition. Yes.

Behind, Sapphire was laughing.

He balled his hands into two dark fists, although of course he wasn't yet at the point where he could really feel his determination. That would take a while, for his system needed time to clear itself of chemicals. But he knew he'd succeed, he'd already made up his mind; he would love her.

Whether she trusted him or not.

THE LEADING EDGE

Roland J. Green

Gene Wolfe, **FREE LIVE FREE.** Tor Books, 1985. $16.95.

Janet Morris, **BEYOND SANCTUARY.** Baen Books, 1985. $15.95.

———, **BEYOND THE VEIL.** Baen Books, 1985. $15.95.

———, **BEYOND WIZARDWALL.** Baen Books, 1986. $15.95.

Paul Preuss, **HUMAN ERROR.** Tor Books, 1985. $14.95.

Anne McCaffrey, **KILLASHANDRA.** Del Rey/Ballantine Books, 1985. $16.95

David Brin, **THE POSTMAN.** Bantam Spectra, 1985. $15.95.

Edward F. Hughes, **THE LONG MYND.** Baen Books, 1985, $2.95 paperback.

Ursula K. LeGuin, **ALWAYS COMING HOME.**
Harper & Row, 1985. $25.00 trade paperback.

Harlan Ellison (Editor), **MEDEA: HARLAN'S
WORLD.** Bantam Spectra, 1985. $10.95 trade paper-
back.

Brian Stableford and David Langford, **THE THIRD
MILLENNIUM.** Alfred A. Knopf, 1985. $13.95 trade
paperback.

Joseph P. Allen with Russell Martin, **ENTERING
SPACE.** Stewart, Tabori, and Chang, 1984. $24.95
1986 trade paperback $17.95.

The average sf writer is wise to make novels compar-
atively easy to follow. A reader who by Chapter Four
has lost track of who is doing what to whom and why is
apt to stop caring by Chapter Seven and stop reading
by Chapter Nine. Some sf writers still choose to culti-
vate what appears to be incomprehensibility for its own
sake. They do so at their own risk, lacking as they do an
important ally of the mainstream writer who wishes to
be similarly self-indulgent: the critical establishment
which may intimidate a reader into confusing incomprehensibility with art.

Gene Wolfe and Janet Morris are two sf writers who
occasionally fail to be completely comprehensible, but
without hiding their art or losing their readers. Both
achieve fine results by sheer fertility of imagination and
splendor of language, reaching their high points in Wolfe's
BOOK OF THE NEW SUN (Pocket Books) and Mor-
ris's DREAMDANCER trilogy (Berkley).

Their most recent works are on a slightly less majestic
scale. Wolfe's **FREE LIVE FREE** begins with elderly
Ben Free inviting people to take free lodging in his
equally elderly house, condemned to make way for a
freeway ramp.

Four oddly assorted people accept this invitation.
Madame Serpentina, a gypsy fortune-teller, uses a com-

puter to cast her spells. Candy Garth, an overweight
prostitute, has a heart that is at least silver-plated.
Ozzie Barnes is a divorced, undersized, and unsuccess-
ful salesman. Jim Stuff is an even less successful private
investigator.

The book takes them through a series of increasingly
bizarre adventures in a winterbound Midwestern city
that has a strong flavor of Chicago (at least to this
twenty-year Chicagoan). No summary can really do justice to these adventures, but it's fair to wager that readers
will keep going because the characters have caught
their interest. It won't be just Ben Free and his quartet, either; there is Sergeant Proudy with his obses-
sions, Mrs. Baker, always ready with the wrong word in
season, and a dozen others.

Eventually the quartet learns that Ben Free is associated with a secret government project going back to World
War II. He himself goes back a good deal further, since
he happens to possess a portable time machine. . . .

It would be easy to say that only Gene Wolfe could
bring off something like this, if Janet Morris hadn't
done very nearly as well with a fantasy trilogy. This
trilogy is the first published spin-off work from the Father
of Shared-World Anthologies, THIEVES' WORLD (Ace).
In devising Sanctuary, Bob Asprin built the proverbial
better mousetrap, and so far the world seems to be
doing a remarkably good imitation of beating a path to
his door (or at least the nearest newsstand). An array of
fine writers has been keeping the mousetrap well oiled,
and Janet Morris has been prominent among them.

The protagonist of the **BEYOND** trilogy is Tempus,
the warrior demigod laboring under the curse of the
storm god Vashanka. It is his curse to destroy any
person who loves him and to be hated by anyone he
loves. Meanwhile, he must lead his Sacred Band (a
force of bonded pairs, like the Theban elite warriors of
the same name) in battle against the Rankan Empire's
great enemies, the Mygdonians.

Morris has peopled the trilogy with a splendid cast of
characters. There is Tempus's sister, Cime the mage-

killer; Roxane, the Nisibisi witch; Nikodemos (war name, Stealth), the tormented young adept and warrior torn between his vows to the Sacred Band and a desire to return to his youthful home; Jihan, a Frost Daughter and Tempus's mistress; and Kama, Tempus's daughter and a member of the Rankan Third Commando, one of the few outfits that can plausibly claim to be as tough as the Sacred Band. There is also a profusion of vividly-drawn cities, camps, houses of varying repute, battles, and brawls, not to mention a daunting profusion of gods and other supernatural beings less easy to classify, none of whom one would really care to meet in a dark temple.

The thread of the story is Tempus's efforts to make his peace with the gods and his own limitations. By the time he succeeds, the number of subplots and fascinating secondary characters may have frayed that thread for some readers. They will still be reading, though, because Morris has done a superb job of making readers what to know *what happens next*.

A book with that virtue will be forgiven many other faults. A book without it will be forgiven very few.

Both Paul Preuss and Anne McCaffrey have composed effective new variations on old themes. With Preuss, it is the old novel of scientific speculation: "What would happen to society if Science/Technology X led to Development Y?" McCaffrey has done a straight-forward space adventure, but with a female protagonist.

Preuss combines computers with gene-tailoring biology. An advanced computer is put on the market, using a tailored virus called Epicell that acts as a self-programming, adaptable chip. Unfortunately, Epicell also tends to infect the computer's users and continue its process of adaptation and growth in a living host.

The first victim is Epicell's developer, Adrian Storey. Adrian dies from Epicell's bungled efforts to cope with its new environment. If Storey's colleague Tony Bridgeman and his lover, psychiatrist Joana Davies, can't communicate with Epicell, it will become a worldwide plague. If they succeed, it may open the door to a new generation of human beings, minds and bodies enhanced by their Epicell symbiotes.

The book moves along as briskly as any thriller, without sacrificing depth of characterization. Preuss has also done a solid job of portraying near-future California and the atmosphere of the computer industry, including its less than scrupulous wheeler-dealers and eccentrics. **HUMAN ERROR** generally invites comparison to the work of Gregory Benford; while Preuss isn't quite up to that very high level yet, he is growing impressively with each book.

The McCaffrey is a sequel to CRYSTAL SINGER (Del Rey). Killashandra Ree must take a vacation from the crystal-mining planet of Ballybran for the sake of her health—and from her lover, the head of the crystal singers' guild, for the sake of *his* health. She travels to the planet Optheria, a "natural" Utopia where the unwillingness of the citizens to leave their planet is beginning to raise eyebrows in the interstellar government.

Killashandra quickly discovers that the suspicions are entirely justified. Except for the despised "Islanders," living a Polynesian-style existence, the Optherians are being kept docile through subliminal conditioning by the music of the planet's famous organs. Killashandra survives a number of well-handled adventures to find an odd assortment of allies. With their aid she brings down the Optherian regime, while one of them, Lars Dahl, becomes her new lover.

McCaffrey remains a good plain cook as a stylist. She also falls into a common error in postulating that a stable interstellar economy could remain dependent on the crystals for as long as she seems to imply. Whether introduced for didactic intent or out of ignorance, the "one key substance" is seldom a recipe for long-term economic stability. Ask any Arab oil sheik or gas-station owner.

It could also be argued that McCaffrey devotes too much time to the sexual chemistry between Killashandra and her lovers. Certainly there's enough of it so that the book has been reviewed in all the romance-fan publications. On the other hand, sexual chemistry that isn't endowed with some Profound Significance or dragged in for titillation is still sufficiently rare in sf and fantasy for my own vote to go with McCaffrey.

More variations on a theme, this time the world after the holocaust.

David Brin has done what is probably the most original post-holocaust novel of the decade. **THE POSTMAN** begins sixteen years after a war that the United States technically "won." Survivor Gordon Krantz is fleeing toward the Pacific Northwest from a Midwest desolated by nuclear winter. He stumbles on an old Postal Service jeep with the body of its driver still at the wheel. Since he has been robbed of his own clothing, he takes the dead postman's uniform and mail sack.

At the next village, he is mistaken for a real postman, sent by a "Restored United States" to reopen communications among the scattered communities of survivors. Krantz realizes that playing up to this role and spreading the myth that the country is on the way back can give hope to people who have lived half a generation without it. As he moves on, his lies become more audacious—and more effective.

His greatest challenge comes from fascist "survivalists" who are trying to turn Oregon into a feudal kingdom. Krantz and his allies (who include a band of Amazons dedicated to weeding out the bullies from the male half of the population) eventually prevail. Their struggle to do so takes up the whole second half of the book, and puts most adventure-sf treatments of post-holocaust struggles for power in the shade.

Brin has done his homework thoroughly on everything connected with the book, from the effects of nuclear winter to the power of myth. He has occasionally let pass flat prose or an undeveloped scene, but on the whole he has left us with a superior book.

Edward Hughes's **THE LONG MYND** is less ambitious than the Brin, but quite successful as the coming-of-age story that is all it tries to be. Daffyd Madoc Llewellyn leaves his native Welsh village and travels to London, discovering in the process that the world is not nearly as simple as he has been led to believe.

In that world, the holocaust came in the late 1980s, as a result of a mutation that produced "Charmers." These men and women were able to rearrange molecules into anything they wished, from shotgun shells and clothing through airplane engines and up to and including nuclear weapons. Daffyd himself is a Charmer, which quickly puts him at the center of a deadly power struggle for the control of London.

"Charming" is never rationalized, so the book skates along the edge of fantasy, but the methods, limitations, and consequences of Charming are worked out so well that the book is *good* fantasy. It also has its share of first-novel raggedness, but in the end leaves the definite impression of the work of an above-average new writer.

In the hands of a good writer, a well-built world can sometimes carry an ill-constructed story. Ursula LeGuin's **ALWAYS COMING HOME** is hardly a story at all, but rather a series of quasi-anthropological studies of the Kesh, a post-holocaust and non-technological people living in the Pacific Northwest. LeGuin's prose and worldbuilding are up to the job of making the book readable and even absorbing, at least in moderate doses.

One does have to ask, however, whether LeGuin has crossed the line between pursuing a personal vision and ignoring her readers. One can say that Wolfe and Morris definitely have not crossed that line; with LeGuin it's less certain. It's also certain that the artwork, music, and poetry included with the book raise its price to a figure that in itself creates a barrier between reader and writer.

The writers in Harlan Ellison's shared-world anthology **MEDEA** have mostly stuck to the craft of storytelling better than LeGuin. They still haven't made their stories the most valuable part of the book, at least in this reviewer's opinion. The 180 pages of material on how Medea was created, from concept seminar through selected correspondence with the contributors, is a treasure trove. If you want to learn more than you ever thought would be put down in print about sf world-building, this is one of the places to start.

Brian Stableford and David Langford are both British sf writers with scientific backgrounds. Their **THIRD MILLENNIUM** is a fascinating hybrid of sf and futurology, a history of the next thousand years consistently written from the perspective of the year 3000. Traditional sf concepts abound—interstellar flight, melting ice caps, world government, biological engineering, contact with alien intelligence—drawn equally from the physical and social sciences. All are handled as they might actually be seen by a future historian. The impressive suite of illustrations, which lends a great deal of additional verisimilitude, uses computer-enhanced photographic techniques that were themselves sf fifteen years ago.

Every reader is likely to find something to disagree with in this book. Most readers will also agree that this sort of book can combine entertainment and education to a rare degree, and that we need more like it.

If I had to pick out one illustrated book on space flight to give as a gift to someone without a technical background, I would probably pick shuttle astronaut Joseph Allen's **ENTERING SPACE.** With his collaborator Russell Martin, Allen has produced a readable basic text and chosen a magnificent array of photographs.

The emphasis in both text and pictures is on the shuttle missions, which lends the book a particular poignancy as I write this column in February 1986, with the *Challenger* tragedy fresh in everyone's mind.

One cringes to read:

"Nearly four years after the maiden launch of the orbiter *Columbia* the Space Transportation System has become operational; launches now follow one another with quick and reassuring regularity."

One also nods grimly at reading:

"Yet for both veteran and novice astronauts, launches will never become routine."

The best monument we can give the *Challenger* astronauts is making Allen's first statement once again the truth, and as soon as possible.

Editor's introduction to:
THE SPACE BEAT

Well, they've finally come out and said it: "That which is not authorized is forbidden." A shame of course, but a freedom that can be alienated by bureaucratic fiat was never more than a pseudo-freedom, a *privilege*. The real question is how have things come to such a pass—and what must we do to remedy the situation?

—JPB

THE SPACE BEAT

THE OTHER SHOE DROPS

G. Harry Stine

On February 28, 1986, two months behind schedule, the Office of Commercial Space Transportation (OCST) published in the Federal Register its rules and regulations governing the launch and operation of private space vehicles and payloads.

Many concerned space advocates have been anxiously awaiting these rules. When the OCST (part of the Department of Transportation) published its original policy guidelines in the Federal Register on February 25, 1985, they raised the hackles of many people who have been pushing for the commercial development of space. See "Waiting for the Other Shoe to Drop" in the last issue of *Far Frontiers*.

In that column, I called attention to the fact that, because of various UN treaties covering accountability, liability, and registry of space vehicles which had led Congress to adopt the Commercial Space Launch Act of 1984, we had effectively given away the solar system, if not to bureaucrats then certainly to the Soviet Union.

I don't wish to imply that the personnel of the United States Congress or the Department of Transportation were somehow working in cahoots with the Soviet Union. I have gotten to know the people at OCST during the past year and have found them to be reasonable bureaucrats—i.e., "Be reasonable; do it our way."

What has made this whole affair even worse is that it has taken place without most space advocates knowing or seeming to care about it. The various space advocacy groups have been embroiled either in internal power struggles or their external activities, trying to attract attention and members. Other starry-eyed space advocates busily argued blue-sky things such as the benefits of lunar mining versus asteroid mining, dreamed up beautiful space colonies that they thought they were going to build some day, or busily built their own egos. No one was watching the store. Thus, the people who might have done something about the current situation were busy elsewhere, their attention diverted into petty earthbound problems or far-out dreams with no real appreciation of how they were going to get to space in the first place.

Although I was concerned that the solar system and the new frontier had been taken away from us, I was willing to withhold judgment until I saw the OCST rules and regulations. It took the United States Postal Service two weeks to transport a First Class package containing the rules from Washington to Phoenix.

However, be that as it may, I have now read the "interim" rules and regulations that will henceforth govern all private activities in space.

We have been had.

Badly.

Furthermore, we've been had with a smile.

No *substantive* difference exists between the February 1985 policy wording and the February 1986 "interim" rules and regulations. However, in the meantime, I have heard some fine-sounding words and platitudes, all seriously uttered by well-meaning OCST personnel who honestly believed what they were saying:

"We don't want to unduly restrict private initiatives in space."

"We aren't in bed with NASA."

"We are simply carrying out the tasks assigned to us by the Commercial Space Launch Act of 1984."

"We are on the side of private enterprise in space."

In a telephone call that came from OCST shortly before I received the rules, I was told that the normal regulatory procedure had been bypassed because of the Challenger accident.

Normally, a federal agency must issue a "Notice of Proposed Rule Making" (NPRM) in advance of implementing rules and regulations. The NPRM is printed in the Federal Register and a minimum of 60 days must be provided for written public comment. However, in the case of the OCST rules, the government invoked "emergency powers" and issued the rules as "interim" instead of "proposed." This means that the "interim rules" are in effect as real rules effective the date of publication, but that the government will accept and consider public comments for 60 days before issuing "final rules." OCST went the "interim rule" route because, I was informed, the *Challenger* disaster "put new pressure on the private launch vehicle industry and therefore it is mandatory that the rules be put in force immediately to handle the anticipated rush of private space ventures."

So the rules are already in place. And, by the time you read this, it will be too late to comment on them.

However, I'm not at all certain that it makes any difference anyway. I'm not sure that anyone really cares about doing it for real because it's so much more fun and less risky to play with utopian dreams of space. It seems that hardly anyone even took the time to go to the public library, look up the Federal Register for February 25, 1985, and read the original proposed "policies" of OCST. Or to write one's congressman and request a copy of these policies. There are about 250 million people in the United States. Some space advocacy organizations boast memberships of 10,000 or more. The readership of *Far Frontiers* is also counted in the tens of thousands. *But only 22 comments on the original OCST policy statements were received!*

In addition to the fact that the Federal Register, difficult as it is to read, constitutes public disclosure of regulatory actions, in July 1985 I managed to get an op-ed piece about the OCST proposed policies and rules published in *The Wall Street Journal*. I will guarantee you that the people in Washington and Houston certainly read that *WSJ* piece!

So no one can say that they weren't warned that the solar system was being taken away from us.

But only 22 of us can honestly say that we tried to do something about it.

(Some lazy people say that an individual can't change proposed government rules. With the help of George S. James of the Rocket Research Institute, and with the support of the National Association of Rocketry, I wrote another public comment on the policies. As a result, the new rules contain an exemption that allows more than a million people every year to fly their model rockets from school yards and public parks without a government permit for each and every flight or a government license and inspection for the launch site, range safety equipment, and etc., *ad nauseam*.)

Most people who responded were upset with the OCST proposed policies which would have permitted OCST to stop the launch of any space vehicle or payload that "was not in the national security or foreign policy interests of the United States." That wording is still in the new rules.

At this moment, the United States government has total and complete power to prevent any citizen of the United States from sending anything into space or from going into space. In spite of all the bureaucratic verbalese, the phrase "in the best interests of national security or foreign policy of the United States," which permits the government to stop a launch, covers a multitude of sins. It has been invoked many times in the past for political purposes, and there is no assurance that it will not be used again in the future by others who may not be as reasonable and approachable as the current personnel of OCST.

The government doesn't even have to get a court order, as Heinlein wrote into several of his early stories such as "Requiem." Government personnel have the right to come right into your rocket or satellite factory, your office, or your private launch site to inspect you and to stop you. And you can be fined for not following their orders or their regulations, said fine amounting to whatever they want to charge you. Administrative law is a whole separate body of legalistic rules in which the government is not only the plaintiff but the judge and jury as well.

Don't think you can get around the new rules by going off to some remote Pacific island to launch you, your vehicle, and/or your payload into space. Or by contracting with Arianespace, Japan, the People's Republic of China, or any foreign government or launch service. Or by working out an agreement to launch your private space vehicle from French Guiana, Kagoshima, or even the Baikonyr Cosmodrome at Tyuratam. The new OCST rules apply to any citizen of the United States (and that includes corporations and other business organizations incorporated in the U.S. or even foreign corporations in which a U.S. citizen or corporation has a controlling interest). You'll have to get your Mission Review, Safety Review, and launch permits from OCST unless an international agreement concerning private launches exists between the USA and France, Japan, the USSR, or whatever country you're going to launch from.

Under the new rules, OCST has the right and duty to poke into every nook and cranny of any proposed space launch, launch vehicle, or payload. You can't keep them out. If you notify them in writing that some aspect of the vehicle or payload involves proprietary or company confidential information, OCST rules say that the confidentiality will be maintained but that you've got to tell them all about it.

OCST people honestly believe that their new regulations will encourage private space development. Time will tell. Irregardless, the rules are now effectively and firmly in place.

Now you've got to get a government permit to go into space.

The worst-case scenario, however, coming on the heels of the *Challenger* disaster, is even less palatable: If the Soviet Union continues its long-term commitment to a manned Soviet presence in space and continues to build its cosmonautic expertise while the U.S. space shuttles are grounded, you may have to go to Moscow to get your passport validated if you want to fly into orbit.

IN THE WAKE OF THE CHALLENGER

The worst-case scenario, however, coming on the heels of the *Challenger* disaster, is even less palatable: If the Soviet Union continues its long-term commitment to a manned Soviet presence in space, and continues to build its cosmonautic expertise while the US adopts a posture of "business as usual" while its Shuttles are grounded, you may have to go to Moscow to get your passport validated if you want to fly into orbit.

—GHS

IN THE WAKE
OF THE
CHALLENGER

G. Harry Stine

The catastrophic failure of the space shuttle Challenger on STS Mission 51-L will be viewed by future historians as a major and critical happening in mankind's conquest of space. It will be ranked with the surprise of Sputnik-1.

But now as then we can rise to the occasion, overcome the difficulties, right the wrongs, and thereafter go on to accomplish great things in a grand manner. We did it after Sputnik. Twelve years after that traumatic day, two Americans walked on the surface of the Moon.

Twelve years from now, free people should be going into space any time they wish at a reasonable price and living in space stations, in the Moon, and on Mars. We only have to want to do it, work toward it, and convince our elected political representatives to lead, follow, or get the hell out of the way.

Sputnik-1 happened because in the decade following World War II Americans liked "space" but considered it to be science fiction and Tom Corbett, Space Cadet, a subject fit only for consumption by dreamers and kids (and there is really very little difference between the two; we kids just get physically older and never stop having Dreams of Glory). Most Americans knew that people would be going into space *some day* in the future, and it was tacitly assumed that those people would be Americans.

At the conclusion of World War II, the United States ended up with nearly all of the German Peenemünde rocket scientists plus about 100 German V-2 rockets looted from the Nordhausen Mittelwerk hours before the Red Army arrived to occupy that part of divided Germany. In spite of some very dedicated American military officers, this enormous technical advantage was allowed to be frittered away by bureaucrats, Congress, and the administration.

Why?

Answer: The American people didn't see the potential of space commercialization (in spite of Robert A. Heinlein's stories in *The Saturday Evening Post*) and therefore didn't back it with risk capital; it was too nebulous. As Heinlein postulated in "The Man Who Sold The Moon," we could have done the commercial development of space with the military development following as a requirement to protect the settlers. But we didn't take that classical, historic road that we'd followed to our terrestrial frontiers. On the other hand, neither did we give our government any encouragement to push ahead in *any* direction by funding rocket and space development. Congress and the administration are extremely sensitive to the wants and desires of their constituents, and with the proper leadership funding a space program could have been accomplished in the decade following World War II. When *Collier's* magazine hit the newsstands on March 22, 1952, with its striking Bonestell cover and the famous Collier's Space Program detailed inside, it could have been the whistle for the kickoff because the American people were ready for it; *Collier's* would never have risked publishing that issue unless its demographics had so indicated. We *could* have launched the first unmanned Earth satellite as early as 1954 if (a) we, the American people, had wanted to do it, and (b) if the various government agencies involved in the piddlin' rocket development of the time hadn't engaged in a monumental battle for bureaucratic jurisdictional turf. But it didn't happen. In 1950, rockets were ventures far to risky upon which to base the defense of the nation. All the top scientists said so, but nobody bothered to ask the engineers. The United States government continued doing what it had done to win World War II: build and operate long-range strategic bombers capable of carrying nuclear weapons. "If it works, don't fix it." Bombers worked. The U.S. had an air-delivered nuclear monopoly which it never used. Rockets weren't needed. The decade from 1946 to 1956 was a frustrating one for American rocket and space advocates. The only high point was the Korean War, which partly awakened the American people to the fact that the Soviets and their satellites weren't interested in the same long-range goals (peace, prosperity, two cars, and a house in Levittown) as we were.

The Soviet Union took a different path. It was unable to develop a suitable long-range strategic bomber even though Soviet engineers faithfully copied the Boeing B-29 Superfortress from examples that had accidentally landed intact in Siberia and been interned. This gave Stalin the Tupolev Tu-4 Bull, which was as underpowered and limited as the B-29 and therefore obsolete by the time the Soviets got it flying. So the Soviet Union did something other than attempt to ape the USAF Strategic Air Command. The Soviets understand technological warfare. They made a flank attack on the West by putting the German V-2 back into production, up-grading it, developing tactical rocket forces, and making an early decision to go for a strategic ICBM force. Less than 60 days after the first Korolev R-7 "Semyorka" ICBM was launched from Tyuratam in August 1957, another R-7 was used to boost Sputnik-1 into orbit.

Suddenly on October 4, 1957, a nation of people perceived by Americans to be backward, ignorant peasants beat America at its own game: high technology. F-80 and F-84 pilots who'd flown against the MiG-15

Fagot over the Yalu had sung, "All I want for Christmas is my wings swept back," and they had some strong feelings about whether or not the Soviets were backward, ignorant peasants. And so had many firearms experts who'd gotten the opportunity to inspect an example of the world's finest battle rifle, the Kalashnikov AK-47, designed to be used by largely untrained peasants under the worst conceivable field conditions.

Americans had been Sputniked, and we didn't like it then. We reacted by beating the Soviets to the Moon. However, we treated the symptom, not the disease. We didn't get to the root cause of the problem: ourselves and our complacent outlook on the future.

In the years to come, the Challenger disaster will be seen to have comparable impact on space activities as Sputnik-1.

By the time this sees print, NASA will have determined why the disaster occurred. NASA will make the engineering fix, and no space shuttle will ever have the same problem again.

The space shuttles may not be flying again by the time you read this. But they must begin flying again, and soon, because NASA has booked payload space, signed contracts, taken deposits of money, made binding agreements with clients ranging from scientific organizations to military commands to commercial customers, while acting as a government business venture. Why? NASA was *told* by the administration and Congress to encourage private shuttle payloads and to engage in the marketing thereof as a de facto government space transportation monopoly. And NASA was *told* by Congress and the administration to totally utilize the expensive space shuttle fleet even to the extent of instructing both NASA and the USAF to quit using such expendable boosters as Atlas-Centaur, Delta, and Titan III.

As of this writing, General Dynamics has shut down the Atlas production line, McDonnell Douglas has shut down the Delta line, and the last five Deltas have been purchased by users. The Martin-Marietta Titan III has been cleared for operation again following its grounding in 1985, when a major flight malfunction occurred in the liquid-propellant upper stage. On April 18, 1986, an Air Force Titan–34 D blew up shortly after launch, thereby putting on hold the only remaining space launch system available in the USA. The United States of America now has virtually *no* space launch capability. The situation is now far worse than this article depicts. In short, except for the Titan III and 34D (just about the same) medium-lift USAF boosters whose design I helped plan in 1957 and which is therefore built with 1960 technology, no expendable space boosters are left in the American stable. We have no new, modern horses left to enter in the race because we've bred none. The USAF was told to shut down the production line. But, like good soldiers have done since time immemorial when presented with an order that flies against all good sense and better judgment, they saluted and quietly kept on doing what had to be done: they kept the Titan III line open and running.

NASA was told by the administration and Congress, representing the American people, to do the whole space transportation job with four space shuttle Orbiters. Now the job must be done with only three because we've lost one-quarter of our space capability. The space shuttle system was an "instrument of national policy" in addition to being a truck line to space. Not only was NASA not allowed to build a fifth Orbiter, but the government rejected offers by commercial organizations to buy one and let NASA use it.

Any bus line, truck line, or airline that attempts to operate with four vehicles scheduled for 100% utilization without a spare vehicle on stand-by to handle emergencies such as maintenance and repair or even loss of a vehicle simply couldn't operate very long. NASA, the administration, and Congress are discovering the truism of this commercial principle. And if what happened to the federal space transportation system had been allowed to occur in a commercial outfit, its managers would be in deep yogurt, the executives would be on the carpet before the board of the directors, the directors would be under pressure from the stockholders and financial interests, and heads would roll because of the abysmal planning.

But heads will not roll at NASA, because the space agency is not a commercial operation, although it is indeed the nation's government-run space transportation monopoly. NASA administrators continually voiced the promise that the Space Transportation System would be run on airline-type commercial operating principles, but all attempts to get them to do so were dismissed and all attempts to "privatize" the space shuttle were literally beaten down. Why? NASA got its marching orders from on top, the administration and Congress. When policy wasn't clear and NASA administrators had to establish it, either the administration or Congress could have reversed it. But they didn't.

We, the people, didn't tell them to do anything different. At least, not enough of us told them in the proper way.

The push toward the frontiers has always been led by a surprisingly few people, and it's never been necessary to get majority approval, much less majority interest. But it took the few to convince the many. It's still done that way. If space advocates had been as well organized as the Wisconsin dairy farmers, an American space station would have been in orbit a quarter of a century ago. . . .

Before Sputnik, there were many fine words spoken about space by politicians and bureaucrats; but the Americna people didn't care or know enough about space to tell their elected and hired representatives to do anything but talk and appropriate barely adequate funds. The space advocacy-then-movement was led by an ex-German nobleman who did succeed in getting us to the Moon but who was unable to gather enough support to do what was needed in spite of his charisma. Want to know why Wernher von Braun resigned from

NASA? He foresaw the mess that the space shuttle was getting into even then, and he was in a position where he was totally powerless to stop it. What was even worse, the pre-Sputnik space advocates fought among themselves and remained disorganized in a series of splinter groups. As late as 1954, the American Rocket Society, the nation's professional organization devoted to the field, publicly refused to assert that the Society's primary goal was space flight or to admit the rocket was not superior to the ramjet for flight in space! In early 1957, Vanguard was being developed on a budget of about $125 million, and even President Eisenhower thought it was too expensive. Today, that sum wouldn't even pay for a single unsubsidized space shuttle flight. . . .

Before Challenger was lost on Mission 51-L, there were many fine words spoken about the commercialization and privatization of space by politicians and bureaucrats, including the nation's chief executive officer, who's a real space buff at heart but can't convince a Congress that hasn't gotten the Word from its constituents or isn't listening. The American people, enthralled as they are about space and proud as they are of the space shuttle, didn't tell their elected and hired representatives to either appropriate enough money to do the job right or get the hell out of the game and let private industry run the truck line to space. As before, monumental bureaucratic turf battles continued to rage in NASA and the Department of Defense, and these were exacerbated by the private launch vehicle industry whose activities managed to bring into the fracas the Department of State, the Department of Commerce, the Treasury Department, and the Department of Transportation, all of whom suddenly began to stake out space turf for themselves. Meanwhile, the space advocates who were not so reticent about speaking out this time made the mistake of preaching to the choir because it was far more comfortable than going out to convert the heathen or convincing people with a lot of money that they should grubstake the struggling new private space transportation industry. And commercial space industry itself fell afoul of several fast-talking con artists.

So we have, in effect, been Sputniked again, but this time we really can't blame it on anyone but ourselves!

How do we get on with the job? Where do we go from here? What can we do in the wake of the Challenger?

Because of the basic European heritage of our American culture, there is absolutely no indication at this time that we will stop squabbling among ourselves; our overseas brethren have been doing so for centuries. The leopard can't change its spots. Our only salvation lies in the fact that all of us can boast ancestors (even the Amerindians) who came here from somewhere else, thereby creating an undefined individualistic, frontier, or pioneering spirit.

Therefore, we'll try to forge ahead and not make the same mistake the same way again. Whether we will succeed or not remains to be seen.

But which way do we go?

Let's look at some alternatives and some scenarios arising from their consequences.

1. NASA does not replace Challenger.

2. NASA replaces Challenger.

3. NASA replaces Challenger and builds a spare Orbiter.

4. NASA proceeds with the development of a "second generation" space transportation system.

5. USAF proceeds with its TransAtmospheric Vehicle (TAV).

6. Congress passes and the President signs a bill guaranteeing that the government will purchase a minimum annual Earth-to-orbit payload amount at a given price per pound.

7. The private space launch vehicle industry receives other encouragements from the government or from financial interests and potential payload customers.

8. In a political and bureaucratic dither of trying to lay blame, cover anatomies, protect friends, placate

enemies, and insure absolute success of future space ventures, nothing happens. In short, we keep right on doing what we've been doing for a quarter of a century or more.

The consequences of #1 are straightforward. The U.S. has lost 25% of its manned space capability. Some consequences have already been felt. Space science was the first loser with the indefinite delay of the Galileo and Ulysses launches. In this regard NASA shot itself in the foot, because the space scientists have believed for years that in a world of a perceived finite pie, they were getting a smaller piece every year because the available funds were going into manned space flight. At the same time, NASA shot itself in the other foot because Ulysses was a joint international operation, and the Europeans are not happy with the indefinite delay, which also applies to many SpaceLab flights in which they have already sunk a lot of money. Do not be surprised if the U.S.S.R. suddenly steps to the fore (it may have already done so by the time you read this) by offering to launch Ulysses *free* on their spare SL-12/13 "Type D" or "Proton" rocket; in 1985, they launched eleven of these, and we know their annual production is twelve, so there they sit with a spare medium-lift launch vehicle. The USAF, who never really liked the idea of having to use the space shuttle in the first place, can and will bump all non-military shuttle payloads because of the absolute necessity to launch its surveillance, reconnaissance, weather, and communications satellites for national security reasons. Those flights not commandeered by the USAF will be co-opted for the Strategic Defense Initiative, although *any* orbital-based phase of *any* effective operational SDI *cannot* be deployed with only three Orbiters. Space station? Forget it! A ten-year delay at the least, provided it isn't studied to death first. Commercial payloads? Profit-making companies must count on getting their satellites into orbit on schedule and within budget. They are likely to beat a path to the door of Arianespace, Japan, the People's Republic of China, or even the U.S.S.R., and that means dollars flowing out of the country, further irritating the nation's international trade imbalance, balance of payments, value of the dollar, and so forth. No matter what the U.S. does, it cannot continue to be a major spacefaring nation with only 75% of its launch capability.

If #2 is the game plan, this doesn't put the U.S. back where it was before January 28, 1986. It will take at least 36 to 42 months to build a Challenger replacement. In the meantime, a lot of the consequences outlined above for #1 may have taken place. In short, the U.S. may not be able to catch up with its international competition no matter how fast it moves to build a new Orbiter. And what happens if *another* Orbiter is lost? The space shuttle system was intended as a reliable, safe, low-cost operational space transportation system. It is none of these, as many of us have been trying to point out for years. At best, it is a development space transportation system based on 1970 technology. And it's wearing out already. Even with an SRB fix, there are still far too many failure modes in the system. The probabilities of losing yet another Orbiter are high. When another Orbiter is lost, we may find ourselves back in January 1986 again—unless some of the other alternatives are exercised, and depending on when the loss occurs and how far along the alternatives have progresed toward operational status.

That brings up #3. Some people are saying that, whatever the real costs of building a new Orbiter are, it won't cost twice as much to build two more while you're at it and have the production line up and running. A competent manager doesn't run a truck line or an airline without a spare vehicle, expensive as it might be; that's the cost of doing business. Other people say that it will be four to five years before a sixth Orbiter can join the fleet, so why put more money into an obsolete system when there may be a second-generation system available by then? The major problem with *not* building a sixth Orbiter lies in the fact that there is no second-generation system that NASA can bring on line in four to five years. Under NASA's own operational procedures, some dictated by federal law, the government development pace for the second generation system will be glacially slow, as it was with the current shuttle system. Do not look for a second generation space shuttle system or even a major upgrade or stretch of the current shuttle before 1991 or 1992. It is far better to go with what you have, poor as it may be, until you have a better bird in the hand and ready. We lost 15 years between Apollo and the space shuttle because NASA quit building proven man-rated medium-lift (Saturn-Ib) and heavy-lift (Saturn 5) expendable launch vehicles and forged ahead on a chimeric system, the space shuttle. Note: This is exactly the way the Soviets run all their aerospace programs, aircraft and spacecraft; they keep up-rating, improving, and using an existing, known design until its successor is available; the MiG-21, Tupolev Blinder/Backfire, and the Korolev R-7 Semyorka (the 30-year-old first ICBM booster still used for Soyuz and unmanned probes) are testimony to this. They may not be as technologically slick as the NASA spacecraft, but boy, are they consistent!

This leads inevitably to a discussion of #4, where NASA proceeds at once with the design and development of a second generation space transportation system. Many of the comments made thus far are also applicable to this. It will require five to ten years and it will be expensive because that's the way NASA is set up to do things. It may also turn out to be a political turkey, after being subjected to ten years of budgetary battles and politically-forced engineering compromises. Political pressures may force NASA to design a system that is absolutely safe but too expensive to operate and/or with such limited performance that it can't really do anything. The British could have told us all about this sort of thing . . . and some of them have. Please see "Slide Rule" written by Neville Shute, in which the British government's program for design, development, and construction of dirigibles is described in great detail. Or read up on the British government's development of the Barbazon transatlantic airliner, which ended up being too expensive, too slow, and obsolete in the face of Boeing's risky but successful private development of the Model 707 jet airliner. On the other hand, the joint British-French Concorde SST paid off, even though it took ten years of operation to become profitable—while the U.S.-funded Boeing SST was stillborn, probably because of the differences in the organizational, management, and funding procedures between the two SST projects. When are *we* going to learn that government-developed systems fare badly in comparison to or competition with those of private enterprise? Maybe Challenger will teach us that lesson . . . but I doubt it.

One way or the other, the USAF will proceed with the development of its TransAtmospheric Vehicle (TAV), so alternative #5 is assured. The Air Force calls it Copper Canyon, while President Reagan in his February 1986 State of the Union message referred to it as the "Orient Express." The Air Force fighter jocks *love* Copper Canyon; line-up with the runway, light off the Aerojet aeroturboramjets, suck the stick into your lap, fly into orbit (with the last gasp), go through the fiery entry, and touch down on a runway. This sounds neat, but you do not equip a passenger or cargo airline with F-16 fighter planes; you buy Boeing 737-300s or McDonnell Douglas MD-80s for short- to medium-hauls and Boeing 747 versions for long-haul services. The chance of us getting a second-generation space transportation system out of Copper Canyon are slim even if it could be converted for such a use. No naval warship has ever been converted into an economical commercial liner or cargo ship. No bomber aircraft has ever succeeded as a commercial transport, and that includes the commercial version of the Boeing B-29/B-50, the Boeing 337 Stratocruiser, which was plagued with maintenance problems; only 55 were built, and the four airlines that bought and operated them replaced them with Boeing 707s as quickly as these became available. Copper Canyon may turn out to be an analogous system. In any event, it *may* not be available before 1991–1992. And it may not be amenable for use as a space transportation system unless it is a compromised design intended for both uses, in which case it probably won't do a good job of either.

Alternative #6 offers an interesting new approach to space transportation. Therefore, it stands a much lower chance of becoming reality. In the first place, it requires that politicians *do something* and that bureaucrats stay out of the way while they're doing it. History tells us that it's very unlikely. However, for a short time after the Challenger disaster, it appeared that the political climate was amenable to the introduction of a bill in Congress that would encourage the development of private launch vehicles by means of permitting agencies of the federal government to guarantee by contract the annual purchase of X pounds of payload lifted to low-Earth orbit for a maximum price of Y dollars per pound. Such a governmental incentive would provide a badly-needed stimulus for an infant private space launch vehicle industry. Yes, such an industry is out there. There are several potentially economical and feasible vehicles well along in the design stage—Pacific American Launch Systems' Phoenix, Third Millennium, Inc. and its Space Van, and Truax Engineering with its Sea Dragon, among others. Some of the best rocket design and development engineers this nation has produced are directly involved. The proposals look good on paper, most of them using well-proved technology and requiring little in the way of technology development. Furthermore, it appears that they will be cheaper to develop, build, and operate than the space shuttle by a factor of ten or more. Costing models have used the data from the Ariane, the SR-71, and other high-tech, high-risk aerospace projects carried out over the last 25 years. Armed with all this information, the private launcher firms have approached the financial community. In turn, the financiers have been suitably impressed. However, nearly all of them have said, "We'd like to have some independent experts look over your design and data." And where have they gone to find the experts? NASA and the aerospace companies, that's where! (Where else are they? Well, I can tell you if you really want to know.) And what is going to be the reaction of people whose rice bowl is filled by NASA who in turn runs a very expensive space transportation monopoly? You've got it right the first time. While never managing to say, "It won't work," the independent experts have managed to cast serious doubts by making such statements as "We worked on such an idea back in 1962, and it turned out to be infeasible for numerous reasons." Deep down inside, however, every one of these experts honestly believes that no space system can be designed, developed, and put into operation for less than the space shuttle on the high end or several billion dollars on the low end because they've always built spacecraft for the federal government doing it the government way . . . and they know what that costs. It is impossible for them to conceive of any other way of doing it. Most aerospace engineers would have great trouble working for other companies producing products for commercial or industrial customers, although many of them have managed to re-learn their profession after being laid off at Offwego Aerospace Company and having to take a job at Industrial Widget Corporation. I did.

Therefore, #6 may not pan out, but we should be pushing for Alternative #7 which would offer some sort of government carrot in the form of risk sharing or risk reduction scheme to the private launch vehicle industry. For a decade now, I've been thinking about this, and I haven't come up with a class act yet. There are too many show-stoppers. Most of these are political. However, numerous feasible and succesful ways suggest themselves to anyone who has bothered to read American history. Unfortunately, nearly every history book completely ignores the overwhelming dominance of industry and commerce over human affairs in the last 200 years. The magnificent ten-volume *Story of Civilization* by Will and Ariel Durant doesn't mention the word "corporation" even once. Neither does the classic *Outline of History* by H. G. Wells. This shortcoming has been noticed by many people now in staff and liaison positions in Washington. The mere fact that the Communications Satellite Corporation (Comsat) was set up to be the chosen instrument of the United States in satellite communications back in the early 1960s rather than a federal agency is heartening, and Comsat has certainly been enormously successful. It has proved again that private enterprise can and does outstrip government enterprise in terms of speed, efficiency, costs, and return on investment. There isn't a single taxpayer dollar involved in Comsat, yet Comsat pioneered and made possible the ubiquitous satellite communications network we take for granted today. Perhaps if we want to move more quickly in space, it's time we had another close look at how to do it with private enterprise while at the same time help keep the NASA and aerospace rice bowls full until people have had the opportunity to adjust, phase over, and thus not feel threatened. But right at the moment, the mere suggestion of private launch vehicle carrots sends NASA into a defensive frenzy, and the agency begins to act like a loose cannonball on deck.

Alternative #8 is scary because it's the easy way out for bureaucrats and politicians if we, the American people, permit them to take the easy way out—which we shouldn't because we're paying them to do the difficult things we can't do ourselves. It's far easier for a bureaucrat to reorganize a branch, shift a few people around, establish a new office, and contract for "additional studies" than it is to make a decision that may turn out to be wrong. Therefore, the ruling procedure in government service today is to delay making a decision either in hopes that the situation will change, thereby eliminating the need to make that difficult decision, or that the study contract will come up with more items that should be studied. With these prevailing operational procedures in the federal government today, the United States would never have built a transcontinental railroad or the Panama Canal, would never have been able to win World War II, could never have developed the atomic bomb, would never have succeeded in making an ICBM or the Polaris SLBM work, or have gotten a single astronaut to the Moon, much less to low-Earth orbit. When a NASA official states that it will take ten years to develop a "second-generation" space transportation system, fifteen years to get a space station in orbit, or twenty years to get back to the Moon, someone should loudly remind them that starting from practically zero we had enough of a primitive space transportation system to put a man in orbit three years after the gun went off, that we put up a space station called Skylab in about four years, and that we got to the Moon from a standing start in eight years. Alternative #8 is the result of our elected officials, appointed administrators, and hired experts suffering from hardening of the neurons, which manifests itself in failure of imagination and failure of nerve. Alternative #8 is frightening because it has the highest probability of occurring unless we do something about it . . . and quickly. We've seen it evolve, we've watched it grow, we've agonized over it, but we haven't done anything about it . . . yet. Time to do something about it.

Naturally, thousands of different scenarios can be developed from a combination of these eight alternatives. Some of them are ridiculous from the start and can be eliminated. Each reader can come up with a favorite combination or two or three. Let me inflict my choice upon you:

Let NASA and the aerospace Gun Club build two more Orbiters. That will keep them busy and their rice bowls full. It will also ensure that the expensive space transportation system in which we taxpayers have already invested heavily will continue to function until something better comes along.

Let the Air Force build Copper Cnayon. Sure as hell, they'll learn a lot doing it, and it will undoubtedly create spinoffs that will be useful to the civilian side of the space transportation equation. The Air Force-financed development of the J57 jet engine and the high-bypass turbofan engine helped reduce the technical risk and make possible the commercial jet airliner and the wide-bodied jet airliner, for example.

Adopt the gauranteed purchase of payload capability by the government from private launch vehicle manufacturers and operators. Get private enterprise into space transportation as quickly as possible in order to get the cost to low-Earth orbit reduced by a factor of ten. Even if the cost could be reduced only by a factor of five, this would provide sufficient incentive to many companies wanting to get into space to do things but finding the lift costs too expensive. One and only one thing is retarding the further development and utilization of space at this time: the high cost per pound to get something into orbit. Make that reduction by a factor of five (or ten, if it can be done), and the space frontier will figuratively blossom.

And it will mean that seven of our finest people will not have died in vain.

THE GREAT BEER SHORTAGE

When assaulted by a culture with superior technology, the time-tested solution is to swipe first the enemy's weapons, then his techniques. But what if the enemy's military superiority is inherent in his genetic makeup? Why, steal that, of course . . .

THE GREAT
BEER
SHORTAGE

Janet Morris and David Drake

"Sauron fucking *super* soldier!" the young troop leader was yelling at the closing door of the officer's bar from which he'd just been thrown. "I didn't *ask* for this—not to be born like this, not this duty, not any goddamn bit of it!"

It was night, Catseye long set up there somewhere beyond massed clouds that hid all starlight. The troop leader didn't mind that at all—he saw best in the dark. He liked it black. And black as a Haven woman's heart it was out here in the boonies at Firebase Three—black as Troop Leader Merari's mood.

No goddamn beer for his troops, though they'd been out on long recon for ten days, fighting the Haven resistance, the pirates, whatever the hell moved on this hostile planet.

Back at the *Dol Guldur* they'd have beer, you bet, like the Assault Leaders and the cyborgs had it here.

Not that the desk jockeys outside Shangri-La'd share it with the guys out here who weren't brass, guys who got their butts shot up following orders. *And it ain't just the orders that're pisspoor either, it's the damned planet and the "plan" that got us here.*

Trash the local government, vaporize Haven's industry, that was the plan. *Take 'em out from orbit, hose 'em down from aircraft and hovers, and when you're done with that, Field Marshal Lidless Eye and all your mechanized Division Leaders, some guys got to go bleed all over the damned jungle to clean out the scattered pockets of resistance you cyborgs created.*

The troop leader had just brought his boys in, what was left of them. Didn't matter to anybody but the body-counters that you took a tenth of the casualties you inflicted. Didn't matter to his wounded or his dead.

They deserved the best Firebase Three had to offer—they deserved some goddamned beer, if anybody did.

Troop Leader Merari put his hands on his hips and hollered at the closed bar door: "You wouldn't treat me this way if I had my Gatling. I'm goddamn coming back with my Gatling and then we'll see you throw me out."

Backing away as the door opened and a three-star Assault Leader glowered at him, Merari might have left it at that.

But the three-star said, looking huge in that doorway spilling light like the blackout-curtained bar windows couldn't, "Come on, son, take it easy. There's booze in your own bar. RHIP, Soldier."

"RHIP?" Merari shouted hoarsely, pumped up on the rotgut he'd found in Artillery's own bar, where there was nary a drop of beer for a chaser. "I got all the RHIP I can eat, *Sir!* I got blood that clots so quick it'll probably give me apoplexy or an aneurism by the time I'm forty. I got great night vision, so great I'm near dayblind here. I got reflexes so enhanced I might just spasm to death for the hell of it. So you don't want to get me excited, *Sir*. No, you don't. And you want to let me and my boys in there, or you want to give us a few barrels of beer—we bled for it, we deserve it."

Goddamn, but that didn't go down well. Back into the blindingly bright bar went the three-star and out came MPs even bigger than Merari himself—older, meaner, and wiser, with Haven AKs pointing right at his gut while they waltzed him back to his troop's barracks—a flimsy bunch of decidedly unkevlared tents out at the firebase's perimeter.

When they left him there, telling him he was lucky he hadn't gotton himself manacled and tossed into the stockade, Merari glared away everybody who came near him.

Fuck 'em all. No women was bad enough, but no woman and no beer . . . .

He *was* going to go get his Gatling, or some shit. He was going to stick a cal fifty right up that Assault Leader's ass and see how good *his* breeding was.

The indigs called the soldiers "Saurons." Maybe they deserved the name, but not the sneer. And some of the genetically-engineered soldiers were better engineered than others. Luck of the draw, quality of the mother. It all varied. Some Saurons were more equal than others. Merari was one hell of a night-fighting machine, enough of one to know he wasn't going to live to sit in the officer's bar. His kind didn't. He was too fast, too strong, too damned enhanced to survive to an old age or a high grade—and too smart not to know it.

You didn't volunteer for this outfit, you were born into it, like some family curse. And now what was left of that family was going to make or break it on Haven, a miserable loo of a planet full of hostiles. It wasn't quite running with your tail between your legs. But it was hiding, and hiding wasn't what Merari was bred to do.

You weren't supposed to know so much about the hows and whys of this fucked-up LZ, and why it was permanent—not down in the ranks, you weren't.

But Merari was too smart for his own good, and he had friends up at Intelligence, back where the *Dol Guldur* was being salvaged into bits and pieces.

A long stay. A new home. And the Lidless Eyes hadn't given a damn what kind of welcome the troops were going to get. They just blew the hell out of Haven's planetary defenses like that was going to solve the problem.

Now there was a fucking insurgency to deal with, if

you wanted to dignify it with a name like that. And Merari's boys were on the front lines.

He didn't even know where the hell he was, in relation to Shangri-La. He knew his quadrant, and every damned hill's number, so maybe he could get his boys in and out of strike zones, but that was it.

You could find Firebase Three, no sweat—it was where the brass was. The fucking enemy could find it, too. Military Assitance Command Haven—MACH—squatted out here and thumbed its nose at these locals, hosing down surrounding territory, and then was surprised that the indigs didn't bring their women in voluntarily so the brass could lay 'em flat.

Goddamn crazy way to run an occupation, if you asked Merari. But nobody did, not even his own troop when he started trashing his tent and then, in the following silence, slipped out the back.

Cal fifty ought to set those fuckers straight.

He went charging through the undergrowth, short cutting to the motorpool, sure that blackness all around would conceal him, in just his grays and a flak vest. Full kevlar was too hot, too constraining, and Merari was feeling like the superman he'd been bred to be, jacked up enough to start a war of his own.

He heard a noise when he'd nearly reached the motorpool and reflexes overrode his rational mind the way they were supposed to: he was hitting the dirt, rolling for cover, and drawing his issue side arm before he could blink and try to focus on the motion in the dark.

He ought to be able to see it. His nightsight was the best in his outfit.

But he couldn't. He couldn't see a damned thing.

He stopped stock still on his belly in the dirt, propped up on his elbows. Rolling in this damned brush was noisy. He went to listening, holding his breath. He could hear insects screwing, his boys said.

But when the unmistakeable pressure of a gun's barrel conjoined the base of his skull, it caught him totally by surprise.

"Freeze, Sauron," came the voice from behind.

Picked up the few words they needed to know of a civilized language, these indigs did.

Every muscle strained and still, Merari said, "I'm frozen." He wanted to hear that voice again. There'd been something funny about it, funnier than just the accent. He was pretty good at accents. He wanted to know who and what had caught him with his pants down, and he wanted to know why.

"Good. Drop the hand weapon; drop your belt; drop your pants and don't ask questions."

"What the *fuck?*" Now he knew what had been odd about the voice he'd heard—it was husky, deep, but it was a woman's voice, almost certainly.

"Now you're getting the idea."

"Wait a minute, lady," Merari objected.

The muzzle of something slapped stars into his medulla oblongata. "Drop 'em, in that order. Then roll over, slow."

Balls, he hoped nobody came upon him while this was happening. The only plus he could figure was that, once he rolled over, he'd have lots more options. And when he did, he could see his attacker.

But it was goddamn degrading while he was still on his belly, especially once he'd dropped the gun in the leaves and seen a blackened hand, shadowy in the black night, reach out to take it and realized how small and frail that hand was. His quick-release webbing buckle came off easy, and with that went the rest of his weapons, beyond what breeding had given him.

Roll over and you've got weapons at hand, boy, he told himself, but the sting of being captured by a female wasn't helped much by that advice.

When he did roll over—slowly, because she knew just how to make sure he couldn't scissor her down and she kept the muzzle of her expropriated Sauron gun against his skull, and then his forehead, the entire time—she straddled him, sliding the gun down his face, until its muzzle was pressed against the soft skin under his chin.

"Okay, Soldier, I bet you can guess what happens now." And she reached down for him, one knee firmly planted on the tangle of pants confining his thighs. "Just lie still, fella. If you're a good boy, it won't hurt at all."

It didn't, though at first he wasn't sure she was going to get what she came for.

She kept the gun under his chin and it's hard to keep up your end of a conversation that way. So he didn't make a sound until she got what she wanted.

Finally, she sat up on him: "Set a land speed record that time . . . corporal, isn't it?"

The pressure under his chin eased and he knew he was supposed to answer. Hell, so far, not too bad. If nobody heard about it, not bad at all. But she wanted ID, he knew: "Troop Leader Merari, at your service—in another half hour or so, if you care to wait."

She said, "Don't get cute, superboy," but he heard her chuckle. Damn, why couldn't he see her? Was she black skinned? Or just covered with blacking? He could see eye-whites and teeth, like she was some Cheshire cat, but that was all.

Or almost all. When she raised herself, he saw a flash of white upper thigh, a slash of white lower belly and pale pubic hair. Camouflaged, then.

"Up, come on, Soldier. Sit up and put your pants on, nice and slow."

The gun came away from his flesh and he could see her shadow move as she pulled up her own pants.

Now! Take her while she's distracted.

But it was only an instant and somehow he didn't want to wrestle her to the ground and take her in for interrogation—where everybody'd know what she'd done to him. And he definitely didn't want to kill her, which was probably because she'd taken some of the fight out of him the best way that can happen.

"How come you did this? How come you picked me?"

"Did this?" came the woman's voice as she backed a few, slow steps away, soundless as a cat. "Well, there's an old saying . . . if you can't beat 'em, join 'em. As for picking you, you just happened to be in the right place at the right time."

"Shit, and I thought you'd been stalking me for months, crazy in love."

"Right," she said. "I'll be back to try you again next month, Troop Leader Merari, if this doesn't do the job. That's the best I can do."

What was he supposed to say? Thanks? But while he was thinking it over, she slipped a few paces farther into the bush and the last thing he heard before she broke for parts unknown was: "Count to a thousand before you pick up a weapon, or you're dead meat, meat."

Nasty bitch, but he stayed there. He really didn't want any commotion about this. Never live down being raped by an indig who weighed maybe a third what he did.

Sauron fucking superman, he was.

There was only one thing to do for his wounded ego and his soldierly pride.

He retrieved his belongings, buckled on his weapons belt, and resumed sneaking up on the motorpool. When he got back to the officer's bar with his gun-jeep, they were going to give him all the beer he wanted.

You bet.

The stockade at Firebase Three was reasonably comfy, considering what the Senior Assault Group Leader, MACH, was trying to keep inside.

They had an exercise area fenced with electro-wire—pointing in at the top, of course. They had a nice dark hole for the real bad boys—it would have been for solitary except there were too many bad boys in the stockade for private rooms—and that was where Merari ended up.

There were two other guys in there, and he could see 'em clear as day at night, though they turned to gray shadows whenever anybody opened the slot for the breakfast feeding.

One of them never said anything, he just glowered at the far wall, night and day. Once in a while he'd get up and run headfirst into the far wall repeatedly, until he knocked himself unconscious, but that was all. He didn't bother Merari, and he didn't bother the other soldier in the hole, the guy with a fifteen millimeter cartridge around his neck on a chain like some sort of jewelry.

Two weeks after Merari had been thrown in here for shooting up the officer's bar at point-blank range from his gun-jeep, the guy with the chain around his neck said something to Merari for the first time:

"Hey, I'm Section Leader Coleman," he said very quietly. "Call me Coley." He held out a huge, scarred hand.

Merari hesitated before he took it. He'd thought none of these guys ever talked. They weren't supposed to—you were supposed to maintain silence, because this was solitary confinement, no matter how many of you there were. He looked at the Runner, as he'd nicknamed the guy who bashed himself into walls. The Runner was staring at his booted feet. They all observed basic discipline: guards came by to check that you were dressed for daytime, stripped for night, like it mattered.

Grasping Coleman's hand at last, Merari said, "TL Merari—or used to be. Whatcha in for?"

"I'm a sniper."

Did he mean his section was the sniper unit? Merari shivered: you didn't see those guys, but you heard about them. Or did he mean he'd shot somebody, or lots of somebodies, probably at regiment level or above where you wouldn't hear about it in the ranks? "Oh yeah?" said Merari aloud. "That's nice, Coley. That's real nice."

"Nah." The sniper reached in his blouse pocket and pulled out a smoke. Merari had seen Coleman smoke before, and couldn't figure out which guard was slipping the stuff in to him.

"Want?" The sniper held the pack out.

Merari took one. He'd have firebombed an enemy

village for one of these, when he'd been with his troop.
Now, he'd steeled himself against the vice, ignoring
Coley whenever the other prisoner smoked his hoarded
butts. He'd had dreams about Coley offering him one.
When the match came, his hands were shaking.

"Thanks, man. I trashed the officer's bar, but it was
their fault. They had beer and they wouldn't give us
any . . ."

"I heard," said the sniper. Then he came up on one
knee and his neck bulged as, smoke loose between his
lips, he stuck his head close to Merari's.

The coal of the smoke, so close, was nearly blinding.
But Merari's ears worked fine:

Coleman said, "I've got 117 notches on my AK's
stock—personal kills at close range."

"Great. Nice shooting." What did you say, closed up
with a fuse like this guy?

"Doc says I'm going back to the Citadel soon, for
observation. Funny, that was what they called what we
were doing—Observations."

Merari laughed nervously in the pause he was supposed to fill.

Over in the opposite corner, the Runner looked at
them both, hissed like a snake, covered his ears with
his arms, and turned his face to the wall.

The cartridge on its chain around Coleman's neck
swung freely, back and forth, as the sniper leaned even
closer. "Know what this is, Merari?"

"Bullet."

"Bullet that's going to kill me. That's what they don't
know at Regiment—they can't kill me, long as they
don't have this."

"But you're going back there—to the Citadel." Wearing it, asshole.

"Yeah, that's what I'm sayin'. Tomorrow." The sniper
sat back and with a fluid motion looped the chain over
his head and held it out. "Keep it, buddy? Wear it for
me? Till I get back."

"Sure thing." I'll take the damn thing, anything
you want, you crazy bastard. If I had a gun, I'd solve

your problem and all that would be left is spent brass.

But they didn't give you guns in the stockade hole.

Coleman watched carefully, pupils dilated, as Merari looped the cartridge's chain over his own neck and tucked it inside his blouse. Then the sniper leaned back against the wall, finished his smoke and went to sleep. Coleman's snoring could have waked the dead.

Merari didn't sleep at all that night, just sat and watched the bigger man, feeling the cartridge burn against his bare chest.

Crazy. Sniper outfits weren't on anybody's duty rosters. This guy had a whole *section* like him, back where he came from? Spooked the hell out of Merari, just thinking about it.

The next morning the door opened and Merari was blind in the sun.

When it closed again, Coleman was gone.

The Runner started to jog in place. Merari ignored it. Next to the sniper, the Runner wasn't any sort of trouble.

A week after the sniper had gone, the Runner spoke to him for the first time: "That guy, Coleman?"

"Yeah?" Merari was happier without chat; he didn't want to know anything about this wingnut; he was out of here in a week's time.

"He won't get back to the Citadel, you know—not alive."

"I figured something like that," Merari said wearily, and turned his own face to the wall.

The next night, all hell broke loose outside: the *swup* of shells; the crack and whistle of hypersonics; the blinding glare of flames.

Merari was up and beating on the door in seconds, yelling his heart out. He had a real aversion to being oven-baked.

There was a lot of shooting. It must be an indig attack. They won one every once in a while, and that meant expropriated weapons.

Expropriated weapons made him think about the girl who'd got his pants down last month.

And, as if he'd dreamed it, there she was beyond the cell door jerked suddenly open.

With her was Coleman, covered with black grease and smoke and blood, big as an APC. "C'mon, buddy," Coleman ordered.

And to the woman (—the tiny, black-on-black woman with the golden hair between her thighs that he could see as clearly as if she were naked—) holding a shotgun on him, Coleman said, "See? My friend. Got my luckpiece. Told you he'd still be here."

"Out of there, Merari!" The woman's voice was husky. "Move, Soldier. You don't want to get dead fighting for the privilege of staying in jail."

"It's awright, kid, trust Coley," said the big sniper. "None of these'll be around to tell on either of us. We'll just roll on back to the Citadel and give 'em whatever story we want—the sole survivors. They'll believe us." Coleman raised his automatic rifle, pointing it past the troop leader.

Merari glanced back at the Runner, curled in his customary corner. "Hey, *no*, man," he said hastily to the sniper. "He won't talk."

"Well," said Coleman. "Yeah . . ." But he fired anyway, a short burst thunderous with its echoes. He reached out his hand.

Merari stepped from the hole, slipping off the cartridge's chain and giving it to Coley. "Yeah, all right. Maybe it'll work."

Maybe saying so would keep him alive a little longer.

But as things worked out, he did get back to the Citadel, and so did the sniper named Coleman.

It took a while. They had to get the little woman pregnant first, before she'd let them go.

BAEN BOOK CLUB ANNOUNCES THE ADVANCE PLAN

The Very Best in Science Fiction and Fantasy
at Super Savings

BUILD A LIBRARY OF THE NEWEST AND MOST EXCITING SCIENCE FICTION & FANTASY PUBLISHED

Having trouble finding *good* science fiction and fantasy? Want to build up your library without tearing down your bank account? Sign up for Baen Book Club's Advance Plan and enjoy super savings on the world's finest selection of science fiction and fantasy.

NEW BOOKS, HIGH QUALITY, LOW PRICE

With the Advance Plan, you'll receive 6 to 8 *new* paperback books every two months—the very best from your favorite science fiction and fantasy writers—*as they are published*. All books are new, original publisher's editions, and you pay only half the cover price (paperback cover prices range from $2.95 to $3.95). There are no additional costs—no postage or handling fees.

SAVE EVEN MORE ON HARDCOVER EDITIONS

To increase your savings, you may choose to receive all hardcovers published by Baen Books, at the same half price deal. With this option, you receive all paperbacks and hardcovers. (Hardcovers are published six to eight times per year, at cover prices ranging from $14.95 to $18.95.)

Sign up today. Complete the coupon below and get ready for the biggest and brightest in science fiction and fantasy.

Yes, I wish to take advantage of the Baen Book Club Advance Plan. I understand that I will receive new science fiction and fantasy titles published in paperback by Baen Books every two months (6 to 8 new books). I will be charged only one-half the cover price for books shipped, with no additional postage or handling charges. Charges will be billed to my credit card account. I may opt to receive hardcover as well as paperback releases by checking the box below. I may cancel at any time.

If you wish to receive hardcover releases as well as paperback books, please check here: [ ]

_____
Name   (Please Print)

_____
Address

_____
City

_____   _____
State   Zip Code

_____
Signature

_____
VISA/MasterCard Number   Expiration Date

MAIL TO:
Baen Book Club
260 Fifth Avenue, Suite 3-S
New York, NY 10001

Please allow three to six weeks for your first order.

WE PARTICULARLY
RECOMMEND . . .

ALDISS, BRIAN W.
Starswarm

Man has spread throughout the galaxy, but the time-less struggle for conquest continues. The first complete U.S. edition of this classic, written by an acknowledged master of the field. **55999-0 $2.95**

ANDERSON, POUL
Fire Time

Once every thousand years the Deathstar orbits close enough to burn the surface of the planet Ishtar. This is known as the Fire Time, and it is then that the barbarians flee the scorched lands, bringing havoc to the civilized South. **55900-1 $2.95**

The Game of Empire

A *new* novel in Anderson's Polesotechnic League/Terran Empire series! Diana Crowfeather, daughter of Dominic Flandry, proves she is well capable of following in his adventurous footsteps. **55959-1 $3.50**

BAEN, JIM & POURNELLE, JERRY (Editors)

Far Frontiers – Volume V

Aerospace expert G. Harry Stine writing on government regulations regarding private space launches; Charles Sheffield on beanstalks and other space transportation devices; a new "Retief" novella by Keith Laumer; and other fiction by David Drake, John Dalmas, Edward A. Byers, more. **65572-8 $2.95**

BUJOLD, LOIS MCMASTER
Shards of Honor

A novel of political intrigue and warfare on a par with Poul Anderson's "Polesotechnic League" stories and Gordon Dickson's *Dorsai!* Captain Cordelia Naismith and Commander Aral Vorkosigan, though on opposing sides in an ongoing war between wars, find themselves thrown together again and again against common enemies, and are forced to create a separate peace in order to survive and bring justice to their home worlds.　　　　　　　**65574-4 $2.95**

CAIDIN, MARTIN
Killer Station

Earth's first space station *Pleiades* is a scientific boon— until one brief moment of sabotage changes it into a terrible Sword of Damocles. The station is de-orbiting, and falling relentlessly to Earth, where it will strike New York City with the force of a hydrogen bomb. The author of *Cyborg* and *Marooned*, Caidin tells a story that is right out of tomorrow's headlines, with the hard reality and human drama that are his trademarks.　　　　　　　**55996-6 $3.50**

The Messiah Stone

What "Raiders of the Lost Ark" should have been! Doug Stavers is an old pro at the mercenary game. Retired now, he is surprised to find representatives of a powerful syndicate coming after him with death in their hands. He deals it right back, fast and easy, and then discovers that it was all a test to see if he is tough enough to go after the Messiah Stone—the most valuable object in existence. The last man to own it was Hitler. The next will rule the world . . .

65562-0 $3.95

CHALKER, JACK
The Identity Matrix
While backpacking in Alaska, a 35-year-old college professor finds himself transferred into the body of a 13-year-old Indian girl. From there, he undergoes change after change, eventually learning that this is all a part of a battle for Earth by two highly advanced alien races. And that's just the beginning of this mind-bending novel by the author of the world-famous *Well of Souls* series.   **65547-7 $2.95**

DELANEY, JOSEPH H.
In the Face of My Enemy
Aged and ailing, the tribal shaman Kah-Sih-Omah is prepared to die . . . until peaceful aliens happen upon him and "repair" his body, leaving him changed with the ability to survive any wound, and to change shape at will. Thus begins his long journey, from the time of the Incas to the far future, as protector of Mankind.   **55993-1 $2.95**

DICKSON, GORDON R.
Hour of the Horde
The Silver Horde threatens—and the galaxy's only hope is its elite army, composed of one warrior from each planet. Earth's warrior turns out to possess skills and courage that he never suspected . . .
                                        55905-2 $2.95

Mindspan
Crossing the gap between human and alien minds as only he can, Gordon R. Dickson examines the infinity of ways that different species can misunderstand each other—and the dangers such mistakes can spawn. By the author of *Dorsai!* and *The Final Encyclopedia*.
                                        65580-9 $2.95

Wolfling

The first human expedition to Centauri III discovers that humanity is about to become just another race ruled by the alien "High Born". But super-genius James Keil has a few things to teach the aliens about this new breed of "Wolfling." **55962-1 $2.95**

DRAKE, DAVID
At Any Price

Hammer's Slammers are back—and Baen Books has them! Now the 23rd-century armored division faces its deadliest enemies ever: aliens who *teleport* into combat. **55978-8 $3.50**

Ranks of Bronze

Disguised alien traders bought captured Roman soldiers on the slave market because they needed troops who could win battles without high-tech weaponry. The legionaires provided victories, smashing barbarian armies with the swords, javelins, and discipline that had won a world. But the worlds on which they now fought were strange ones, and the spoils of victory did not include freedom. If the legionaires went home, it would be through the use of the beam weapons and force screens of their ruthless alien owners. It's been 2000 years—and now they want to go home. **65568-X $3.50**

FORWARD, ROBERT L.
The Flight of the Dragonfly

Set against the rich background of the double planet Rocheworld, this is the story of Mankind's first contact with alien beings, and the friendship the aliens offer. **55937-0 $3.50**

KOTANI, ERIC, & JOHN MADDOX ROBERTS
Act of God

In 1889 a mysterious explosion in Siberia destroyed all life for a hundred miles in every direction. A century later the Soviets figure out what had happened —and how to duplicate the deadly effect. Their target: the United States. **55979-6 $2.95**

KUBE-MCDOWELL, MICHAEL P., SILVERBERG, ROBERT, & SPINRAD, NORMAN
After the Flames

Three short novels of rebirth after the nuclear holocaust, written especially for this book. Kube-McDowell writes of a message of hope sent to post-holocaust humanity via the stars. Silverberg tells of the struggle to maintain democracy in America after the destruction of the government. Spinrad adds his special sense of humor with a tale about an Arabian oil baron who is shopping for a bomb. Edited by Elizabeth Mitchell. **55998-2 $2.95**

LAUMER, KEITH
Dinosaur Beach

"Keith Laumer is one of science fiction's most adept creators of time travel stories ... A war against robots, trick double identities, and suspenseful action makes this story a first-rate thriller."—*Savannah News-Press*. "Proves again that Laumer is a master."—*Seattle Times*. By the author of the popular "Retief" series. **65581-7 $2.95**

Retief and the Pangalactic Pageant of Pulchritude

Once again Retief stands up for truth, beauty and the Terran way—this time at the Pangalactic Pageant of Pulchritude. He escorts a Bengal tiger to the gala affair, where the most beautiful females of the galaxy gather to strut their stuff. But Retief has a penchant for finding trouble—and there's plenty of trouble ahead when he discovers that the five-eyed Groaci intend to abduct the pageant beauties, and blame it on Earth . . .
65556-6 $2.95

The Return of Retief

Laumer's two-fisted intergalactic diplomat is back— and better than ever. In this latest of the Retief series, the CDT diplomat must face not only a deadly alien threat, but also the greatest menace of all—the foolish machinations of his human comrades. More Retief coming soon from Baen!   **55902-8 $2.95**

Rogue Bolo

A new chronicle from the annals of the Dinochrome Brigade. Learn what happens when sentient fighting machines, capable of destroying continents, decide to follow their programming to the letter, and do what's "best" for their human masters.   **65545-0 $2.95**

MARTIN, GEORGE R.R.

Tuf Voyaging

On a colonial world in the far future, struggling trader Haviland Tuf stumbles across the find of the century —a long abandoned Earth Ecological Corps seedship, a repository of every bit of scientific knowledge once known—and since lost—to man, as well as the tools to recreate any form of life. Tuf turns the ship into a gold mine, but not without paying a price. *Hardcover.*
55985-0 $15.95

MORRIS, JANET (Editor)
Afterwar
Life After Holocaust. Stories by C.J. Cherryh, David Drake, Gregory Benford, and others. This one is utterly topical. **55967-2 $2.95**

BEYOND *THIEVES' WORLD*

MORRIS, JANET
Beyond Sanctuary
This three-novel series stars Tempus, the most popular character in all the "Thieves' World" fantasy universe. Warrior-servant of the god of storm and war, he is a hero cursed . . . for anyone he loves must loathe him, and anyone who loves him soon dies of it. In this opening adventure, Tempus leads his Sacred Band of mercenaries north to war against the evil Mygdonian Alliance. *Hardcover.*
55957-5 $15.95

Beyond the Veil
Book II in the first full-length novel series ever written about "Thieves' World," the meanest, toughest fantasy universe ever created. The war against the Mygdonians continues—and not even the immortal Tempus can guarantee victory against Cime the Mage Killer, Askelon, Lord of Dreams, and the Nisibisi witch Roxane. *Hardcover.* **55984-2 $15.95**

Beyond Wizardwall
The gripping conclusion to the trilogy. Tempus's best friend Niko resigns from the Stepsons and flees for his life. Roxane, the witch who is Tempus's sworn enemy, and Askelon, Lord of Dreams, are both after Niko's soul. Niko has been offered one chance for safety . . . but it's a suicide mission, and only Tempus can save Niko now. *Hardcover.*
65544-2 $15.95

MORRIS, JANET & CHRIS
The 40-Minute War

Washington, D.C. is vaporized by a nuclear surface blast, perpetrated by Islamic Jihad terrorists, and the President initiates a nuclear exchange with Russia. In the aftermath, American foreign service agent Marc Beck finds himself flying anticancer serum from Israel to the Houston White House, a secret mission that is filled with treachery and terror. This is just the beginning of a suspense-filled tale of desperation and heroism—a tale that is at once stunning and chilling in its realism.   **55986-9 $3.50**

MEDUSA

From the Sea of Japan a single missile rises, and the future of America's entire space-based defense program hangs in the balance. . . . A hotline communique from Moscow insists that the Russians are doing everything they can to abort the "test" flight. If the U.S. chooses to intercept and destroy the missile, the attempt must not end in failure . . . its collision course is with America's manned space lab. Only one U.S. anti-satellite weapon can foil what *might* be the opening gambit of a Soviet first strike—and only Amy Brecker and her "hot stick" pilot have enough of the Right Stuff to use MEDUSA.   **65573-6 $3.50**

HEROES IN HELL™—THE GREATEST
BRAIDED MEGANOVEL OF ALL TIME!

MORRIS, JANET, & GREGORY BENFORD, C.J. CHERRYH, DAVID DRAKE
Heroes in Hell™

Volume I in the greatest shared universe of All Times! The greatest heroes of history meet the greatest names of science fiction—and each other!—in the most original milieu since a Connecticut Yankee visited King

Arthur's Court. Alexander of Macedon, Caesar and Cleopatra, Che Guevara, Yuri Andropov, and the Devil Himself face off . . . and only the collaborators of HEROES IN HELL know where it will end.

65555-8 $3.50

CHERRYH, C.J. AND MORRIS, JANET
The Gates of Hell

The first full-length spinoff novel set in the Heroes in Hell℠ shared universe! Alexander the Great teams up with Julius Caesar and Achilles to refight the Trojan War using 20th-century armaments. Machiavelli is their intelligence officer and Cleopatra is in charge of R&R . . . co-created by two of the finest, most imaginative talents writing today. *Hardcover.*

65561-2 $14.95

MORRIS, JANET & MARTIN CAIDIN, C.J. CHERRYH, DAVID DRAKE, ROBERT SILVERBERG
Rebels in Hell

Robert Silverberg's Gilgamesh the King joins Alexander the Great, Julius Caesar, Attila the Hun, and the Devil himself in the newest installment of the "Heroes in Hell" meganovel. Other demonic contributors include Martin Caidin, C.J. Cherryh, David Drake, and Janet Morris.

65577-9 $3.50

POHL, FREDERIK, & WILLIAMSON, JACK
The Starchild Trilogy

In the near future, all of humanity lives under the strictly enforced guidance of The Plan of Man—a vast, oppressive set of laws managed by a computer security network. One man vowed to circumvent the law and voyage to the farthest reaches of space—but he has been found out and sentenced to death. A mysterious Power is on his side, however, and it demands not only clemency for Boysie Gann, but an end to the Plan of Man itself. If her rulers refuse, Earth's sun will be snuffed out . . .

65558-2 $3.95

REAVES, MICHAEL
The Shattered World

Ardatha the sorceress and Beorn the thief unite with the cult of magicians to undo the millennium-old magic that shattered the world into fragments. Battling against the Establishment, which fears (perhaps rightly) that the pair can only destroy what little is left, they struggle to fulfill their self-assigned destiny of making the world whole again.   **55951-6 $3.50**

SABERHAGEN, FRED
The Frankenstein Papers

At last—the truth about the sinister Dr. Frankenstein and his monster with a heart of gold, based on a history written by the monster himself! Find out what really happened when the mad Doctor brought his creation to life, and why the monster has no scars. "In the tour-de-force ending, rationality triumphs by means of a neat science-fiction twist."—*Publishers Weekly*   **65550-7 $3.50**

SCOTT, MELISSA
A Choice of Destinies

Macedonians vs. Romans in a world that never was . . . this brilliant novel shows what might have happened had Alexander the Great turned his eyes to the west and met the Romans, instead of invading India and contracting the fever that led to his early death. An exciting alternate history by a finalist in the 1985 John W. Campbell Award for Best New Writer.

65563-9 $2.95

SHEFFIELD, CHARLES
Between the Strokes of Night

The story of the people who leave the Earth after a total nuclear war, living through fantastic scientific advances and personal experiences. Serialized in *Analog*.   **55977-X $3.50**

VINGE, VERNOR
The Peace War

Paul Hoehler has discovered the "Bobble Effect"—a scientific phenomenon that has been used to destroy every military installation on Earth. Concerned scientists steal Hoehler's invention—and implement a dictatorship which drives Earth toward primitivism. It is up to Hoehler to stop the tyrants.

55965-6 $3.50

WINSLOW, PAULINE GLEN
I, Martha Adams

From the dozens of enthusiastic notices for this most widely and favorably reviewed of all Baen Books: "There are firing squads in New England meadows, and at the end of the broadcasting day the Internationale rings out over the airwaves. If Jeane Kirkpatrick were to write a Harlequin, this might be it."—*The Washington Post*. What would happen if America gave into the environmentalists and others who oppose maintaining our military might as a defense against a Russian pre-emptive strike? This book tells it all, while presenting an intense drama of those few Americans who are willing to fight, rather than cooperate with the New Order. "A high-voltage thriller ... an immensely readable, fast-paced novel that satisfies." —*Publishers Weekly* **65569-8 $3.95**

WREN, THOMAS
The Doomsday Effect

"Hard" science fiction at its best! The deadliest object in the universe will destroy Earth in seven years—unless a dedicated band of scientists can stop it. The object is a miniature black hole trapped in our gravity field; experts show that the singularity will dive in and out of the Earth, swallowing everything in its path, until the planet collapses. But how do you stop something that is smaller than an atom, heavier than a mountain, and swallows everything that touches it?

65579-5 $2.95